LUNA MARE

LUNA MARE

Book One
The Luna Duet

by

NEW YORK TIMES BESTSELLING AUTHOR
PEPPER WINTERS

Lunamare
Book One
The Luna Duet
Copyright © 2023 Pepper Winters
Published by Pepper Winters

All rights reserved. No part of this book may be reproduced or transmitted in any form, including electronic or mechanical, without written permission from the publisher, except in the case of brief quotations embodied in critical articles or reviews.

This is a work of fiction. Names, characters, businesses, places, events, and incidents are either the products of the author's imagination or used in a fictitious manner. Any resemblance to actual persons, living or dead, or actual events is purely coincidental.

This book is licensed for your personal enjoyment only. This book may not be re-sold or given away to other people. If you would like to share this book with another person, please purchase an additional copy for each person you share it with. If you are reading this book and did not purchase it, or it was not purchased for your use only, then you should return it to the seller and purchase your own copy. Libraries are exempt and permitted to share their in-house copies with their members and have full thanks for stocking this book. Thank you for respecting the author's work.

Published: Pepper Winters 2023: **pepperwinters@gmail.com**
Cover Photo: Cleo Studios
Cover Design: Cleo Studios
Edited by: Editing 4 Indies (Jenny Sims)
Proofread by: Christina Routhier
Translation & Authenticity Reader: Betül Silence is Read
Sensitivity Reader: Sedef

OTHER WORK BY PEPPER WINTERS

Pepper currently has close to forty books released in nine languages. She's hit best-seller lists (USA Today, New York Times, and Wall Street Journal) almost forty times. She dabbles in multiple genres, ranging from Dark Romance, Coming of Age, Fantasy, and Romantic Suspense. She has won awards for best Dark Romance and is a #1 Apple Books Bestseller.

For books, FAQs, and buylinks please visit:

https://pepperwinters.com

Subscribe to her Newsletter by clicking here or following QR code

To grab three of Pepper's books for free (Tears of Tess, Pennies, and Debt Inheritance) Please CLICK HERE or use the QR code

SOCIAL MEDIA & WEBSITE
Facebook: Peppers Books
Instagram: @pepperwinters
Facebook Group: Peppers Playgound
Website: www.pepperwinters.com
Tiktok: @pepperwintersbooks

Dedication

To my French-Canadian husband.
I was born in Hong Kong to English parents.
You were born in Montreal with traces of Montagnais blood.
We come from different cultures, different languages, different worlds.
Despite our origins, we met in a country that wasn't ours…Australia.
We met by chance, by luck, by fate.
And I knew I was meant to find you the moment our eyes first touched.
You are the reason I can write romance.
Because you are my friend and protector, home and heart.
And I know the day we part from this life, we will find each other in another…

**Digitally Signed
By
Pepper Winters**

Thank you so much for reading.

*Love,
Pepper*

Letter from Author

This book is a tale of blended culture, languages, and love that overcomes every obstacle. Sensitivity readers have been enlisted for authenticity and research has been conducted to provide as accurate and respectful a tale as possible. Creative license has also been used as the characters are their own person and their evolution is unique to them.

This book is intended for audiences who enjoy graphic sexual descriptions, intense emotional challenges, and are familiar with my darker work. This is a life story, a coming-of-age story, and ultimately, one of the most poignant love stories I have ever written, but it does deal with topics such as death of family, rape (on page), and other mental health challenges.

Please read responsibly.

Pepper
x

Prologue

NERIDA

(*Sea in Latin:* Mare)

"I SUPPOSE MY FIRST QUESTION HAS TO be the one that everyone is dying to know." The reporter cast a shy look my way, cheeks flushed, eyes bright, hope clinging to every word for the story of her career.

I sighed, knowing this question would come but hoping it could have waited until *after*. After I spoke so eloquently of my life's work. After I gave every piece of my legacy. Instead, my broken heart would have to bleed all over the rest of her questions because I wouldn't be able to staunch the flow once she asked.

"Perhaps we should ask about Lunamare first?" Dylan said, shooting a reproachful stare at his colleague, all while adjusting the microphone in front of me.

"Oh yes, of course." Margot sat back on my comfy wicker furniture, the soft ocean breeze playing in her strawberry-blonde hair. She winced. "I'm sorry. I just…ever since I heard about you two, I can't stop imagining your love story."

I smiled softly.

Was I once like her? Diamond-eyed and untouched by time? So full of magic and wonder?

Yes.

The answer was yes.

Yes, I'd once been like her.

And I'd lived a life worth living.

A life worth telling.

Even now, with time carving relentless lines across my face and stamping its unforgettable memories into my weathered skin. Even now, with that very same clock *tick-ticking* in the back of my mind of what I faced once this interview was over…I still glowed with gratitude.

So, *so* much gratitude.

"You can ask," I said softly. "I don't mind."

Dylan stiffened a little, a dark beard framing his mouth with harsh expectation. His article on my unparalleled creation seemed to be overshadowed by true love.

And wasn't that always the way?

You could fashion the tallest building.

Build the fastest car.

But in the end...the greatest achievement of your life would always be what you loved the most, and what loved you the most in return.

"Is it true..." Margot scooted closer, her notepad and pen forgotten on her lap, her burnt-yellow sundress swaying around her knees. "That you pulled a lion from the ocean and fell in love with him?"

Tears pricked.

Heart swelled.

The sea called to me with its soft *hish-hish-hish* upon the crystalline sands.

"It's true." I smiled.

"And is it also true that you descend from a line of sirens? That your very name means nymph, and that your lion loved you back because you sang to him like all sirens do and captured his soul forever?"

"Jesus, I'm so sorry about her." Dylan snorted, tossing his rakishly long hair off his forehead. "I swear she comes highly educated." Pinching her in the side, he muttered, "This isn't a fantasy, Margot. This is real. This is a once-in-a-lifetime opportunity to interview the greatest visionary of our time. A woman who not only gave her life to the sea but also made living beneath the waves a reality."

Margot deflated a little, nodded sadly, and consulted her little notebook. "Nerida, how did you envision Lunamare? Did you always believe you could create a liveable undersea biosphere?"

"It's not just a sphere anymore," Dylan interrupted. "Over a thousand people now list their address as the Coral Sea." His eager hazel eyes met mine. "How did you go from being a marine biologist to the architect of a new world?"

I looked back and forth between the two reporters.

I glanced down at my weathered hands, and the pangs in my bones spoke of time running out. I'd agreed to this interview because Lunamare was worthy of every publication possible, but...my heart was weary and nostalgic.

Tipping up my chin, I smiled at Margot and gave her the answer to the question she truly wanted. The question that followed me around every time I stepped on shore.

"It is true that I captured the heart of a lion. That I plucked him from the sea when I was just twelve. It's true that I fell in love with him at first sight, all while he was stubbornly blind. And it's true that he fell for me...eventually, not because I'm a nymph or siren or some other fantastical myth or legend. He fell because we belonged to each other." I sighed wistfully. "All it took was for our eyes to touch and our hearts to beat, recalling the song we'd always known, slipping into sync where we belonged."

"Wow." Margot blinked. "That's—"

"A wonderful tale. A romantic one to be sure." Dylan sniffed. "But not the one we came to—"

"Is he here?" Margot scooted even closer, looking like she'd fall off her wicker chair with eagerness. "Do you think he'd share his side of the story while you shared yours?"

"Margot—" Dylan shot daggers at her, all while her eyes remained soft and dreamy.

I pitied this spritely thing. She hadn't met the one who would change her life. Not yet. I wanted to tell her that when that love of a lifetime found her, she would know the deepest abysses of despair and the highest hills of joy.

That each day would be perfect, even if there were tears and fears, and none of them would be long enough.

I hid my flinch from her question and covered it smoothly with a smile. "He's not here, I'm afraid."

"Oh." Margot's face fell. "That's too bad."

"Yes…it is." My lovelorn heart squeezed like it always did when I thought of him.

Lunamare might be my legacy, but Aslan?

He was my reason for existing.

Thanks to him, my lips had been kissed beneath a million sunsets. Our blood had turned to salt from a thousand moonlit swims. And our love gleamed brighter than all the stars.

"How did you come up with the name Lunamare?" Dylan asked, looking pointedly at the microphone and trying one last time to follow the script.

I wasn't prepared for the kick in my chest. "It's Latin. My mother was always fascinated with languages and swore she'd be fluent in all of them before she died."

"And was she?" Dylan asked.

"Not quite. But she did know more Latin than anyone else I knew."

Margot wrinkled her nose. "Luna…means moon, right?" And mare means…"

"Sea." I held her stare, willing memories not to drown me.

"So you just combined the two words?" Dylan kept a close eye on me, tasting my reluctance to share.

This tale I wanted to keep close. But…if I wanted to do this, *truly* do this—truly leave behind the purest parts of me, the truest parts and ugliest parts, I had to pour all my hardships and heartaches into their hands.

Do I have the strength?

Sucking in a breath, I tasted the words before speaking them, learning how it would feel to be honest. To give them everything.

"*You said without the moon and the sea, we would never have met,*" he whispered.

My heart hiccupped. "*Thank goodness for the* ay *and the* deniz *then.*"

"*For the* luna *and the* mare," he whispered, his eyes locking onto mine and making the world drop away.

I sat taller, my chest aching and so full of love. "It was Aslan who joined the two, many, many years before I ever dreamed of creating something so extraordinary."

A rush of memories.

Star glow and moonlight.

Desire and desperation.

My cheeks heated, and it was my turn to lean forward.

If I shared my innermost parts, I could relive them again. I could rewind time that was whispering of my end and go back to the very beginning.

I could touch him for the first time again.

Kiss him for the first time.

Love him until the end of time.

I need that.

One

last

time…

Brushing down my wave-foam green dress, my bare feet longed to step into the cool wetness of my home. I'd been on shore for far too long.

But it wouldn't be too much longer.

And then…

I sat taller with determination. "It was the moon and the sea that brought him to me. Without either, we would never have found each other." I smiled as a vibrant memory swept me up. "It became a bit of a vow between us. A wedding troth, if you will."

Dylan sucked in a breath.

Margot swooned. "How old were you when he realised he loved you back? I mean…how old were you when you first slept together? I mean—"

"*Margot.*" Dylan reared back, rolling his eyes. "Jesus Christ, I'm so sorry." He pinched the bridge of his nose. "This interview is not turning out how I thought it would."

I chuckled under my breath, running my thumb over the ring on my wedding finger. The inscription burned against my skin as if it were only yesterday.

The night he'd placed it there.

The crashing wave of love.

Longing caught in the back of my throat. I whispered, "I'll tell you what. Let's forget about the interview. We'll ignore your scripted questions. We'll forget about why you came here today."

"Are you…are you saying you'd like us to leave?" Dylan's spine snapped straight. "If so, I must apologise. We meant no offense. We're just impassioned about your life, Nerida—"

"Please, if I overstepped, I didn't mean—" Margot bit her bottom lip, cutting herself off.

"It's fine." I looked at them both. At their newness and verve. I'd been like that once. I'd been passionate about every fish, whale, reef, and anemone. I'd been besotted with love and embraced every day with joy because I'd been given him so young.

I suddenly wanted to relive it all.

Every moment.

Every kiss and trip and fall.

I sighed, accepting how differently today would turn out to be and how thankful I was that I had this final chance to love him. "I meant...instead of a stuffy interview, I give you a story. A story people whisper about. A story about a nymph and her lion and everything else between."

Margot reached over with the biggest grin and touched the back of my paper-thin hand. "With every part of me...*yes*. Yes, please."

I twisted my wrist and let her link her fingers with mine.

A flashback of my much younger fingers wrapping around the arm of a teenage boy filled my mind.

My thoughts tripped back to that fateful day, and I sucked in a breath as so many others unspooled.

I sank like a stone into a sea of them.

I let them crash over me with waves of tenderness, brokenness, and home.

And when the last one washed away, I focused on the two young reporters.

This story wouldn't be the one they came for.

It would be so, so much more.

"I thought he was dead when I first saw him. I jumped overboard and swam as fast as I could, all while my father yelled, my mother screamed, and the pod of dolphins we'd been studying swarmed around me..."

Chapter One

ASLAN

(*Moon in Latin:* Luna)

I'D NEVER BEEN SO SCARED OF THE sky before.

Never thought clouds could reach down and smother me. Never believed rain could fall fast enough to drown me. Never thought thunder could reach inside my chest and stop my terrified heart with its fury.

BOOM!

My mother screamed. My sister screamed. My cousin screamed.

But my father just kept holding on to all of us. Draped over us the best he could as the boat tossed side to side, desperately trying to cast us out of it.

Lightning forked.

Terror sliced.

Another *BOOM!*

"It's okay. We're okay," my father chanted, his voice long since salt-whipped and hoarse. "There is land beneath our feet. There is always land, even when there is an ocean between us."

My sister pressed tighter against me, huddled into a tiny, storm-dripping ball. "Aslan, make it stop. *Please*, make it stop!"

I tried to be brave like my father.

"It's okay, Melike." I wrapped my arms around her tiny figure, doing my best not to crush her as another wave tipped us high, so high, then shot us soaring down its face, landing back on the churning angry surface as froth splashed high into the sky, clashing with rain, fighting wet with wet.

We landed sideways.

We rocked with horror.

And for a moment, I feared this was it.

The moment we capsized.

But…like all the other moments, the ocean cradled us at the last second, keeping us upright even while drenching us in fresh brine.

Everyone gasped for breath.

Everyone clung to the sides, the benches, the broken rigging, desperately holding on, all knowing our strength was fading with every wave.

"It's okay, *canım*," my mother crooned, using the term of endearment I'd heard a thousand times before. My life. My soul. To my mother, we were all her life, even while that life was so terribly threatened.

She swallowed back tears and did her best to be brave for us. "Listen to baba, Melike. He says the land beneath the waves will save us. We will touch it again soon. You'll see."

"I hate the sea!" my cousin, Afet, yelled over the howling storm.

"Emre, what are we going to do?" My mother shouted at my father just as another wave crested against the savage fork of lightning and smashed heavily over us.

Spluttering.

Coughing.

Our fingers clung to anything and everything.

Each time the hull was battered by another wave, it grunted as if the waves were knives, slowly disembowelling it.

Another thunderclap punctured our eardrums.

The boat groaned a little louder. A dying groan.

We'd started this journey with twelve others.

The small boat had been overcrowded, unbalanced, and with a motor that coughed and spluttered more than it propelled.

I'd had my doubts when my father helped us into it.

But he'd said this was how these things were done.

Covertly, quietly, smuggled across the sea by moonlight.

But the storm had decided that twelve were too many.

The rain had come.

The waves had arrived.

And now…there were only five.

"The storm will pass," my father bellowed, gripping on to all of us as if he could fight the storm and swim us to shore. "Just hold on. The boat will last. We will look back upon this as our greatest adventure!" He forced a grin, his teeth startling white in the storm-churned night. "We will live the life of safety and happiness that I promised. You will see."

My sister didn't buy it. My cousin cried harder. And my mother just looked at all of us as if imprinting our faces on her heart.

Another roil.

This one tossed us into a heap and made us cry out with fresh bruises. Blood coated my forehead from smashing face first against one of the benches. Blood smeared my cousin's upper arm, mixing with seawater until it swirled with morbid patterns.

True fear settled into my heart.

Fear borne from suddenly understanding that my parents weren't magic. They could promise to keep us safe, but they couldn't actually make that promise come true.

They were as helpless as me, and that knowledge—that awful, awful knowledge—made me clutch at my baby sister. "It's okay, Mel. Close your eyes. It will all be over soon."

My mother let out a tattered cry; her dark eyes locked over my shoulder.

She shook her head, her hair plastered to her shoulders, her mouth working in a frantic prayer.

Pure terror sliced through me.

I turned to look, but she threw herself over us, planting salt-stinging kisses on our cheeks. "*Seni çok seviyorum.* I love you so much. *Seni seviyorum.* Love you—"

"Jale, stop that. You're scaring them," my father yelled. "The boat will last—"

The boat made a sickening noise.

Not a groan this time but a crack and a tear and a gush of water sprouted from the ocean-hammered sides.

A rush of nausea and a buffet of vertigo as the ocean surged beneath us, sending us high again, soaring again, dragged up the face of a giant wave as winds whipped and rain fell and sea foam blew agony into our eyes.

"Hold on!" my father yelled.

"Baba, help—" my sister screeched.

"I love y—"

And that was the last time I ever heard my family.

The wave crested.

It broke.

Onto us.

Into us.

Killing us.

The boat smashed into smithereens.

Splinters danced into the sky as a wall of water ripped me from my parents' hold and flung me into the sea.

The icy embrace of the churning depths suffocated what air I had left.

I plummeted from the warmth of my family with such suddenness, it tore open my heart with grief.

I tried to scream.

Salt water poured down my throat.

I tried to swim.

Waves pushed me deeper.

I tried to survive.

Something heavy crashed against my—

Something painful lashed around my wrist.

I mumbled incoherently and tried to get away.

Only…nothing worked.

Everything hurt.

Everything stung and ached and screamed.

"You're okay…I've got you." The pressure moved up my forearm, squeezing. I groaned and tried to push it away.

"Oh no, you don't. You'll sink." The pressure moved up to my shoulder, clamping tightly around me.

"Mum! He's alive!"

I winced.

The words sat heavy in my waterlogged mind.

I recognised them.

English.

My father made us learn so we'd be able to speak when we travelled to a land where we weren't hunted and safe.

"Help me. He's hurt. He's barely holding on—"

Something nudged my legs.

Awareness crashed through me.

Wet.

Floating.

Scratchy wood beneath my cheek.

The slippery nudge bumped my knee again.

My eyes ripped open.

The storm.

The decimation.

The sorrow.

The nudge wasn't just a nudge this time but a shove to my side.

Everything inside me went cold.

Shark.

Shark!

I screamed and struck at whatever held me captive.

Pain tore through me.

Blackness stole my sight.

I sank—

"It's okay. You're okay."

I hated those words.

I *despised* those words.

They were lies and false promises, and they'd stolen *everything*.

"Neri, move away. I need to see how badly he's injured." A male voice rumbled in my storm-deafened ears.

A scuffle sounded but then gentle hands landed on my head, fingers feathering around my skull as if searching for something.

I moaned.

The fingers stopped searching. A shadow loomed over me, blotting out the sun dancing behind my closed eyelids.

"Can you hear me? Can you speak? Open your eyes, mate."

A tap against my cheek. A shake on my shoulder.

Another flash of breath-stealing pain from my ribs, my wrist, my leg.

Darkness feathered over my thoughts again, pushing me down…down…

"It wasn't a shark," a soft, sweet voice suddenly whispered—so close to my ear it tickled. "It wasn't a shark nudging you. It was Sapphire. She's a dolphin. Her pod brought us to you. They saved you. So rest easy, whoever you are, because you're safe now and nothing can hurt you."

My heart fisted.

My throat closed.

Loss crashed over me.

I tried to fight the cloying heaviness.

I did my best to open my eyes and see who spoke so kindly.

I wanted to thank her.

To touch her.

But pain pushed me deep—

Chapter Two
ASLAN

(*Moon in Turkish:* Ay)

THIRST.
Out of all the things that hurt, that hurt the most.
It scratched along my thoughts and clawed through my dreams, layering nightmares with desperation for water and drinking and overflowing cups full of sweet tea that my mother so adored.
Gasping, I slammed awake.
And just like that, my thirst was no longer the worst thing I endured.
A groan tore through my lips, involuntary and guttural as I tried to move.
Flashbacks of heavy rain, blinding lightning, and ear-bleeding thunder shot through me with panic.
Melike! Afet!
I shot upright, the world swimming, my eyes hazy, and my head stuffed full of salt-drenched clouds.
My pain was nothing this time.
They were still out there.
Drowning.
"Mel! Where are you!? I—"
"Hey, it's okay. Don't move. Dad told me you're not allowed to move." Something slight and surprisingly strong landed beside me, hands pressing against my bare chest, pushing me backward.
"No." I fought. "Wait, I need—"
"You're safe but you're broken in places and shouldn't move." The hands pressed firmer. "Do you understand me? Stop fighting. You'll only break yourself more." A firm shove sent me reeling.
My head crunched against something soft.
My body bounced against comfort instead of splinter-splicing wood.
I blinked and did my best to focus.
A girl appeared in my brine-scratched stare.

A girl with sun-streaked dark-brown hair, wild and thick, tanned button nose, and the brightest, bluest eyes I'd ever seen. They were so pale and clear, they reminded me of moonlight on crystal water.

I licked my dry, storm-cracked lips.

My thirst came back with a vengeance. My throat was agonisingly raw. "Who…who are you?" I asked in my mother tongue.

She sat back and narrowed her bright, bright stare but she didn't take her tiny hand off my chest. She kept it splayed and planted, daring me to try to fight again.

"I can't speak your language." She tilted her head, sending a tumble of sea-wavy hair over her bare shoulder. My gaze slid over her, confusion wrapping tightly around my jumbled thoughts.

Just a child.

She was younger than I first thought.

Her willowy body was hidden beneath a turquoise one-piece bathing costume with dolphins frolicking on the chest. Her arms and legs were long and spoke of grace and strength that she'd eventually grow into, but for now, she was as fragile and opinionated as my little sister.

Melike.

Where are you?

My heart spasmed; grief became the worst pain of all.

With a grunt, I grabbed the girl's wrist, shoved her off me, and sat upright.

The room tipped upside down.

Sourness splashed on my tongue as I swung my legs over the edge of whatever I lay on.

I went to stand.

I have to find them—

I stood.

My left leg buckled beneath me, sending me plummeting to the floor.

I blacked out for a second, blinking back spots as the girl dropped to her knees beside me and wrapped a slight arm around my quaking shoulders. "I told you, you're broken. Dad reckons your ankle is fractured. And your right wrist is almost certainly too. And there's a gash on your forehead that probably needs stitches, and I don't know about you, but no one should be as black and blue with bruises as you are, so they need tending to as well."

I fought the urge to throw up as wave after wave of debilitating pain crashed through me. Heavy and relentless, just like the waves from the storm.

Horror clutched at my throat. "Please…take me to them. You have to take me to them." I shook my head and clutched blindly at her hands, losing myself in a whirlpool of despair. "I'll do whatever you ask. Just please. Please, let me see my family."

Her fingers clutched hard around mine, her eyes sad even as she smiled and refused to answer me. "I knew it." Her closeness interrupted my spiralling sorrow. "I knew you spoke English. Mum wasn't sure, but I knew you screamed the word shark when I touched you."

She leaned closer, her body heat sinking into me. "Do you remember me telling you it wasn't a shark? It was Sapphire. She's the leader of the pod of bottlenose dolphins that led us to find you."

I struggled to care about anything that wasn't my family.

I'd done this.

I was the reason we were fugitives—

Swaying away from her, I cursed the rock and roll of my head. Sitting on the floor, I felt a different rock and roll beneath me, blending with my sickness. The steady slap-slap of water, the constant drum of sea rushing past a hull.

A hull that didn't groan as if it were butchered or break apart into pieces.

A boat.

I'm on another boat.

I glanced upward, flinching at the white ceiling, sun-beaming window, kitchenette, and table full of paperwork, mugs, and plates.

This wasn't just a boat.

It was a floating kingdom.

If my father had commissioned a vessel like this to carry us, he might still be alive.

This ship wouldn't have capsized. This boat would've protected us.

A tearing kind of anguish ripped through my chest.

An awful keening knowledge that I might have survived but everyone else—

A sob caught in my throat.

The *guilt*—

I tried to scramble away from the girl but I had no strength. I only had horror as I dropped my stare and froze.

My t-shirt was gone.

My shoes were missing.

The hand-woven friendship bracelet Mel had given me had torn off my wrist and most likely rotted at the bottom of the sea. Every inch of my skin was mottled and discoloured as if the very sky had taken offense to us trying to escape and done its best to scar me.

My bags were gone.

Every worldly possession we'd carefully packed and stowed was missing.

The only thing I had left was my torn and crinkly-dried grey shorts that my father had bought for my sixteenth birthday.

Stinging tears shot to my eyes.

Eleven months since our lives were normal. Eleven months of hiding, fearing, running…

Swallowing hard, choking on fear, I caught the clear-bright stare of the girl who sat far, far too close. "Please..." My accented voice sounded so different to her sunny, effortless rhythm. "Did you...did you find anyone else?"

The girl's pretty face froze as her eyes turned even sadder. She bit her bottom lip and her gaze flickered as if to leave mine, but with a fierce inhale, she held my stare and slowly shook her head. "You were the only one."

My chin tipped down.

My nape tingled with despair.

And I couldn't help it.

I'd drunk enough seawater to last a lifetime and now it poured hotly out of my eyes.

My ankle bellowed as I drew my legs up to my chin.

My wrist screeched as I wrapped my arms around them.

And my heart shattered as the girl who'd saved my life scooted closer and wrapped her slender embrace around me.

She shook and shuddered with me, holding on to me so tight.

Tight enough to keep me from being washed away by my tears.

Chapter Three

ASLAN

(*Moon in French:* Lune)

"NERI, WHAT ON EARTH—"

"It's okay, Mum. He fell. That's all." The girl ripped her arms away from me and leapt nimbly to her feet. She threw me a worried look. "His family is missing."

My heart fissured and it took everything inside me to stem my sorrow. Sucking gulps of air, I swiped angrily at my face, wiping away wetness, hissing as my damaged wrist screamed not to be used.

The girl's mother stepped warily toward me, throwing a glance at the long bench with its sun-faded baby-blue upholstery along the wall where I'd woken and promptly tumbled off. A streak of my blood marred a white cushion, staining it, ruining it.

I had absolutely nothing to my name, and, if I was honest, I would rather be at the bottom of the sea with my mother, father, and sister—

Tears welled again; I gritted my teeth.

But I was alive.

And that meant the politeness that'd been drilled into me by my uncle who was the reason my family was *dead*—

I fought another crest of grief.

Fuck, I can't do this—

An image of Melike speared through my mind.

Her innocent laughter. Her trusting eyes.

It wasn't fair.

It's not fucking fair!

"It's okay." The girl's mother approached me warily. "You're okay."

That word again.

I *hated* that word. *Despised* it.

If I never heard it again it would be too soon.

Anger was good.

It dried up my misery and gave me strength.

Straightening my spine, I shoved away my shipwrecked emotions and tipped up my chin.

I had nothing and no one.

These people had saved me.

It didn't matter I would rather they'd let me drown.

I owed them my thanks, and what had I done?

Ruined one of their cushions.

I sank into a lifetime of respect and obedience, taught with love and compassion but expected with a firm hand and harsh command. "I apologise for the stain. I'll…I'll replace the pillow. I'll find a way to repay you." I tried to stand but without two hands and two workable legs, I only succeeded in cursing with agony.

"Stop that." The girl strode back toward me and planted her delicate hand on my suddenly sweaty shoulder. "I told you not to move. You didn't listen to me the first time and now you're on the floor. You better listen to me now. Otherwise, your bones will break even more."

I shot her a look, anger flushing to be instructed by a child, but there was also something else. An odd kick in my heart that a total stranger cared enough about me to protect me, even from myself.

"Neri, let him go." Her mother drifted closer, holding out her hand as if I was a threat to her daughter. Her sun-lightened brown hair swayed in its ponytail as she shook her head kindly. "And I don't care about the cushion. I'm just glad you're awake and breathing."

I shifted the best I could, highly aware the girl called Neri hadn't removed her hand. Her delicate fingers burned my skin.

I looked up at her looming over me.

Her crystal-blue eyes met mine.

I couldn't suck in a breath.

Her mother looped an arm around Neri's shoulders and pulled her firmly away from me.

Neri tripped back with her, but her gaze never left mine, fierce and bright, perceptive and clear.

Prickles broke out over my nape as I swallowed hard.

Looping her arms over Neri's shoulders and clasping her hands over the dolphins on her daughter's flat chest from behind, the woman said, "My name's Anna. Anna Taylor. And you've already met my daughter, Nerida. My husband, Jack, is above deck. We found you amongst some wreckage—"

"It wasn't us who found him, Mum." Neri twisted to look up at her mother. "It was Sapphire. I told you the pod was acting strange. They came to get us and then swam so fast the boat barely kept up."

"They were merely wanting to surf the bow wake. Like they always do."

"No. They knew. They knew he was about to die and took us to find him." Neri turned back to face me, her jaw set with determination and eyes glittering with belief. "We found you for a reason. I'm so sorry we couldn't find the rest of your family, but don't be sad. They're with the whales now. They're swimming and happy and free."

A dagger pierced my chest.

Visions of my little sister trading her legs for fins brought fresh tears but also…incredibly…a little comfort.

I nodded once, even as my teeth gnashed together so hard they threatened to crack.

"What's your name?" Neri asked, sweeping me up in her questions, once again saving me from the undercurrent of my sadness. "Where are you from? Where were you going?"

"Neri. Hush, love." Anna shook her gently. "Give the poor guy time to breathe." Pausing, Anna narrowed her eyes and asked a question of her own. "Do you remember what happened?"

Storm-swells and thunder.

The sting of salt.

The horror of my mother's goodbyes.

I gritted my teeth all over again and swallowed—swallowed and swallowed so my tears couldn't drown me. I needed to look somewhere else, anywhere else, other than at the intense little girl who never took her gaze off me.

I glanced at the circular window where sun speared.

I flinched.

The perfect blue of unending sky had been replaced with the spiers of boat masts and seagulls. The faint noise of laughter and footsteps pounding on a pier drifted in.

How long did I lose myself to grief?

I stilled and noticed the quiet and stillness for the first time.

No more sea rock.

No more drone of waves and engines fighting against one another.

The woman sucked in a breath as something banged above and a man's voice intertwined with another in conversation.

"We're docked at port," she said. "We've already called ahead, and the hospital staff are aware you're coming. We'll take you and get you fixed up, alright? Once you're tended to, then we can talk."

I froze.

All the lessons from my father rushed back.

We were illegal.

We were supposed to slink ashore, unseen and undetected. To slip into society with silence and secrecy, doing our utmost to avoid any forms of authority or law enforcement.

We…

My heart broke.
Not anymore.
I was the illegal one.
I was the one who had to ensure I was never sent back.
Just me.
Panic overrode my sadness. "I-I'm fine." I fought to clamber to my feet again.

I have to leave.

Now.

I went to push up, but my ankle refused, sending a thousand bolts of pain up my leg.

I cried out.

"Don't." The girl struggled to come to me, held fast by her mother. "Don't move. Not until a doctor has patched you up. We have good doctors. I promise they'll make you better. Mum. Tell him to stop moving. He's hurt."

The girl's eyes welled with tears as if distraught at my pain. A boy she'd never met before but somehow felt so responsible for his well-being.

I could survive a storm and run from murderers, but for some reason, I couldn't fight her.

I fell back down, breathing hard.
I caught her stare.
My chest tightened.
And I nodded.

I nodded to them taking me to the hospital. To the risk of being deported. To death that continued to stalk me.

A man suddenly leapt down the short steps by the kitchenette, his bare feet nimble and well used to nautical life. He froze as he noticed us, his brown hair and blue eyes were darker than his daughter's but just as shrewd. "Ah, you're awake. I was hoping you would come round."

Striding forward in red swimming trunks and a white t-shirt, he clapped his hands and beamed. "I've pulled many things from the ocean, but never a boy before." Squatting down to face me, he dropped his attention to my wrist and ankle. "Didn't Neri tell you not to move? Never mind. We're on land now. Just a short drive, and you'll be right as rain in a jiffy."

I didn't have time to move or refuse as his strong arms wrapped around me, hoisting me to my feet with a powerful wrench. "There you go. Good as new."

My chin tipped downward as sickness crashed through me.
Pain and vertigo.
Lightheadedness and nausea.
I moaned and swayed in his hold.

"Easy does it, mate. Just give me a heads up if you're gonna hurl and try to hop on your good leg." Leading me toward the short flight of steps to the upper deck, he huffed under his breath. "This isn't gonna be fun, but I carried you down here, and I can carry you back up. You're a lean bean, and I'm used to wrangling whales, don't you know."

I groaned again as my vision washed in and out, and then…somehow, I was in his arms. Scooped up as if I weighed nothing. He grunted as he hauled me to the top deck.

I screamed as my ankle bashed against the safety barrier.

"Oops, sorry. Watch out for your appendages." The guy tripped forward, keeping me tight in his arms. "Hold on to my neck. There you go. That's a good lad."

"Dad. Careful. You're gonna break him even more." Neri's voice slipped through my ringing ears, giving me an anchor as the world swept in and out.

The black spots were back.

Woozy waves crashed over my mind.

"Jack, be careful. The deck is slippery." Anna's voice sounded farther away. "Neri, grab my bag. I'll help your father with our piece of flotsam here. Actually, how about you run ahead and get the Jeep started so you're not underfoot?"

"Okay. I'll drive it down to the pier."

"No. No driving. I told you last time—" Jack bellowed.

But it was too late.

The little girl with hair the colour of sun-streaked chocolate and legs as tanned as mine dashed into the captain's cabin, snagged a black bag, then hurled herself over the edge of the boat.

My heart seized.

Images of my sister being flung out of my arms and into the sea made me sick.

But then the thud of her feet on wooden planks came and the sight of her sprinting to shore stole all my remaining strength.

The black spots won.

I passed out.

Chapter Four

ASLAN

(*Moon in Māori* : Marama)

I RAN MY FINGERS OVER MY RIGHT wrist, following the bumps of a fresh cast that imprisoned me. My thumb and most of my palm were free but half my forearm had been encased with stiff plaster.

At least my wrist didn't scream as much, cocooned in protection and dulled by over-the-counter painkillers.

Continuing my exploration, I raised my hand and stroked the neat row of stitches in my forehead. According to the doctor who'd sewn me up, my skull had been showing, thanks to a nasty thwack and throw by the storm. Seven internal stitches and eleven external ones meant I was no longer bleeding.

Glancing down my body, I narrowed my eyes on my left ankle.

At least they hadn't bound me in a second cast.

X-rays had shown a fracture—just like my wrist—but they'd opted to strap me into a plastic boot rather than something porous and semi-permanent.

I was grateful for that.

Grateful for the care I'd been given, the kind smiles I'd been offered, and the lack of questions I'd been asked.

I hadn't passed out again after I'd come to in the back of a rough and rugged four-wheel drive, my head on Neri's lap. Her fingers had paused their journey through my salt-dry hair the moment my eyes opened and locked onto hers.

I'd frozen.

I'd struggled to breathe.

But then she just ran her fingers over my scalp again, sending a flurry of goosebumps down my arms and inside my heart.

The moment had stretched far longer than it should before the 4WD lurched to a halt, and Neri's father wrenched open the back door.

He'd helped me hop into the hospital as my vision hovered between opaque and clear, dropping me into a wheelchair as two nurses approached.

I'd looked back as I was wheeled through double doors.

I'd swallowed my fear as the doors closed on the Taylor family and the little girl who watched me so fiercely.

I'd done my best to stay alert for the past few hours, but my concentration was failing now I'd been left alone. The doctors said I had a probable concussion, contusions and bruises on almost every inch of my body, and whispered it was a miracle I'd survived.

They seemed to know about the shipwreck.

They seemed to know how I'd ended up here.

Yet no one asked anything more, focusing on fixing me rather than learning who I was.

Their lack of interest begged me to relax, but each time someone entered the room, I prepared to leap to my feet and run. I had visions of uniformed officers appearing, slapping me in cuffs, and marching me out of the hospital. Nightmares of dragging me past the girl who'd saved my life, all while knowing that the moment they sent me back home, I was a dead man anyway.

But no one came.

No one looked at me as if I didn't deserve to be there.

No one refused me care.

I sighed, dropping my hand and staring at the ceiling.

Images of my parents crowded in my head.

My mother's desperation telling us she loved us.

My sister's scream—

I clenched my jaw and forced myself to think about another girl.

Would I ever see her again or had they gone? They'd done their duty and delivered me to doctors. They had no reason to return.

I hated that beneath my never-ending grief for my family, I had enough sadness to spare at the thought of never seeing them again.

My stomach snarled, interrupting my tired thoughts.

My thirst had been steadily growing more and more excruciating the longer I'd been tended to. Despite the doctor's wonderful care on patching up my obvious injuries, no one had stopped to think how dry and desiccated I was after drinking an entire ocean of salt.

My eyes fell on the basin in the far corner of the ward where I'd been placed. Other beds were occupied, kept private with curtains with flowers and stars printed on them. I was closest to the wall. Nearest the window.

At least there was a way out.

Gritting my teeth, I forced my battered body to move.

First, I would drink. Then I would see about stealing some clothes to replace the open-backed gown I'd been dressed in.

And then...I was leaving.

Grabbing hold of the safety rung around the bed, I gingerly lowered my legs to the floor. I didn't leap down. I took my time, easing myself to standing while the world threatened to turn black on me again and my throat closed around fresh nausea.

Hissing between my teeth, I managed to stand. Barely.

The sink and its tap seemed a million miles away.

Fuck.

My chin tipped down as exhaustion clotted my mind.

My mouth was so dry. My head so heavy.

But I couldn't fucking move because if I didn't have something to hold on to, I'd fall.

Furious tears pricked. Exhausted rage-thick tears.

I'd never been so weak or so helpless. Never forced to see just how fragile I truly was. After eleven months of running from my uncle's killers. Eleven months of stepping up to help my father protect our family. Eleven months of becoming a man and so stupidly believing I was strong enough to take on anything and anyone, I finally accepted I was *nothing*.

Nothing but a boy who could so easily be snuffed out.

Fuck, what a fool I am.

I'm so sorry. My grief swelled. *So sorry I'm the reason you're dead—*

"What in the freaking seashells are you doing out of bed?"

My head whipped up, and I slashed at the tear rolling down my cheek. Everything stilled inside me as Neri marched toward me with tiny hands on dainty hips, and a peach sundress wafting around her lanky legs. "Are you that pig-headed that you don't obey anyone or are you just stupid?"

I scowled. "Don't call me stupid."

"I can call you stupid if you're doing stupid things, and right now—" She crossed her arms and looked me up and down. "You're being stupid."

I was suddenly very aware of my lack of clothing and the breeze running over my bare ass. With a wince and a groan, I hitched myself back onto the bed and breathed heavily. "I thought you and your parents had gone."

"We did." As quickly as she'd snapped at me, she grinned. Dropping her arms, she skipped to my side and sprang onto the bed, making it shudder. "We went home to change and grab supplies."

"Supplies?"

"Yeah, you know like food and stuff."

"Stuff?"

She plucked at the starchy bed sheets. "This isn't very comfy. It's all stiff and smelly."

I couldn't keep up with this girl. "You're annoyed at the bed now?"

"I'm not annoyed." She looked up, blowing strands of wavy, chocolatey hair out of her eyes.

Once again, I couldn't look away.

Her eyes were unique. Too blue. Too bright. Too *seeing*.

"You okay?" she whispered, her voice so gentle and sweet it made me jolt with a wave of homesickness, heartache, and sorrow.

I knew I should look away.

I should probably *move* away.

But the longer she looked into me, the more I found myself in her, and I fucking drowned all over again.

She blinked.

The spell broke.

I shook my head and tried to speak. "I…I—" I coughed, clearing the scratch and dryness. "Please don't ask me that. I never want to hear that word again."

Her innocent forehead scrunched up before her eyes widened with understanding. "Okay. I promise not to say okay. Oops, I said okay to not saying okay. Darn, I said it again. Okay, I'll stop now. I mean, crap—" She swatted her hand against her mouth, mumbling. "I'm done."

A smile teased the corners of my lips.

It caught me by complete surprise.

I never thought I'd ever smile again, let alone be on the brink of a chuckle.

What sort of magic did this girl possess?

I sighed with all the weight of this new world I'd been thrust into. "Do you…do you think you could do me a favour?"

Her eyes lit up and her shoulders pinned back with importance. A silver chain around her neck glittered with a whale tail charm.

I caught myself wanting to touch it. To touch her. To ask her about her necklace and why she seemed so at home on the sea and why she could speak to a pod of dolphins and just who the hell *was she*.

But then I blinked again and forced myself to truly look at her.

To see the child she was.

A child who beamed with trust and newness and purity.

"Of course! I mean…it's not like I didn't do you a favour by saving your life or anything. After that big favour, everything else will be tiny." She leaned forward, her nose wrinkling adorably. "Let me guess. You want…" Peering around the room, she tapped her lips with pink-painted fingernails. Her gaze fell on the sink in the corner. "Water! You want a drink. I always want a drink after swimming. Mum doesn't believe me, but I reckon my skin soaks up the salt. I get ever so thirsty."

Launching off the bed, she charged for the sink, grabbed a paper cup from a strange-looking holder beside it, and filled it.

I practically fell off the bed with desperation as she brought it to me.

I snatched it off her.

I poured it down my throat.

Two swallows and the meagre amount was gone.

I lost all concept of politeness. "More. A thousand times more."

With a stern little look, she took back my empty cup and marched to the sink again. This time she filled it to the brim, sloshing precious water all over her hand as she crossed the distance and handed it to me warily.

I did my best not to snatch it from her this time, but it was difficult.

She didn't wait for me to drink.

Running back to the sink, she looked around for something bigger and settled on the measuring jug one of the doctors had used to measure the plaster ingredients before wrapping my arm with bandages and smearing hot goo all over me.

My lips smacked together as she filled it.

So long.

It took *so long* for it to fill.

And when it was full, she struggled to carry it, clutching it tightly to her chest, dousing herself as she walked with utmost concentration across the ward.

I took it from her as if it was liquid gold.

I drank from it as if it contained holy water.

And only once the last droplet landed on my grateful tongue did I slowly lower the jug, wipe my mouth with the back of my non-cast hand, and look up. "How old are you?" I asked quietly.

She startled as if she hadn't expected me to ask. With a tilt of her chin, she held out her arms for the empty jug. "Twelve. How old are you?"

Twelve?

"Sixteen," I muttered. "I turn seventeen in December."

"Wow, you're old." She placed the jug on the side table where a board of medical buttons and important-looking wires reminded us exactly where we were. "I mean, you're like *ancient*. I should probably have let the sharks eat you. You're so over the hill it's not even funny." Planting her hands on her hips again, she grinned. "You know what? My dad has a speargun. I'll get him to put you out of your misery, okay? Ah shoot." She smashed her hands over her lips again. "I did it again."

This time, I did chuckle.

My belly was uncomfortably full from so much water and my heart kept bleeding for what I'd lost, but for the first time, the heaviness in my head had faded, and with it, some of the heaviness in my soul. "I'll tell you what. You can use that word in any other context, as long as you're not using it to ask how I am. *Okay*?" I smiled as I forced myself to use it. Forced myself to face a fear that I refused to bow to.

"Deal." She stuck out her tiny hand.

I reared back as if she'd aimed the promised speargun at me.

She didn't lower her arm, although an embarrassed flinch crossed her face. She tried to cover it with a grin, but I couldn't unsee it. Couldn't unsee the way she watched me with the same sort of longing I'd looked at the jug full of water.

My heart quickened.

There was...*something*.

Something that shouldn't exist.

I couldn't stop myself as I reached out and wrapped my much bigger hand around hers.

She sucked in a short breath, making my nape prickle. Her blue, blue eyes landed on our linked hands, and with the softest exhale, she whispered, "It feels different, doesn't it?" She looked up, freezing me in her far too bright stare. "I mean...different to when I touch my mum or dad. Different to when I touch my friends. Different to even when I'm stroking Sapphire and her babies."

Her fingers flexed in mine, sending the faintest current through me.

I tugged my hand from hers, burying it beneath my casted one. "It's because you saved my life."

"It is?" Her eyebrows met her hairline. "Why?"

I flexed my fist, willing the tingle to cease.

A flash of my mother making up stories for Melike when she struggled to sleep haunted me. Those stories had been the only thing that could calm Mel enough to dream, especially as we ran for our lives.

Swallowing against another onslaught of despair, I murmured, "In my language...my name means lion. Lions don't belong in the sea, and if you hadn't found me, I would've sunk and—"

"Become a sea lion." Neri giggled. "There are sea lions, you know. They don't have paws, but they do have big teeth and strong flippers."

"Are you going to let me tell the story or not?"

"Is it a happy story?"

"Aren't all stories happy?" I winced.

I'd learned the hard way that wasn't true. Not at all.

"Not sometimes," Neri whispered. "Not always." Coming closer to me, she rested her hand on my cast.

I was grateful I couldn't feel her skin against mine, but her nearness did worrying things to my heart.

"I'm so sorry. About your family. I meant what I said about them being with the whales now. I know you're sad, but they're oka—I mean...they're safe now. Just like you are. Here. With me."

I couldn't breathe.

Couldn't move.

She looked down then back up again, keeping her chin low and watching me beneath thick eyelashes. "What's your name? It must be cool if it means lion." She hopped onto the bed, making me shift away. "My mother called me Nerida because it means sea nymph. That's cool too. Or at least, I think it is.

She said a fortune teller at a local fair told her that one day I would live beneath the waves." Her eyes turned dreamy. "I can't breathe underwater yet, but I keep trying. Keep scaring my dad when I manage to hold for ages, and he's probably going to have a heart attack when I figure out how to be a real fish, but...oh well."

I held her stare.

I fell into everything about her.

Guilt roared through me.

Grief made me suffocate.

I needed her gone.

Crossing my arms, my tone cooled. "I think you should probably go."

"Go?" Her mouth parted in shock. "But why? I thought..." Her shoulders slouched. "I thought we were friends."

Her pain became my pain.

I flinched.

Ah, fuck.

How had this happened?

I squeezed the back of my neck. "Look, I—"

"Are you harassing that poor boy again?" Neri's father appeared around the flower curtain.

I scrambled farther away from his daughter as if I'd been caught doing something punishable by death.

His weathered face broke into a grin as soon as he saw me. "You're alive. And hopefully, back in one piece."

I clutched my cast and bowed my head in respect. "Thank you, sir. Thank you for getting me care—"

"Jack. Please. Call me Jack. And you're more than welcome." Raising his hand, he dumped a heavy duffel on the end of the bed next to his daughter. Giving her a quick squeeze, he tapped her on the nose and tutted good naturedly. "We told you to stay with us while we finished filling in the paperwork. Yet what did you do, little fish? You ran away again." He huffed and rolled his eyes as he stood to his full height. "Always slipping through my fingers. Making me wonder where you've swum off too."

"I came to see if he was alright. I overheard the nurse say which ward he was in."

"You're too smart for your own good." Jack ruffled her hair and turned to his wife as she appeared. "Anna, look at where our no-good daughter ended up. Harassing the patient."

Anna smiled, her pretty face so similar to Neri's with big eyes, petite nose, and expressive mouth. Her hair was darker but only just, losing the battle with salt and sun. "I'm glad to see you're stronger," she said, throwing me a smile even if it was a little reserved.

Striding forward, she ordered, "Neri, help me with this table. We'll scoot it closer to the bed and have ourselves a picnic before we go."

"Go?" The word slipped from my lips despite myself.

"Yes. It's getting late. We have to be up at four again tomorrow. The humpbacks have begun migrating back to warmer waters to calf."

That was not the answer I was expecting. "You help whales give birth?"

Jack chuckled. "Nah, we just watch. And take photos. And notes. And everything else really that will document their habits and secrets." He helped Neri wheel a large table that'd been pushed by the window toward me on the bed. "My wife and I are marine biologists."

"And me!" Neri piped up, throwing herself back on the bed beside me as if she belonged there.

I forced myself not to look at her, focusing on her parents. "I've never met a marine biologist before."

"Well, now you have." Anna dropped the brown paper bags and drinks she'd been carrying, before dragging two hardback chairs from behind the curtain separating us from another patient. "We get to spend every waking moment doing what we love."

"And one day, I'll be the bestest biologist there ever was." Neri grinned, tearing into the bags and passing me something wrapped in grease-shiny paper. "Here. It's from our favourite burger joint. I made Dad grab you something to eat before we came back to check on you."

Jack huffed and unwrapped a juicy burger full of crisp lettuce, battered fish, and oozing white sauce. He bit into it. "It's called the Nemo burger. Kinda wrong, really, to name a food after a children's movie, and even more wrong for people who study fish for a living to eat it, but…hey." He shrugged and took another huge bite. "That's life, I guess. Food chain and all."

Neri munched beside me, watching me intently as I slowly unwrapped my burger.

Just like my thirst had attacked me and made me lose all decorum, my hunger snarled to shove the food into my mouth as fast as humanly possible.

"Here." Anna passed me a box of golden french fries.

My mouth watered so much I almost drooled.

"That's super rude, by the way!" a voice yelled behind the flower curtain. "I can smell that deliciousness all the way from my bed."

"Sorry!" Jack yelled. "Can't share. Don't know what drugs you're on."

"I'm allowed whatever I want," another patient yelled. "Go on, share!"

"Ah, damn, but would you look at that!" Jack shouted. "All gone. Our shipwreck survivor just inhaled every bite."

Cracking a smile, shocked once again that I could do such a thing, I did exactly what he said.

I shoved the french fries so fast into my mouth, I choked.

"Easy," Anna admonished. "There's plenty more. We bought two of everything in case you hadn't eaten in a while."

Neri never looked away as I finished the fries in a few massive mouthfuls and raised the burger to my mouth.

I bit into it.

She grinned as I groaned.

Whatever the sauce was, it was divine.

How long had it been since I'd eaten?

A day? Two? Three?

We'd nibbled on bananas and rice balls on the long journey from Indonesia, but that was barely enough to sustain us. A full month since I'd left Turkey, first by plane, then by boat, leaving behind everything I ever knew for a reason I wasn't told until we were at sea and unable to turn back.

No one spoke as we focused on eating.

I lost myself to chewing and swallowing, slowly feeling more and more alive with every bite.

It might've been a month since I'd left my home, but we'd been on the run for almost a year. A year of looking over our shoulders, hiding in earthquake-cracked villages, and relying on the kindness of strangers.

Tears sprang to my eyes as I finished my meal, and Anna passed me another burger without a word.

Her caring attentiveness reminded me of my own mother.

My mother who was now a meal herself for every creature under the sea.

My appetite fled.

I felt sick.

With trembling hands, I pushed away the unwrapped burger and shook my head. "I...I can't. I'm sorry."

"Don't apologise," Jack muttered, wiping his hands with a napkin. "You've endured something not many people have. It will take time to move past it." Taking two soft drinks from the cardboard holder, he kept one and passed one to me.

I nodded my thanks and raised it to my lips.

I shuddered as icy sweetness hit my tongue, suffocating me, all over again, with memories of my mother's addiction to sugary tea.

I sucked on the paper straw, my mind sinking deeper into sadness.

I couldn't stop it.

Couldn't swim back to the surface where these people were so incredibly kind.

Whatever lightness Neri had granted blinked out, and I sighed heavily. I cursed the crushing pressure of a sob just waiting to crawl up my throat.

I wanted them to go.

To leave so I could break in peace.

Jack sensed my unravelling composure and clasped my shoulder. "Look, you're being kept here overnight to monitor your concussion. You'll be warm and dry and can get some rest." He arched his chin at the duffel he'd tossed onto the bed. "I brought you a few clothes. They might be a little big, but they'll do for now. When you're discharged in the morning, get the hospital to call me." Letting me go, he pulled out a card from his wallet. A crinkled, corner-curled card with the same whale tail that hung off Neri's necklace. His name was stamped in blue along with a phone number and an address.

"Here. Keep this safe." He pressed it into my greasy hand. "Once you're feeling a bit better, we'll talk and figure out where to go from here. Sound good?"

I fisted the card.

My eyes burned hotter.

"Is there anyone in Port Douglas we can call?" he asked. "Were you travelling to family already here?"

I choked on grief, barely managing to shake my head.

Jack was perceptive and merely nodded. "Enough questions for now. We've filled in all your paperwork as best we can, so you don't need to do that tonight, but there is one thing they need to know."

I raised my heavy head, sorrow swirling thickly. That damn whirlpool was back, sucking me down, down, down. "What?" I asked stiffly. "What do you need to know?"

"Your name," Neri said quietly.

Her voice cut through my despair, ripping my gaze to hers.

I tripped over my badly stuttering heart. "My name?"

Didn't I tell her?

I thought I told her.

"You said it means lion…in your language."

Her parents shared a look I didn't like. A look with raised eyebrows and suspicious curiosity. I ought to care what they thought.

But I was exhausted and lost and the only thing keeping me from being swept out to sea on a wave of tears was her.

"Aslan," I whispered.

"Aslan?" She licked her lips, drawing all my attention.

My broken heart gave another strange kick.

"My name is Aslan Avci, and I owe you, Nerida, for every breath that I take. From this moment, until my last moment."

Her cheeks pinked.

Her father wrote my name on the form.

Her mother gathered up the packages from our meal.

And then…in a vortex of darkness and misery, they gave me words of comfort and goodbyes before gathering up their daughter.

They left me on that bed.

All while Neri never took her eyes off me as they dragged her away.

I felt her eyes on me long after she'd gone.

I felt her watching as I tipped to my side, drew up my knees, and lost myself to grief.

Chapter Five

ASLAN

(Moon in Chinese : Yuèliàng)

"ASLAN AVCI? CAN YOU WAKE UP FOR me?"

I ripped awake, snapping upright, searching the darkness for guns and bastards.

My heart thundered for sounds of shots and screams.

Someone touched my shoulder.

I reacted the way I'd been taught.

I struck without question.

I hit before they could hit me.

An *umph* sounded with a pained exhale before a click and a wash of light.

I cringed away from the brightness, my head pounding and my battered body stiff from surviving.

"You're safe. No harm will come to you. Are you awake and aware, or do I need to get reinforcements?"

Rubbing my eyes, the terror of being hunted faded. Memories of the storm overshadowed memories of home, and I slouched. Raising my head, I blinked at the pretty young nurse with dusky-olive skin and brown-black hair watching me.

She rubbed at the side of her neck, letting me know where my strike had landed.

I hung my head and dug my fingers into my throbbing head. "I'm sorry. I didn't mean—"

"It's okay."

I clenched my jaw.

That damn word again.

"You weren't really supposed to sleep. You're on concussion watch, but all hands were needed for an emergency. We're a small hospital with typical staff shortages, so I apologise that no one has been around to check on you." Dropping her arm, she consulted the forms that Jack Taylor had filled in on my behalf.

I watched her carefully as she skimmed whatever he'd written. A slight frown pinched between her eyes. "Your next of kin is Anna Taylor? The marine biologist?"

I flinched.

She knows her?

How sad was it that my world had been reduced to no one.

Everyone I ever loved or loved me was gone.

And a total stranger was listed as my next of kin.

I didn't have the energy to explain, and a whisper in the back of my mind warned me to tread carefully. Trying to change the subject, I asked, "What...what time is it?"

She stood taller and flicked her wrist, checking a rose gold watch gleaming in the soft light. "Two a.m."

I didn't even remember falling asleep.

My thirst was back, along with hunger, but both urges were nowhere near as excruciating. And, unlike the other times when I'd woken from being unconscious, I wasn't woozy or sick. The burger and water had replaced my strength, and I sat a little straighter in bed.

An awkward silence fell while the nurse glanced at my casted wrist, booted ankle, and the stitches in my head. Finally, she asked, "How are you feeling? Any significant discomfort? Do you need pain relief?" She scowled a little. "Not that we can administer anything stronger than paracetamol, seeing as your list of allergies and medical history hasn't been filled in."

Slipping a pen from her breast pocket of her uniform, she moved to one of the chairs Anna had dragged round to enjoy our picnic. Sitting down, she hovered the pen over the paperwork. "Can you tell me your date of birth? Your nationality? I'll fill in the rest for you, so tomorrow, when border control officers arrive to interview you, they'll have all the relevant information."

My heart stopped. "Border control?"

She nodded slowly. "It's protocol. You were found out to sea. We often receive asylum seekers trying to illegally enter Australia. It's nothing personal, you understand. We merely want to ensure you have someone to help, money to survive, and a home to go to."

Panic coiled through me, cold and sharp. "And if I don't have a home?"

"Then we can arrange transport back to the one you left behind."

Ice.

Freezing ice down my spine.

I swallowed hard, desperately willing my battered brain to figure out what to do. "When—" I cleared my throat. "When will the officers arrive?"

She gave me a searching look. "They're usually here around ten o'clock. Gives the morning rotation time to assess you, perform any last-minute tests, and confirm that you're fit for discharge."

I nodded.

It was all I could do.

My throat closed up.

My eyes flew to the window, but then I forced them back to her. I did what I'd done ever since my uncle was killed and we were forced to run. I smothered down my terror and embraced the cold. "Do you mind if I get some more sleep then? Tomorrow sounds like it will be busy."

She studied me for a moment before nodding. "Pass our final concussion test and I'll leave you be until daybreak." Striding toward the bedside table and its collection of buttons and wires, she opened the drawer and held up a laminated piece of paper. "Read this fully and completely."

I frowned but obeyed as she passed it to me.

It was nothing more than nonsense.

Utter stupidity of a dog chasing a mouse and failing, along with a few extremely basic arithmetic.

I handed it back to her. "Why did I have to read that?"

Keeping it tucked to her chest, she smiled gently. "If you remember the story and the sums and can recall which way the mouse ran, it's safe to say you aren't suffering a concussion."

Striding away, she said over her shoulder. "I'll be back in thirty minutes."

I was waiting for her when she returned.

Thirty minutes had felt like an age but really it passed in a blink.

At least I had a plan now.

A plan that would probably get me killed, but it was a far sight better than being sent home.

"So?" The nurse smiled. "Do you remember the story?"

"The dog with fourteen spots heard a rustling and saw a hungry mouse. The dog counted to five and chased the mouse but lost it when it turned left at the willow tree. The dog sniffed around the tree four times and barked thirty-three barks but still couldn't find it. After waiting fifty-seven minutes, the mouse appeared, and the dog chased it into the farmer's back garden, destroying twenty-nine dandelions in his hurry."

The nurse raised her head from reading along. Her eyebrows raised. "You said it verbatim. No one ever does that."

I hadn't been taught that English word, but it didn't matter. I took her shock as a good thing. "Did I pass?"

"You're definitely not concussed."

"Does that mean I can sleep now?"

She frowned and studied me. "You don't happen to have an eidetic memory, do you?"

Yet another English word I wasn't aware of. My pulse skittered. "I'm not sure—"

"If I asked you what twelve times fifty-six was, you'd say—"

"*Altı yüz yetmiş iki.*" I flinched. "Sorry, in English, I'd say six hundred and seventy-two."

"How about forty-seven times ninety-two?"

"Four thousand, three hundred and twenty-four."

Her eyes widened. "Have you always been good at math?"

My heart folded in on itself. "My father was a math professor."

"Oh." She nodded and stood, her eyes still locked on mine. "I suppose that explains it." Moving toward the drawers, she slipped the concussion test sheet back inside and closed it quietly. "I'm sorry…about what happened."

My throat closed up.

I said nothing.

She hovered over me for the longest moment, almost as if she wanted to say something else. But then she rolled her shoulders, forced a smile, and said softly, "I'll come check on you before my shift is over." She went to leave, but at the last second, she placed her hand on my cast, wrenching my eyes to hers.

"You'll be okay, I promise. I know it's scary to be interviewed by officials but just tell them the truth, and you'll be fine. You seem very special and…they'll see that. They'll know what an asset you could be to this country."

Tell the truth?

I swallowed a morbid laugh.

The truth would get me slaughtered.

Pulling my hand from beneath hers, I fluffed up the stiff and bleach-smelly sheets that Neri had wrinkled her nose at. "Goodnight." I lay down on my side, giving her my back.

A few lingering seconds before a shuffle of her shoes and a quiet sigh. "Goodnight, Aslan."

I waited until I could no longer hear her.

I waited longer just to be sure.

I waited until the patient next to me behind the curtain started snoring again.

Only then did I rip back the sheet, swing my bruised legs out of bed, and bite my tongue to silence my groan as I dropped to my feet and grabbed the bag Jack had left me.

With shaking hands and fighting the awkwardness of my cast, I quickly tore off the backless gown, shoved my legs into black boxer-briefs and navy shorts that were far too big for me—cursing the boot around my ankle the entire time—and shrugged into a cream t-shirt that dwarfed me. In the bottom of the bag rested a belt that I notched to the tightest hole and flip-flops that stuck out behind my size eight feet.

I only needed one shoe, thanks, once again, to the damn boot.

I turned to go, but something caught my attention.

Cash.

A bundle of pretty-coloured notes folded in half and secured with a paperclip waited in the bottom of the duffel.

My sorrow chose that exact moment to crush me.

Tears burned, and despair choked.

I'd lost my family, yet another had been so incredibly kind to me.

Kind enough to fix me, feed me, clothe me, pay me.

They deserved to be left alone.

They owed me absolutely nothing.

I owed them absolutely everything.

Yet I had nowhere else to go.

Snatching the money, I crept to the window and yanked off the insect screen. With my heart in my mouth, I eased it open.

It stopped halfway, as if rigged to prevent people from using it as an unofficial exit.

In another life, the crack wouldn't be big enough.

But in this one, where I was malnourished from living on the run and desperation made me determined, I shimmied my shoulders through, sucked in my belly, and slithered like a snake into the wilting flowers below.

Chapter Six
NERIDA

(Sea in Turkish : Deniz)

"SO, YOU SAVED A BOY'S LIFE WHEN you were just twelve. You fell in love with that boy without knowing a single thing about him, and when you confessed it felt different when you touched him, he merely said it was because his life was now yours?" Margot clutched her notebook to her chest. "I mean…wow."

She blinked back the stars in her gaze. "That is so crazily romantic and—"

"Stupid," Dylan muttered.

"Dylan!" Margot whacked him with her notebook. "It's not stupid. It's fate. It's love at first sight—"

"Forgive me," Dylan said, catching my eyes with a wince. "But…I'm not one for destiny. Surely, you look back now and admit that what you felt back then was just an…infatuation? A strong one but nothing more than that."

I laughed under my breath, not offended by his lack of belief. After all, until it happened to you, it seemed as far-fetched as a fairy-tale. "It was the biggest infatuation of my life." I stroked my wedding ring. "My *only* infatuation."

"No one else?" Margot asked, her eyes crinkling with eagerness. "You mean, he was your first and your last? Oh God, could this tale get any sweeter?"

I didn't catch her misty gaze.

I couldn't answer that question without reliving the two worst moments of my life.

So I didn't.

"I'm never going to live this down." Dylan groaned under his breath. "Not only did I brag to everyone I know that I was chosen to interview *the* Nerida Avci, but now I'm going to have to sign my name to an article full of taboo romance and pubescent angst."

I chuckled softly and shook my head, dispelling the future and what I'd have to share. "I promise our tale has more than just longing, Mr. Collins." My laughter drifted away as my thoughts nudged at the wound that would never truly heal. "There is darkness. A lot of darkness. There are bad guys and murderous plots. There's torture and—"

"Hold up. *Torture?*" Dylan sat dead straight. "Whose? Yours, his—?"

I swallowed hard.

That part of the story would also not be easy.

In fact, looking back, our love had endured so much.

So, so much heartache and pain and suffering.

God, the *suffering*.

But I would live it all over again to be with him.

"If you don't mind, Mr. Collins, I'd like to unfold the events as they did in the past." I gave him a smile, softening my tone. "If I'm going to do this, I'd like to bask in the freshness of new love a little longer, if that's okay with you."

I wanted to relive the falling, the wanting, the first touch and stolen kiss and everything else between.

Margot glanced at Dylan before reaching across the short distance between us and patting my knee. Her eyes caught mine, wide and eager. "Tell us everything. I don't know about Dylan, but I'm not going anywhere. Give me every juicy, delicious detail."

Settling back against the lacy cushions, I said, "Okay then. Well, I was an impressionable young girl. I was raised a little wild and given freedoms not granted to many. My days were full of sea life and sunshine. My nights were full of watching my parents laugh and love. I wanted so very much to be loved in that way, so I suppose, when Aslan told me that his every breath, from then until his last, was mine, I fell so hard I became his in return."

I plucked at my floaty dress. "I believed the sea had chosen him to be mine, you see. A shipwrecked boy delivered to me by a pod of dolphins that I'd grown up swimming with. I was just lucky I had kind parents who believed it was their duty as humans to help anyone and anything who needed it. If they'd been anyone else, our story would've ended before it'd even begun."

Dylan wiped his mouth and angled the microphone closer to me. His lips were pursed but he couldn't hide the light in his hazel eyes. The curiosity to see where this story would go. "You said your parents took him to receive care? That you went back to check on him—with takeout no less—and then you left because of an early start?"

"The hours of a marine biologist are all over the place. Some nights, we'd work until two a.m. studying phosphorus luminescent plankton. Others, we'd get up at dawn to chase the dwarf minke whales or dive on the reef to see hundreds of baby turtles fresh out of their nest."

"But you were twelve." Dylan scowled. "You weren't working with them, surely? What about school and things?"

"I was home-schooled until I finished primary. They tried sending me to school on land, but it never stuck. I'd run from class, stowaway on some fishing trawler, and appear from behind their nets when we were far out to sea, demanding the poor fishermen radio my parents on *The Fluke* to come get me."

"*The Fluke?*"

"Our research boat." I grinned. "My mother often said she'd doomed them the moment she delivered me in a home water birth. That my affinity with the ocean could never be undone."

"She was right." Margot laughed. "I mean, you figured out a way to live underwater. Just like you said that fortune teller prophesized."

"I don't think she quite meant I'd one day create a biosphere capable of recycling air, reusing waste, and providing a dry and wonderful home to land-locked humans, but yes. I did. But not without a lot of help from my business partners."

"I really would like to know more about Lunamare," Dylan said. "How did you figure out the construction? How do the fields of seaweed work? How do you channel CO_2 into energy?"

"Later, Dylan." Margot waved him away. "Not important. What *is* important are these two lovebirds." Planting her elbows on her knees, she rested her chin in her upturned palms. "Go on, Nerida."

I studied both journalists and let myself sink back into the head and heart space of a twelve-year-old besotted little girl.

"He was there, at our house, when we returned from the sea, the day after we found him. Fast asleep in the driftwood sala that my father made for my mother on their tenth wedding anniversary. He'd raided the veggie garden that I'd been put in charge of, and I distinctly remember being cross at the hole where he'd helped himself to a carrot."

My eyes no longer saw the beach or the reporters.

They only saw Aslan as I nudged him with my tiny, pink-painted toes, and said—

Chapter Seven
ASLAN

(*Moon in Indonesian:* Bulan)

"YOU KNOW, STEALING ISN'T VERY NICE. IF you'd just asked, I would've given you anything you wanted."

My eyes shot wide.

Evening sun blinded me, glowing around the palm tree swaying by the corner of the house. Scrambling upright, I winced as my wrist throbbed in its cast and my ankle protested in its boot. One of the Velcro straps had come loose across my foot.

I'd walked far, far longer on it than I probably should have. I'd limped my way through the local town and down suburban streets, clutching Jack's address, doing my best to be as inconspicuous as possible, all while kids pointed and whispers chased after me.

Any loud noise or growling car behind me made my feet quicken in fear.

Would the officers come after me? Would they hunt me down and arrest me?

All day I'd walked in terror, doing my best to avoid people.

I hadn't stopped to use the money Jack'd so kindly given me.

I didn't buy food or drink, and by the time I limped through a neighbourhood full of sunny-painted houses and hobbled past tropical gardens, I'd been close to passing out beneath a bush for some much-needed shade.

A shadow fell over me as Neri blocked out the setting sun, her silhouette stern and scolding. "I make pocket money by growing those you know. By my calculation you just cost me a dollar fifty." Her hand shot out. "Pay up and then tell me what you want to eat, and I'll go make you anything you want. We have leftover lasagne or…if you liked the Nemo burger, I can get Dad to pick you up another meal."

Her voice rang in my ears. Her presence too much for my raw and flayed emotions.

Squinting, I patted the wooden floor beside me. "Can you sit down? The sun is hurting my eyes."

She promptly flopped to her butt next to me as if she lived to do whatever I commanded. "That's probably your concussion, you know. Bright lights can hurt if you have headaches. Did the hospital fix you already? I thought you were broken."

I sighed and did my best to chase away the fog in my head. The nap I'd taken in the weathered gazebo seemed to have made my exhaustion worse, not better. "I don't have a concussion." I raked my good hand through my dark brown hair. It'd grown longer than usual, thanks to hiding from society for so long, but it was clean enough.

Neri watched me unnervingly, sending my heart skipping in that worrying way.

Dropping my arm, I shifted awkwardly.

What did you say to the girl who saved your life?

What could you possibly do to show your thanks, all while secretly cursing her for preventing you from being with your family?

Tearing my eyes from hers, I looked toward the house that glowed orange around the edges thanks to the sun setting behind it. It wasn't overly big. The cream brick and dark grey roof needed a refresh and the wooden fence around the sun-bleached grass had seen better days. But I could understand why the marine biologists had picked it.

It was only a few houses away from the beach and the entire garden—minus the vegetables growing around the edges—was a natural looking pool.

Neri caught me looking at it and brought her legs up to her chest with a happy grin. "Dad built it. Just like he built the sala we're sitting in."

I looked up at the rafters and thatched ceiling. Patches of sunset shone from areas where the thatch needed tending, but it'd been a good shady spot. The steppingstones leading toward the house skirted the pool with its rocks and palms. Sand glittered in the shallow end, leading up a gentle incline where their very own beach waited with shells and driftwood.

"He seems talented in many things." I ran my finger under the edge of my cast, cursing the sweat encasing my wrist beneath. Memories of my own father teaching me algebra quickly morphed into how to wield a knife.

"You're thinking about them." Neri lowered her legs, her smile dimming. "Aren't you?"

I stiffened and sniffed back the sorrow that was my biggest wound of all. If it was anyone else asking that question, it wouldn't hurt so much.

But her?

Her kindness caused me the worst kind of pain.

Swallowing hard, I murmured, "I was thinking about my father. Yes."

"What was his name?"

"Emre."

"Strange name."

"Not where I'm from."

"And where is that exactly?"

I caught her curious stare, not quite ready to tell her my life story but willing to give her that one answer. "Turkey."

"Oh, I *love* Turkish bread. It has little indents in it that catch melted butter when my mum toasts it. Yum!"

A chuckle caught me by surprise, dragged along into a normal conversation despite the not-so-normal circumstances. "My mother used to make delicious homemade pides."

"Oh, I can just smell them." Neri sniffed the air. "I love when my mum bakes. It smells like home. What's your favourite food?" She eyed up the dirt I'd brushed off the carrot and the wilted carrot top that was all that was left of my foraging. "Surely, it's not boring veggies."

My heart panged, remembering my mother's skills in the kitchen and some of the incredible meals we'd shared thanks to the hospitality of people welcoming us into their homes as we ran. Everything tasted divine when it was made with love.

Shoving those memories away, I smiled. "Well, your carrot was one of the best I've had. Completely worth the money you're charging."

She snorted and rolled her pretty blue eyes. "Liar."

"Truth." I patted my chest, trying for light-hearted, but a shred of despair made me far too serious. "If that carrot were my last meal, I would die happy."

A shiver worked down her spine. "But you're not about to die, though…right?"

"Right." I sat taller, my tone turning colder than I meant. "You made sure of that."

Her head tilted; I couldn't look away from the sudden sharpness in her gaze. "Are you…are you *happy* about that?" Her voice lowered to a whisper. "I mean…you're glad Sapphire brought us to you, aren't you? I know you're alone, and your heart is broken at the moment, but…you have me now. And…and…well, I know I can't replace your family, but I'll do my best to fix your broken heart…you'll see."

A rock lodged in my throat.

I had no idea what to say.

The ice inside me threatened to crack. "Neri…I—"

"Ah, there you are!" Anna appeared, walking over the steppingstones without even looking for the cracks. "You have *got* to stop doing this, Nerida. I'm going to go grey if you keep disappearing on us. One minute, you're on the shore; the next, you're gone."

Neri smiled, big and bright, dispelling the tension between us as if it'd never been. "Sorry, Mum." Leaping to her feet, she ran to her mother and stood on tiptoe to press a kiss to her cheek. Without pausing, she tore off her lime-green sundress, revealing a red one-piece underneath. "Just wanted to get home, that's all." She hurled herself into the pool, sending a wave over the natural edge and soaking into the suffering lawn.

When she broke the surface, Neri pointed at me. "I wanted to see if Aslan was okay."

Anna focused on me with a frown. "Hi, Aslan. I'm glad to see you're looking better. Please don't take this the wrong way, but…how are you here, and how did my daughter know you'd be waiting for us?"

I stood and brushed off my borrowed shorts. Goosebumps darted down my spine as I glanced at Neri swimming at the bottom of the pool and back to her mother.

"I…I have no explanation for how Neri knew. I don't think she did. She's just saying that."

Anna narrowed her eyes. "My daughter exaggerates, that's true, but she isn't a fibber."

"I didn't mean—"

"I know. It's fine. Nerida is her own kind of special. I swear I'll be an old woman before I fully understand how she senses things she shouldn't. Do you know she almost always guesses where we'll find the sea creatures we're trying to study? She's more reliable than a fish finder." She laughed under her breath. "She's wild and free and frankly scares me a little."

I cracked a smile. "She's definitely a force."

"Oh yes. A force that can knock you over if you're not careful." Her eyes darkened, and I swear a warning laced her words. "Anyway, you were saying….How did you get here?"

"I walked."

"*Walked*?" Her eyebrows raised as she looked at my boot. "On a fractured ankle?"

"It doesn't hurt."

"I'm sure that's a lie if I've ever heard one."

I dropped my head, truth spilling free before I could censor. "I've had worse. Please. Don't worry. You and your family have already been so nice to me. I'm fine. Truly."

For a moment, she didn't reply.

She just stared at me as if she was as in-tune as her daughter and could sense things I would never say. Finally, she nodded. "So you were discharged early, and you came here?"

I fidgeted. "I-I wanted to come and say thank you. Again. For everything." Throwing a quick look at Neri, she popped up, took a breath, then vanished underwater again.

I added quietly, "I know I shouldn't have come. You've already done so much, but I…" I shrugged all while my eyes stung. "I…"

These people had saved my life, but now I was trespassing in their garden.

Why would they help me further? Why did I think I'd be safe here when it was their legal obligation to hand me over to the authorities and let them deal with me?

Air was suddenly hard to come by.

I squeezed the back of my neck.

A giant splash wrenched my head up and spun Anna around.

Water went flying, followed by a girl's squeal.

I stood frozen as Jack tossed his daughter into the sky, letting her rain back into the pool with a waterfall of droplets. His t-shirt lay discarded on a rock. The same rock he'd probably just jumped from.

Neri screamed a war cry and launched herself onto her father's back, scrambling to his shoulders and grabbing fistfuls of his hair. "I win. I win—"

Jack ducked underwater, taking Neri with him.

Anna rolled her eyes. "I live with water babies. I swear. Been on the ocean all day and spent most of that freediving on the reef and what do my beloved husband and daughter do when we get home? Go straight back into the water."

Jack appeared again, swiping his face free from wetness. "Aslan! Hey. You found us then!"

Neri swam between her father's legs and popped up in front of him, waving at me. "You're staying for dinner, right?" Spinning in the water, she faced her father. "Go pick up more Nemo burgers. Aslan wants one."

"No. I'm fine," I rushed. "I don't expect—"

"I have a hankering for pizza." Jack winked. "Homemade with lots of mushrooms and mozzarella."

"Yes!" Neri swam to the sandy shore and jumped out of the pool. "I'll go get changed and help you make them."

She tore off into the house, leaving me alone with her parents.

One dry and wary.

One wet and welcoming.

No one said anything for a long moment.

Jack clambered out of the pool, grabbed his t-shirt and looked me up and down. "I figured my clothes would be too big on you. For your height and build, you're slightly underweight."

I didn't know how to respond so I just tipped my chin in acknowledgment.

Glancing at his wife, they shared a look before Jack pinned me with a stern stare. "Do you know why I gave you our address, Aslan?"

I shook my head.

Anna mumbled something, but Jack ignored her and strode toward me. Placing his wet hand on my shoulder, he squeezed me once. "It's because I know what you are, and after what you've lost…I wanted you to have at least one safe place to go."

My eyes shot to his. "You know…what I am?"

Letting me go, he nodded. "You're here illegally."

Ice frosted around my heart.

"I figured you'd probably run before they could interview you. You're alone without anyone to rely on. You also know you'll either be detained or shipped offshore for processing. Or worse…be deported back to your home."

The ice thickened, blowing a blizzard in my lungs.

Jack's voice turned husky. "Answer me two things. Give me honesty and then we'll eat dinner and afterward…we'll talk. Properly. With no fear that we'll tattle on you."

The rock was back in my throat.

"Ask." I balled my good hand.

"Where are you from?"

"Turkey."

"How the hell did you end up here of all places? Turkey is insanely far. If you had to leave, why not stick closer to home? Europe perhaps, or—"

"Australia was my father's goal."

"Why?"

"Because it was the farthest country he could get to without moving to Antarctica."

"And you sailed the entire way?"

How much could I tell them? How much was *too* much?

Weighing every word carefully, I said, "My family wasn't poor. We had passports and money. We left the usual way—on a plane, just like everyone else. But…" I tensed and did my best to forget the many airports, the many flights, travelling a little farther from Turkey with each one. By the time we landed in Indonesia, my parents' panic had reached manic levels to rid themselves of our identities by any means necessary. Next thing I knew, Afet, Melike, and I were somehow on a boat, surrounded by other nationalities, sailing out to sea.

"We traded planes for a boat on the final journey," I admitted.

Jack studied me for a while before nodding and accepting my unwillingness to share more. Inhaling heavily, he asked, "If you get sent back home. If I tell our government about your status and they choose to ship you back the way you came, would you survive?"

I held his stare.

I stood as tall as I could.

And I uttered the most honest words of my life. "The moment I step foot back there, I will be caught, tortured, and probably be made to beg for death before they grant it."

Jack stared into me as if searching for a single lie. He flinched. "You are never to tell Nerida that, do you understand me? Not a single hint that you're in danger."

"You have my word."

After a long pause, he sniffed, cleared his throat, and grinned. "Then let's eat. I'm starving."

Chapter Eight

ASLAN

(*Moon in Irish:* Gealach)

I STAYED QUIET WHILE THE TAYLORS SQUABBLED over what to put on the homemade pizzas. I sat on a barstool, resting my hands on the granite countertop as Anna lifted ingredients out of the dinged-up fridge, danced around the white kitchen, and Jack and his daughter tormented one another relentlessly.

At one point, they picked a sword fight with two sticks of bread.

Anna merely rolled her eyes as if their bickering was perfectly normal and let them get on with it. She didn't even flinch as freshly picked spinach went flying, landing in Neri's wavy chocolate hair.

Once the pizzas were made, Anna tapped Jack on the shoulder, interrupting an impromptu game of naming the latest humpback calf they'd witnessed being born.

"You're up," Anna said. "Go put those in the oven."

Jack smirked, kissed Anna on the cheek, and collected the tray of delicious-looking vegetarian pizzas. "Tell that wench we call our daughter that I want to call the calf Moby."

"Moby was an albino sperm whale. You're not calling him that." Neri planted her hands on her hips, her hair airdried from her swim and her lithe body encased in a flower-print dress that flowed to her ankles. "Koholā is much better." She flashed me a smile. "It's Hawaiian for humpback."

"How do you even know that?" Jack asked, pushing open the insect screen with his hip and disappearing onto the small deck where a pizza oven had already been stoked and warmed.

"Gee, I dunno, Dad. Google translate?"

"I'm gonna take that phone off you. Learning all these new-fangled words."

Anna laughed and hugged Neri close. "I adore that you love languages as much as I do. You might fail at the school's curriculum, but no one can deny you're a smarty-pants."

Neri caught my stare. "I get my smarts from Mum. Did you know she can speak like four languages."

"Four?" My tone deepened with respect. "That's...impressive." Watching their ease around each other made my heart crave my own family. Their ghosts swarmed inside me; I found myself admitting, "I only know two. And my education with English was rather...intense."

"Intense?" Neri asked.

"My father was a teacher. He's always spoken to us with English words interspersed with Turkish, but it wasn't until..." I cleared my throat. "It wasn't until almost a year ago that he forced our entire family to only speak English."

"To prepare you for moving here?" Anna asked.

There was another reason, but I nodded. "Yes."

"Well, you'd never know you're rather new to our tongue." Anna smiled kindly. "You obviously have an aptitude for learning. Let me know if you want to learn another. I pride myself on knowing a lot of Latin—mainly for the correct names of all the creatures we study—regardless that it's utterly pointless in everyday life."

I held her eyes. "No word is pointless."

"Teach me a Turkish one," Neri demanded, fluttering her thick eyelashes at me. "One that means a lot to you."

My heart felt as if she'd suddenly bled it dry.

Every word of my homeland vanished. The only one that remained was excruciating, echoing in my ears with roars of storm and thunder.

"Please?" Neri implored.

Balling my hands, I croaked, "*Canım*."

"*Canım*?" Her eyes narrowed with intelligence. "What does it mean?"

I winced.

Anna stiffened. "Neri, how about you let Aslan have a night of peace. He'll answer your questions when he's feeling better."

Neri never looked away from me as her shoulders slouched and sadness etched her face. Without a word, she padded barefoot around the kitchen bench, pushed one of my knees aside to widen my legs, then slotted herself between them and wrapped her thin arms around my waist.

I turned absolutely rigid.

All the pain.

All the grief.

It crashed against the walls I'd started building around my aching despair, pounding and thrashing, desperate to let go. To let go and purge, all while this beautiful girl embraced me.

My breath hitched.

My vision wobbled.

And just like the first time she'd embraced me on the floor of the boat when I awoke to a life I didn't want, I didn't have the strength to return her affection.

I hoarded everything she gave me.

Every shred of compassion and comfort.

Last time, I'd broken in my misery. This time, I held on just long enough for her to let me go, stand on her tiptoes, and press the softest kiss to my cheek.

"You don't have to tell me yet. I can wait until your happiness is healed. The doctors may have patched up your broken bones, but I'll be the doctor of your broken heart." Drifting away, she added, "Your heart will never be perfect again, though. Losing loved ones always leaves cracks, but…eventually…those cracks become the strongest part of you."

Turning on her heel, she skipped outside.

Leaving me shattered and shaking.

Anna cleared her throat, wrenching my gaze to hers.

Her tanned skin had whitened; her gaze glimmered with tears. "I'm sorry, Aslan. I'm sorry for her perception, her vibrancy, her determination to fix everyone." Coming toward me, she clasped her hands and shook her head. "I told you she was sensitive. And I mean it. She always seems to know impossible things." A single tear rolled down her cheek. "It all started when she was six. Her best friend from down the street—a little girl she practically grew up with—had a tragic accident. This is the part where people expect me to say it was Neri who found her, Neri who witnessed Sophie's death. But…she wasn't. Neri was in bed. It was close to midnight. The neighbourhood was quiet and still. That was until Neri started screaming."

Anna shivered. "She screamed and screamed, then tore outside and bolted down the road. Jack and I followed, only to find Sophie in the middle of the street. What she was doing out there alone at that time of night, we don't know."

She dropped her attention to her entwined hands. "She'd been badly mauled by a loose dog. No one knew where it'd come from, and it ran before anyone could deal with it. Sophie was taken to the hospital, but we all knew it was too late. Ever since that night, Nerida has seemed…different. Almost as if she hears and feels things that others cannot."

Slashing at her tears, Anna blinked back into the present. "Oh my God, what on earth am I doing? I'm so, *so* sorry, Aslan. I didn't mean to bring death here tonight. Especially when you've lost—" Waving her hand, she mumbled, "I merely wanted to say…Neri might unnerve you. She might say things that spook you. She might even speak of Sophie because she claims she can still talk to her, even now. She is unique, and for that, I love her with all my heart."

I let her words hover between us.

As awful as it was, her tale had mercifully distracted me from my own brush with death. Slowly, I stood from the barstool with legs that no longer trembled. "It means darling, sweetheart, my dear, but it's true essence translates from my life, my soul." I wiped my mouth. "*Canim*. It's a term of endearment. It's used so often these days that it's lost a lot of its meaning…but my mother never used anything else."

Anna winced. "Sounds like she loved you very much."

My throat tightened. Pulling my shoulders back, I murmured, "Thank you for telling me…about Nerida. It helps to know she'd be this kind to everyone. It helps dull some of the intensity she brings."

Not waiting for Anna to reply, I stepped outside and leaned against the house as Jack and his daughter squabbled over where best to place the pizza and salad on the table.

Anna swept past me with a jug of water.

Jack announced it was time to eat.

And Neri smiled at me as if she'd singlehandedly heal every crack and crevice within my broken, bleeding heart.

I sat at the glass-topped table, and the rest of the evening passed by in a daze of delicious smoky pizza, a family who joked often but loved deeply, and the ever-creeping knowledge that once the food had been eaten, I'd have to tell Jack anything he asked.

And once I did?

I honestly didn't know what would happen next.

"Time for bed, little fish." Jack stretched and yawned.

The table where we'd eaten outside, with a bug coil smoking beside us that was said to keep the mosquitoes at bay, was littered with empty plates, crumpled serviettes, and discarded water glasses.

In front of Jack rested three bottles of beer.

He'd offered me one but Anna had given him the side-eye and he'd given me a Sprite instead.

It made me wonder if Anna could guess my age or if she just didn't want me drinking because I'd been shipwrecked and still suffered the aftermath.

Not that I cared.

My stomach was unpleasantly full from eating more than my body was used to, and I felt lightheaded again from the long day and building stress of what would happen next.

Where would I sleep tonight?

What would happen tomorrow?

As lovely as these people were, as much as I appreciated Anna revealing a little about her daughter and their way of life, *my* life waited in their hands, and I couldn't rest, couldn't relax.

My gut churned with anxiety.

"It's only eight, and it's Friday." Neri crossed her arms. "And besides, we have a guest."

Jack bopped her on the nose with his finger. "We have another early start in the morning, and you have all the homework that you were supposed to finish yesterday. That means you don't get a weekend, and our guest isn't going anywhere. You'll see him tomorrow."

"I will?" Her eyes brightened. "Can he come with us to see Koholā?"

I blanched.

Go back on the ocean after it stole my entire family?

No fucking chance.

"We'll discuss it tomorrow." Jack pointed at the sliding door leading into the house. "Now, git."

Neri glanced at me, her gaze sharp and far, far too seeing. Chewing on her bottom lip, she looked at her mother and then her father and shuffled deeper into her chair. "You know…you might as well let me stay and listen to whatever it is you're about to talk about." She crossed her arms. "I'll just eavesdrop anyway. No matter where you go, I'll just sneak around until I hear everything."

"Nerida. This doesn't concern you," Anna scolded gently. "Go to bed, love."

Determination etched Neri's young face, making my heart skip. "It *does* concern me." Pointing at me, she said firmly, "I'm the reason he's here. I'm the reason he's alive. He belongs to me just as much as I belong to you. Whatever you have to say to him does concern me because he said it himself."

My heart raced as she leaned forward, never taking her intense stare off me. "His every breath is mine now, and I think I have a right to know where he's gonna live while taking those breaths." She looked at her mother, a plea entering her tone. "He's alone, Mum. We're all he's got. I want to be here to make sure you're not gonna send him away. He needs us."

"Neri, enough," I whispered. "Go to bed."

She scowled. "Don't tell me what to do, Aslan. I'm staying. Whatever you're about to say to my parents, you can say to me."

Jack hung his head and slouched in his chair.

Anna sucked in a tired breath.

And Neri stuck up her chin, knowing she'd won.

She was definitely a force.

A tiny hurricane.

A tropical cyclone far more terrifying than the storm that'd smashed apart my world and left me clinging to life because I had an awful, awful feeling if she ever smashed apart my life like that storm did...I wouldn't survive the wreckage.

"Aslan...it's your decision," Jack finally said. "We can go for a drive and leave my troublesome child to wander the streets searching for us, or we can talk here." His eyes shot a blatant message. *Say nothing that might scar my child or cause her nightmares.*

After what Anna had told me about Neri's childhood friend being killed and Neri somehow knowing about it, I agreed with his request.

She didn't need any other darkness staining the bright, beautiful light she shone.

Besides, I was well used to keeping evil as far from innocence as possible. I'd done my utmost to keep Melike naïve to why we were running and what would happen if we were caught.

Neri never looked away from me, her crystal-clear blue eyes drowning me in so many things. Beneath her determination to hear things she shouldn't lingered hurt and fear.

Hurt not to be included.

Fear that I might not be here when she woke.

The way she watched me sent alarm bells clanging in my head.

My chest tightened, and I knew I shouldn't. I cursed myself that I did. But my heart gave another strange kick, and I found myself bowing to every demand she made.

"She can stay."

The smile she gave me made air hard to come by.

"Thank you," she whispered. "I promise I won't utter a thing you say to anyone." She drew a cross over her chest.

I cleared my throat and looked away.

Jack caught my stare, his dark blue gaze churning with things I didn't want to see. Throwing a quick glance between his daughter and me, he leaned forward and clasped his hands on the table. "Alright then...let's begin."

Anna stood and disappeared into the kitchen, returning a few moments later with a jug of water to top up our dry glasses.

"How old are you?" Jack asked.

I sat taller, grateful the questions would start off easy. "Sixteen."

"And how many of you were travelling?"

"Five. Me, my cousin, my sister, and my mother and father."

Jack swallowed with a wince. "And...did you see what happened to them? Is there any chance they might still be alive? That they've been found by others and are looking for you?"

My heart panged with vicious, cutting hope.

I hadn't even thought of that.

My hands shook as I clutched my glass. "I-I—a wave ripped us apart. My last memory was huddling with my mother, sister, and cousin, and then...I wasn't." My voice thickened. "I suppose there's a possibility they were able to stay afloat like I did. That they drifted to another rescuer."

Anna reached over and patted my hand. "I'll ask around the fishermen. They'll know." Sitting back, Anna asked, "Where were you and your family heading to? Do you have contacts here? Anyone who might be expecting you?"

I shook my head. "It was just us. We were aiming to reach Perth—"

"*Perth?*" Jack choked on a mouthful of water. "I hate to tell you, but you overshot that by a few thousand kilometres."

I couldn't comprehend that much distance.

"I suppose the storm knocked you off course?" Jack mused.

Old anger over my father's dealings with the smuggler rose. I couldn't stop my voice from hardening. "The guy who agreed to take us didn't seem very qualified. His boat wasn't suitable. He boarded too many people. I'm surprised we even ended up in Australian waters before the storm hit." Choking on my fury for the guy who'd killed my family but also lost his life, I asked, "Where...where am I?"

"Only the best town in all of Aussie, mate." Jack grinned. "Port Douglas."

I frowned, doing my best to remember the map my father had made us all study. "By Cairns?"

"Close. Cairns is about an hour's drive away." Placing his elbows on the table, Jack rubbed his mouth and studied me. "I'm not going to ask about your life back at home." His gaze flickered to Neri, who sat quiet and curious in her chair. "Not yet, at least. It's getting late, and we have a busy day tomorrow. So...I'll only ask the important bits."

My spine prickled.

This was it.

I braced myself for him to say goodbye.

"Okay..." I laced my fingers tightly together. "Do you wish me to go?"

"Do *you* wish to go?" Jack asked with a brown eyebrow quirked.

Neri shifted in her chair, drawing up her knees and hugging them.

My heart skipped as she rested her chin on the flower print of her dress, her gaze fierce.

She didn't speak, but her silence was deafening.

I should say I wanted to go because if I stayed, I'd have to continue enduring Neri, and I honestly didn't know how long I could withstand her, but I also had nowhere else to go. No other people I would rather be with now that mine had been taken.

"No. I don't wish to go."

"Good, you'll stay with us then."

"Jack...what are you proposing here?" Anna asked quietly. "He's illegal. He can't just slip into society unseen forever. Eventually, they'll come for him."

"Not if we make him legal," Neri piped up. "Get him a passport. That sort of thing."

Is that even possible?

My father had never spoken of what would happen when we got here. Only that we did.

Jack glanced at his wife and daughter before finally saying, "I'm proposing a week."

A week?

How could seven days seem like both a lifetime and a single second?

"A week to heal, regroup, and then figure out where to go from here. Anna is right that your situation here is precarious. People are close-knit in this town, but if they're told you're with us right from the beginning, you'll be safe enough. No one is out to hurt anyone with gossip or narking, but you'll have to stay under the radar."

"I understand."

"You can stay with us for a week. You can take the guest room and have our absolute word that we'll keep you safe, but…I will ask for one thing in return."

My gaze flickered to Nerida, then settled on her father. "What thing?"

Jack saw me look at his daughter, and his jaw clenched briefly. "You work for us."

"Excuse me?"

"I've been meaning to hire a deckhand for a while now. We're marine biologists that do all the grunt work but not so much the lab work: hunting and gathering data, if you will. We send off samples to those who request them, so it's not a boring inside job I'm offering. It's laborious and worthwhile and we've made do up to this point, but it would be extremely beneficial for us to have someone on deck while we are beneath the waves, monitoring, recording, providing what we need, etcetera."

"I…" I ran both hands over my face. "I don't mean to seem ungrateful, but I don't think I can step foot back on the ocean, sir."

"Jack. Call me Jack. We've discussed this. And I'm well aware it won't be easy, but you can't avoid the sea your entire life. Especially if you're planning on making Australia your home. We're surrounded by it, if you haven't noticed. The ocean is part of our culture, and you'll stick out like a sore thumb if you don't embrace it like the rest of us do."

My heart pounded.

The ground beneath my feet seemed to roil and swell, mimicking the waves that'd stolen everything.

"Try for one day," Anna said, sharing a silent conversation with Jack before directing her words to me. "One day to see if you can forgive the sea. We'll show you what we need help with and then, tomorrow night, you can make the call. Stay a week and prepare to leave. Or stay a week and embrace this new country as your own."

Jack leaned back with his arms crossed. "There's your offer, Aslan."

Anna waited for my reply.

And Neri…

She just raised her head, her dark sun-touched hair wild around her shoulders.

Our eyes locked, and all it took was a whisper from her. "You can say goodbye to them out there. That's your sanctuary now. You should at least visit them to let them know you're okay." She flinched. "Sorry, didn't mean to use that word."

A small smile twitched her lips, somehow turning mine.

Whoever these people were.

Whoever this girl was.

They were dangerous.

So fucking dangerous to my cracked and waterlogged heart.

Dropping my gaze, I studied my empty glass. "Why…why are you doing this for me?"

A shift of positions and a circle of stares before Jack finally murmured, "Because if Anna and I were ever lost at sea, I'd want someone to love and look after Neri as if she were their own. You're someone's son, Aslan. A son who is now an orphan…unless we can find your parents—ocean willing. Hopefully, they'll be found in a week, and you'll have far easier decisions to make, but for now, you're with us and you have a home here."

He laughed, dispelling the weight of the evening. "But only if you work for your room and board. Growing teenage boys aren't cheap, you know. In fact, if you don't pay your way, I might be tempted to throw you to the sharks. Save my bank balance."

"Jack. Oh my God." Anna rolled her eyes. "Your sense of humour sometimes."

"That was funny, Dad." Neri giggled.

I surprised myself by cracking a smile. "The sharks could've already eaten me, but they decided I wasn't to their liking."

"Not salty enough, huh?" Jack chuckled. "Well, we can fix that. Come on *The Fluke* with us and you'll soon embrace the sea as if you were born to it."

Neri stood and pushed her chair back, coming to stand over me.

Goosebumps darted down my arms as she stuck out her hand. "We don't feed you to the sharks and you come on the ocean with us tomorrow. Deal?"

Jack cleared his throat, drawing my gaze to his.

Once again, I got the sense that he was aware of the strange closeness forming between Neri and me. I wanted to assure him it was purely because I'd lost my little sister, and, even though no one could ever replace Melike, Neri's innocent presence was a much-needed cure.

But then Jack slouched and smiled, nodding as if to give me permission to touch his precious daughter.

Slowly, I placed my hand in Neri's.

It wasn't the first time we'd touched.

I doubted it would be the last.

But it felt *different*.

Binding.

Eternal.

And when I tugged my fingers from hers, I swear those warning bells in my head stopped ringing.

They stopped ringing because they already knew it was too late.

Chapter Nine

ASLAN

(*Moon in Japanese:* Tsuki)

"WHERE IS HE?"

I clutched Melike closer, wedged beneath our parents' bed where our mother had shoved us the moment the front door flew inward, and five men dragged our father into the living room by his hair.

"Tell us!"

"We don't know," my mother yelled. "We haven't seen him for weeks!"

My father bellowed, "You have no right to barge into our home and—"

"Oh, we have every fucking right. Blood comes with consequences. You are liable for what he's done." Something smashed, and Melike buried herself deeper into my arms, doing her best to stifle her sobs.

"What has my brother done?" my father asked. "Tell me and—"

"We shall give you one chance. Tell him to face us. Tell him to confess. Tell him to give back what he stole from Kara, or all of you will pay instead."

"We've done nothing wrong!" my mother screamed.

"Yet you'll still die." Heavy footfalls sounded on our wooden floors. "You have until tomorrow night. Find him."

The door slammed.

A hand grabbed my shoulder.

Reflexes kicked in to protect my sobbing sister.

I swung—

"Ouch! Ow, ow, ow!"

The dream-memory dissolved.

I shot upright in bed, wincing as a flash of pain worked through my casted wrist.

Where the fuck am I?

My heart rate galloped as my gaze swung to all four corners of the homely room with a chest of drawers, seashell-bordered mirror, and white curtains that I hadn't drawn. The faintest tinge of sunrise made everything glow a dark orange.

A whimper came from the floor.

My heart stopped galloping and froze.

Melike.

Throwing myself out of bed, I collapsed to my knees with a grunt.

I stiffened as two stunningly blue eyes met mine, dancing with tears and dawn light.

Not Melike.

Everything came slamming back.

The storm.

The Taylors.

Neri…

"Fuck, Neri." I reached out and cupped her cheek.

Her skin was hot, and she flinched as I drew my thumb along her reddened jaw. "It's okay. I'm okay. Crap, I'm sorry. I didn't mean—"

"Say the damn word as much as you want." I dropped my hand, swallowing hard. "I hit you."

"I shook you. You didn't hear me when I said it was time to get up. I'm sorry. I didn't mean—"

"Stop apologising." I cupped her cheek again, tracing the strike I'd given. A strike I'd delivered with my casted hand that was wrapped in hard plaster and struck like a rock. "I'm the one who should be apologising. I'm unbelievably sorry, Nerida. I didn't know it was you. I…" I swallowed again, still in the fear-space of the night when everything changed. "I was dreaming and…"

"It wasn't a dream." She shifted away from me, nursing her cheek before jiggling her jaw and dropping her hands. "It was a nightmare."

I sniffed and looked away.

Even now, even with her sun-streaked hair and heart-stopping blue eyes, I still saw Melike. Saw her glossy dark hair and terror that broke me because she was far too young to know such emotion.

"You're right," I murmured. "It wasn't a good dream. But that's no excuse to hurt you. I just…" I sighed and plucked at my cast. "Don't touch me if I'm asleep, alright? Poke me with a stick or something."

She half-smiled. "How about with a harpoon?"

"That will work." I forced myself to grin. "With the pointy end."

"*Definitely* with the pointy end." Her half smile bloomed into a soft laugh. "Anyway, the pain is going. You only really grazed me. I have pretty good reflexes."

"I'm glad. But you should probably put some ice on it."

"Nah, no time." She smoothed down her dress, this one with jellyfish all over it. "You're awake now. Dad said you have twenty minutes to get ready.

He's left a spare toothbrush in the guest bathroom and a plastic bag for your cast. Do you need help unstrapping your moon boot?"

Shifting, I slowly stood and offered her my good hand.

Looking at it once, she pursed her lips and slipped her fingers silently through mine.

The faintest tingle between us made our silence seem painfully sharp as I wordlessly pulled her to her feet and severed our connection. "Moon boot?"

"That." She pointed at the plastic contraption protecting my ankle. "We call it a moon boot."

"I'm fine. I don't need help."

"Even undressing?"

"Definitely not undressing."

Her cheeks pinked. "Just offering."

"And I appreciate you looking after me, but at no point will I ever accept such an offer."

Her eyes flared. "Never?"

My stomach twisted. The way she asked that question hinted things weren't as simple as I wanted to believe between us. Balling my hands, I cooled my tone. "Never."

Her lips turned down for a heartbeat but then curled back into a smile. "You might change your mind. One day."

Padding barefoot to the open door, she grabbed the handle and spun back to face me. "Twenty minutes. Don't be late."

She left without another word.

***

"How're you doing, Aslan?"

I swallowed around the grief and terror lodged painfully in my throat and forced a single word. A word I was learning to live with. "Okay."

"It will get calmer when we get to the reef. Just a little farther. Just focus on the horizon."

I clutched the co-captain's chair where Jack had told me to sit when we'd arrived at the port and boarded *The Fluke*.

I'd been hauled onboard last time, dripping wet and barely breathing, yet I remembered it so clearly. I remembered the tidy deck, gleaming rigging, and the small kitchenette with its table and benches below.

It wasn't an overly large vessel, but it cut through the water with a powerful purr.

Once again, it made me rage at the feeble boat my father believed would be our salvation. We should've taken the chance of flying here. We could've used our passports one last time before he burned them. But then again, after what he told me in the boat about why he'd made us nameless and homeless…I now knew why leaving clues behind would've led to our death.

They're dead anyway…

"Have you heard anything from the fishermen?" I asked, cursing the hope in my voice. "Any other people hauled from the sea?"

Jack gave me a sympathetic look. "Not yet. We put out a call last night and again this morning." He pointed at the impressive radio and dials surrounding the helm. "We're in constant contact with seafolk, so we'll know the minute anything or anyone is found."

I nodded and looked back outside.

The view had changed from the seaside township of Port Douglas to the open waters of the Coral Sea. Anna had given me a lesson on suburb names as we'd driven the short distance to where *The Fluke* was moored, but now she stood at the front with Neri, their hands wrapped around the stainless steel barriers, riding the waves as their hair snapped and danced behind them.

Neri's jellyfish dress tore around her legs as she pointed at something to the right.

Anna turned to look at Jack through the glass frontage of the captain's quarters. Shrugging, she pointed at Neri and then laughed.

Jack groaned under his breath, following what his wife was silently saying all while I floundered. With a flick of his wrist, he turned the boat in the direction where Neri waved.

The sun blinded me off the water.

Curiosity itched, shoving back my horror at being back on the ocean and the sorrow just waiting to drown me. "What does she see?"

Jack shot a look my way. "One of these days, I swear I'm gonna have her tested."

"Excuse me?"

"Nerida." He laughed as a dolphin suddenly launched itself out of the water in the exact location Neri had pointed at. "She always does this."

"Does what?"

"Seems to hone in on wherever Sapphire and her pod are." He pressed harder on the accelerator lever, making us skim over the water. "But it's not just the damn dolphins. It's the whales and the turtles, the migrating humpbacks and the octopus. She even seems to know where we'll find saltwater crocs when we're tasked with providing new data on their locations."

"Has she ever told you how she does it?" I wiped away a droplet of sweat from my temple, grateful for the shade of the cabin and dreading going out on deck where the sun beamed relentlessly.

"Nope. She just says she has a nudge. A little push deep in her belly."

"You sound jealous."

"I am." Jack laughed. "Don't get me wrong. Anna and I are very open-minded. We're fully self-funded by grants and other projects given to us by universities and researchers, and we've come across our fair share of unique and interesting people. We even travelled to Southeast Asia when Neri was eight to learn from the Bajau people. Some of them can hold their breath for up to thirteen minutes."

My eyebrows shot up. "That's impossible."

"That's what we thought. But then we went and trained with them. Their tribe has spent so much time in the sea that their bodies have adapted. They have much larger spleens than most and spend up to eight hours a day freediving. We wanted to learn how to protect ourselves if our oxygen tanks ran dry or if something happened while we were underwater. What we found was a way of life that embraced things that shouldn't be possible –a way of life that is slowly going extinct, unfortunately—and it opened my eyes that just because we're all human, it doesn't mean we don't have different adaptations that make us uniquely qualified."

I mulled over what he said, trying to picture people who could swim underwater for so long. But Neri laughed as a dolphin broke the ocean and spun in the air, sending a wash of sun-gleaming droplets over the deck.

My heart squeezed.

Trying to ignore the annoying kick, I forced myself to focus on Jack again. "How long can you hold your breath for?"

Jack slowed the boat, quietening the purr to a gentle putter. "On a good day, just over three minutes."

"Damn."

"But that hasn't come easy. That's come from a lot of training and daily dedication." He winked. "Anna can do over four minutes." Cutting the engine completely, he stood from the captain's chair and pulled on a baseball cap with the whale tail symbol I guessed was his business logo. "And Neri? Well, I call her my little fish for a reason."

"How long can she hold it?"

"Five." Brushing past me, he strode out of the captain's cabin and headed to the front of the boat. Anna smiled in welcome, and Neri waved at the dolphins.

A sudden wash of loss clutched me around the throat.

They were so happy together. So safe and *alive*.

My eyes strayed to the turquoise sea, unable to fight the images of my parents, sister, and cousin floating underneath…nibbled and bloated.

Fuck, stop.

Pinching the bridge of my nose, I willed the stinging in my eyes to fade.

It'd only been two days, but I was sick of the heaviness of grief. Sick of the cloying stickiness of tears that never left me alone.

I just wanted to wake up and find this was all a nightmare. To wake in the hills where we'd been hiding and hug my family, just like Jack hugged his.

"You're safe, Aslan. I promise the boat won't sink." Jack's voice ripped my head up. I blinked back everything I couldn't survive and went to join them.

Clearing my throat, I braced myself. "You brought me out here to work. So…put me to work."

He studied me for a moment before nodding and pointing at my cast. "You can't get wet. Therefore, you're stuck on deck. There's an area of coral below us that's becoming a hybrid reef. That means parts have been lab-grown in a new venture to replace the dying Great Barrier Reef with a more robust coral that will hopefully withstand warmer sea temperatures. They were transplanted here a few months ago, and it's up to us to see how the natural reef and fishes are interacting with the lab-grown coral."

My eyes widened.

I had absolutely no idea any of that was possible.

For all my education, I'd never spent so much time around someone who not only held such passion for their calling, but held so much knowledge too.

"What do you need from me then?"

"I'm glad you asked. Come with me." Jack led me to where strapped down boxes of equipment, scuba gear, and oxygen tanks waited to be used. "If you survive the day and are willing to come back out tomorrow, I'll give you the rundown on how all of this works, but for now. All you need to use is this." Pulling out a hard-topped briefcase, he carried it to a table bolted in place by the bow and unlatched it.

Neri came to stand beside me as her father opened a heavy-duty laptop, along with sensors, wires, and an electronic drawing pad.

Angling the screen toward me, Jack said, "When we're down there collecting samples, the computer will automatically record our findings. All our equipment is linked through an in-house Wi-Fi. However, sometimes the connection gets interrupted and can cause the data to file into the wrong columns. What I need from you is to keep track of the data coming in, and if there's a glitch, keep it filing in the proper place."

"That's it?"

"For now." Anna smiled. "Let's start easy."

"It's when you start swimming with us that the real fun begins," Neri said softly, wrenching my gaze to hers. "It's a whole other world down there. A world that is so pretty and colourful and *big*."

Images of her swimming and bumping into a corpse of someone I loved shot into my head.

I suddenly felt sick.

I swayed a little and Anna murmured, "Are you nauseous from the waves, Aslan? If so, we have seasick-reducing bracelets that push on pressure points. They work surprisingly well."

Moving away from Neri, I focused on the computer. "I'm fine."

Jack pulled up a plastic chair from where it'd been stacked and strapped in place. "Get familiar with the program. Feel free to click on a few things and learn how it works while we get our gear on."

"I'm not wearing a tank today, Dad," Neri announced.

"Oh yes, you are." Jack crossed his arms. "You know the rules, Nerida. You may free-dive ten metres or less. We'll be at least twenty today. You are wearing a tank, or you're not going."

Neri pouted. "But it gets in the way when I play with Sapphire."

"I don't care. I like you alive."

"Well, I'm not wearing a suit, then. I'll just wear fins."

"Heaven help me with you, child." Jack threw his arms at the sky. "Don't come complaining to me when you start shivering from being down there for too long."

"I wouldn't dream of complaining." Neri smiled a triumphant smile. "And besides…the cold never bothered me anyway."

Anna groaned and tugged on Neri's wild hair. "Stop quoting *Frozen*. And get in the water, before I throw you overboard."

The Taylors left me sitting in silence as they dressed each other in weighted belts, oxygen tanks, and flippers, before giving me some last-minute instructions, waddling with their flippered feet to the side of the boat, opened the side to reveal a sturdy staircase, then fell backward into the blue.

Chapter Ten
ASLAN

(*Moon in Korean:* Dal)

AN HOUR PASSED.

An hour where the sun blinded me, burned me. Its relentless siege on my skin made me coat my already tanned flesh with liberal amounts of sunblock from the huge dispenser next to the cage where the scuba gear lived.

It helped stop the burning, but it didn't stop the heat. My eyes grew blurry from watching numbers automatically appearing on the screen as Jack and Anna did whatever they were doing down there.

Occasionally, the column where raw data was collected would skip to a random one-off page, leaving me to track down where it was recording, copy and paste it back into the correct area, then realign for the next lot of information.

The glitches were frustrating, and I could see why Jack wanted a deckhand. It was mind-numbing work but would save time when it came to correlating later.

I couldn't get over the fact that whatever equipment Jack was using on the seafloor had the capacity to talk to a computer up here.

Time continued ticking onward, and I kept doing what I'd been tasked with before a strange noise wrenched my head up.

Hoping that the connection wouldn't glitch, I stood and headed toward the side of the boat. My plastic boot clunked on the deck, and my bare foot burned from the hot planks. Grabbing the sun-sizzling railing, I looked down and froze.

The water undulated and twinkled.

Bright blue and perfect—the exact opposite of the black massacre that'd come for us in the storm. This looked like it wanted to be my friend, promising a cool embrace and a place to rinse away my sweat and strain.

But it wasn't the sea that made my heart pound harder.

It wasn't the memories swirling like spectres behind my eyes.

It was her.

Nerida.

Or at least, I thought it was her.

Quicksilver images flickered beneath the surface. Grey and sleek along with skin-flashes and chocolate streaks.

The grey wobble shot toward me, breaking the water with an elegant dive, blowing out and inhaling before it vanished back down again.

My mouth fell open.

A dolphin.

I'd never been so close.

Never been so near I could reach out and touch it.

Bending farther over the railing, I tried to see beneath the rocking waves. Another few grey blurs appeared, circling around the flashes of a sea-swallowed girl.

I frowned.

If Nerida was down there, where were her parents?

As quickly as the dolphin had broken the surface, the girl-shaped shadow grew more and more solid just as her head popped up, and she spat out her mouthpiece. With a lungful of fresh air, she ripped off her mask, then tipped her head back into the water, smoothing down her hair.

A dolphin circled her on its side.

Fear crawled through me.

I'd heard dolphins liked humans.

They weren't killers, but nevertheless, watching Neri be circled by three of them sent my pulse skyrocketing.

"Get out of the water." I gripped the hot railing with white fingers.

Neri gasped and looked up. Her innocent eyes wide and full of things she'd seen below. Things that still enraptured her and made her somehow even more pretty than usual.

My heart did that frustrating little kick, and I marched toward the staircase.

Neri swam beside me, blinking back saltwater. "Hi! How's it going up there? Did you figure out the data? Dad used to make me do it, but I kept jumping overboard to join them." She giggled as she reached the stairs. "That showed him."

"It's fine," I muttered, planting my casted hand on the railing, and bracing myself across the open side of the boat. "It's not hard to do."

"Stinking hot, though, right?" She struggled with the buckles and straps of her scuba tank, wriggling in the water as an inquisitive dolphin nosed her legs. "I should've told Dad to set up the sail for you. It shades the table. Sorry I forgot."

Nervous sweat ran down my back. "Neri. Get on the boat. Now."

She stilled and cocked her head, her eyes seeing way too much of me. "It's okay, Aslan. It's only Bubbles, Rocky, and Seaweed."

"I'm sure they're your friends and you've swum with them countless times, but I really must insist." I held out my hand, leaning as close to the water as I dared. "I'll pull you up. Come on."

Dropping beneath the surface, she reappeared with a grimace, holding up her tank. "Take this. It's super heavy, and I'm over it." Not letting me say no for an answer, she placed the straps of the heavy tank into my hand, followed by the belt with small weights on it. "You're the best." With a quick grin, she duck-dived, splaying me with seawater as her flippers pushed her deep.

The dolphins crested the surface, blew air in my face, then chased after her, their blurry grey forms becoming more and more ghost-like the farther they swam.

Fuck.

Dragging the heavy gear onto the deck, I placed it carefully by the other oxygen bottles, then hustled back to the side.

I peered so damn hard into the water, begging her to reappear.

Jack would kill me.

His daughter had vanished, without any air.

My heart thundered as I glanced at the sun-bleached clock bolted to the side of the captain's cabin. How long had she been under? How long had Jack said she could hold her breath? Four minutes? Five?

The second-hand ticked past excruciatingly slowly.

True fear cracked through my bones and the horror of losing everyone I ever knew to the sea made nausea crawl up my throat. When the clock showed she'd been gone two minutes—not including the time it took for me to stow her tank—I couldn't do it anymore.

Bending down, I tore at the Velcro locking the boot around my fractured ankle.

Images of my little sister crowded my vision.

Of her choking and drowning and—

Terror suffocated me.

I clenched my jaw in agony as I kicked off the boot and hobbled toward the staircase. I couldn't remove the cast around my wrist, but I didn't care. All I cared about was finding Neri before she could die just like—

"Aslan."

I stopped on the second rung of the ladder.

Twisting to look over my shoulder, I came face to face with Neri.

Dripping wet, her eyelashes sparkling with water, she scowled at my unbound foot. "Why is your moonboot off?"

Fury poured through me, and I launched myself back up the stairs, hissing as my ankle spasmed. Dropping to my knees, I slid to my belly and grabbed her unceremoniously beneath the arms.

"Hey! What do you think you're doing?"

"Getting you out of the damn ocean." It was awkward, and she was heavier than I expected, but I somehow managed to wriggle backward and drag her onboard.

Depositing her on the deck, I swear the planks sizzled as she rained ocean all over them. Breathing hard, I sat on my ass and drew up my knees. My ankle protested, and my heart crashed against my ribs. I was coherent enough to understand that my panic wasn't about Neri.

I didn't know her.

Her father himself called her a fish after a lifetime of being around the sea.

She didn't need me acting as if I'd just saved her from an unmentionable death.

Yet I couldn't get my fear under control. My despair. My all-consuming panic of losing someone else.

Brushing back her wet hair, Neri yanked off her flippers, tossed them aside, then sprang to her feet and headed straight for my discarded boot.

Shaking her droplet-streaming hands, she scooped it up and padded back toward me.

She stood silently before me, her breathing calm, her black one-piece tight and far too revealing.

Raking both hands through my hair, I flinched as she sat on her haunches and passed me the boot. "It's okay. I know why you're worried. And you don't have to be. You never have to be worried about me and the sea." Hesitantly, she placed her cool hand on my knee. "It will get easier. One day. Perhaps not soon. Maybe not for a long while. But…eventually—"

"I'm fine. I overreacted. Forget about it."

She shrugged and licked at a droplet by the side of her mouth. "You can talk to me, you know. I know you probably think I'm just a kid but—"

"You *are* just a kid." I snatched the boot from her and made a show of inserting my broken limb and hissing between my teeth as I strapped up the Velcro. "I'm fine. Everything is fine."

"Things obviously aren't fine if you travelled halfway across the ocean and left behind everything you ever knew."

I went cold. "Enough. I mean it."

"But I want to get to *know* you. What do you miss most about Turkey? I want to know—"

"I said, *enough*." Pushing myself awkwardly upright, I towered over her.

But she sprang up, temper flaring in her eyes. "You can't just appear in our lives and not tell us who you are, you know."

"I didn't *ask* to appear in your lives. You're the one who found me, remember?"

"And I'm glad I found you before you died—"

"*You're* glad? What about me? You didn't think to ask what I wanted, did you?" The scorn and hurt dragged confessions from my soul. "You just saw me, floating there, alone and mostly dead, and thought to yourself. 'Oh, I know. I'll go save him. He looks like he has *so* much to live for.'"

Neri shrank back. "What?" Her forehead wrinkled with pain. "Why are you saying it as if keeping you alive is a bad thing?"

"Because it is!" My snarl cut between us, slicing through my sickly fear and making my chin drop to my chest. "*Kafami sikeyim.*" Sucking in a gust of air, I shook my head. "Look, I'm—"

"What does that mean?"

I blanched. "Nothing. Forget I said it."

Her eyes churned with quick-fire intelligence. "It means fuck, doesn't it? It's a swear word."

"Was that a good guess, or do you like languages as much as your mother?"

'Fuck' wasn't quite the translation, but no way would I elaborate and tell her it meant 'fuck my head' which loosely meant, 'fuck me'.

"Good guess." She crossed her arms. "And don't distract me. You wish you died. You wish I'd never found you—"

"I didn't say that."

"Yes, you did! You literally just said it was a bad thing that you're alive!"

I winced as her fury clashed with mine, causing vicious sparks.

This wasn't right.

In what world did the rescued yell at the rescuer?

She's just a kid.

A kid who didn't know how awful the world could be.

I couldn't blame her.

I couldn't curse her.

She didn't have a clue why we'd been running or who I truly was.

Choking back my endless guilt for surviving, for being the very fucking reason my family was gone, I snapped, "Look, I'm sorry. I didn't mean—"

"Yes, you did." She crossed her arms over her flat chest. "You blame me for this."

Did I?

Was that what this was all about?

Sighing, I said softly, "I don't blame you."

"I saw it in your eyes." She sniffed. "You wish you'd had the easy way out. That you'd died with them."

I flinched.

I had no words.

Silence chilled the air around us.

Finally, I shrugged helplessly. "I'm tired, probably have sunstroke, and let my fear run away with me that you'd be drowned by dolphins." Stepping toward her, my hand came up as if it knew exactly where it belonged. My palm tingled, urging me to do something I really shouldn't do.

The hurt in her crystal eyes.

The hurt I'd put there.

I stopped fighting the indescribable urge and cupped her cheek.

Platonically.

Gently.

Instinctually.

She sucked in a breath as I touched her like I had this morning when I'd struck her. My fingertips burned, my heart clenched, and another blade of pain cut me deep. She was just a girl. A girl trying to be good and fix all the broken and unhappy in the world.

Could I blame her that I wasn't ready to be fixed?

That it would take time and most likely a shit ton of space and sadness?

"*Özür dilerim.* Shit, I keep slipping. I mean…I'm sorry. For hurting you. I didn't mean what I said. I just…I really miss my family." My voice was barely loud enough to carry over the salt-heavy air. "I'm sorry for this morning, and I'm sorry for now." I trembled a little as she wrapped her fingers around my wrist, holding me in place as I went to pull away.

She didn't speak.

And words got caught on my tongue as I croaked, "You want to know something about me? Fine, I'll tell you." My fingertips stung against her soft cheek. "You absolutely terrify me. You're so alive and sure and *painful*. And I—"

The whoosh of air and murmur of voices wrenched both our heads up.

I yanked my hand from her cheek, leaving scratches of her fingernails on my wrist as I ripped out of her hold.

Our eyes caught.

The sparks that'd appeared between us from our fight exploded into brighter stars, just as Jack popped up from the staircase, threw his flippers onto the deck, and hauled his heavy bulk with its tank and weight belt onboard. His jaw clenched as Neri linked her hands together and smiled an unconvincing smile. "Hi, Dad."

Jack froze, hearing things in her tone that I wished he didn't.

His gaze shot to my wrist and the red lines his daughter had marked me with.

Guilt roared through me; I tucked my arms behind my back like a thief.

Jack looked between us, his stare a solid, flat blue as it settled on me. The connection between Neri and me—a connection that throbbed with my grief and her kindness—a connection that meant nothing more than what it was, was suddenly ever so wrong.

Shame heated my neck; I couldn't hold Jack's eyes.

I wanted to tell him it wasn't what he thought.

That I was all kinds of torn and tattered, and Neri had somehow gotten mixed up in the knots within my bleeding heart, but he stomped onto the deck and raked a hand through his dripping hair.

Anna followed him, grunting a little at the weight of climbing the ladder with her tank.

Jack wordlessly helped her out of the scuba gear before glowering at Neri. "Go get dressed, Nerida."

His tone was curt and cold.

Anna shot him a surprised look, then glanced at me.

Confusion etched her eyes, but Jack didn't enlighten her.

I didn't even know what there was to enlighten.

But I knew, deep in my gut, that I'd done something forbidden by touching her and that would be the last time I would ever slip.

Nerida was not Melike.

It didn't matter that my sister instigated lots of affection, and our parents encouraged closeness between our family.

She was *not* my family.

She was a girl four years my junior.

She was off-limits in every way.

Bowing my head, I muttered, "I did what you asked, sir. I mean…Jack." Did he even want me calling him Jack after this?

Shrugging away his tension, he smiled, but it didn't reach his eyes. "You didn't find it too complicated?"

"Not at all."

"Good." Grabbing a towel from the rack just inside the captain's cabin, he scrubbed at his hair. "In that case, consider that your task for the week."

I didn't have the strength to refuse.

Anna looked back and forth between us, unzipping her wetsuit and peeling it off her slim shoulders. She didn't say anything, but her questions stabbed me anyway.

"Right. I'm hungry. Let's go back." Jack strode into the cabin and switched on the engine. The faint whirring of the anchor being raised was the only noise as Neri drifted to the side of the boat to wave goodbye to the dolphins, and I slunk to the back, all while cursing the sea, Nerida, and this new existence that suddenly seemed so much more dangerous than the one I'd left behind.

Chapter Eleven

ASLAN

(*Moon in German:* Mond)

"RUN INSIDE AND COLLECT OUR ORDER, WILL you, little fish?" Jack twisted in the front seat of his Jeep and passed his credit card to Neri in the back. "Just use payWave, but you know my pin if you need it."

She flashed me a look where I sat beside her before palming his card and opening the car door. Her jellyfish dress had been covered with a white jumper now that the sun had gone down. "Be right back."

The moment her door closed, leaving me trapped in the 4WD with Jack and Anna outside the local Italian restaurant, my heart started hammering.

Rubbing my sweaty palms on my borrowed shorts, I sat stiff and barely breathing.

The tension increased until finally Jack unbuckled his belt and turned to face me, his hand on the steering wheel, his face stern. "I'm only going to say this once. I'm a firm believer of trust, and in the few short days of knowing you, I can tell you are a decent, honourable guy. You might be young, and you might be adjusting to an entirely new life, but you were raised with morals. Am I right?"

I swallowed and nodded. "Yes, sir." I bit my tongue to let him speak, but I rushed, "What you thought you saw today? It wasn't like that. I...I panicked when Neri threw her oxygen tank at me, then dove below without any air. I couldn't stop thinking of my little sister. Of those I've lost and...and I let my temper colour how I spoke to her."

I rubbed my nape. "What you saw was me apologising. That's all. I know what you're going to say. But you don't have to say it. I already know."

Anna stayed sitting forward, but her soft voice pinched my heart worse than any harsh word. "You're a good kid, Aslan. We will do all we can for you, but there are boundaries you must never cross."

"Boundaries that will mean the end of our hospitality. Do you hear me?" Jack asked calmly. "You are welcome in my home, on my boat, and in my family, but if you *ever* touch my daughter in a way that is anything more than platonic, you will be on your own so fucking fast you'll wonder how it happened." His gaze narrowed. "And I don't do second chances."

I held his stare.

I placed a fist over my heart. "I will never give you a reason to doubt me."

"Good." Twisting back in his seat, Jack rolled his shoulders and said in a much happier tone. "You did good today. The data was kept where it should be. You're going to be a great help."

"For a week at least."

He turned and caught my eyes. "For a week at least."

Nerida wrenched open the door and struggled to climb inside with bags of delicious-smelling food. Reaching across, I took the paper bags from her, flinching under Jack's intense stare.

"Thanks." Neri gave me a grateful smile and buckled into her seat.

I placed the food between us.

The scents wafting from the containers sent another wave of guilt through me. I couldn't repay these people. I had no way of thanking them for all the meals, the welcome, and the willingness to keep my illegal status a secret.

It wasn't just about how much Jack could trust me around his daughter but also my refusal to take advantage of anything that belonged to him.

The cash.

Shit.

I totally forgot I still had the money Jack had given me at the hospital.

Tearing into my pocket—his pocket—I yanked out the folded notes held together with a paperclip. Leaning forward, I tossed them into Jack's lap.

He started and looked down. "What's this?"

"I can't pay you for any of this. I can't take your money either."

He gave me a look. "You can keep it, you know."

"No. I can't."

He studied me before nodding quickly. "You're a good kid, Aslan." Catching Anna's stare as he turned to face the front again, he wedged the money into the console, then threw the Jeep into gear. "Let's go home."

The takeaway bags had hidden the best meal of my life. Better than the Nemo burger or handmade pizza. The creamy spaghetti, zesty pesto penne, and cheesy garlic bread were simply sinful.

Every mouthful had wracked me with guilt and gratefulness.

Guilt that my family would never taste Australia's multicultural cuisine and gratefulness that I could.

It was the first moment I stopped cursing being alive.

The first night that I allowed life to interrupt my despair, and I settled into it as peacefully as I could. I didn't speak much at dinner, preferring to listen to the Taylors discuss their plans for tomorrow, scold Neri for still not doing her homework, and the upcoming conference that Jack and Anna had to attend on the breeding habits of deep-sea tuna.

I didn't know if it was the extremely rich meal or my lack of endurance from being on the sea all day, but my eyelids grew heavy the moment the last morsel was gone.

I swayed in my chair; Jack chuckled. "Go to bed, Aslan. We're up early again tomorrow, and I assume you're coming with us?"

I nodded.

Never again would I let this man down.

I'd let my father down.

I'd let my uncle down.

Jack Taylor would be the one man I didn't.

"Of course. I'm willing to do whatever you request of me."

"Even though it means working on the ocean?" Anna asked carefully, her sun-browned hair catching the string of lights hovering above the outside deck where we sat like last night.

"I'll make peace with it." I shot Neri a look. The first look all night. "Eventually."

She understood what I was saying.

That I was accepting her wisdom that I'd heal…eventually.

She gave me a smile, blushed a little, then looked at her plate.

Her usual energy and sunny vibrancy seemed dulled, as if clouds had cast over everything that made her Neri.

I wanted to make things right between us.

I wanted to apologise again for not handling my grief and all this newness well.

But I never wanted to be alone with her again—not because I didn't trust myself but because I wanted Jack to trust *me*.

Standing, I gathered my dirty plate and reached for Neri's.

"What are you doing?" Jack waved his hand and yawned. "No need to do that. We have a dishwasher, and its name is Nerida."

"Aw, Dad. Really?" Neri pouted. "I have homework."

"And if you want to earn your pocket money this week, you will do the dishes, water your veggie garden, and then do some of that homework."

"Fine." With a huff, Neri snatched the plates from my hands and stormed inside.

I stood there.

Not quite sure what to do.

Anna saved me from lingering like a fool. "Goodnight, Aslan. I'll knock on your door when it's time to wake up in the morning."

I raked a hand through my hair and nodded. "Goodnight."

Striding into the house, I deliberately didn't look toward the kitchen and the clanking of plates in the sink. I didn't catch Neri's stare even though I felt it burn into me. I didn't go anywhere near her.

I strode straight to the guest room and firmly closed the door.

I woke with a start.

I sucked in a haggard breath, tasting salt, hearing thunder, my fingers torn from—

Sitting upright in bed, I blinked away the nightmare.

The guest room sat calm and still around me, its chest of drawers standing watch, and the haphazardly drawn curtains shielding me from everything the night sky could bring.

It didn't feel like I'd been asleep all that long, but the urge to use the bathroom had me swinging my legs out of bed and shuffling in my boot to the door. I didn't know if I was meant to sleep in the damn boot, but after taking it off today and feeling how painful my ankle was, I opted to keep it on.

Cracking open the door, I went to hobble down the corridor, but I pulled up short at Neri's voice. "You can't just forbid me from being friends with someone, Dad. That's just stupid."

"I'm not forbidding you from being friends with him. I'm forbidding you from harbouring any fantastical ideas that it could be more."

"I'm not a child anymore."

"Being twelve is the definition of a child."

"Says who?" Nerida demanded.

"Says life." Jack's tone hardened, but didn't grow louder, staying just above a harsh whisper. "I know you love saving things and nursing creatures back to health. I love your caring heart and will never say no to you when you demand we bring back a sick octopus and somehow cajole me into donating to the damn cat shelter again, but I *am* putting my foot down when it comes to that boy."

"That boy has nothing. He needs a friend."

"So be his friend, but so help you if you try to be anything more."

"You can't stop what's going to happen anyway."

Jack groaned under his breath before muttering, "Whatever you think is going to happen, Nerida, let me tell you once and for all that it will *never* happen beneath my roof. Aslan is sixteen. You are twelve. He's a nice boy, but we know absolutely nothing about him. If you want him to stay and give him a chance at a life here, then you will be his friend and *only* his friend, got it?"

"Okay, Dad, but don't get angry when I marry him."

"*Marry* him—" Jack huffed and uttered a stream of unintelligible curses. "Heaven help me, child, one of these days I'm going to toss you overboard and leave you out there. You won't be able to cause this much nonsense if you lived with those bloody dolphins."

"But you'd miss me too much." Neri's tone brightened with a smile. "And don't worry, Dad. He has to want to marry me too, and right now…he barely wants to be alive. So you have nothing to worry about. Friends only. But I am going to be the best friend he's ever had because he needs one, and I'm not going to shy away from the responsibility I made by pulling him from the ocean when he would rather have sunk beneath it."

Fuck, I told her that in confidence.

I'd barely even acknowledged those thoughts myself. What the hell was she doing spilling my darkest confessions to her father?

Her voice quietened. "He's hurting, Daddy. He told me that I should've asked him before saving him. And you know what…I get what he means. I've done my best to put myself in his shoes—moonboot and all—and I honestly don't think I'd be able to breathe if I lost you and Mum and suddenly lived in an entirely different country with no one I knew."

She sighed before adding softly, "Don't stop being nice to him, Dad. I cross my heart that he's just a friend. And besides, you wouldn't want to hate on your future son-in-law, would you?" Her quiet laughter slipped down the corridor and licked around my ankles.

Chills shot up my spine.

There was no way that would ever happen.

No way.

I would be gone in a week.

I had my own life to figure out.

And she's twelve!

"You're gonna make me wish I was born a eunuch and was never able to produce you, aren't you?" Jack asked with a groan-chuckle.

"What's a eunuch?"

"Never you mind." A rustle of clothing and a grunt of a violent hug. "I love you, you crazy fish. Even if you terrify me."

"Aslan said I terrify him too," Neri murmured, barely audible.

My stomach churned; I held my breath.

Kafami sikeyim.

Turned out she was spilling all my secrets.

"He said that?" Jack's question sliced with sharpness. "Why?"

"I don't know. That's when you interrupted." Her voice turned louder as if she'd extracted herself from Jack's arms. "Now, if you're done nagging me, I'm going to bed. I did all my chores and all my homework. That means, I get to play in the sea on my terms tomorrow."

"We'll see."

"You'll see me play with baby Koholā, you're right."

"I disown you," Jack mock-growled.

"And I was born to make you pay for whatever bad stuff you did in a past life."

Silence before Jack muttered, "I shouldn't say this. I already kinda regret saying it and haven't even said it yet, but, Neri…one piece of advice from a man who once said the same thing to a girl that Aslan said to you."

Neri didn't speak and Jack took his time to formulate words into sense.

"Next time a boy says he's terrified of you, listen to him. It's not a compliment. It's the truth. It means you have a power over him he doesn't like and frankly makes him dangerous."

"Why?" Neri asked quietly.

"Because, most of the time, it's not you he's afraid of but the way you make him feel. And this is where real talk comes back in, daughter of mine. You are permitted to be his friend. But beware of the force that you are and give the poor boy a break. He knows my rules, and I trust him to abide them, but no one can withstand you if you don't obey them too."

I pinched the bridge of my nose and swallowed a furious groan.

I cursed them both for talking about me.

I hated that they discussed me as if I had no control over myself just like I had no control over my life or death.

"What happened with the girl who terrified you?" Neri asked.

Jack laughed loudly, dispelling the tension and making me fold deeper into my room. "I bloody well married her."

"Ah, see!" Neri laughed like a windchime. "I *told* you I'd end up marrying him."

"I'm done. I literally…I can't with you anymore." The sound of a kiss smacking on Neri's cheek echoed just before Jack's flip-flops disappeared down the corridor, heading away from me.

I shut my door as quickly and as quietly as I could.

I rubbed at my thundering heart.

I looked at the sleep-warmed bed with its covers thrown to the side and the chest of drawers standing watch, daring me to break any of Jack's rules.

A wash of sickly despair clutched my stomach.

The Taylors laughed about love and family, but they didn't know what it was like to have that richness turn into such awful destitution.

Jack thought I'd told Neri she terrified me because I was a stupid sixteen-year-old boy with no morals and a shit ton of hormones, blinded to what was touchable and what was not.

But the honest to God truth was…

Neri terrified me because she threatened everything I was.

Every lesson I'd been taught and every dream I'd ever dared hope for.

She terrified me because she *threatened* me.

And the longer I remained in her company, I would have no choice but to change to withstand her. I'd be swept away by her hurricane, and by the time I stopped drowning, I wouldn't have just lost my family…*I'll have lost myself.*

I really should've taken that thought for the premonition it was.

I should've run from the Taylors' kind hospitality that night.

But I didn't.

I slipped back into bed, yanked the covers over my head, and condemned myself to everything that came next.

Chapter Twelve
NERIDA

(Sea in French: Mer)

"I THINK IT'S TIME I TOLD YOU how the twelve-year-old version of myself saw Aslan Avci." I glanced at the two reporters, already feeling younger than I had in years.

Slipping back into who I'd been was like slipping into the sea after the sun punished you on shore. It was soothing and calming and brought a welcoming sort of belonging that calmed my heart and soul.

"Did they ever find his relatives?" Dylan asked.

I shook my head. "No."

"They literally vanished?"

"Unfortunately. Bodies tend to do that at sea."

"You sound as if you have experience." Dylan smirked.

I held his eyes. Remembering another body. Another disappearance. One that I was responsible for. "I have enough." I twirled my ring, a nervous habit that'd begun on the worst day of my life.

I hadn't stopped since.

Whenever something pushed my emotions into unease, I found myself twirling. Always twirling. As if trying to turn back the clock and erase what had happened or avoid what was next to come.

Sighing, I shoved aside the dark parts of our tale and focused on the light. The parts that warmed my heart to recount and reminisce. "When I first found Aslan, storm-battered and spat out by the sea, he was borderline malnourished. Once upon a time, he'd known the luxury of regular meals, but it had been a while. Far longer than a smuggler's voyage. Far worse than losing his entire family. The reason they left Turkey took a toll far crueller than he admitted."

I sighed and stared at the soft waves. "You have to understand, when Aslan looked at you, you could tell he carried a million secrets. You could see everything he would never say, swirling in his coal-black eyes. You could witness it in the way he moved, as if he expected the world to know who he truly was and to punish him for it."

"Why did he think he'd be punished? Did he carry guilt for his family drowning?" Dylan asked, taking notes despite his reluctance documenting my unplanned autobiography.

"Oh yes. To this day, he still carries that guilt. It will never go away. Neither will the inherent belief that he deserves to be sentenced for being responsible."

"I don't understand…" Margot murmured.

"You will…eventually." I curled my hands on my lap. "For now, what I can tell you is…Aslan Avci was a walking contradiction." I caught both their inquisitive stares, trying to explain. "He was tall for his age, yet seemed uncomfortable in his height. He was strong with his words and fierce in his actions, yet always seemed to swallow down the ferocity of his feelings. His lips knew how to smile, yet his eyes held a horror that never quite faded. His mind was bright and sharp, yet he hid his intelligence as if he feared it. The more I got to know him, the more I realised…he was hiding. Hiding from himself. Hiding a part of himself that he didn't want, couldn't accept, and for so many years, I had no idea what part that was."

"When did you finally know?" Dylan asked.

"When he told me."

"And were you right?" Margot tensed. "That he was hiding?"

"Oh yes. He's been hiding his entire life. I think, even now, a part of himself still pretends he isn't who he truly is."

"But why would he hide for so long? What on earth could be so bad that he never accepted himself?"

"That's a question I can't answer," I said. "Soon, perhaps. But not yet."

Clasping my hands, preventing myself from spinning my ring, I said clearly, "Of course, I know every secret and sin there is to know about my husband now. I know too much if I'm honest. Some of what he's told me, shown me, has caused me to wake up screaming and break into sobs. I was naïve back then to think I could cure him of his sorrow. High on my own belief that I could singlehandedly crash my way into his heart and stitch it back up with everything I felt about him and every thread of connection I wanted to share. I should've heard what he was telling me. What his body was telling me."

"And what was he saying?" Margot asked softly.

"That his past had once been bright but was now ever so dark. That he'd run from something far worse than death, and the fact that I'd kept him alive, when he was almost free of that darkness, was one of the things that kept him cursing me for far longer than I could stand."

I looked at my lap. "He was malnourished for a reason. He woke from nightmares with explosive violence for a reason. He knew how to hold a knife and use it…for a reason."

Neither reporter spoke as I settled back against the pillows. "Aslan at sixteen was as much a force as I was. I'd grown up believing I was a sunshine hurricane—destined to shed light on anything I chose to help. It gave me purpose. It gave me pride. But Aslan? His force was different. It was like a riptide. A silent, unseen force that operated beneath the surface, so elegant in its ruthlessness that you didn't even know you were trapped before you opened your eyes and realised the shore was gone and you had drowned in its hold long ago."

"That's quite the claim," Dylan muttered. "You're saying he hurt you?"

I smiled, but it tasted sharp. "Oh, he definitely hurt me. He's the only one who has ever made me wish to die. The scars he's left me with—scars that can't be seen with the naked eye but are felt with a heart—are long and deep and silvered with history."

"Wait. Are you saying he *beat* you?" Dylan reared back. "He hit—"

"Never. Not once." My eyes narrowed. "Not even a little. Circumstances beat *both* of us. Life made us suffer such terrible things. If you knew…" Pressure built behind my eyes; I swallowed hard. "If you knew what he did, what he overcame—all in the name of love—well, I doubt this interview would appeal to the science world but would be eaten up by romance readers."

Margot looked at Dylan before she caught my gaze. "Why do I get the feeling this love story isn't as Disney as we believed?"

"Because it's not." I shrugged. "We've endured things I wouldn't wish on my worst enemy. But those circumstances didn't make us who we are. We became who we are despite them. We found each other in *spite* of them. We loved one another, all while despair did its best to break us apart."

Tiffany, my wonderful housekeeper who kept this on-shore property functioning and kept us alive while we dwelled in it, appeared with a tray of freshly squeezed lemonade.

Giving me a quick smile, her kind eyes wrinkling with age, she passed me a sweating glass before nodding at Margot and Dylan to take theirs.

We all sipped.

I mouthed a thank you to Tiffany and then returned willingly to the past.

"The night my darling father tried to give me firm boundaries for the first time in my short life, I went to sleep concocting dastardly plans. How I knew Aslan was going to feature so heavily in my life, I still can't say. Just like I could never explain how I always seemed to find the creature I was looking for in the ocean. It's a gift I've never questioned, and one that has steered me well, so…naturally, I trusted that little nudge deep within my belly that said he was the one.

"I woke the next morning with steadfast belief that Aslan had been sent to me for a reason. I fizzed with excitement as the poor shipwrecked boy joined us on *The Fluke* for another day of research. He survived that day. And the next. He begrudgingly learned to live in a world that he'd been so eager to leave."

"Why do I get the feeling he was there for longer than a week?" Dylan grinned, scribbling notes.

"Because he was." I welcomed the haze of memories again. "Every night for that first week, I buried my face into my pillow and thanked the stars that'd guided me to him. The more I was around him, the more I gravitated toward him as if he was the planet on which all those stars shone. But he was also the blackhole that threatened to swallow those stars if I dared get too near.

"After the conversation on the boat, where he'd confessed he wasn't sure he wanted to live, Aslan kept his distance from me and did exactly what my father told him. He threw himself into working, as if staying busy could stop his grief from finding him. He'd occasionally look over at me but would glance away if I tried to catch his attention. There were no more tense moments. No more secret stares. He shut me out—obeying my father's strict rules to avoid me…even if that meant avoiding my friendship too.

"Whatever fear Aslan had of the open water was soon replaced with an almost aggressive desire to master it. He didn't let his fractured ankle or wrist slow him down. He didn't look for handouts or free passes. He made sure to battle his demons, all while being an asset to the ones who'd found him, but he couldn't quite hide his flinch whenever my mother would pass out homemade sandwiches on the boat or Dad would have me run in to pay for dinner on the way home. I knew he felt like a burden. I knew he hated that he couldn't pay his way. He didn't see his work as payment. He didn't truly know what his help meant to my parents.

"But I did.

"My parents had finally found the worker they'd needed ever since their small company had gotten notoriety and attracted long-term research projects. It didn't matter that he worked harder than all of us and offered no complaints. He streamlined the computer data storage in the second afternoon. He reorganised my father's folders on the third. And by the end of the first week, it felt like Aslan had lived with us all along."

My eyes glazed as I relived everything my young, impressionable heart had felt back then. How my twelve-year-old obsession slowly morphed into something with substance.

"Aslan had only promised us one week, and we'd made no offer for more. My tender heart skipped with worry at dinner on that final night, knowing Aslan was supposed to stay and be mine, but not so sure my parents would agree. I came up with a crazy plan of sneaking him out of the house while they slept and sailing him to Low Isles. I'd hide him there, and we could live happily ever after on an island."

Margot sighed dramatically. "Oh, I can just picture it. Him building a shack and waiting, oh so patiently, for you to become old enough to be his."

"Jesus Christ," Dylan muttered under his breath. "You really should have been a novelist instead of a journalist with that sort of carry on."

Margot laughed and poked Dylan in his ribs with her pen. "You're into this. I see you scribbling. I see you annoyed at me for interrupting."

"If I'm going to partake in recording Nerida Avci's autobiography, then I want to have every fact perfect."

"Liar." Margot giggled under her breath. "You're a romantic."

Dylan scowled and focused on me. "So what happened? Did he stay in the end?"

"He stayed but not without a lot of discussions. Aslan was every bad word you can think of: illegal immigrant. Overstayer. Tax avoider. Visa dodger. Every day, his status overshadowed his safety within our lives, which made every day so precious because we never knew if he'd have another.

"We all felt it. And we all wondered how long we could keep him unseen, but thanks to my wonderful parents, they chose Aslan and all that came with it. We sat down at the dining room table and had one of the most influential conversations of my short life. My father laid it all out there. He said everything we were thinking and more: Aslan could never get complacent. He'd always have to look over his shoulder. He could never travel. Never work. Never rent or buy a home. Never marry.

"His only two options were...hand himself in and let the paperwork fall where it fell or...stay with us."

Dylan cocked an eyebrow. "But why would your family take on that sort of risk? Surely, there are consequences for people who harbour asylum seekers?"

"You have to understand that for all the work my parents did, it was still very much reliant on grants and donations. They had a fabulous reputation and were able to afford their own craft and crew—even if it was just them. They were always very proactive about sourcing research firms who needed trustworthy scientists in Australia, but...they couldn't afford to hire another biologist. They couldn't even afford to hire a skipper."

"So they hired Aslan under the table?" Dylan wrinkled his nose. "Isn't that taking advantage of a minor and an unpapered one at that?"

"Definitely." I laughed. "My father and mother hired an illegal immigrant and paid him under the table."

"And that sat okay with you?" Margot asked quietly.

"Of course. He wasn't some nameless statistic on TV or some random refugee. He lived with us. He hid the depth of his pain and gave the best of himself to us, all while trying to repay us for the life he still wasn't sure he wanted. He was just a boy. A boy who would be affected by our decision and entirely reliant on our willingness to step outside the black and white lines of the law. My parents needed help they couldn't afford. And Aslan needed a chance at a new existence. The agreement benefited both parties."

"So that was it? You plucked a total stranger from the sea, and he became family?" Dylan asked with an edge.

I didn't like that edge, but I kept a smile on my face. "Not quite. We all agreed on six months. Six months to see if it would work and give Aslan time to figure out what to do next. The very next day, my father announced Aslan couldn't stay in the guest room for that amount of time, and we all travelled to the local Bunnings where we filled up a trailer full of building supplies."

I stopped speaking, reliving that chaotic day of taking Aslan into town for the first time. He'd been so nervous walking beside us. So twitchy whenever a sales assistant came too close. And downright terrified when we got stopped on the way out of the wood yard to show our receipt for the timber strapped inside the borrowed trailer.

My mother hadn't thought it wise to parade our recently acquired illegal overstayer in public, but Dad argued that if he was staying, he had to be seen with us *now*, not later. He had to spread the narrative before someone else could spread a damaging one. From that day on, Aslan was a distant friend of a cousin, and he'd come to learn the trade.

Remembering to talk and not just silently travel down memory lane, I said, "When we got home with all the building supplies, my father commanded us to carry everything to the sala overlooking the pool. The sala that he'd built for my mother but had seen better days after a few tropical storms.

"I remember watching Aslan's reaction to being demoted to living in the garden as my father got building, blocking in the walls to make the sala weather tight, and placing shingles on the roof to make it rain proof. I expected to see shock, annoyance, trepidation even. But you know what I saw? From the homeless, sea-orphan boy?"

Margot shook her head, her eyes locked on mine.

"I saw relief and utmost gratefulness. It was as if a guarded piece of himself finally felt as if it didn't have to swim anymore. That he could rest, for a little while…even if this wasn't the shore he'd wanted to find."

I rubbed at my chest, feeling the same crest of feelings I had back then. "That was when I knew that he'd survived things I could never understand. He'd escaped things that still haunted him, and once the sala had been transformed from a rarely used garden ornament into somewhere to protect our newest family member, my mother disappeared to pick up something to eat and came back with a double-sized mattress, a simple black bedframe, and bags of fresh linen and cosy grey blankets."

"Aslan slept there that night?" Margot asked.

"And for all the nights he lived with us."

"How long was that?" Margot stopped writing, giving me her full attention.

I rubbed again at the pang in my heart. It surprised me how much it hurt. How much I would struggle when I had to tell the part of the story that came after all the newness and falling. "Almost six years."

"Six? Wow, that's a lot longer than what I thought you were going to say." Dylan sipped his lemonade. "And he worked for your family that entire time?"

"Every day. Through storm, sun, and sickness."

"Do you think he would've stayed that long if it wasn't for the fact he couldn't get another job or home without the risk of deportation?"

I flinched at Dylan's question, but nodded and accepted his judgement. "I asked myself that a lot. I feared Aslan stayed with us out of obligation. That he wanted to leave, rather than live in our garden as a fugitive, but I know now—thanks to hindsight—that if we'd given him the choice and he actually *had* a choice, he would've stayed far, far longer than six years."

"Why didn't he, then?"

I sagged back against my cushions, tiredness creeping over me. "You'll find out soon enough. For now…let me indulge in the newness of feelings. To share the first stirrings of love from a girl who'd found everything she ever wanted in a boy. A boy who wanted nothing to do with her."

"Oh, now we're talking." Margot finished her lemonade and sat forward with her chin in her hands, abandoning her writing and letting the microphone capture my tale. "Go right ahead. I'm here for all of it."

I smiled and drifted. "It all began when my father cut Aslan's cast off…and I forced him to go swimming."

Chapter Thirteen

ASLAN

(*Moon in Welsh:* Lleuad)

"HOW WERE THE CLAMS?" I ASKED, LOOKING up from the laptop where I'd been tweaking another data system to try to streamline Jack's saved files with keywords and locations instead of time stamps and gibberish code that meant nothing to him.

The sun had been extra hot today and the ocean extra blue. My eyes ached even behind sunglasses, but at least the shade sail kept my skin from crisping like the first day.

"They were good. Samples show the water is healthy at the moment, so I'm happy," Anna said, wringing out her hair and heading to the cage where the scuba gear was stored. Methodically stripping off her tank, belt, and wetsuit, she smiled. "How's your wrist?"

I stuck my arm out, scowling at the slightly paler skin and the weaker-looking muscles. "Pathetic."

She laughed as Jack clambered on board, speaking to Neri who threw her flippers past his face and jumped up behind him.

"It will take a few days to get used to the cast being off," Jack said as he copied what Anna had done and stripped his gear, leaving him in black boardshorts. "Sorry we couldn't take you back to the hospital. It would've been good for a check-up, but well, you know…circumstances aren't exactly ideal." He winced. "Does it feel healed at least? When I cut it off this morning, I didn't see any deformities, and you said nothing crunches or hurts when you move…so that has to be a good sign, right?"

"It's fine, Jack." I smiled at the man who'd turned his garden sala into a bedroom for me. Who kept me safe and lied for me. Who gave me a second chance…all when he didn't have to.

I rolled my healed wrist as Neri drifted past, giving me a cool smile and looking at my exposed arm. Up until this morning—when I'd complained of how itchy the cast had become and Jack had announced it'd been seven weeks and should probably come off—I'd been beholden to the temperamental nature of plaster of paris and water.

Showering with a plastic bag on my arm had become the worst part of my day.

Not being able to help clean the dishes made me feel like I took advantage.

But now…I was free.

Finally.

Free from everything trapping me since I'd been tended to at the hospital.

My stitches had dissolved a long time ago, and the wound on my head had faded into a pink scar. My cast was now in hacked-up pieces in the Taylors' rubbish bin. And I'd discarded the moon boot after week four—even though Neri had scowled and tried to persuade me not to be an idiot.

But I'd reached my limit.

I was sick of not being able to move without a hobble and even though my ankle still ached in bed and twinged if I decided to do anything more than walk, I was happy enough that it was mending.

Seven weeks I'd lived with the Taylors.

One week in their guest room and six weeks of sleeping in my sala-bedroom in their garden, listening to the gentle lap of their pool as the underwater vacuum kept it clean, and a bone-deep longing to slip into the coolness kept me awake. I'd lost my fear of being on the ocean through forced exposure, but I had no desire to swim in it.

The Taylors' pool, however?

I was past the point of desperation to get away from the stagnant Port Douglas heat.

A few nights last week, I couldn't stand it anymore, so when the lights turned off in the house, I'd waded into their pool up to my waist, keeping my arms above the waterline.

The moment I'd stepped into the water, memories of screaming, sadness, and storms crowded me. My mouth went dry. My heart beat faster. The relief from finally being cool was immediately overshadowed by sorrow and guilt that I'd survived and they hadn't.

Water had stolen everything from me.

Didn't matter if it was salt or chlorine.

I'd waded out as fast as I'd waded in, guts churning and breath tight.

I'd stood in the quiet garden while everyone slept and balled my hands, hating that just because I wanted something so fucking badly didn't mean I was ready.

Ever since that awful epiphany, I'd made a show of groaning about how eager I was to swim when the Taylors jumped in their pool after a long day, cursing my cast and sitting on one of the man-made rocks with rolled eyes and a frustrated huff.

No one knew that a huge part of me was grateful that I had the cast to blame. I was glad I could blame a physical ailment rather than a mental one.

But now, it was off.

And I had no more excuses.

Well, I had one.

One very real excuse but one that already grated on me.

From here on out, I'd have to live a very careful life.

I couldn't afford to get hurt, sick, or push myself to extremes because medical care would be tricky. When we'd all had the chat about where I would go and what I wanted to do, Jack had been explicitly honest about how careful I would have to be if I stayed.

After running from the hospital that first day, the Australian government had my name on file and most likely a record of me vanishing into the night, never to be seen again.

I'd expected someone to knock on the Taylors' door—especially seeing as the nurse recognised Anna's name, but…so far, I'd been lucky.

And I needed that luck to keep flowing because I now lived in a country full of the world's most poisonous and venomous creatures. Neri had been the one to tell me about the monsters I now shared a home with when I'd gone to pick up a spider in the kitchen to throw it outside.

She'd yelled at me.

She'd yanked me back.

I'd thought her overreaction was like my littler sister's would have been—a typical arachnophobia response—but that was before she'd stalked to their small bookcase in the lounge and marched back with an encyclopaedia on all the man-eating, flesh-devouring, biting, stinging, tearing, mauling animals that lived here.

Nowhere was safe.

And I had a horrible thought that I might die, not because I was deported home, but because some murderous snake would bite me in my sleep.

"Guess it will take time to build up strength in your wrist again, but it will happen," Jack said, rubbing his wet hair with a towel. "Least you're free of it now! Free of any reminder of what you survived. You can swim and do everything you've wanted to do."

"Great." I nodded, glad my sarcasm wasn't noticed. Touching my wrist briefly, I saved the spreadsheet I'd been amending and closed the laptop. Seven weeks was long enough for my bones to heal, but my heart? That was still a gaping, bleeding mess.

I still had nightmares.

I still asked if any of the fishermen had found anything that belonged to my family.

Hope still sliced me, not letting me accept the stark truth that they'd gone.

Clenching my teeth, I stowed the laptop back inside its hard-case cover and stepped around Neri, who stood wringing out her hair like her mother had done. She splashed my bare toes as I walked past, catching my eyes but not smiling.

My chest tightened.

Ever since that first day on the boat, when I'd confessed things I shouldn't and Jack had caught us touching, Neri had kept her distance.

I never told her that I overheard the conversation between her and her father and her quips about marrying me. The first few days afterward had been insanely awkward. I didn't know how to act around her. Didn't know if I should bring it up with her or pretend everything was normal.

What exactly *was* normal?

Nothing about our relationship or how we came to be sharing a life was normal.

Therefore, I chose not to say anything at all, and I was both grateful and suspicious when Neri toned down her friendship. She continued to speak to me, laughed at my half-attempted jokes at dinners, and seemed to watch me far more times than I was aware, but gone were the attempts at pulling me out of my depression. Gone were the impassioned explanations that she'd heal my heart because she'd found me for a reason.

To be honest, I was grateful for the space.

Yet something niggled, and I felt as if I'd lost something before I'd even realised that I wanted it.

My ankle burned a little as I crouched and inserted the laptop case into its secure shelf. A bead of sweat rolled down my spine beneath one of the seven t-shirts Anna had arrived home with a few weeks ago, along with a bag of hoodies, socks, shorts, underwear, and swimming attire.

I'd accepted the clothing…what else could I do when I had nothing but Jack's borrowed things? But it didn't mean I was happy about it.

I worked doubly hard to ensure she knew how grateful I was.

It was a daily fear that I'd come across as a leech, made worse by Jack paying me for my help every Friday.

To start with, I'd refused to accept. They paid for *everything*. They gave me a room, food, and safety. They kept my secret. They didn't have to do any of it.

But he'd argued.

We'd ended up in a heated discussion.

And Anna had to intervene, stating time worked was time paid. It was fair even though I felt utterly indebted.

She forced me to accept the money. Jack gloated, pressing the envelope into my reluctant hand, and promised to take me into town if I ever wanted to buy anything.

I'd stopped fighting, and every Friday, I'd wedge the latest envelope with all the rest, untouched and hidden beneath my mattress.

One day, when I found my feet and could think about tomorrow without breaking apart over yesterday, then I would give him back the money. I would find a way to repay him for everything.

Jack strolled to the large chiller containing water, soda, cut honeydew melon, and packed sandwiches. Plucking out a ginger beer, he looked at his wife, daughter, and stowaway. "Anyone want anything?"

Anna finished wrapping a purple sarong around her black one-piece and drifted toward him. "God, I'd kill for an ice-cold Sprite."

Jack kissed her on the lips as he passed her a dewy can. "Neri? Anything?"

His daughter slipped by me, her body free from its wetsuit and wearing her usual outfit of nothing but Lycra. Her never-ending supply of bathing costumes put my meagre wardrobe to shame. Today, she glowed in a burnt-gold one-piece with frills on the hips and bronze stars across her flat chest.

"Are we staying here for a bit?" she asked, not answering her father. "Or are we heading back to shore?"

"Why?" Jack asked suspiciously. "Where do you think you're going?"

Neri threw me a look I couldn't decipher and shrugged. "We're near Low Isles. If we're not leaving yet, I'd like to go swimming on the reef."

"You just went swimming." Jack took a drink. "That's literally what we've been doing all morning. Swimming with the clams and noting any changes to their habitat with increased boat traffic and tourists."

"You know I hate swimming with tanks and things." Neri looked at me again. A glint appeared in her blue gaze, sending my instincts on high alert.

What is she up to?

"I much rather swim with nothing."

"Take a snorkel, at least," Jack muttered.

Neri grinned, her pretty face a little pink from the sun. "I'll take my fins. Final offer."

"Fine. But stay where we can see you. And don't be out for hours. We have plans tonight with Carol and Tim from down the road."

Neri groaned. "You're not dragging me too, are you? I'd rather stay at home and do schoolwork than be bored at their place."

"You know the rules. You're too young to stay at home, especially with a swimming pool in the backyard."

"A pool that I've swum in since I was born."

"A pool that I'd hate to find you drowned in—not from lack of skills on your part, little fish, but a horrible accident. I don't trust you to stay out of it while we're gone. Therefore, that's a firm *nope* on you staying home alone."

Neri's face softened. "There won't be any horrible accidents."

"Exactly. Because you're coming with us," Anna said. "You can be sociable and—"

"Aslan can watch me." Neri crossed her arms over the bronze stars glittering on her chest.

I spluttered. "Excuse me?"

"You live in the garden. If my parents are so worried about me drowning, then you'll hear me." She smiled coyly. "I mean…it's not like you have any plans tonight, is it?"

I scowled. "That was low, even for someone as short as you."

She stuck out her tongue. "Sorry but not sorry. You know no one else in Australia. You'll be there, and I'll be safe with you." She flicked a glance at my naked wrist. "You can get wet now. So it's not like you can't jump in and save me."

"I-I'm not babysitting you, Neri." I crossed my arms.

Anna nodded. "He already has a job, Nerida. We're not going to ask him to watch you when you're perfectly fine coming with us."

Neri never looked away from me, her head tilting sideways a little. Her gaze sharpened, tearing through me, rifling through my sins. Finally, she muttered, "You can't swim. That's why you don't want to watch me."

"What?" My forehead furrowed. "Of course, I can swim."

"Prove it."

I looked at Jack for support. "I don't have to prove anything—"

"You don't have a cast on anymore, Aslan. Jump in the ocean. Have a cool off. Go swimming with Neri. She'll show you the starfishes and clownfish and the parrotfish who absolutely love bananas. You can take one with you and have a cloud of fins surrounding you in a second."

"I'm good. I don't need—"

"'Course you do. It's a great idea." Jack headed toward the chiller and its contents. "I have no idea how you've lasted these seven weeks, working in the heat without a reprieve. You deserve to jump in and have a break."

"Not interested." Crossing my arms, I did my best to bottle up my sharp fury. I knew my temper came from fear, but I hated that I couldn't contain it. Couldn't stop my words from getting short or my heart from getting annoyed. "I have no intention of stepping foot in the sea."

"Whoa, what?" Jack's eyebrows shot up to his damp hair. "No intention? Like…ever?"

"Never."

"Eh…" His gaze flickered to his wife, then back to mine. "I hate to remind you, Aslan, but you're working with marine biologists. You have to know what that entails, right?"

"It means I continue doing what I've been doing." I waved at the sleeping laptop. "I run your data. I look after the boat when you're down there."

Anna finished her Sprite and came toward me slowly. "That is just one of the many tasks we hope to show you. We've been waiting for you to heal, Aslan. You've done an amazing job with the computer and numbers side of our business, but that's just the surface."

"Literally," Nerida said. "Beneath the surface is where the real work is."

"And you guys can do that while I stay above it." I fought the urge to run. "I'm not going in there."

"You can say goodbye to your family down there," Neri breathed, pouring her awful adolescent understanding all over my anger and making me explode.

Every muscle in my back tensed to stone. "I can say goodbye to them wherever I damn well want."

"Not the way you need to." Her eyes pooled with sadness. "Your body might have healed, but you haven't even begun to attempt to heal the parts of yourself that we can't see."

I tripped back a step. "You know nothing."

I hated that she echoed my own thoughts.

I hated that she could *see* me, even so young and naïve and, and…*young.*

Too young to have this effect.

Too young to have this power.

"I know enough that you were using your cast as a reason not to go near the water."

"The fuck I was—"

"Aslan. Language," Jack scolded. "Neri. Leave him alone." Pointing at both of us, he barked, "No one has to do something they don't want to do. Aslan will go into the ocean when he's ready."

"Don't talk about me as if I'm not here," I snapped.

Instantly, regret pressed on my shoulders. "I'm sorry. I didn't mean to get angry or curse. I just…I don't want to go in the ocean, and if that means I can't be your assistant anymore, then…I don't know what to say."

"You don't have to make a decision now," Anna said gently, smoothing over the rough patch I'd caused. "You'll change your mind."

"I'll work on the sea but not in it. That's a hard line for me." I backed up, trapped and itchy to run. "And I'm not crossing it. Ever."

"It's fine, Aslan—" Jack's words were silenced by a loud splash.

My eyes ripped to where Neri had been standing.

She was gone.

Chapter Fourteen

ASLAN

(*Moon in Vietnamese:* Mặt trăng)

"ARE YOU SURE ABOUT THIS?"

I looked up from the sudoku workbook I'd found at the pier the other day. I'd tried to hand the rumpled book into whatever management ran the pier, but Jack assured me that it would've been forgotten about already, and for the three buck price tag, no one would care if I claimed it for my own.

So I did.

And I'd done almost every puzzle inside, scratching down figures in my sala-bedroom, feeling closer to my dad with every number I placed correctly.

"Of course. I wouldn't have offered if I wasn't." I swung my legs off my bed and forced myself to smile politely at Anna. "I'm sorry for my behaviour on the boat this afternoon. Accept this as me trying to make amends."

Anna ran a hand down her silky ruby dress. I'd never seen her so dressed up and wondered what exactly was happening tonight down at Carol and Tim's. "You honestly don't have to babysit her. She can come with us. I'm so sorry she pushed you today. I've had a chat with her, and she knows better than to use your grief as motivation."

"It's fine." I raked my fingers through my messy hair. "I shouldn't let her get to me so easily. It's my fault."

"It's not your fault. Don't ever think that." Giving me a final smile, she said, "We shouldn't be too late. Neri will be fine as long as she stays in the house, so you might not even see her tonight. But…if she does sneak into the pool, please keep an ear out and just supervise."

"You have my word."

"Thank you. The house we'll be at is about seven doors down on Helmet Street."

"Got it." I clutched my sudoku book. "You and Jack have fun."

"We'll try. Thanks again."

I stayed sitting up as she closed the pre-made door that Jack had purchased from a store shelf almost two months ago. The sala got stuffy at night, but I was grateful it had a door. The two windows he'd put in had Perspex instead of glass and slid open for a much-needed breeze, but I wouldn't have survived without the fan in the corner.

Flicking it on, I reclined on my bed again, opening up the puzzle I was almost finished with.

Memories of playing math games with my cousin came and went. Toward the end of a year in hiding, we were used to packing up in the dead of night and fleeing before we could put the kind-hearted strangers who housed us at risk. We never stayed in one place too long, and my parents ensured whoever welcomed us was well compensated for their generosity. Despite being homeless, the hospitality of my people ensured we never went hungry or without a roof.

Whenever we'd step into a different village, seeking somewhere new to hide, my mother would always whisper angrily that we were putting them at risk. I hadn't known what we were running from back then. Only that nowhere was safe. It was why we'd taken the risk to return to İstanbul and catch a flight.

The day we flew away, was the day I knew what true terror looked like on my father's face. He'd sweated and twitched in the city, breathing hard as we checked in, never relaxing until we were in the air.

I'd thought he was insane back then.

But now…now I knew what he was running from, and it was all my fucking fault—

Fuck, stop.

Pinching the bridge of my nose, I forced the ghosts to recede, laid the sudoku book on my chest, and closed my eyes.

I woke with a grunt.

My fingers stung from trying to hold onto my sister.

My ears rang with my mother's screams.

Bolting upright, I rubbed my face and tried to get a hold of my breathing. Only…

Something splashed.

Water.

Neri.

Shit!

Scrambling out of bed, I ripped open my door and tripped into the garden.

The palm tree and scant flowers hid beneath the dense darkness with thick clouds in the sky, preventing any moonlight. If it wasn't for the solar lanterns ringing the vegetable patch along the fence, I wouldn't have made out the shadow on the bottom of the pool.

My heart stopped.

I didn't think.

Limp-sprinting to the water's edge, I jumped onto one of the man-made rocks and hurled myself into the pool.

Water crashed over my head.

Everything that I'd been running from crashed with it.

The pressure of the sea as it forced me down.

The churn of bubbles as I fought to swim.

The oppressive silence that wasn't truly silent as I struggled to survive.

I quaked as I fought instinct to leap for air and arrowed to the bottom instead.

I'd wanted this, hadn't I?

I'd been desperate for a swim, despite not being ready for it.

But now I was submerged, it felt like drowning, not swimming.

My lungs splintered as I snatched at the shadow beneath me and yanked it into my arms.

Shoving off from the bottom, I exploded into the evening and looked down at the girl in my terrified embrace.

I buckled beneath images of her dead.

Of yet another girl gone because I hadn't been good enough, quick enough, strong enough to save her.

But Neri's intelligent, all-seeing stare met mine.

She didn't try to untangle herself from me.

She didn't try to stand.

She merely floated in my arms, hair swaying around us like seaweed, water raining over her lips as she parted them and sucked in a delicate breath.

For a moment, I couldn't separate fact from fiction.

I couldn't stop seeing the nightmare of dead things and fallen families, but then Neri reached up and placed her small hand on my sodden t-shirt, pressing her fingers directly over my thundering heart.

I lost it.

With a groan, I dropped her back in the water and waded to the sandy shore. My ankle screamed as I rolled it a little on the uneven bottom; the weight of my shorts and clinginess of my t-shirt felt claustrophobic as hell.

"Wait."

I froze, but I didn't turn around.

"Aslan, are you…are you okay?"

That word no longer affected me, but her voice did.

Her innocence did.

Everything she represented and everything that I'd lost.

My chin dropped and a wash of pure rage worked through me, tainting my grief, blotting out my fears. I should keep walking. I should get as far away from her as possible but…

I found myself turning.

I found myself hurting.

So.

Fucking.

Much.

And I couldn't stop myself.

"Am *I okay*?" My lips twisted into a snarl. "You're asking if *I'm okay*. Of course, I'm not *fucking* okay. I agreed to watch you. I made a promise to your parents—parents who hold my very life in their hands—and what did I do? I almost let their fucking daughter drown."

"I wasn't drowning—"

"What sort of fucked-up twelve-year-old decides to swim on her own, at midnight, the moment her parents leave?"

"It's not midnight. It's only ten—"

"What sort of girl likes to swim beneath the sea with no air supply? What sort of girl doesn't care that there are sharks and jellyfish and stonefish and poisonous fucking coral just waiting to end her life? What sort of girl is so oblivious and carefree when living in a goddamn country where everything is trying to kill you?! You have no survival instinct. None. You're going to get yourself killed before you're my age and—"

"I was improving my breath hold." Neri stood to her full height, her balled hands just beneath the surface. "That's all. And Australia might be dangerous, but I know your home was far worse if you ran from it." Her voice hardened even while her cheeks pinked with apology. "I should've told you I was swimming. I know that. But…after your refusal to swim today and the way you got so angry with me, I…" She shrugged, choosing an easier excuse. "I thought you might be sleeping. I didn't want to annoy you again, and I practice every night, so it's not like I did anything wrong."

"Everything you do is wrong!" I roared. "Everything you say to me is wrong."

Her forehead scrunched. True pain sliced through her gaze. "I…I don't understand."

I didn't, either.

I had no idea where that had come from or any explanation why I felt that way.

She'd been nothing but sweet and welcoming and…*young*.

Yet…she saw me like no one else did.

She saw what I hid from, what I wasn't brave enough to face, and it made me hate her, because while I lived with her, I could never just brush my grief beneath a rug and forget about it because she wouldn't fucking *let me*.

Sighing heavily, all my fight evaporated.

I felt sick for yelling at her.

I felt wrung out from all the emotions I still couldn't process.

Pressing knuckles into my eyes, I wished I could squeeze out the mess inside me. My wrist sent a small spasm of pain, but it was my heart that was absolutely shattered.

How long would it be until I felt sane again?

Before my heart would return to keeping me alive instead of making me wish I was dead?

Neri waded silently through the pool.

I dropped my hands and glowered at her as she came to a stop before me. The water lapped her knees, her baby-blue bathing suit almost navy in the night. "Come swim with me."

Everything stilled.

The cicadas in the garden quietened.

The waves down the road seemed to crash gentler on the shore.

"W-What?"

She hugged herself. "I'm so sorry, Aslan. I hate it when you're cross with me. I…I told myself to give you space these past few weeks, so you could become my friend on your terms, but…you don't seem to want to be my friend. And…if you don't want to be my friend, then I have nothing to lose by making you even more angry with me."

She trembled but bravely held my stare. "You need to start grieving. I know you think I'm a kid who knows nothing, but I lost someone when I was young and—

"I know." I cut in. "Your mother told me. I know about Sophie."

"You do?" Her eyes glittered, and she looked over her shoulder to the driveway and the street beyond. Slowly, she looked back at me. "I'm not saying losing a friend is the same as losing a sister or a mother, but…I do know that you can't keep fighting it."

"You sure about that?" I asked with a grimace. "Because I'm getting pretty good at it."

She gave me a half-smile. "You can become a master at it, but you'll never truly be happy. You might always be angry when you want to be sad."

Such a simple sentence spoken by such an innocent girl, yet it harboured wisdom that stabbed me through the chest and made me gasp.

For the first time in weeks, I stopped adding bricks to the wall between us and stood before her with nothing in the way. I met her eyes with no barriers, and sucked in a haggard breath as yet more words tumbled from my lips unbidden. "Who *are you*, Nerida Taylor?"

The tension in her shoulders flowed into the pool and her half-smile turned into a full one. "If I told you, you'd probably run."

Once again, absolute shock that she could make me feel anything other than furious caught me by surprise. I wanted to say something light-hearted. To crack a joke. To do my best to be *normal*. But my tongue disobeyed. "I heard you, you know." I flinched and cursed myself.

What was it about this girl that kept me failing at keeping secrets?

Why did it feel so wrong to just *talk* to her when her parents were gone and the night hid so much?

"Heard what?" She trailed her fingers on the water's surface.

I could back out.

I could swallow everything that I'd heard her say in the corridor with her father, but I found I didn't want to choke on yet another thing. She wanted to be my friend? Well, for the first time…I actually contemplated it.

A sixteen-year-old boy who'd had to run from all his friends without a goodbye was ready to accept a kid as his confidant and most likely fucking therapist.

Scrunching up the bottom of my t-shirt, I wrung it out as I murmured, "I overheard Jack telling you the boundaries that have to exist between us. I was heading to the bathroom and didn't mean to listen, but…" I shrugged. "I didn't leave. I have no excuse. And at the end you said—"

"That I was going to marry you." She laughed loudly and sank into the water but popped up again, her eyelashes twinkling with droplets.

Her reaction wasn't what I expected.

Where was the embarrassment? The denial?

I watched her warily.

"Do we need to have a chat about those boundaries your dad explained?" I crossed my arms.

She shook her head, laughing again. "Nah. I'm good."

"So…what you said in the corridor…" I raised an eyebrow. "That was a joke?"

"No. It wasn't a joke." She held my stare. "I know you're special, and I know I found you for a reason, but…if that reason is just to help you find a new life after your old one has been stolen, then…I'm happy with that."

"Oh."

"You sound disappointed." She winked. "I mean…why wouldn't you be? I'm pretty freaking awesome."

"Pretty freaking annoying more like." I chuckled as she splashed water my way, amazed that she'd defused my temper and somehow made all of this—us and night and water and friendship—utterly understandable and acceptable.

It was the first time I could take a breath without the ghosts inside me trying to steal it. The first time I could just be, without fearing what came next.

I sighed heavily. "I think…I think I rather like you, Nerida Taylor."

A flash of something in her blue eyes before she dipped her chin and replied quietly, "I think I rather like you too, Aslan Acee."

"It's Avci."

"Oh, sorry. I suppose I better learn how to spell it if it's going to end up being mine."

I froze.

But then she threw herself backward and swam in a lazy stroke. "Relax, Aslan. It's a joke. Friends can joke. Friends can tease. Or at least, here we can." Her gaze landed on my soaking clothes. "Now…seeing as you're already wet, join me."

"I don't think—"

"There are no piranhas in here." She splashed me again, the droplets not reaching the shore. "Nothing to be afraid of. First step to reclaiming water: start with the pool. Otherwise, I might be tempted to push you overboard next time we're on *The Fluke*."

"You wouldn't dare."

"I would, and you know it."

I glowered at her.

She glowered back.

And as much as I didn't want to admit it, agreeing to be friends with Nerida—officially and wholeheartedly, on my terms and not being coerced—set me up for a world of pain.

Pain that I hoped would eventually heal me…somehow.

Pain that I knew would break me in so many other ways.

"Fine." Trying not to second-guess myself, I stripped off my t-shirt and slapped it against a rock. Leaving my shorts on, I waded back into the pool, doing my best to ignore the swirl of sorrow.

It was just a pool.

I'd been in it before.

Yet being in it with Nerida felt like a baptism.

A forced new beginning.

A beginning I wasn't ready for.

A beginning that would end with far more than just broken hearts…

…it would end with broken everything.

TWO YEARS LATER

Chapter Fifteen

ASLAN

(*Moon in Greek:* Fengári)

"SO…." I LOCKED THE CUPBOARD WHERE THE expensive sonar equipment lived and turned to face Nerida. The boat rocked beneath my bare feet, tugging on repressed memories of another life, another family, another world.

I hadn't dealt with my grief.

I'd shoved it in a box and tossed it overboard.

But every now and again, it would float like a badly bloated corpse, rotting and offensive, doing its best to haunt me.

Nights were when it hurt the most, but during the day…I'd become a master at segmentation. I had walls within walls and rooms within rooms in my mind. Everything had its place, and the places I no longer wanted to go had locks and chains barring them from affecting me. For a while now, I'd been able to convince the Taylors that I'd gotten over my tragic beginning.

They no longer asked how I was.

They no longer worriedly searched my eyes for signs I wasn't coping.

They only saw what I wanted them to see and what they saw was a boy quickly turning into a man. An eighteen-year-old who was no longer a bumbling idiot on their boat but an indispensable member of their business.

"So…?" Neri glanced up, her sunglasses perched on the end of her cute nose, her favourite hat glowing purple in the sun with an embroidered seahorse on the front. "Is there more to that conversation or did you just feel like saying two little letters?" Her lips twitched. "Because you know, I could help with that. Teach me a few more words in Turkish and then you can forget all about English…seeing as you're not very good at it."

I smirked, padding toward her. "I see someone is feeling extra feisty this morning."

"Frustrated more like. What was the phrase for fuck again? *Kafami sikeyim?"*

"Don't swear."

"That's right, though, isn't it?"

"It means 'fuck my head' which translates to 'fuck me' but close enough." She grinned. "What's another curse word?"

She played this game often. She never wanted to know the words for simple things but everything she shouldn't. "I've suddenly forgotten every letter in my language."

"How do you say fuck off?"

"Why? You gonna say it to me?"

"Maybe." She laughed. "Never know when it will come in handy."

"*Siktir git,*" I muttered under my breath. "And if I catch you using it, you're in trouble. It's offensive. Fuck off in English is preferable."

"I won't be in nearly as much trouble as my parents are in for leaving me up here. This sucks." She leaned back in her chair, keeping one hand on her workbook on the table so the much-appreciated breeze didn't snatch the pages, and the other on the e-tablet where she scribbled whatever notes required. "How do I say balls?"

"Bouncing balls or—"

"The other kind. The swear-word kind. You know, balls. Testicles—"

I laughed under my breath. "Your selective vocab is going to seriously scare someone one day. And it's *taşaklar*."

"*Taşaklar.*" She rolled the letters on her tongue, making that annoying kick in my chest return. "I'm going to knee my dad in the *taşaklar* if he forces me to do homework again when the water is singing to me."

I shook my head with another laugh. "Your frustration is definitely showing."

"I told you." She tipped her head to the sun and groaned.

My gaze landed on the graceful curve of her throat, and my stomach clenched. Tearing my eyes away, I focused on the blinding sea. The sun was relentless today, and I was both jealous of her parents working on the seafloor and grateful it wasn't me.

Two years of living illegally in Australia and I'd stayed true to my vow never to step foot in the ocean. However, my promise hadn't come true from the lack of Neri's attempts to get me wet. We swam together almost every night in her pool, and I'd well and truly gotten used to living in the Taylors' garden, but no matter how refreshing I found our nightly swims, I still couldn't stop the ice-cold frost at the thought of even dipping my big toe into the sea.

I was sure a therapist would have a fucking field day with that.

They'd strip back the many layers I'd wrapped myself up in and demand I do a deep dive into everything I'd repressed.

How convenient that I couldn't get help, even if I wanted to.

"Why are you frustrated? You're out here. Sapphire came to say hi before. It's the perfect office to do your schoolwork." I used the hem of my white t-shirt to wipe some of the sweat off my face. The scent of coconut suncream caught my nose, reminding me that just because my skin was naturally slightly darker than Neri's, I still burned in this intense Australian sun.

"I wish I'd never said yes to high school."

I chuckled. "It's not like you had a choice. You're fourteen. You can't just wake up one day and say I'm done with education."

"I wish I was still home-schooled."

"You were the one who said that if you wanted to follow in your parents' footsteps, you needed a school with labs and biology programs. The entry requirements for a bachelor in marine science is tough. You've told me so plenty of times."

"I know." She slouched. "Doesn't mean I like staying on land while you guys spend all day at sea, though."

"I'd trade you in a heartbeat if I could. The sea is my mortal enemy."

"One of these days, I'm going to figure out a way to get you to jump *willingly* into the brine, and when I do, you'll realise that this fear you have is ridiculous."

"Not a fear." I scowled. "A choice."

"A choice that makes no sense living in this country." She huffed, bored of a topic that always got us tetchy with each other. "Argh, my brain is fried in this sun." She looked longingly at the sparkling turquoise surrounding us in every which way. "I wish I was below with Mum and Dad."

"They're not doing anything fun." I stretched where I stood beside her, my t-shirt hem rising. Her gaze locked onto the exposed part of my belly before she swallowed hard and looked away.

Dropping my arms, my voice was a little rougher as I said, "Think they're collecting sea cucumber slime. And before you ask, I have absolutely no idea why. I'm merely the guy who has to catalogue it when they come back."

"Did you know the sea cucumbers' proper name is 'Holothuroidea?'"

"See, all that schoolwork is paying off. Good job."

She groaned. "I like that part. The learning part. It's this shit that I don't like. The staying on land Monday to Friday, and when I do get to come on the boat, I have to do stupid homework instead of playing with Seaweed and Bubbles."

"This shit?" I swallowed my chuckle. "Language, Nerida Taylor. And before you ask, I'm not teaching you that in Turkish."

She stuck her tongue out at me and hunched over her workbook again.

Sitting in the spare chair beside her, I leaned close and read the textbook she was studying.

Maths.

My favourite subject.

"I can help you if you want." I caught her stare, careful to control that annoying, frustrating little kick in my heart that never went away around her.

Two years.

Two long, suffering years I'd lived with her family and every day I forced myself to see her as another sister but…where Neri was concerned? The boxes I tried to put her in and the labels I tried to stick on her never quite stuck.

"Why are you such a nerd for numbers?" she asked, wrinkling her nose. "You're always scribbling away in those silly sudoku books."

"They're not silly. They keep your brain sharp."

"If yours was any sharper, you'd cut me with it."

"A strange image but I'll take it as a compliment."

"Not sure it was one, to be honest." She pouted, bridging the line between kid and the woman she'd grow into.

The past few months, puberty had kicked in, and I cursed the curve of her new breasts beneath her swimming costume. I felt uncomfortable each time she stripped from a wetsuit or jeans, revealing the lengthening of her legs and the rounding of her hips.

I'd caught Jack looking at her a few days ago with the same stare I did.

The one that said…fuck.

She was growing up, despite both our wishes.

Another few years, and the things she'd be getting frustrated at would be boys and kisses, not math homework and school.

Even though she now dabbled with hormones and all the other mess that came with getting older, she'd somehow retained all the annoying, fascinating, lovable parts of her that I'd fallen for the night in the hospital when she'd given me as much water as I could drink.

She'd been so kind then.

So sweet.

She still was.

But she could be sour too.

And a little haughty and moody.

Would Melike have gone through the same stages if she'd survived?

I killed that question as suddenly as it had appeared.

"What's the word for seahorse?" she suddenly asked, running her fingers over the embossed stitching of the one on her lilac cap.

"Seahorse." I grinned.

"In Turkish, you ass."

"Again with the language."

"Yes, I want to learn a language. *Your* language. Mum has been learning with her apps. I know you help her practice sometimes. Help me. Teach me and then I won't have to call you an ass because you won't be one."

I tried to keep a stern face but failed. Pinching the bridge of my nose, I shook my head with a low chuckle.

"I'm glad I amuse you." She winked. "Now...teach me more words. Otherwise, I'm going to jump overboard and go see Mum with her hands full of sea cucumbers."

"Finish your math homework and then I'll give you a few more."

She crossed her arms. "Words then maths."

I copied her. "Not gonna be coerced, Neri. It's Sunday. You've put this off all weekend. Jack told you explicitly what would happen if you left this boat without every single one of those questions filled in."

"You do it, then." She shoved her e-tablet and workbook toward me. "You didn't even finish school. Bet you can't answer half of them."

I stilled.

I'd deliberately never answered any questions about my past with her, yet I supposed it wasn't hard to conclude some of them. I'd been sixteen when she found me. I'd already been on the run for almost a year. And I had no ability to continue studying now that I lived here illegally.

For all her quips about my intelligence, curiosity got the better of me, and I picked up her e-tablet, careful not to smear the screen with sweaty fingers.

She sucked in a breath as if she hadn't been expecting me to obey. Staying quiet, she inched closer, the tips of her sun-streaked chocolate hair tickling my forearm as I scooted her textbook nearer, looked at the equation, and didn't even have to use the method it recommended to work it out.

Colours bloomed in my head.

Inherent knowing chased after them.

I scribbled an answer down in the appropriate place, enjoying the satisfied rush.

So much more fun than sudoku.

I might technically be a dropout, but...my brain didn't know that.

"How did you do that so fast?" she asked.

I shrugged. "I've always been good at numbers. They feel smooth in my mind and arrange themselves most of the time."

"Feel *smooth*?" She cocked a delicate eyebrow. "That makes no sense."

"Doesn't it?" I looked away, annoyed that I'd slipped. My father had actually arranged for me to be tested when I was about her age. He'd watched me like she did now, eyes wide and shocked.

It'd all happened the night I'd asked if I could try some class problems that he'd created for his university students. I found school far, far too simple and regularly searched for harder.

He'd grinned and patted me on the back. "Don't be sad if you don't get any, son. I don't make them easy. It's why I'm known as The C Professor. I very rarely hand out grades any higher because no one can crack my tests."

I'd fallen quiet as he'd passed me a pencil and continued his work. Meanwhile, I'd sat beside him, my brain on fire, colours flowing with every number until I only saw in rainbows. My blood crackled as each equation danced and dipped, smooth and bright, forming the right one.

I'd finished in thirty minutes.

My father had almost fallen out of his chair.

And later that night, I heard him on the phone to my uncle who had his own successful accounting business—not because he was reasonably priced or did a passable job—but because he was said to be a genius when it came to numbers, using his skills for asset protection and fudging profits.

The back of my neck prickled as I ignored Neri's question and shoved her tablet back toward her. "*Denizatı.*"

"What?" Neri licked her lips.

"The word for seahorse. It's *denizatı.*"

"That's really pretty." She smiled then murmured, "The word you call me sometimes…when you're sleepy or loose and don't catch yourself in time…what does it mean?"

I froze.

She was right that I only ever used it when I was tired or more relaxed than usual.

Anna knew what the word meant, and she'd thrown me a look the first time I'd slipped when addressing Neri. I went out of my way to ensure Jack and Anna never suspected I felt anything more than a brotherly-sisterly bond with Neri.

But that one word…

Fuck.

"Another time."

"Tell me now."

"It's not important."

"I would've believed you if you'd just spit it out, but now I'm beginning to wonder if it's some secret code."

"Code?"

She fluttered her eyelashes, reminding me she was still the little she-devil who thought she could fix me, cure me…marry me. "Code for I love you."

"*Seni seviyorum* is I love you. Have you ever heard me say that?"

She held my eyes, her shoulders slouching. "No."

"Exactly."

"But you do…right? Love us?"

My heart pattered painfully. "Of course, I do. You're the reason I'm alive. Your parents are the reason I'm not in some refugee camp or deported."

"But you never say it."

"Don't take it personally." I stood, unnerved by this conversation and ready to use work as an excuse to get away from her. "Finish your maths—"

"Tell me the word you use. What is it? Janum or Janniim…something like—"

"*Canim*." I glowered at her, cursing that, without fail, she always got under my skin.

"That's it." She pinned me to the spot with her crystal-blue stare. A stare that I'd never get over or stop comparing to the sea. "What does it mean?"

Regretting it already, wishing I could lie but knowing if she asked Anna she'd find the truth, I muttered, "It can mean different things in different contexts. It's lost a lot of its meaning with overuse, but my mother said it a lot to us and—" I cut myself off. Clearing my throat, I finished almost coldly. "It means…my life, my soul."

She stilled.

Her eyes never left mine.

And ever so quietly, she murmured, "Oh."

I turned my back on her.

Yes, oh.

It was such a common phrase back home. But to me? Saying it to her? It meant far more than it should.

"Enough, Neri," I said over my shoulder. "Get back to work."

Placing the hatch back over the engine bay after completing the weekly inspection, I wiped my oil-black hands on the rag set aside for such a thing. I'd become more than just a kid paid under the table; I was pretty fucking handy now, if I did say so myself.

Jack and Anna continued to attract research projects, and I slowly learned every task there was to being a marine biologist's assistant. Every gizmo, gadget, and expensive piece of technology I'd mastered, and knew more about the ocean than most eighty-year-olds, let alone teenagers.

Every day, Jack would try to convince me to swim, and every day, he failed. Because of his annoyance and my stubbornness, he'd put me in charge of literally everything else.

I became the skipper, the fuel filler, and the equipment checker. I was left to my own devices to improve computer programs and tracking software.

On the days where we had to hunt down a whale's location, using its already-tagged tracker to gather fresh data, Jack would leave me to scan the depths with sonar and radar, teaching me, but making me complete every step.

Every menial and important job somehow became my responsibility.

And I worked my ass off to be the best damn help the Taylors could ever ask for.

I never forgot where they'd found me or where I would be if they hadn't.

I never once complained.

Days off were rare.

Evenings were cut short in favour of sleep for predawn starts.

And mornings were full of discussions about migration, breeding patterns, and anger at yet another human contamination that had threatened the livelihood of some mollusc, fish, or crab.

When a storm blew in last year and kept us landlocked for a few days, Jack had sat me down at the dining room table and gone over every part of the engine, using the thick manual to coach me, then drill me, forcing me to memorise how to fix it if we were ever stranded at sea.

Once he'd crowded my head with theory, he took me to *The Fluke* where it bobbed on churny seas, and made me huddle in the engine bay, repeating every bolt and gear, regardless of my seasickness from the storm's fading waves.

Ever since the first six months passed—when Jack and Anna said we'd trial me living and working with them—life had become…perhaps not easy, but definitely not hard.

I stopped looking over my shoulder when Jack would drag me into town to run errands. I let my guard down a little with Geoff who filled the oxygen tanks and ran the local dive shop. I grew comfortable driving the Taylors' old Wrangler to the supermarket and to pick up specialist equipment that sea scientists require.

I'd even agreed to a few days of volunteering at the local aquarium that focused on rehabbing and releasing.

That was Neri's fault.

She still had a bleeding heart where animals were concerned and I'd somehow been roped into dropping her off (on the rare instances that Anna couldn't) and ended up staying while she cleaned tanks, tested waters, and monitored healing aquatic life.

I'd ended up helping her; our hands slimy and our shoulders touching as we scrubbed old habitats.

When I'd driven Neri home, she'd demanded words in my language for every creature in the aquarium, keeping my mind on her and not on the whisper of fear that if I was pulled over, I could be deported.

It was risky to drive without a license or identification.

Risky to go into the supermarket or downtown or literally anywhere.

But…thanks to Jack and Anna (everything I was, was thanks to them), most of the locals had accepted me as part of them now.

No one questioned where I'd come from because Jack told the same exact story every time: I was a distant family friend here to learn the trade. "I hope he stays for years." He'd laugh. "He's a part of our family now." He'd chuckle.

I quickly learned that Jack was savvy when it came to using the truth to hide the lies, and slowly, I sank into his confidence that no one saw me as different or illegal as long as I didn't act like it.

Cutting through the captain's cabin, I glanced at the weathered clock.

Almost forty minutes had passed since Jack and Anna went below, which meant they should be almost done. Grabbing a spare hat from the cupboard where flip-flops and suncream lived, I jammed it on my head, wishing for a reprieve from the sun.

My eyes fell to the table.

I froze.

No Neri.

Her workbooks were all tidied away, her chair back in the stack to be locked into position for sailing.

Where the hell is she?

Spinning on my heel, I sucked in a breath as I found her standing at the back of the boat, her arms folded on the stainless-steel railing, her chin on her arms, staring into the sea below.

At least she hadn't jumped overboard to find those wretched dolphins.

Breathing a little easier, annoyed that her well-being always fell to me when her parents dived, I padded over to her.

She huffed as I pressed up against the railing.

"You were a while," she sighed. "Engine give you trouble?"

"Nothing a wrench couldn't fix."

"So we're not gonna be washed out to sea and become beached on some tropical island where we have to drink from coconuts and fashion houses from driftwood then?"

"What?" I chuckled. "Of course not. Is that what keeps you up at night?"

Turning to face me, she rested her cheek on her forearm. "Yes. But as a dream, not a nightmare. Most days I wish I could do that, don't you? Turn your back on all of this and just go wild."

"All of this?" I cocked my chin at the boat, the sea, the knowledge that their work mattered. "I thought you loved all of this."

She sighed. "I do. I just don't love the stuff on land."

"Having another moment where you wish you were a whale, Neri?"

She scowled and looked back at the sea. "Is it my fault that I was a fish in another life? I have a hankering to go back. I want to live down there. Amongst the coral and the currents."

I laughed. "You cannot possibly know you were a fish. And besides…who's to say we have anything more than this life. It could all be over with when we die." I hid my wince at the thought of my family suddenly unexisting.

I'd grown used to Neri's insistence that my parents, sister, and cousin were still out there. They might not remember me and might not be human, but they still existed. And that offered a bit of comfort to the grief I refused to deal with.

Neri didn't reply with her usual snark.

Instead, her spine stiffened; she leaned closer to the water. "Is that…? Oh my God!" In a flurry of speed, she kicked off her sandals, ripped off her hat, and shimmied out of her calico sundress, revealing a yellow one-piece.

I jerked upright. "What the hell do you think you're doing?"

"It's a broken net. There's a turtle…see." She pointed wildly at the water where the sun spangled on the surface, blinding me.

"It's dying." Grabbing the railing, she climbed to the top rung and leapt off, executing a perfect swan dive and vanishing into the blue.

"Neri!" I bent in half over the rail, watching her watery form kicking fast, vanishing the deeper she swam. "*Nerida!*" I punched the side of the boat, hoping the thumps would be heard underwater.

But she didn't stop swimming, and she didn't return.

A flurry of bubbles erupted on the surface.

Shit.

My knuckles whitened as I glowered at where she'd disappeared.

This wasn't new.

She often leapt overboard if the dolphins came to visit. She'd given me a heart attack when she went swimming with a fever of stingrays (learned that word thanks to my new profession). Yet each time, it never got easier. Each time she disappeared for minutes on end. My chest would tighten and my bones would crack, desperate for her to breach the surface and return.

Tearing the cap off my head, I raked both hands through my hair. I paced as I always did, waiting for her to come back and breathe.

My eyes strayed to the clock.

I started counting.

Two years had proven that the Taylors were freaks when it came to holding their breaths. Neri regularly went five minutes as if it was thirty seconds to her. She'd even pushed it to six in the swimming pool, laying like a starfish on the bottom and forcing me to time her.

But out here?

On the open water?

Dealing with swells and dangers?

The clock's hand completed a circle.

One minute.

My feet thudded on the deck as I paced faster. I locked my gaze on the ocean, begging to see the shimmery image of her swimming back to me.

Two minutes.

Fuck, Neri…

I balled my hands and forced myself to stop pacing.

She's fine.

She does this all the time.

She's not Melike.

There is no storm.
Three minutes.
Fucking hell.
I locked my knees and clutched the railing. Bending as much as I could over the top, I studied the undulating water below, trying to see what she had seen.

Slowly, a different world came into view.

Obscured and wavy but I made out images underwater. The dark spot that I assumed was the turtle and red flashing lines in the otherwise pristine blue that hinted at the net.

Four minutes.

My gaze landed on another shadow.

Long and fragile, swaying with whatever currents existed down there with a glint of yellow Lycra.

Loose and unmoving—

"NERI!" I pounded on the boat. I hit it so hard my hand throbbed. "NERIDA!"

The shadow didn't react.

Didn't stop swaying, red lines intersecting the whiteness of her legs.

Shit.

Shit!

Tearing back to the captain's cabin, I ripped open the cabinet that held the speargun and diving knives.

Snatching the largest one, I shuddered as the blade felt familiar. How the handle reminded me of a different life, a different world.

Fisting the handle, I tore off my t-shirt, grabbed a snorkel mask, and ran back to where Neri had jumped.

Yanking the mask on, I didn't think.

I hurled myself up the railing and plummeted over the side.

Water *crashed* over my head.

Salty and cooler than the Taylors' pool and so, so terribly vast.

Terror latched around my heart.

The storm that always lurked in my mind roared in my ears.

My fingers clenched at the knife as I drowned beneath ghosts and screams.

But then, I looked below.

The mask offered a perfect view of a stunning world of coral, glittery fish, and rocks covered in starfishes and shells. And hovering in the middle, stuck between the surface and the depths was Neri.

Her hair clouded around her face, her arms loose and floating, her legs tangled in the net.

I swam.

All my fear of what I'd endured at the sea's moods vanished.

Anger filled me.

Such fucking rage.

The salt had taken my family.

It won't take her too.

Kicking as fast as I could, ignoring the burning of my lungs, I grabbed the loose, algae-smeared net and slashed it as if it were my mortal enemy.

I hacked at the nylon as the current tried to trap me in it too.

Panic swirled in my fiery chest.

I grabbed Neri's ankle and sliced away the strands.

I sliced as fast and as furiously as I could, hacking, sawing, noticing the turtle by Neri's unconscious hand that'd already died thanks to the noose around its throat.

Fish dangled in the net, suffocated and gone.

Even pieces of bleached coral hung as if the net had dragged along the seafloor, scooping up its victims and keeping them as trophies.

My vision greyed around the edges as I fought the overwhelming urge to bolt for the surface.

Just a little more.

She'll die if you don't.

Brushing away the sliced net around her other leg, I wrapped my arm around Neri's slender waist.

I went to kick.

The net washed around her shoulder, tangling in her hair.

Fuck!

Letting her go, I snatched it and hacked.

I kept hacking until there was no more net to trap her.

My entire body *screamed* for air.

I grabbed her wrist and swam.

I kicked and fought and howled as the surface seemed impossibly far.

Black dots danced on my vision as I shoved the knife into my waistband and put everything I fucking had into surviving.

I hadn't been able to save my family.

I would die trying to save Neri.

She floated behind me, her hair obscuring her face as I burned and battled the urge to breathe.

I have to…

fucking…

breathe!

I crested the surface just as every organ snarled at me to inhale.

I gasped and choked, water streaming down my face as I sucked in lungfuls after lungfuls.

I shook and had no strength but I dragged Neri up and rolled her onto her back, keeping her face pointing toward the sky as I brushed aside her sodden hair.

"Breathe, Nerida. Take a breath!"

Nothing.

No cough.

No spasm.

"FUCK!" I coughed and swam for the staircase. Keeping my arm wrapped around her upper chest and beneath her arm, I did my best to keep her head out of the water.

It took absolutely everything to climb the four steps into the boat.

Every muscle screamed.

Every bone fractured.

I grunted as I turned and hoisted Neri out of the water, dragging her onto the boat, not caring that her one-piece was torn around her hip where I'd hacked with the knife. Not caring that her legs got caught on the railing on either side of the stairs.

The moment she was on her back, I shot to my knees, brushed away her hair again, and did what Jack had taught me to do. The first-aid course he'd made me sit through a year ago. The dummy he'd made me practice on when he'd taken me down to the local school for safety training—just him and me.

I let instinct take over as I pinched her tiny nose, tipped her chin up, and planted my mouth over hers.

I exhaled as much as I could, filling her chest before rocking on my heels and taking my own much-needed breath.

I pressed my lips to hers again, exhaling every part of my life into her.

Fisting my hands, I found the right placement on her fragile chest and sank all my weight above her heart.

One, two, three, four, five—

Fuck!

I had to give her more air. Her lips were an awful shade of blue. Her cheeks sallow and cold.

Pinching her nose again, I forced air down her throat.

Another one.

Sweat burned my eyes as I returned to compressions, hard and cruel, not caring about bruising or breaking. The heart was too well protected. You had to use force to reach it.

"Come *on*, Nerida!"

Pinching her nose again, I bent over her.

Her lips were ice cold as I fed her air.

I reared back to breathe.

I bowed over to feed it to her—

Her body jolted upright, her shoulders launching off the deck, her ribcage flying upward.

She choked.

I rolled her immediately onto her side, swiping away her seaweed clinging hair and thudding her back.

Seawater spewed out of her mouth.

Her legs came up as she convulsed and choked, coughed and cried.

"That's it. Get it out."

I couldn't stay upright anymore.

Pressing my forehead to her shoulder, I rode out her convulsions, shaking so much my teeth rattled.

Finally, her coughs subsided, and she tried to roll onto her back.

I didn't let her.

Lying down beside her, I wrapped my arm around her waist and kept her on her side. "Breathe. I got you. Just breathe, Neri. You're safe."

Her breath rattled and wheezed, but she obeyed, slowing down, finding her natural rhythm, a shiver wracking her as shock replaced her blood.

I lost track of time.

I should get her a blanket.

I should radio for aid.

I should use the whale song that Jack had recorded for emergencies and play it under the waves to bring him and Anna back.

But I couldn't do a damn thing as Neri slowly pushed away from me and sat up.

I sat with her, cursing my trembling, unable to stop.

Visions of her unconscious kept coating my mind, making me sick and anxious. "Are you…are you alright?"

She nodded slowly, rubbing where I'd compressed her chest with a wince. "I—" She coughed and wiped her mouth. "I-I…think so?"

She traced her lips with her fingers, her eyes turning inward for a moment.

I stiffened.

Had I done it wrong?

Had I bitten her?

Slowly, her eyes met mine and her white cheeks flushed with colour. "Did you…give me mouth-to-mouth?"

I cringed. "I-I had no choice. You…you weren't breathing. You weren't fucking breathing, Nerida, and—"

"Thank you." She placed her hand over my shaking ones. "Thank you so much for saving my life, Aslan."

And just like that all my fear, my terror, and my panic dissolved. "I suppose my debt is paid now. A life for a life."

"I suppose it is." She smiled.

I sighed raggedly, letting my chin drop to my chest. "Don't ever, *ever* do that again."

Time passed, the ocean lapped at the boat, and my shaking subsided by the time she finally laughed.

Just a tiny, quiet laugh but it ripped my head up and I glowered at her. "What the hell is so funny?"

Her gaze dropped to my mouth before scooting back to my eyes. "I did promise you, didn't I?"

"Promise me what?"

"That I'd find a way to get you to willingly jump into the sea."

Fury poured through my veins; I scrambled to my feet. "If this was a sick prank to—"

"No, no, it wasn't." She pushed to standing, wobbling a little but far stronger than I expected after almost drowning. "I would be dead right now if you hadn't come for me." She stood dripping wet with her hands clasped in front of her, meek and contrite. Something poked through her fingers, but she kept it hidden from sight. "I overestimated myself. When the net wrapped around my legs, I panicked. I forgot how to control my heartbeat and my breathing. I just...I got scared."

The echoes of her fear lingered in her voice.

I'd spent the past two years living with this wonderful girl. Swimming with her, eating with her, helping her with her vegetable garden, listening to her moan about school and life.

I might have complicated feelings when it came to Nerida Taylor.

She might be four years my junior and absolutely forbidden.

But...she was my friend.

Regardless that my heart might stray over the line sometimes, following Anna and Jack's rules wasn't a hardship. I could touch this girl with nothing more than platonic affection. I could laugh at her, play with her, and feel so lucky that I'd been given a second chance at having a sister.

But right then...in that moment...

With her slowly coming back to life and blinking up at me with all the years she still had in front of her, years that I'd saved and given back to her, I couldn't stop myself.

Stepping into her, I hugged her close.

Her slim arms wrapped around my bare waist.

And we stood there.

Just breathing.

Thanking.

Touching.

"I'm glad you're still alive, Nerida Taylor," I whispered into her hair before pulling away and dropping my arms.

She rubbed at her goosebumps, her hand still cupping something I couldn't see. She gave me the gentlest smile. "I'm glad you're still alive, Aslan Avci."

The way she said my name always sent a secret thrill through me.

And she made it a thousand times worse by adding, "I never imagined our first kiss would be like that but…I'm glad we got it over with."

I froze. "First *kiss*?"

She giggled. "You did have your tongue in my mouth."

"I did *not* have my tongue in your mouth. I was feeding you air, you ungrateful sea urchin. I was trying to keep you alive."

"With your tongue."

"With my *mouth*."

"Ah, so you *do* agree you kissed me. Our lips were plastered together. That's a kiss, I hate to tell you." Fire glittered in her ocean-blue stare, and my mixed feelings of horror and despair hovered on a knife's edge.

I wanted to spank her.

I wanted to stalk away.

But…as she winked at me with as much finesse as a kitten trying to seduce a tiger, I snickered. Every sharp and tangled emotion she dragged out of me transformed into the only thing it could.

Laughter.

"Hey. Laughing at a girl isn't nice, you know." She pouted but it was playful. "You'll scar me from ever hitting on another boy for life."

"Good." I chuckled harder. "I hope you become a nun."

"Nuns can't wear skimpy bathing suits. And I'd drown in their stupid robes and hats."

I shook my head, still laughing. "You are literally going to be the death of me."

She grinned. "Almost entirely likely. But I'll make it feel good."

Heat shot through me.

My laughter faded.

Something painful lashed between us that shouldn't exist.

Glancing at the staircase, my ears straining for sounds of her parents returning, I bent close to her and dared to say, "You're fourteen, Neri. I work for your parents. I exist by the grace of their mercy. So please…please don't tell me you're still harbouring stupid ideas of—"

"Marrying you?" She patted my shoulder as if giving me sympathy on a life sentence. "It's inevitable, Aslan. I suggest you stop fighting it, and—"

"Stop fighting what?" Anna's voice sailed from the staircase, making me trip away from Neri. My nape prickled, and I spun to face her mother as she hoisted up the rest of the red net that'd almost killed her daughter.

"Nothing," I snapped, rushing forward to grab the sea-laden mess. The turtle carcass was mysteriously absent, but the dead fish stank in their half-decomposed state. "Let me help with that."

Anna flicked me a smile. "Thanks, Aslan." Her eyes narrowed. "Wait…why are you wet? Did you…?" Her gaze dropped to the knife in my waistband and Neri dripping seawater behind me.

Jack appeared behind Anna, removing his mouthpiece and pushing his mask off his face. He hovered in the water, his eyes shrewd and far too good at reading his daughter.

"Nerida. What happened?"

Anna looked at Neri. "Someone speak. Right now." Hauling herself onboard, she threw her fins to the side and planted her hands on her hips, still with her tank and wetsuit on.

Neri raised her hand with a deliberately innocent chuckle. "Nothing happened. Aslan decided to go for a swim, that's all—"

"Neri went to save the turtle that drowned in the net you found. She almost drowned herself. I went in after her and did CPR, but she needs a doctor. Her lungs were full of water by the time I got her onboard, and I might have bruised a rib or two giving her compressions." Marching toward the captain's cabin, I muttered, "I'll haul up the anchor."

I left the Taylors to yank their daughter aside, studying every inch of her.

I didn't go back out there, choosing to skipper *The Fluke* back to shore where Neri would be forced to go to the hospital, I'd be able to stop worrying about her getting sick, and I could get some much-needed space from the girl who made my life both a joy and a misery.

Chapter Sixteen

ASLAN

(*Moon in Zulu:* Inyanga)

THE FIRST TIME SHE SNUCK into my room, I'd been furious.

I'd shoved her out the very same door she came in through and marched her back to the main house across the garden. The stars had twinkled and the pool had glittered, and by the time I had her safely deposited back into her bedroom, I'd been wide awake and pissed off.

I'd gone for a walk.

Down the street to the beach at the end of the road.

I'd paced the sand and listened to the waves and begged the moon for any hint on what I was supposed to do.

She'd been thirteen the first time.

It'd been the night after her thirteenth birthday when I'd helped Anna supervise six young girls swimming in the pool with unicorn rubber rings and mermaid lilos. I'd suffered between second-hand enjoyment from Neri's excitement at officially becoming a teenager and agonising grief that I would never be able to be a chaperone at my own sister's birthday.

Nothing ever got washed up to hint they'd survived.

No fishermen mentioned survivors being plucked from obscure islands.

Jack had done what he could to find out information and even requested all the paperwork that would be required to turn me from illegal into citizen.

We'd huddled over the documents for days, trying to find a loophole for someone already living here under the radar. Someone who had no official identification or itinerary on how they got here. Someone who'd been living secretly in the back garden of the nicest family I could ever have been found by.

Visited by their daughter who didn't take no for an answer.

"I know you're not asleep. I can tell by your breathing," Neri whispered, hovering by the cracked door as she peered into my room.

In the two years since this gazebo had been mine, I'd changed nothing.

I still had the bedside light and side table that'd been dragged here from the guest room. The chest of drawers that I'd salvaged from the side of the road, and the extension cord feeding electricity from the house. The money I got paid had morphed into a substantial amount, spent only if I needed something essential or if I wanted to find a way to repay the Taylors by buying them dinner or treating Neri to something for school—even though it still felt strange to buy them gifts with their own money.

"Go away, Nerida." I curled up tighter on my side.

Flashbacks of saving her a few days ago still flickered behind my closed eyelids. I hadn't been able to sleep well ever since diving into the ocean after her. My blood felt sharp and slicing. My veins felt thin and feeble. I felt as if my entire body was rejecting this comfortable, safe life by remembering the tragic, painful one I'd done my damnedest to forget.

"But I brought a thank-you gift." Her bare feet shuffled quietly on the floorboards of the sala. Moonlight spilled over my bed before being forbidden to enter as she closed the door.

The energy in my room intensified every time she stepped foot in it.

Tonight was no different.

If Jack and Anna knew she regularly paid me midnight visits, would they care?

They trusted me.

They trusted me even more now that I'd set aside my own issues to save her life. Jack had pulled me aside the evening they got back from the hospital. Neri had undergone a full check-up and was put on antibiotics just in case she got a bacterial infection from breathing in seawater. Her ribs were bruised but not broken, and she'd make a full recovery without too much special attention.

I'd never seen Jack as fragile as he had when he brought me a beer and sat on the edge of my bed, fumbling for ways to thank me.

I'd done my best to assure him it was the least I could do.

He'd already done so, so much for me.

He'd clasped my hand with a bruising promise that I was welcome to stay with them for however long I wanted. Decades. Centuries. Forever. He'd embraced me so fiercely, I'd remembered how it felt not to breathe under the sea, and then he let me go and marched back to the kitchen.

The next morning, I found a basket of muffins, fruit, and ten sudoku books waiting outside my door with a simple thank-you card from Anna signed: *You saved my heart, and I will never be able to repay you.*

And now it seemed as if that heart of hers was determined to ruin mine.

"I don't need any gifts, Nerida. The only gift I'm interested in is you going back to your own room and letting me sleep."

"You suck at sleeping. You can't deny it." Tiptoeing across the small dark space, she hissed under her breath as her toe found a splinter. She landed heavily on my bed.

I growled at her as she sat on my ankle.

The ankle that'd well and truly healed but still ached every now and again. "Goddammit, Neri." Groaning, I swung my legs out of her way and sat up. Rubbing my face with my hands, I glowered at her in the faint moonlight coming through the Perspex windows. "These visits have got to stop."

"Ask nicely."

Damn this girl.

"Please, Ms. Taylor. Go. Away."

"Nice try but nope." Her teeth flashed white in the night. "Here." Passing me a small velvet bag, she hitched up her legs and hugged them. Her pale-pink nightgown encased her body with frills and capped sleeves.

She looked every inch of fourteen, and my heart firmly behaved.

No strange kick.

No annoying tension.

I paused as a stray thought appeared.

Perhaps the reaction I had toward Neri was from *her* rescuing *me*...not because I felt anything that I shouldn't. Perhaps now that I'd rescued her in return, that debt would no longer have any hold over me.

With hope unfurling, I took the little bag and bowed my head politely. "Thank you. But you really didn't have to."

"I know." Her gaze burned into mine as she watched me undo the string and pulled out...a spiny shell.

I looked up. "A shell?"

"I dove down to grab it from the reef. I was stupid to leap in without a knife. I thought the shell's spines would be sharp enough to cut the net." She shrugged, struggling not to fidget. "It wasn't, obviously."

"You acted before you thought." I ran my thumb over the smoothness of the shell and winced as I pricked my thumb on one of its sharp spikes. Its faint colours of peach and cream were barely visible in the darkness. "So this is what you were holding when I gave you CPR?"

"Yeah...crazy, huh? I never let go of it."

I couldn't look at her. The strangeness in my blood was back, bubbling with warning. "Just...promise me you won't let your heart rule your head next time."

She smiled softly. "My heart always rules my head. You already know that."

I stiffened and placed the shell on my knee. "Regardless. Think next time."

"Oh, I think a lot." She plucked the shell from my leg and held it in both hands. "This is a spiny frog shell. I've forgotten the scientific name, and I was lucky its inhabitant no longer lives inside, but...when I woke up, thanks to you, I was still grasping it. I don't know how or why but...I think..." She sighed and looked at me beneath her eyelashes. "I want you to have it."

I held her stare, despite the prickles down my back. "Why?"

"Because..." She huffed and rolled her shoulders. "*Kafamı sikeyim,* this is harder than I thought it would be."

"Language," I murmured. "Just because you said fuck me in Turkish doesn't mean it doesn't count."

She laughed quietly before whispering, "I got it from the sea. I held on to it while I almost died. And...I had it when you brought me back to life. I think...I think you were meant to have it because it's been in both worlds now. It might allow you to talk to your family. You can whisper whatever you want to say to them into the shell and hear them whisper back with the song of the sea."

I reared back, my blood going cold. "They're gone, Neri. I don't need—"

"I think you do." Resting the shell back on my knee, her touch soaked into my bare skin with a scalding kind of heat. Her fingertips lingered before pulling away. She stood gracefully. "How do you say thank you...in Turkish, I mean?"

My heart skipped a beat, but I forced myself to reply. "*Teşekkür ederim.*"

She smiled, and it wriggled painfully into my chest. "*Teşekkür ederim,* Aslan." Her cheeks pinked. "How do you say I love you again?"

Words fled my tongue; I shook my head. "Don't remember."

She rolled her eyes. "Spit it out."

"Nope. Sorry. Completely forgotten."

Her hands planted on her nightgown-clad hips. "It was something like senee sevee or uum."

I flinched at her butchering my tongue. "*Seni seviyorum.*"

"That's it." Her lips twitched into a shy smile. "*Seni seviyorum,* Aslan." Her hand came up in surrender. "And before you kick me out and wrap your door in chains and locks, I love you as my friend. I love you for saving me. I love you for helping my mum and dad. I love you because you exist, and not a day goes by that I'm not super thankful to have you living with us." That blue fire returned to her gaze. "Even if you keep denying we've had a first kiss, I promise our second one will be *so* much better."

I groaned and threw my pillow at her. "*Defol,* you little monster. *Hayatında bir kez olsun uslu dur.*"

Her eyes widened as her tongue licked her bottom lip. She caught my pillow and hugged it close, damning me to inhale whatever soap and shampoo she'd used tonight for the rest of my non-existent sleep.

"What does that mean?" she breathed.

"It means go away and behave for once in your life."

Tossing back my pillow, she blew me a kiss. "Oh, I'll behave. The day I'm no longer too young for you is the day I stop driving you crazy."

"The day you aren't a young girl anymore, I'll be certifiably insane."

"Part of my evil plan. To make you so nuts about me, you won't be able to survive without me."

"I'll be so tangled by your games that I'll probably kill you by accident."

"Kill me with love you mean."

"Get the hell out."

"Okay, okay…" Her sweet laughter trailed after her as she slipped through my door and returned back to her room, leaving me with the shell, the sound of the ocean, and ghosts swirling thickly around me.

Chapter Seventeen

NERIDA

(*Sea in Māori:* Moana)

"HOW EXTREMELY LUCKY THAT HE OVERCAME HIS aversion to the ocean to save your life," Margot murmured, pulling up her legs and getting comfortable. "Did he go in the sea regularly after that? Seeing as he'd put aside his trauma and jumped in?"

I blinked back the past, struggling to return to the present.

Margot's question jerked me from my story, and I scowled, desperate to go back to Aslan. My heart fluttered like it always did back then, full of desperate knowledge of how many moments were about to unfurl. How many times that boy would break my heart. How many instances I almost gave up forcing him to *see me*. How many fights I'd have to go through to snap him out of the role he'd assigned me.

I was his friend.

His replacement sister.

His *responsibility*.

Not that my father had helped in that regard whatsoever.

Ever since the day Aslan performed CPR on me from the stupid net incident, my father had lost any aversion he might have had to Aslan and I becoming close. If fact, he actively encouraged it. He basically assigned Aslan as my bodyguard, tutor, and guardian angel.

And Aslan accepted his duties with steadfast determination and commitment, just like he did everything else.

It got to the point where the butterflies in my stomach whenever I was around Aslan became furious moths instead.

His possessiveness started to grate on me.

His constant watching made me want to rebel.

And not because I didn't want to be watched by him, but because he watched me for all the wrong reasons. He didn't watch me like I watched him. He didn't linger on my mouth or shift nervously if I caught him staring.

To him, I was a fragile child that could, at any moment, attempt to die again, and it was up to him to prevent that from happening…all because my parents had asked him to.

I knew better than to point out that his undying loyalty to my parents might not be entirely healthy. I tried to encourage him to live his life and not just the one they offered.

In the years he lived with us, he never did anything for himself.

Never sought out his own interests or requested time off.

Never spoke of dreams he might have had or goals he wanted to achieve.

It was as if he took his illegal status to mean he had to live entirely in the shadows where only secrets dwelled.

Clearing my throat, I finally untangled myself from my thoughts and answered Margot, "It took almost a year, but I did manage to get him back into the sea, yes."

"And did he like it?"

"God, no." I laughed softly. "He hated that I managed to coerce him for the second time and promised if I ever did it again, he'd hate me too."

Dylan raised an eyebrow. "Hate you for what exactly? You were just trying to help him get over unresolved trauma."

"Yes, but I went about it the wrong way." I brushed down my dress, deliberately not meeting his eyes. "And he had a right to hate me. For many things, really."

Would they judge me for how the rest unfurled? Would they understand the things I'd done and the events that came to pass? Could an outsider ever truly sympathise with another's life story when they might have done things differently and changed the entire course of how the years unfolded?

But it was too late to change my mind now.

I'd wanted to do this.

I wouldn't stop just as it was getting good.

Sitting taller, I said, "I managed to get Aslan back into the sea the night after my fifteenth birthday."

"Oh, that's a tricky age." Margot smiled. "So many urges. So many new feelings swirling around and making young bodies grow up."

I smiled at her, remembering those tormented, tangled years. "I agree. I was fairly young when I officially became a woman, but I felt so worldly, so old and ready for life to begin. Fourteen was when my first cycle struck, and my breasts grew big enough to become a nuisance whenever I wriggled into my wetsuit. I'd hoped, as my body stopped looking so much like a child's, that Aslan would start seeing me differently, but…ever since he saved my life, he seemed even more determined to only see me as Jack and Anna's daughter.

"Off-limits.

"Too young.

"Entirely forbidden on the threat of ostracization.

"Needless to say, having him hover over me at my father's bequest and having him accompany me wherever I went, all while harbouring such feelings for him—feelings that only grew stronger—I steadily became a bit of a wreck."

"When you say he accompanied you wherever you went, surely you don't mean literally." Dylan looked up from scribbling down a note, his eyes fixed on mine as if waiting for me to prove I'd just exaggerated part of my tale.

"I meant what I said. Apart from marching into school and sitting beside me during class, Aslan was in every moment of my teenage years."

"How exactly?" he asked.

"Well, for example, I'd ask my mother if I could go to the movies with my friend Zara and the local boys who'd been flirting with us. Sure, she'd say…but only if Aslan chaperones. I'd spend the entire movie feeling his eyes on the back of my head, unable to even smile at the boy sitting next to me for fear Aslan would either punch him or tell my father what I'd gotten up to.

"On the nights I'd lie and say I had a study session with some girlfriends, Aslan would knock on my bedroom door, jiggling the borrowed Jeep keys, asking me where he had to drive me for my study session."

I rolled my eyes with a reminiscing smile. "Of course it wasn't study sessions I wanted to go to but underage house parties. I was literally the only girl in my class who hadn't been kissed by a tipsy boy or gotten tipsy herself on stolen parental liquor. And the worst part was, it wasn't because of strict parents but because I had a sexy-as-hell nineteen-year-old boy with morals purer than Jesus following me around."

Margot groaned with a grin. "That sounds like an absolute nightmare."

"Oh, believe me, it was." I shared her smile. "It was even worse when he scolded me in Turkish. Over the years, I'd hounded him to teach me, but by the time I turned sixteen, he regularly slipped into his mother tongue and cursed me with words I didn't fully understand, yet somehow made every part of me burn alive."

I fanned myself dramatically. "Here I was, a young woman desperate to act on the urges he gave me, frantic to kiss him, going crazy with the need for him to look at me the same way I looked at him, and he'd just chuckle if I made a blatant attempt or glower if I tried to be sneaky."

"Sneaky?" Margot asked.

My cheeks heated, even now, so many years later. "I remember the first time he shot me down so badly, my chest literally felt like it would crack in two, and I cried into my pillow for hours. It made things extremely strained between us."

I didn't mention that the strain lasted until I did something even more stupid. I'd done something that finally pushed Aslan over the edge, and if I counted him giving me mouth-to-mouth as our first official kiss, then our second…good God, I would burn in hell for how he'd made me feel.

"Okay, now I'm dying to hear all of it." Margot jiggled in her chair. "But…seeing as we're going chronological, tell us about the second time you got him into the sea."

I smiled at the fresh-faced journalist and sighed.

She would eventually feel everything I had and get the opportunity to experience the highs and lows of exquisite lust and everlasting love. I would be jealous if I hadn't found the love of my life at twelve and spent the last six decades loving him.

I'd had my happily ever after, and I was ever so grateful.

Getting cosy, I settled into my tale again, but this time, I didn't narrate like a storyteller. I let myself fall back, way back, all the way back.

I stepped into the shoes of Nerida 'little fish' Taylor: a fifteen-year-old girl, marine biologist wannabe, and young woman desperately in love with the boy who lived illegally in her garden.

Chapter Eighteen
NERIDA

AGE: 15 YRS OLD

(*Sea in Chinese:* Hǎi)

"SO, CAN I GO? *PLEASE?* IT WOULD mean so much to me. I swear Zara's parents will keep me safe, and it will be so good for me to experience a few nights in the rainforest and not the sea. They've already booked the site, said they'll keep us fed and safe, and I promise I'll do all my chores without you having to nag me. I'll do all the gross jobs on *The Fluke*, and I solemnly swear I'll stop moaning about going to a school on land while you guys spend all day on the ocean. Come on, Dad. It's my birthday. I didn't ask for a big party. I'm not giving you grey hairs by sneaking out with boys—even though I totally could. I'm a saint, really, and I'll literally do whatever you want if you just let me go camping with—"

"Dear God, I give up." Dad chuckled, placing his hands over his ears in mock protest of my lengthy stream of pleading. "I yield. I yield. You can go."

"Ah! Really?" I leaped up and danced on the spot, not caring that it would seem juvenile to the brooding, ever-watchful boy finishing off his beer beside me where we sat outside.

Tonight had been homemade pizza night, and we'd all had fun designing our own toppings before Mum brought out a dolphin-shaped cake with fifteen candles stuck into the poor creature's silver-grey icing.

Wrapping paper from my gifts littered the floor around my chair, almost catching fire from the smouldering mosquito coil beneath the table.

I hadn't wanted a big party. I'd wanted to spend it exactly like we had, with the added bonus of finally wearing my father down.

"Oh my God, thank you, thank you, *thank you!*" I ran to where Dad sat at the head of the table and wrapped my arms around him. Planting a big kiss on his sea-weathered cheek, I grinned. "I'll never ask you for anything else. I swear."

"You said that last week when I finally caved and bought you that monofin for your birthday. Wish I hadn't to be fair. You'll only kill yourself faster."

"Monofins are what all the free-divers are using." I couldn't wipe the smile off my face. "Plus…it makes me look like a mermaid. Bi-fins are totally out."

"Bi-fins are so much safer," Dad argued. "They don't trap your legs into one, and you can turn so much faster underwater—"

"But they don't have as much propulsion, and if I want to chase the freediving record, I need to make every kick count."

"Not getting into another debate with you, Neri. Just…promise me you'll be safe, in all your endeavours, that's all I ask."

I nodded madly. "I promise. I promise." I kissed him again before straightening and jiggling with pure happiness. I never in a million years thought he'd agree. This was massive. This was the first taste of freedom.

I could feel it.

This was the year when I'd finally be allowed to live a little. To ditch my constant chaperone and catch up with my school friends in their shenanigans. Perhaps I might even kiss Zara's older brother, Joel, while we camped out in Daintree.

He'd been flirting with me at school, and I'd gotten sick of not living as recklessly as my fellow students. I'd been a good girl for long enough, and this camping trip was the start of a whole new me.

I flicked a glance at Aslan as he stood and started gathering up the dirty plates from dinner. I couldn't recall the moment he'd started cleaning up after us, but I didn't like it.

Now it was just his thing.

My parents didn't put up a fuss as they always lost to his assurances that he wanted to. Whatever guilt he still felt for us rescuing him tainted everything he did…even three years later.

He did it so slyly, so quietly, that the dishes were done and the dishwasher was sloshing in the corner before Mum and Dad even realised the kitchen was sparkling.

It made me feel as if Aslan didn't believe he was truly part of our family and kept himself firmly in the position of hired help.

Marching toward him, I tried to take back my plate. "I'll do it. You just sit down and relax. You were complaining of a headache on *The Fluke* before. Not surprised with the number of hours you guys are putting in at the moment with the whale migration."

His lips pursed, tipping over the little jar in my belly where I imprisoned all the butterflies he caused. The butterflies that weren't permitted to flutter around with their annoying love-struck wings.

I'd done my best to stop my feelings for him.

I'd gone as far as to try self-hypnotism so I could forget about all the ways he made me feel and all the ways he trespassed on my dreams.

But...no matter what lies I told myself, or how I forced myself to form crushes on other boys, none of them were him. None of them were this honey-skinned, sable-haired, ebony-eyed, dark-humoured illegal immigrant who'd been gifted to me by the very same sea that I wanted to live in forever.

I'd never told anyone that my ultimate dream—the one thing I wished would come true more than anything—was one day figuring out how to live beneath the waves. I wanted to spend my life amongst the anemones and octopus. I wanted to open my curtains in the morning and wave to a humpback and not Mrs Starkins across the fence.

But I didn't want to do it alone.

I wanted to do it with *him*.

With the boy who hated the sea for everything that it'd taken from him.

It hurt that he couldn't accept that the yin to that yang was that it might have taken his past, but it had given him *me*.

I was there.

Just waiting for him to open his damn eyes and choose me.

"It's fine, Neri." His husky, accented voice wriggled through my blood like it always did. "It's your birthday. No one expects you to do the dishes on your birthday."

"And no one expects you to do the dishes every night, either, yet you do."

He grinned and ducked from his tall height. Pressing a chaste, respectable kiss to my cheek—which somehow burned a hole through everything I was and made my tongue tingle for an entirely different kiss—he murmured, "Sorry I haven't gotten you a gift yet. Each time we dock for the night, the shops are closed and—"

"It's fine. I don't need anything."

Well, I do need one thing...but you'll never give it to me. Just give me a kiss, Aslan— a single proper, 'I need you more than air' kiss, and you'll never have to be alone again because I'll be yours...through and through.

I shrugged, hiding my inner thoughts that I'd grown bored of. I was sick of falling so stupidly hard for this boy, only to splatter at the bottom of the cliff without him there to catch me. "Honestly, you don't have to give me anything."

"But I want to."

Our eyes held.

The black depths of his gaze trapped me, and my stomach bottomed out like it always did. I stood there like an idiot trapped in quicksand, sinking into the abyss of his soul—the soul I wanted to capture in my butterfly jar and make mine forever.

Oh my God. Stop. You're fifteen now. Enough of this childish infatuation. He'll never look at you that way.

Get. Over. It.

Smiling like a crazy person, I let go of my plate, letting him stack it with the others balancing on his palm. "Well, whatever you get me, I'm sure I'll love it. And thanks for doing the dishes. You're very helpful."

"I do my best." Skirting around the table, he gave me another smile before heading toward the open sliding door and the kitchen beyond.

I watched his every step, drinking in the strain of his white t-shirt over well-defined back muscles, dropping to his firm ass beneath his cargo shorts.

"Nerida." My mum's voice wrenched my gaze to hers, where she sipped on a glass of white wine.

"Um?" I blinked. "I mean, yes?"

"You can go to Daintree rainforest. On one condition."

Dad snickered into his beer bottle. "You beat me to it, my love." Cocking his chin at me, he said, "The one condition—for us to find it acceptable to let our only daughter go camping in the rainforest for three nights—is that Aslan goes with you."

A jangle of crockery as Aslan spun around, doing his best not to drop the plates. "*Me?*"

Dad shifted in his chair, smiling at his employee, secret overstayer, and unofficially adopted son. "You're the only one I trust to keep her alive. As proven by your impeccable track record."

"But..." Aslan marched back to the table and dumped the plates down with a clang. "I've read about that rainforest. It's home to an insane number of dangerous creatures. Saltwater crocs, death adders, taipans, redbacks—"

"Precisely why you need to go. You have your eyes open to everything that can kill my precious little fish. She has her eyes full of hearts as if they're going to fall in love with her, not murder her."

"I do not have eyes full of hearts."

Dad huffed. "Did you or did you not ignore me when I told you to get the hell away from that tiger shark last week?"

"It was only a juvenile. It was harmless. It cruised on by and—"

"And could've turned around and devoured your leg."

I crossed my arms. "I would've punched it in the nose, and it would've let me go. I'm not stupid, Dad. I know how to defend myself. I know to line up with their attack head-on. I know the best way to avoid being bitten is to hold onto their nose, do my best to flip it upside down so it goes into a catatonic trance, or failing that, whack it in the gills."

"Knowing isn't the same as doing, Nerida." Dad's good mood faded a little. "We love you. Most dearly. We trust Zara's family to keep you safe, but don't think for a moment that I'm going to kiss my only daughter goodbye and let her go sleep in the bush without someone watching over her. And I only have one tent, so guess who you'll be bunking with."

Aslan groaned under his breath. "Jack, I really don't think—"

Dad ignored him, chuckling. "I mean...it could be worse, Neri. *I* could come with you. Would you prefer that? I'll share your tent and check your shoes each morning for snakes. I'll even stand guard while you pee against a tree to make sure nothing bites your—"

"Stop. Please stop." I shuddered. "Please don't even joke about that."

"Aslan's going, or you're not going." Mum smiled, her voice kind but sharp.

"Don't I get a say in this?" Aslan growled. "We have a busy week. I just put in the order for more testing apparatus for the water samples that Sydney Aquarium ordered. I thought you wanted me to—"

"We can survive a few days without you. It's Neri we can't survive without." Dad lowered his voice and patted Aslan's crossed arms. "Please, mate. Think of it as a forced vacation. You work too much as it is. You haven't seen any part of Australia apart from our boat, this town, and our garden. There won't be any government bureaucrats out there. No threat to your status on our shores. You'll have fun."

"Fun?" Aslan groaned again. "None of that sounds fun."

"You'll be with Neri; she'll force you to have fun."

"That's what I'm worried about," Aslan muttered.

Dad laughed and stood up, stretching his spine from a long day. "I don't trust anyone as much as I trust you, Aslan. Please tell me you'll keep my daughter safe. And enjoy yourself while doing it."

My cheeks heated as Aslan's dark gaze snapped to mine.

I got the feeling he heard the same sordid invitation I did. An invitation my father definitely did not mean but echoed between two teenagers who had history—regardless if that history was purely one-sided.

I would give anything for Aslan to 'enjoy' me.

He could enjoy me in every which way he wanted.

Running my tongue over my bottom lip, my blood turned hot as images unfurled of him kissing me in the rainforest. Of him silently undressing me in our tent and relieving me of my virginity, all while my friends slept in the next tent, none the wiser.

Aslan's narrowed glare landed on my mouth.

He stiffened and shook his head, as if he could read my wayward thoughts. With a long suffering sigh, his shoulders sagged and he gave in. "Okay, Jack. I'll watch over your daughter for you."

"And say you'll have fun together."

Aslan refused to meet my eyes all while I couldn't control my smirk. "I'll have fun with her."

"Good lad." Dad patted him on the back. "You'll love it out there."

"I'm sure I will." Aslan croaked, flicking me another stare before stepping away from all of us. "I'll make sure to bring her back to you in one piece."

My heart pounded.

He could break a tiny piece of me.

A virgin piece that no one would see but would firmly bind me to him in body and soul.

Dad had no idea the secret undertones between Aslan and I, but it gave me a cheap thrill to believe the boy I cursed for chaperoning me had just promised to have *fun* with me.

We're going to share a tent…

I shivered as a flurry of excited goosebumps cloaked me.

"I've got some old camping gear, the tent I mentioned, and some other supplies that you can take," Dad said to Aslan. "Tomorrow morning, you and I will go shopping so that you'll have all the essentials."

"Essentials being…?" I asked, tearing my gaze from Aslan's discomfort.

"A first-aid kit to rival any hospital, that's for damn sure," Mum said, standing and swirling the last mouthful of her wine. "I want antidotes and EpiPens. I want cures for every bite there could possibly be and a freaking tracking beacon so we can come and get you if anything goes wrong."

"Nothing is going to go wrong, Mum," I muttered. "You've met Zara's mother and father. They're insanely knowledgeable from all their trips abroad. They've been in far more dangerous places than Daintree."

Not that they're going…

That was a lie.

And one I did not feel guilty about.

I was fifteen now. Fifteen and ready to *live*.

"Sleeping in the Serengeti isn't the same as the Australian wilderness," Dad muttered. "One has hungry lions you hear coming, and one has creepy-crawlies that can kill you without a sound."

"Fuck, are you sure you want Nerida going to a place like that?" Aslan asked stiffly. "It's reckless for someone who isn't equipped. I don't agree, Jack. I think you should say no."

"Oh, don't you start." I glowered at him. "I'm going. And I guess that means you're going to." I flashed a tight smile. "We leave tomorrow afternoon. I suggest you get ready to have some *fun*, Aslan."

Hating that I sounded bratty but really needing some space, I disappeared into the house and slipped into my room.

Throwing myself face first onto my bed, I screamed into my pillow.

I screamed, not because I was still being treated like a child or even that I was the overly protected one bringing a damn bodyguard into the jungle.

I screamed because that bodyguard would be sharing my tent.

He would be watching over me as if my very life was his.

He was going to make it absolutely impossible for me not to kiss him at some point and I already knew how that would go.

I would kiss him.

He would hate me.

And the distance that he never let fade between us would grow impossibly, horribly wider.

Chapter Nineteen
ASLAN

(*Moon in Finnish:* Kuu)

I SAT IN THUNDEROUS FURY AS NERI danced with her best-friend Zara, their feet kicking up dried leaves, their laughter loose and free.

I hated that all she wore was her tangerine-coloured bikini, matching Zara's decision to strip off her clothes almost the moment we arrived here.

I hated the guys sitting on their camp chairs, sipping beer, whispering to each other as they watched the girls spin and sway.

My hands balled into fists.

The lies she'd spun.

The tale she'd sold.

I had a good mind to wring her perfect little neck and take her back to Jack in a damn body bag. Because that was probably how this trip would end.

With me killing her.

Or killing Zara's older brother, Joel.

Or maybe the other two guys Joel had brought.

Fuck, I might even murder the two girls sitting at the feet of the guys on garish bright blankets, their breasts barely covered by skimpy bikinis, their legs glistening from insect repellent.

They definitely looked closer to eighteen than fifteen, passing around a flask of something potent, giggling at something Joel said.

I sat alone.

Leaning against the tyre of Joel's Ute, unable to take my eyes off Neri, incase a snake appeared or a spider bit her or a fucking goanna launched at her from the bush.

Four hours we'd been here.

Four hours where each group had staked out a patch of the rented site, erected our mismatched tents, and placed the eskys (a new slang word I'd learned)—holding the food and copious amounts of alcohol that Joel and his friends had brought—in the most shady, coolest spot we could find.

Four hours and I was already fucking exhausted.

I'd gone through all my reserves just keeping an eye on Neri as she laughed at something Joel said and shot him a heated look when he touched her bare waist.

I'd almost ripped his arm off for that.

I'd almost snatched Neri, thrown her into the Ute, and driven away.

But I hadn't because I'd made a promise.

A promise to keep her safe. To have fun.

Fuck.

Fun?

This was an utter nightmare.

I'd rather be anywhere but here.

I'd rather be scrubbing barnacles off the bottom of *The Fluke* than be forced to watch Neri flirt and dance, humming with sexual invitation and recklessness.

My gut clenched.

My blood turned white-hot at the thought of one of the guys taking Neri's hand and disappearing down the overgrown path to Noah Beach.

At least my visions of sleeping in a dense jungle with no facilities or help for miles had been wrong. The trip here had taken almost two hours, but I was grateful to find a proper campground with toilets and other campers who took it upon themselves to police any newcomers, making sure we obeyed the rules of no bonfires or drunken idiocy.

That ought to appease me.

I should be able to enjoy Joel's slightly-flat beer and accept that this was my new home for three days.

But…*she* had made that impossible.

I'd begun to suspect she'd lied the moment she'd ordered Jack to drop us off at Zara's house. Jack drove away with a smile, leaving us alone with all our gear dumped on Zara's front lawn.

The front door had opened.

Zara had shot out and whisked Neri up in a hug with a fair amount of excited screaming.

I'd stood with my hands jammed into my cargo short pockets, not saying a word.

I'd met Zara over the past few years as she came round for play dates and a couple of sleepovers with Neri. The first time I'd met her, she'd been floating around the pool on a zebra lilo, high on sugar, and giggling the way only thirteen-year-old girls could do, celebrating Neri's birthday.

She'd grown up since then.

She was taller, prettier, with breasts on full display in a tight turquoise bikini, short-shorts, and a baggy grey tank-top that gaped every time she bent forward.

While Nerida reminded me a little of my lost sister with her kind heart, intelligent eyes, and desire to be good, Zara reminded me of my cousin with her sly brown eyes and desire to be older than she was. Despite the fact that Afet had black hair and Zara was blonde, the similarities in their moods and disregard for rules made me sick.

I might be the reason my family died on that boat, but my cousin was the reason we were there to begin with.

While I watched Neri and Zara giggle and gossip, I waited for Zara's parents to appear, only…that never happened.

Joel had marched out of the house, chucked all our gear into the back of his dinged-up blue Holden Ute, then commanded we all hop in.

Neri had leapt in the back with Zara.

I'd climbed reluctantly in the front with Joel.

We'd met up with two other cars as we'd driven out of suburbia, hit the highways, and it became abundantly clear that these three days would have no parental supervision whatsoever.

Jack was right to send me to watch her.

Only problem was, I didn't know how long I could stand just watching. I had an awful suspicion that I'd end up doing something she'd hate me for, all because I would do absolutely anything to keep her safe.

And these assholes were not safe.

They'd come here to drink, party, and fuck.

And Neri was far, *far* too fucking young for that.

My teeth ground together.

"Yo, mate. Allan, is it?"

I blinked back my anger and stared at the guys a few metres away.

Keeping half my attention on Neri as she figured out how to light the camp stove that Zara had set up to cook on, I focused on the shaved-head guy who'd already had enough beers to be well over the limit.

"It's Aslan."

"Cool name." He toasted me with his half-empty bottle.

"Isn't that the name of the lion in the *The Lion the Witch and the Wardrobe*?" one of the girls sitting by Joel's feet asked, flicking me a smile. "Narnia or some shit."

"It's not shit," Neri piped up, glaring at the girl. "The Chronicles of Narnia are a classic."

"The witch was pretty hot, I'll admit." Joel laughed. "Especially when she turned all those creatures into ice. Or was it stone? Either way, she was an unapologetic bitch."

Joel's mate snickered, cocking his chin at me. "My name's Gareth, and this is Hadleigh."

I nodded. "Hey."

"I'm Rita, and this is Molly." The redhead wearing a bikini wrapped around her torso with a thousand gemstone strings smiled. "We all go to the same school. We're two years above Neri and Zara but figured...they're sensible enough to drink responsibly." She laughed as if she was hilarious.

"She's not." I crossed my arms. "Not old enough to drink or do whatever else you're planning on doing here."

"Aslan," Neri snapped. "You're not my father. Shut up."

I glowered at her. "I'm here *because* of your father. And thank fuck I am, seeing as you lied about how this trip would go."

"I didn't lie." Neri hunched. "I just...fibbed that parents were coming."

"Parents are most definitely *not* coming." Rita chuckled, dropping her eyes and looking me up and down. "We're here for fun. Everyone is free to be who they want and *do* whoever they want." Before I could growl that those sort of rules weren't gonna fly with me, she asked, "How old are you, Aslan?"

Doing my best to keep my temper in check, I replied, "Nineteen."

"So you finished school? Which one did you go to? Do you work, or are you at uni? If I'd known Nerida had a hot older brother, I would've popped by."

"You didn't even know Nerida until today," Zara quipped, placing a pan on the small flame coming from the camping stove.

"But I do now." Rita wriggled her fingers at Neri. "Hi, Neri. Do you think you could hook me up with your brother?"

"Not my brother," Neri muttered, her face stern and any sign of a smile gone.

"Oh?" Rita crossed her legs and leaned forward, flashing me the crotch of her bikini, revealing the tiniest scrap of material that hid everything between her legs.

Despite myself, I hardened a little.

Taking a swig of luke-warm beer, I said, "I'm a friend of the family's. Been staying with the Taylors to learn the family trade."

The well-rehearsed line I'd heard Jack say so many times spilled effortlessly.

"Oh? What trade is that?" Molly asked, her eyes just as hungry as Rita's as she studied me.

"Marine biology," I replied, my voice husky and harsh.

"That's so cool. So you, like, swim with whales and sharks all day?"

"I—"

"He flatly refuses to go in the ocean." Neri stood upright, planting her hands on her indecently curved hips. "Don't you, Aslan?"

My nostrils flared as I glowered at her across the small space. "If you're trying to shame me, it won't work."

"Shame you?" Neri placed a hand over her heart. "I'd never dream of doing such a nasty thing. I'm merely trying to save you the horror of being asked to go skinny-dipping later."

Rita laughed loudly. "Ooo, you're gonna be fun." She patted the blanket next to her. "Come sit by me, Nerida, and tell me all about your family friend's secrets."

My heart almost broke through my ribs.

She wouldn't.

Would she?

I subtly shook my head as Neri brushed away leaves stuck to her knees.

All it would take was for her to tell them what I truly was.

In a single drunken whisper, she could sign my death warrant.

"Neri…" I murmured, never taking my eyes off hers. I couldn't say the word, but I shouted it as loudly as I could with my stare.

Don't.

With a shiver and a strange look in her stunning ice-blue eyes, Neri abandoned the camping stove and sat next to Rita.

She didn't speak to me and jumped a little as Molly passed her a bottle full of heinously pink liquid. "Watermelon vodka. I think it's time we got this party started, don't you?"

With a smile that didn't reach her eyes, Neri nodded. "Right. Let's have some *fun*."

She stressed the word fun.

She made my heart patter the same way it had last night when Jack had told me to *enjoy* his daughter.

My skin had tightened.

My body had hardened.

And I'd cursed myself the moment Neri had stormed to her bedroom because as much as Jack had meant it innocently—as much as Jack trusted me to keep Neri safe and had given me his ultimate faith the moment I saved her from drowning—he had to be absolutely blind not to sense the hum of electricity between his daughter and me.

A hum that only grew louder as Neri grew older.

When she was twelve, it'd been ignorable.

When she was thirteen, it'd been a gentle burn.

When she was fourteen, it'd been an itch I couldn't scratch.

But now she was fifteen?

Fuck me, it was agonising.

I'd done my best to fight it.

I'd told myself again and again that it was nothing.

Each year, I hoped the unexplainable connection to her would fade.

Each year, it only grew worse.

And now?

I honestly didn't know how much longer I could withstand the pain.

Chapter Twenty

ASLAN

(*Moon in Croatian:* Mjesec)

GRABBING THE BOX I'D HIDDEN IN MY borrowed sleeping bag, I cracked it open.

I struggled to see anything in the dark tent, but smiled a little, knowing what was nestled in the royal-blue velvet.

The sun had well and truly gone to bed.

Most of the campground had joined it, and we'd already received one warning from other campers to keep it down as Joel and his mates steadily drank more and more, becoming less and less inhibited.

The friendly game of UNO had been traded for strip poker about an hour ago. I'd panicked about how to grab Neri and tie her up in the tent before she could flash everyone. But she surprised me in a good way by shaking her head and sitting the game out, sipping on a Sprite instead of a vodka mixer.

It didn't mean I relaxed or stopped watching her every move, but I was grateful that despite her lies and reckless endangerment by agreeing to come out here with these older teens, that she was still the same sensible girl who would rather live in the sea than on land.

I'd caught her yawning twenty minutes ago and was insanely grateful when she disappeared into the tent, grabbed a plastic bag holding her toothbrush and night things, and walked across the dark-shrouded camp to the toilet block in the distance.

The urge to follow her had been vicious, but I'd forced myself to stay where I was.

The camp was safe enough.

The signs about dangerous wildlife and warnings to be crocwise in a rainforest full of crocs had hopefully instilled some common sense to be aware of her surroundings. She walked straight enough so she wasn't drunk. And besides, she'd lived in this dangerous country all her life.

She knew far more than I did.

With her gone, I spied my opportunity to grab her birthday present so I could give it to her before another day passed.

I felt fucking awful last night for not buying her anything.

Last year, I'd settled with a heavy glass paperweight that looked as if it had a red and gold sea anemone trapped inside. It'd been one of the rare times I'd used the cash Jack and Anna paid me, doing my best to make up for the lack of a gift on her thirteenth.

But this year…this morning, when Jack dragged me to the huge department store that sold literally everything, piling a trolley high with things his daughter might need for safe camping, I'd snuck to the jewellery counter and looked at what they had.

I'd almost walked away before I saw it.

Saw the perfect present for the most perfect ocean-loving girl.

A girl who was the reason I was still alive and doing my damnedest to live a life my parents would be proud of.

Fisting the box, I ducked and stepped out of the tent.

I grunted as I ran straight into Rita.

Her arms flew toward me, her hands clamping around my waist as if keeping me upright when I was completely steady on my feet.

I'd only had two beers.

I'd ended up frying the eggs and hashbrowns when everyone else had become too tipsy to bother.

I'd somehow taken on the role of cleaner, cook, and guardian.

Not that that role was new to me.

Even at fifteen, I'd done my best for my sister and parents. Happily pulling my weight as we hid from death that stalked us.

Our eyes met, and I had the sneaky suspicion that it wasn't me Rita was trying to hold up, but herself.

Stepping back a little, I broke her hold on me and shoved Neri's present deep into my cargo pocket. I winced as the spikes of the spiny frog shell Neri had given me the night I'd saved her life warned that that pocket was already occupied.

"You off to bed too?" I asked, listening to the night chorus of bugs, birds, and whatever else lived in this damn jungle.

She hiccupped and licked her lips. She'd slipped into an oversized light pink hoodie and it slipped off her right shoulder, revealing she'd removed her bikini…or had it stripped off, thanks to losing at poker.

"Is that a proposition?" she asked. "I'd happily crawl into bed with you."

My heart leapt but I locked my knees and tried to be as gentle and as polite as I could. My mother would have expected nothing less. "You're a lovely girl, Rita, but—"

"Hey, we said we'd ask him together," Molly growled, stepping from the darkness and linking her arm with Rita's. She winked at me, swaying a little as alcohol affected her balance and judgement. The grey sweater dress she wore barely skimmed below her ass.

"Ask me what?" I asked, wariness colouring my tone.

Across the campsite, Joel, Gareth, and Hadleigh had dragged their sleeping bags into the back of Joel's Ute. They chuckled and traded a bottle of bourbon between them.

Whatever this group of inebriated teens would do tonight was not my problem.

The moment Neri returned from brushing her teeth, I was shoving her inside the tent and zipping it up tight until morning.

The guys laughed again, pointing at something in the bush surrounding us.

They didn't seem to care that the girls were with me, looking me up and down as if starving for a second meal.

"We wondered if you wanted to go to the beach with us." Molly tripped forward, dark hair swinging, her eyes slightly glazed but also sharp with determination. "You don't have to swim if you don't want to. We actually have a *much* better idea than swimming."

Rita stepped into me, running her finger down my chest. "Have you ever had a threesome, Aslan?"

I jerked as her fingers traced my waistband and boldly followed the zipper down the front of my crotch.

Snatching her wrist, I pulled her hand away. "No, and I don't plan on—"

"Oh, come on." Molly pressed against my side, kissing my ear and running her tongue down my neck.

I convulsed.

It was the only word I could use.

A full-body convulsion thanks to the slippery, intoxicating sensation of her tongue on my skin.

Fuck.

"Ooo, are you that sensitive?" She licked me again. "That's good to know."

My eyes snapped closed despite my control.

I'd never felt anything like it.

Never had anyone this close or this forward.

A hand rubbed against my rapidly hardening cock, making me choke on a groan.

The rubbing stopped as suddenly as it'd happened.

Molly whispered, low and husky, "Rita…I can't believe a guy who looks like this. A guy who has spent the entire evening watching out for us as if it's his sworn duty to protect us, jumps like a virgin."

My eyes shot wide. "What? That's not—"

"Don't worry, your secret is safe with us. You're trembling from a single touch." Rita sucked on her bottom lip, her red hair flaming in the night, and cupped me through my shorts. "You've never fucked a girl, have you?"

I slapped her hand away; embarrassment made my voice icy. "That's not any of your damn business."

"But, see, we're *making* it our business," Molly murmured. "We don't care if you have or you haven't. We've spent all night watching you, and when it came time to decide who would approach you, we couldn't agree who would be the lucky one."

Rita smiled with hooded eyes. "We want to fuck you, Aslan. No strings. No worries. Both of us. Together."

"I'm good." My voice was strangled. "Thanks for the offer, but—"

"You've refused to drink, you've refused to play strip poker, and you've refused to flirt with us." Molly kissed my cheek. "You've had a shit night so far, and we want to make it better. We won't take no for an answer—"

"Come to the beach, and we'll show you why having two girls is better than one." Rita pressed her breasts against me, rising on her tiptoes to plant a kiss against my lips.

Two things happened.

Three things, actually.

One, I very nearly grabbed her and kissed her back. All the years of living in the Taylors' garden, of working and worrying and watching Neri grow up had left me ready to explode.

Two, I tried to shove her away. To get control of the rampant throbbing in my shorts and the crazed palpitations in my chest.

And three.

Fuck, three.

A gasp cut right through all my roaring, thundering urges.

A simple, soft little gasp that I would recognise anywhere.

My eyes flew wide, my hands landed on Rita's shoulders and pushed her away, just in time to see Nerida drop her bag, her eyes welling with tears.

A single second for her face to fall.

Another second for her to bolt so fucking fast.

And the last thing I saw was the cute polka-dot night shorts and button-up shirt that her mother had bought for her birthday vanishing into the rainforest.

Chapter Twenty-One
ASLAN

(*Moon in Thai:* Dwng canthr̀)

"NERI!"

I went to charge after her, but sharp fingernails wrapped around my wrist, keeping me pinned. "Let her go, Aslan. She's just being silly."

"Let me the fuck go," I snarled, yanking my hand.

Rita didn't obey, pouting unattractively. "I have no idea why she's acting like a two-year-old. I saw her smiling when Joel kissed her before."

"What?"

"You know…when she snuck off to get some fresh water? He went too. She knows Joel wants to fuck her. That's why we figured we'd take you to the beach. That way she can use your tent."

My heart stopped.

I couldn't speak.

Rage flowed out of me, making my entire body quake.

Molly cleared her throat. "Eh, what Rita means to say is Neri and Joel have been flirting for weeks. She agreed to come with us because she knew—"

"That Joel wants to fuck his little sister's best friend?" I snarled.

Rita giggled. "Well, when you say it like that—"

"He's not going to lay a single finger on Neri."

Molly narrowed her eyes. "Why? You jealous or something?"

I saw red.

Literal blood-red dripped over my vision.

Snatching my wrist out of Rita's talons, I bared my teeth. "I'm responsible for her well-being. To keep her safe from everything—including horny fucking bastards who think they can get lucky with a damn *child*."

"Oh, for heaven's sake." Rita threw up her hands. "She's not a kid. She's fifteen. I lost my V-card when I was her age. I gave my first blowie at fourteen—"

"Nerida is not you," I hissed.

"Oh, please. All girls at that age are like me. We want. We hunger. We ache." She pressed her hand over my out-of-control heart. "You can't stop her from growing up and—"

"Watch me." Shoving her away, I broke into a run.

My bare feet flew over fallen leaves and twigs, kicking up plumes of sand. "Nerida!"

"What the hell is his problem?" Rita's annoyance chased me as I bolted past the two posts announcing the trail to Noah Beach. Signs dotted the entrance with pictures of crocodiles and other dangerous creatures.

I didn't stop to care.

"Neri. Get your ass back here!"

No response.

No sound of her running up ahead.

The night swallowed me completely as I balled my hands and raced faster.

The path seemed to go on for miles, an endless tunnel of darkness and claustrophobic trees before it finally spat me out on the most stunning beach I'd ever seen.

I didn't stop to gawk.

I didn't care how the thick bush suddenly ended, giving way to golden moonlit sand.

I didn't look at the huge glowing disc in the sky as the moon granted its silver light, pouring it all over the calm ocean. The faintest lap of lazy waves licked at the sand, refracting the night sky above, glimmering with a million salty stars.

My heart pounded as a shadow flung itself toward the sea. A shadow that tripped and flew, sun-lightened chocolate hair streaming behind her.

"Nerida!" I threw myself after her. "Get back here."

I didn't know why she'd run or why I hurt in the pit of my stomach.

She was being immature and stupid, and the moment she stopped, I was gonna make damn sure she understood that this sort of behaviour wasn't on.

Neither was kissing drunken boys or lying about a chaste camping trip, only to find out it was a ruse for a fuck-fest.

Her parents are going to kill me.

"Neri! *Koşmayı bırak ve benimle konuş!*" I flinched as I slipped into my mother tongue. Repeating myself in English, I yelled, "Stop running and talk to me! You're going to twist an ankle running so fast!"

She didn't stop or look back.

Jack would never forgive me if I returned her damaged.

My teeth ground together.

He'd also never forgive me if I returned her, and he found out she'd spent the night with a seventeen-year-old moron like Joel.

A splash and spritz of moon-glimmering water as Neri barrelled into the sea, ran until the water lapped at her thighs, then dove under.

Gone.

I slammed to a halt on the sea's edge, panting hard, heart chugging. "Neri!"

My gaze skimmed the gentle waves, wishing the sun shone and not the moon, desperate to be able to see her.

Terror of her drowning like she almost had with the net suffocated me.

I paced the shore, seawater wetting my feet and ankles, warm and whispering.

I didn't have a watch.

I couldn't time her.

She'll come up for air soon.

How long has it been?

A minute?

Two?

Dragging both hands through my hair, I kept pacing. Madly, furiously, kicking the ocean out of my way as my eyes stayed locked on the spot where she'd gone under.

No bubbles.

No ripples.

She'd disappeared without a trace.

I dropped my arms, rubbing my mouth as I looked at the moon, the forest, the sand, the stars.

Nothing could help me find her.

Every instinct screamed to launch into the sea and snatch her from the depths. But...the grief I hadn't dealt with threw itself against the walls in my mind.

The creak of the boat as it broke apart.

The throb of my bruises as the waves threw us around as if we were nothing.

The scream of my mother—

"Nerida!" I stopped pacing the shore and turned to wade deeper into the sea, ignoring the thundering in my ears and the horror in my heart.

Water lapped over my knees, soaking the hem of my shorts.

Fuck, how long has it been?

Too long.

Far, far too long and new images came to mind.

Images I couldn't shove back into the waterlogged box where they belonged because these were all too real, too true.

What if she was stabbed by a stingray?

What if she was stung by a Portuguese man o' war?

What if a shark smelled her or a saltwater croc—

I turned to ice as a shimmer of movement appeared where Neri had vanished.

It looked like the swish of a croc's tail. The ridges of its reptilian spine. The power of death hunting the one girl I'd fucking die for.

I hurled myself into the sea.

Fully clothed, pockets full of precious things and belated birthday gifts, I forgot all about myself and only thought of her.

I dove under and swam.

Fuck, I swam as fast as my arms and legs would allow.

I opened my eyes underwater, begging to see signs of Neri—in one piece, alive, unbleeding.

Gentle waves carried me, rising and falling with the sea's currents.

My eyes burned from salt.

Nothing.

Nothing but blackness and darkness and—

A terrifying shadow to my left.

I choked on a mouthful of brine as I shot to the surface and planted my feet on the sandy bottom. Images of poisonous stone fish and barbed sea urchins ready to impale my feet couldn't scare me as much as the shadow racing toward me.

I braced myself for teeth.

I sucked in a breath to fight.

And that breath exploded with a grunt as Neri popped up beside me, eyelashes sparkling, pretty face dripping, moon-drenched hair plastered to her slender shoulders.

Fuck.

She looked absolutely stunning.

Stunning and hurt and young.

So, so young.

But...also not.

The way she watched me.

The way she held her shoulders back, fully ready to go to war, all while her lips turned downward with pain.

She burned with so many things, barely hidden in her churning stare.

The urge to protect her from all of it roared through me. Every drop of brotherly instinct kicked in, followed by the not-so-permitted rage of a man who didn't think of this girl as his family.

Not at all.

She was my nemesis and saviour.

My dream and tormentor.

All the lies I told myself of feeling nothing for her went up in fucking flames because I'd never been more aware that she wasn't Melike. She wasn't my sister. She wasn't the second chance at a family after losing mine.

Our eyes locked.

She opened her mouth to speak.

But I couldn't do it.

I'd either strike her, kiss her, or try to drown her.

I was livid.

Irrationally ropable at her for putting herself in harm's way.

"Don't say a single word." I snatched her wrist and jerked her toward the shore. "I thought you were a damn crocodile."

She came without protest, wading beside me as the sea gradually grew shallower, allowing us to walk free without croc teeth or shark jaws killing us.

Something splashed between us as we walked the final few steps and sand welcomed us back to the world I preferred. Ripping my hand away from her, I swiped back saltwater dripping from my hair.

I couldn't catch a proper breath.

I couldn't see straight. Couldn't stop the tattered hammering of my heart.

I braced myself for her excuses.

Turning slowly, I prepared to fight with her even though all I wanted to do was make sure she was alright.

What had possessed her to do something so dangerous?

Why had she kissed Joel?

What else had she done at school when she ought to be learning instead of flirting?

In the silver moonlight, Neri bent and plucked something from the lazy waves. Cradling it gently, she straightened and tipped her chin at me. "What's this?"

I frowned. "No idea. Sea trash. Throw it back."

"Throw it back?" Shaking her head, she cracked it open and gasped. "It didn't come from the sea." Her eyes shot to mine. "I think...I think it fell out of your pocket."

"What?" Standing my ground, I trembled as she padded toward me and held out the blue velvet box I'd stuffed in my pocket before Rita and Molly had accosted me outside the tent.

Her lips dared raise in a tentative smile. "Is this...is this my birthday present?" Darkness clouded her face as she recoiled. "Wait...did you buy it for someone else?" Glancing past me, she flinched. "Is it for her?"

I groaned and pinched the bridge of my nose. "*Kafami sikeyim*."

Her shoulders sagged. "It is, isn't it? It's for—"

"You're going kill me. You saved my life only to make it a living hell." Marching into her, I grabbed her rolled shoulders and shook her. Hard. "Ignore that. That's not important. What is important is: what were you thinking? Running through a rainforest in the dead of night? Running into the sea where a million signs warn you about crocodiles and jellyfish?"

"I—" She struggled to get free, but I didn't let her. "Your father ordered me to keep you safe. How am I supposed to do that if you go running around letting any monster take a bite?"

"Any monster being…Joel?" She cocked her head, distracting me.

More temper flowed. "He definitely acts as one."

"Does not. Joel's nice."

"*Nice?* He isn't nice. He's thinking with his cock and—"

"At least he's willing to touch me! Unlike some."

"What the hell is that supposed to mean?"

"It means my father told you to enjoy yourself with me, yet I doubt that will ever happen."

I blanched. So she'd heard the taboo invitation in Jack's innocent remarks too. "He didn't mean it like that, and you know it."

"I know you look at me as if you want to."

I reared back. "Like hell I do. You're his daughter. You're—"

"Right beneath your nose, and you're too scared to do anything about it."

"You're fucking fifteen!"

"And you're just some boy I plucked from the sea. I think you use my family as an excuse not to do what you want!"

"In case you forgot, I *can't* do what I want. Any day, I might be found out and sent back home."

"No one cares you live with us, Aslan. You're free to do whatever you want with me. I would *let* you do whatever you wanted—"

"Fuck, Neri, I never thought you'd be so crude."

"Well, being subtle hasn't exactly gotten me very far, has it?"

"For the last time, Nerida—"

"If you say I'm fifteen again, I'm going to knee you in the balls."

My fingers dug into her shoulders, I struggled to speak in English and not slip into Turkish. "Fine. I admit you're not twelve anymore. Believe me, I'm highly aware of that after watching you drink and walk around half-naked—"

"I'm wearing the same exact bikini I wear onboard *The Fluke*."

"That's different."

"No, it's not."

"Believe me, it is."

Her eyes heated. "And there you go again, making my heart trip and my belly clench and those damn butterflies fly like maniacs inside me."

"What the hell are you talking about?"

"I'm talking about *you*, you idiot! Me and you. *This.* Whatever this is. It's been there since we first met and it's only getting worse."

"You saved my life, Neri. Of course, there's going to be a connection—"

"And you saved mine. That makes us even. You said it so yourself. So why hasn't this—whatever it is—faded? Why does it keep getting stronger? Why do I catch you watching me as if you feel the same exact way, only for you to hide it the moment I—"

"You're underage. You're Jack and Anna's daughter. You're—"

"Going out of my mind." She groaned.

I sucked in a breath, my fingers burning where I held her. "Look, let's just forget about this and—"

"Joel kissed me tonight. My first official kiss that wasn't CPR." Her lips stretched into a sarcastic smile. "He's older than me. He's seventeen, yet had no qualms at all about—"

"Enough." My grip tightened as fresh rage poured through me. "I've heard all I want to know about that bastard sticking his tongue down your throat."

"Why?" Her eyes glittered dangerously. "Jealous, Aslan? Is that why you're angry? You're not pissed off I went for a midnight swim, but because I kissed him?"

My jaw clenched. My teeth ached. I struggled to control my temper.

She made it worse by saying, "Want to know why I went for that swim in the first place?" She wedged the gift I'd bought her against her heart. "Seeing her kiss you? Seeing the way she touched you? It made every part of me feel as if I'd explode."

Fuck, I know the feeling.

"At least someone wants to kiss me," she murmured. "At least I can try to move on with someone if you're not strong enough to touch me yourself."

Fury roared.

I tripped well and truly over my limit. *"O sadece seni öpmek istemiyor. Seni sikecek ve sonra seni tamamen unutacak."*

Her crystal-blue eyes narrowed, glowing in the moonlight. "What did you say?"

"I said he doesn't just want to kiss you. He'll fuck you and forget all about you."

"Maybe that's what you should do so you could forget all about me," she snapped. "Go on. No one will know. We're alone. The government won't know. My parents won't know. You could fuck me, Aslan, and—"

I threw her away, tripping backward, my hands burning and heart smoking as if she'd burned me alive.

"Dur." I choked. "Fuck's sake, Neri. *Dur.*"

"What does—"

"It means *stop*."

Raking both hands over my face, I growled into my palms, "It's late, and you've been drinking."

"I'm not drunk." She planted her feet into the golden-silver sand and raised her jaw.

I caught her stare as she sniffed. "I'm so sick of this. I'm sick of you thinking you have to take care of me. I'm sick of you looking at me as if you don't *see* me. I'm sick of—"

"If you're so sick of me, Nerida, why are you so determined to give me a goddamn heart attack?"

"Because it's the only way you pay attention to me!" she cried, shooting forward and making me stumble in the sand. "You know as well as I do that there's something between us. Just admit that you feel it and—"

"I can't admit something that doesn't exist."

For a moment, the world froze.

No air. No waves. No insects chirping.

Just a stagnant pause where we stood glowering at each other, drowning beneath the stinging, electrifying connection I couldn't stop.

Finally, she nodded.

Her lips twisted. "Doesn't exist, huh?"

I grunted in shock as she threw herself against me, dove her hands into my unruly sun-bronzed hair, and jerked my head down.

Her lips crashed hotly to mine.

Her breasts crushed firmly against my wet t-shirt.

Her hands yanked at my strands, sending bolts of pain and indescribable need.

It happened so fast, I just stood there.

Stood there as she plastered every part of her to every part of me and dove her tongue deliciously into my mouth.

I convulsed.

A full-body shudder that had nothing to do with the kiss but the girl fucking kissing me.

She was the sea all over again, pulling me under, ripping me from everything I knew.

I drowned in her.

I lost myself in her.

I wanted and wanted and…*couldn't.*

I choked on a groan as her tongue licked me again.

And it broke every fucking bone in my desperate fucking body to plant my trembling hands on her ocean-damp shoulders and gently, firmly, *excruciatingly* push her away from me.

She didn't fight.

She gave up.

Gave in.

She bowed her head as tears glittered in her gaze.

Heartache etched her every feature.

And I begged every power there was that she wouldn't see the same heartbreak in mine.

Slowly, ever so slowly, I ducked and grabbed the blue box that she'd dropped in the sand when she'd grabbed me.

Trying to catch a proper breath, I opened the lid and pulled out the necklace with its silver charm.

She stood swaying, not saying a word as I unthreaded the chain, and tucked the box back into my pocket with the shell she'd given me. I would never admit that that simple spiky shell had become my most valuable possession.

Not because I spoke to my parents with it, like she'd suggested, but because I gave it my every confession about *her*. I spoke aloud my secrets when everyone was in bed, hoping it could cure me of the incurable desire for a girl I could never have.

Silently, I stepped behind her.

Her button-up top and night shorts were drenched and almost translucent beneath the polka dots, showing the curves of her body and the shadows of everything I shouldn't want.

Glancing at the chain dripping in my fingers, she sucked in a breath. Without a word, she gathered up her sodden hair, revealing the gorgeous curve of her spine and nape as she kept her gaze firmly on the sand.

My voice was thick as oil as I said, "I bought this for you, Nerida. No one else." Securing the clasp around her neck, I fought the battle of my body to spin her around and kiss her.

To kiss her the way I wanted to.

The way I would never be allowed to: with teeth and tongue and years' worth of torment.

Somehow, I found enough strength to hug her gently, sweetly—perfectly approved for fathers and the strict promises I'd made.

She shivered as I hugged her from behind, resting my chin on her shoulder, keeping my hips and what she'd done to me far away from her perfect ass.

"I couldn't believe it when I first saw the charm," I whispered. "The girl caught my attention first, swimming exactly like you do…so full of grace and power. But when I saw the sea lion swimming with her…the way it looked at her with so much love and joy, I had to buy it for you." Pressing a chaste kiss to the side of her hair, I licked my lips at the salt coating her. "You once told me that your name means nymph, and I told you that mine means lion. You joked about sea lions, which has always stuck with me because I knew, even then, that I could never forgive the sea for what it's taken from me."

Turning her around slowly, I cupped her cheeks and confessed more than I ever had before. "I've lost everyone I ever loved, Neri. I ran from my birthplace and can never go back. And the only people keeping me hidden and safe are your parents. I owe them everything. I'm loyal to them…above everyone."

Running my fingers down the chain and around the charm nestled just above her breasts, I steeled myself against her sharp inhale and whispered, "You're right that there's something between us. You're right that it's been there ever since you jumped overboard and found me. And you're right that it only gets stronger every year, but…nothing can ever happen between us, do you understand? Nothing can happen because…I made a promise to your parents that I would never touch you in that way. And I have no choice but to honour that promise because…"

I swallowed hard, forcing myself to continue. "Because…I'm afraid. I'm afraid of where I'd go if Jack threw me out. I'm afraid of what will happen if the government finds me. But the real reason is, the main reason I will never lay a finger on you, is…I'm fucking terrified of loving you, only to lose you. I wouldn't survive. I'd rather never have you than run that risk."

Tears ran down her cheeks. "No one would need to know…"

"*I* would know." I pressed the softest kiss to her forehead. "If I touch you, Neri, your dad will kick me out. And if I can't stay with you, I'll never see you again because I'll be caught and deported."

"I don't care."

I hid my wince.

She didn't know what she was saying.

By saying she didn't care about me being deported, she admitted she didn't care if I died.

But she didn't know.

Didn't know that the moment I stepped foot on beloved home soil, I would be slaughtered.

Yet another secret I'd kept from her at Jack's command.

"I wouldn't care if you were deported because I'd just follow you," she breathed.

Frosty horror filled me.

If she ever did that…fuck, she'd be as dead as me.

I wanted to shake her and snarl that she could never step foot in Turkey, but that would raise questions I couldn't answer. Instead, I distracted her. With words that would make her heart flutter because they already made mine quake.

Catching her eyes, I whispered, "You asked me once why I never say the words I love you. The simple truth is…I do. I think I've loved you from the moment you dragged me from the sea. You saved me, Neri. You gave me purpose. You gave me something to fight for when all I wanted to do was die. Not a day will go by that I'm not grateful to you, but…that is all I will ever be, do you understand? That is where we end."

She cried silently, her tears looking like jewels upon her cheeks. "But that's where we should *begin*, Aslan. Don't you see?"

Frustration rolled through me, doing its best to tame my need. "I love you. Isn't that enough?"

"No." Her tears rolled in the moonlight. "It will never be enough."

I sighed heavily. "Then I'm sorry for hurting you. That was never my intention. I love you like I loved my family—"

"Bullshit. You love me like I'm yours. I *know* you do."

"I love you, but that is where it stops. No more. No less. I will never touch you. I will never change my mind. Trust me on that."

"So you're choosing to ignore the connection between us all because you're a coward?"

I sucked in a breath, my anger pinching. "I'd rather be a coward than dead."

"*Dead?* What—?"

"Forget it. I didn't mean it. Come on...we should get back to camp." I tried to grab her wrist, but she tripped out of my reach.

"I don't want to go back. We need to talk—"

"We *have* talked," I snapped. "There's nothing more to say."

"For you maybe—"

"It's over, Neri."

"It hasn't even begun, Aslan. How am I supposed to stay away from you? How am I supposed to watch you with others? How am I supposed to stop wanting you?"

Fuck.

Each of her questions flayed me alive and left me bleeding all over the starlit beach. I had the same questions. I never wanted her to find another, all while hoping she found the happiness she deserved.

I hated that I couldn't be the one to give her that happiness, all because I came with so much risk.

All I wanted to do was grab her. Kiss her. Snatch all my promises back and take what was mine to take.

But I couldn't because it wasn't just my life on the line.

If she cared for me as much as she said. If she dared fall for me the way I was desperate to fall for her...

Then the moment I got deported, it would kill her too.

And I could never be responsible for her broken heart because I knew the pain of being left behind.

Never.

I would never put her through such loss, such grief.

I would rather she hated me than that.

"Enough, Neri."

"Don't 'enough' me. *Talk* to me! Tell me the truth. Tell me why you won't even consider—"

"I *have* told you the truth!" My voice cut loudly through the night. "This is not up for debate. We're done here." Grabbing her hand, I dragged her, dripping and spitting up the beach to the campsite.

"We are not done here. We are definitely not done. Tell me why—"

"I've told you. Now shut up. This is dangerous and risky, and I'm *done,* do you hear me? You saved my life. I saved yours. That's all there ever was and all that will ever be. The sooner you accept it, the sooner we can go back to normal and forget all about this."

"I'll never forget about this. Never forget that you chose Australia over me."

My teeth ground together. Truth snarled in my soul.

Wrong...I choose you over myself.
I choose not to hurt you when I'm dead.

I didn't reply as we stalked through the dark, our hearts aching, our feet hissing in the sand, watched over by judging trees and gossiping bushes. By the time we stripped out of our wet clothes and dressed in drier things, the strain between us had reached feverish agony.

I hated that I'd hurt her.

I cursed her for hurting me.

I wished things could be different—that I was free to find my own place, my own work, my own life. A life that was separate from the Taylors so I might, one day, deserve Neri for my own.

But that would never happen.

I would never be given asylum—regardless of what forms I filled in or pleas I made. It would never happen because of what my family was back home. What my last name truly was.

A secret I'd only found out the night we'd boarded that condemned rickety boat.

If Neri ever knew...

Sighing heavily, I listened to her crying in her sleeping bag and couldn't stomach the distance between us.

It was agonising and wide, and in the dark where no one could see, I broke my own rules as Neri gave me her back and her soft sob ripped out the rest of my already mangled heart.

I shouldn't do this.

If Jack found me hugging his daughter like this, he'd most likely punch me.

But nothing could have stopped me from pulling her against me, tucking her head beneath my chin, and letting her break in my arms. "I'm sorry, Nerida. More than you'll ever know."

She didn't reply.

She stayed stiff in my embrace.

But I couldn't give her anything more.

I couldn't fall for her because I had nothing to offer her.

But at least I could give her a tiny shred of my true feelings before I locked them away, hiding them from tomorrow.

Chapter Twenty-Two
NERIDA

(Sea in Indonesian: Laut)

"THAT MUST HAVE BEEN SO HARD, to give all your truth to the boy you were in love with, only for him to refuse you."

I blinked.

For a moment, I forgot where I was. Who was the girl in front of me? How did she know about that heart-wrenching night on the beach in Daintree?

But then, Dylan cleared his throat, and Margot shifted in her chair, waiting for me to answer her, and everything came flooding back.

The interview.

I'm telling them everything.

I shook my head a little, shocked that I'd been steadfast in that decision. I hadn't held anything back. I hadn't hidden the depth of my feelings even when I was so young. The way Aslan made me feel, even to this day, had never been surpassed by anyone.

And it never will.

I'd made my peace with that when I saw those two girls propositioning him all those years ago.

"It was the most painful moment of my life." I looked at both reporters. "And what a privileged life I'd led that I can honestly say unrequited love was my bittersweet tragedy at the tender age of fifteen. Unlike Aslan, who'd already lived through more loss and pain than I could ever have imagined."

I struggled with the ghosts of that time. Feeling, all over again, the way my stomach dropped to my toes and a rush of nausea made me flush with heat. He hadn't kissed the girl back that night, but he hadn't pushed her away either.

Seeing him with another had been such a shock, such a slap in the face, that I'd had an out-of-body experience. I'd stepped out of my younger self and pushed aside silly teenage desires and saw the truth.

A truth that condemned me because no matter how old I became or whatever paths my life took me on, Aslan was *mine*.

I was more sure of that than anything.

I was willing to accept it, even if he never made me his.

And as he'd spooned me that night in the tent, I'd broken for all the things he would never be able to give me.

By the time the sun rose, my heart was irreversibly cracked. And those cracks only grew wider each time I touched the girl and sea lion necklace he'd given me.

A necklace that I lost on the worst day of my life a few years later.

The day I almost died of heartbreak.

Not yet.

You don't have to tell them that part...not yet.

Meeting Margot's eager gaze, I said quietly, "That camping trip opened my eyes to things I hadn't fully respected. I was safe, you see. I was loved and legal and home. I had no threats hanging over my head and no experience with adversity. I believed Aslan lived life the way I did. Bravely and boldly. Ready to make his mark and take what he wanted.

"But he couldn't do that and go unnoticed. He couldn't leave us. He couldn't give my parents any reason to throw him out. I struggled to understand why he would put his promise to my parents above the aching need between us. But I soon learned he was right to be wary. I soon felt the same terror of his deportation. The same horror of him being sent home. Enough so that the desperation within me to be with him was leashed by the very real need to keep him safe.

"I suppose I never got to be a true teenager because of him. I never got the thrill of falling in love with the wrong boy and making mistakes as I figured out who I wanted to be.

"I already knew who I was: I was his. And I already knew what I couldn't have: him."

A long pause as I fell into silence.

Reminiscing was enjoyable but also incredibly hard.

"Your voice has gone quiet, Nerida," Dylan said gently. "Did something else happen between you two?"

A rock lodged in my throat as I swallowed. "Oh, many things happened. Many awful things. But some good, too."

"Want to tell us about them?"

I shivered. "Not really. But I made you a promise, and my life has been nothing but eventful."

"Forgive me if I'm misunderstanding, but...you married Aslan, correct? If you felt this deeply when you were so young, and he felt the same way, why do you sound as if this tale doesn't have a happy ending?" Margot hugged herself. "He's not...dead, is he? Please tell me he's not—"

I held up my hand, my heart pinching at her question. "I think we should take a little break, don't you?"

Her eyes glittered. "Please tell me your love story has a happy ending..."

I didn't answer her.

Happy wasn't the word I'd use. But neither was tragic or hard or awful. It was us.

Quintessentially us and no one else's.

Margot kept me pinned in her stare, and Dylan hung on my every sentence. The mention of a break didn't seem to entice them so...I gave them the only words I could. The words that came next.

"The rest of that camping trip went as well as you'd expect. Aslan kept his distance from me, yet his eyes tracked me wherever I went. Joel tried to kiss me again, but I declined and said I'd changed my mind. Rita and Molly attempted to have their dirty way with Aslan the next night, but he firmly told them it would never happen. We did our best to stay busy with local tours into the rainforest, a bush-educational walk, and took turns cooking bare essentials and learning how to use the barbecue in the campground.

"By the time the three days were over, I'd never been more grateful to get home. Even if my father asked a million questions and my mother flinched when she looked into my eyes, most likely seeing the cracks left in my heart by the boy who lived in our garden.

"Aslan didn't act any differently toward me in their company. He still hugged me, smiled at me, spoke to me, and watched out for me. He didn't tell my parents that I'd lied about being supervised out there. He didn't tell them what'd happened between us or about Joel kissing me.

"He kept my secrets and I kept his, and by the time a few months had passed, we slipped into an understanding that no matter what we felt or how much we wanted, we would never speak of it again.

"That was...until I went and did something that made Aslan well and truly snap."

"What did you do?" Margot asked.

"I tried to replace him."

"Replace him?" Dylan frowned.

"I couldn't have him. Therefore, I had to find someone I could." I sighed. "Needless to say, it did not end well."

Chapter Twenty-Three

NERIDA

AGE: 16 YRS OLD

(*Sea in Japanese:* Umi)

"HEY."

Aslan groaned and pulled the pillow over his head. "Neri, go back to bed."

"I will, don't worry. No one saw me, and I won't be long." Closing his door on the solar lights flickering in the garden, I tiptoed through the dark and sat on the end of his bed.

He moved his long legs to give me room, his lips thin and wary.

Four years he'd lived with us, yet he never changed this sala-bedroom.

Never spent the money my parents paid him.

Never complained that for four years, his routine of hanging with us, working for my parents, and keeping to himself had become a rut.

He didn't have friends because he didn't trust anyone to get close to him.

He didn't have a girlfriend to ease whatever urges he felt because...well, same problem.

On the rare instances when I'd catch him deep in thought and ask him how he truly was, he'd smile, pat my hand, and assure me that he was fine. Better than fine. He found enjoyment in his work. He found peace in his puzzle books. He found contentment with us.

But I worried he lied.

I worried he wanted more. Needed more. And eventually, he'd look for more.

He was twenty, after all.

All the guys I knew had fucked multiple girls and been in numerous relationships.

Yet on the nights when I couldn't sleep and I sat leaning against my windowsill, panicked at the thought of Aslan sneaking out to find someone who wasn't me, I always sighed in relief when he didn't.

He'd never flirted with anyone when he drove me around town or picked me up from school or completed chores for my father.

It was as if he ignored that part of his humanity.

I'd have almost believed he didn't need anyone to touch him or love him if I didn't catch the fire in his gaze whenever he dropped his guard. The last time it happened—when we were watching a movie as a family last week, and I'd laughed at something silly and turned to Aslan to see if he laughed too, I'd been struck breathless at the smouldering, deep, black heat in his stare. With the TV flickering over his face, he looked as if he battled every feral instinct not to snatch me, savage me, and tear me into well-fucked pieces.

But then my mum had turned to see what made me tremble.

And Aslan had blinked.

His throat had worked, and his fists had clenched, and by the time he opened his eyes again, the inferno within him was replaced with bored humour, successfully smothered before my parents could notice.

"What's in your hands?" He sat up in bed, pushing the black sheet to his waist, revealing the hard ridges of his toned chest and stomach.

My mouth went dry.

I forgot how to speak.

The undercurrent that always flowed between us felt particularly vicious tonight.

My nipples pebbled, and my stomach twisted, and it took all my strength to lift my gaze to his. I smiled as if the delicious sight of his pillow-ruffled sun-bronzed brown hair, sleep-hooded eyes, and perfectly toned body didn't make me tingle all over.

Those butterflies that I constantly trapped and suffocated in a glass jar flurried and fought, desperate to be free to leap into bed with him, dive their wings through his hair, and flutter against those lips I'd only kissed once.

I swallowed hard as I always did whenever I thought of that kiss on Noah Beach. How he'd stiffened and stopped breathing. How, for the tiniest of heartbeats, his lips had shifted beneath mine, and the groan that'd escaped him set fire to every droplet of my blood.

But then he'd pushed me away.

He'd told me exactly why it would never happen again.

And I'd respected his reasoning ever since. Not because I didn't want him more than anything, but because I didn't want him to leave…and I was terrified he'd vanish if I pushed him.

"I got you a gift."

"What? Why?" His voice was husky and low. "I don't need anything, and even if I did, you could've waited until morning to give it to me."

"I could've, yes. But I…I wanted to see you."

"You saw me at dinner a few hours ago."

"You and Dad were poring over the nautical maps of Whitsundays. I know you're going with them next week, and I can survive on my own, but…I'll miss you."

He sucked in a breath, his eyes darkening. "It's only four days."

"Four days of being alone."

"You're the one who said you'd rather stay here than crash at a friend's place."

"I know." I shifted the two bulky gifts in my lap. "I'm not regretting that choice. Just jealous that I can't come with you."

"You have exams. School is almost over for the year."

I smiled. "Only one more year to go before uni."

His lips tipped up. "I'm proud of you. You've worked super hard." He chuckled. "And sacrificed untold hours of reef swimming and dolphin diving for being land-locked to study."

"And I've hated every moment of it."

"Ah well, the moment you get your degree, you can be back on the sea. Perhaps, when you officially work for your parents, I can find something that suits my preference for keeping earth beneath my feet."

I stilled. "You know you've become invaluable to them. Just because I'll be a fully qualified marine biologist doesn't mean they won't still want your help."

He shrugged. "Doesn't bother me. I'll be free to find something more suited."

The way he said it was too relaxed, too rehearsed.

Without my parents paying him, he opened himself up to a whole ocean of risk.

Leaning closer, I whispered, "You could work for me instead. I'll get my own boat and research grants and—"

"I'll still have to step foot on the ocean all day."

"Would that be so bad?"

"Yes." He laughed, deliberately keeping things light between us. "Have you not been listening to anything I've said the past four years?"

"What if you could live *beneath* the sea? Would that change things?"

He raked his hands through his hair, making his biceps bunch and pecs bounce.

I crossed my legs together, growing indecently warm.

"The only way you could ever get me to live willingly beneath the sea would be to prove it was safer than living out of it."

"Would you live there if I lived there? Would you trade air for salt if it meant we could be together?"

The air immediately crackled between us. "Neri…don't."

I didn't know what possessed me to skip close to the line we never crossed, but I couldn't stop myself. "If the thought of you going away for four days makes me sick to my stomach, what the hell is it going to feel like when you finally do leave?"

"I'm not going anywhere."

"What if you fall in love and chase after someone?"

He swallowed hard. His eyes ignited with coal-fire.

I didn't breathe, bracing myself for him to brush away such a thing, but he licked his lips and whispered, "I can't fall in love if I've already fallen."

I moaned.

I couldn't stop it.

My skin came alive; my heart exploded with all the instincts and all the moments where I tripped and fell, only to end up broken and bleeding on the ground.

He contradicted everything he'd said on Noah Beach.

He gave me *hope*.

Tears pricked my eyes as Aslan leaned forward and cupped my cheek. His skin was warm from sleeping. His hand slightly calloused from work. His touch achingly tender and desperately right.

I leaned into his palm.

We never brought up what happened in Daintree and the lines between us were no longer drawn in sand but built in stone and concrete. Neither of us had attempted to cross them. Neither of us had slipped or made the other hope everything could be different. Neither of us was brave enough to shove aside the very real problems preventing us from being together and saying fuck it to everything but us.

Yet in that room, on that night, I was so, so horribly close to throwing everything away because I couldn't do it anymore.

"*İşte bu yüzden şu anda dokunduğumdan daha fazla dokunmayacağım sana. Bekar ve gizli kalmaktan mutlu olmamın nedeni, istediğim tek kızın, sahip olamayacağım tek kız olması.*"

I shivered. I recognised a few words from his lessons over the years, but he spoke too fast, too low for me to understand. "What...what did you say?"

He dropped his arm and pulled away. "I shouldn't have said it at all. Let alone repeat it."

"You can't do that." I balled my hands, fighting the rush of sick desire. "Tell me."

Inhaling hard, he pinched the bridge of his nose and whispered, "This is why I will never touch you more than I'm touching you right now. Why I'm happy to stay celibate and hidden because the only girl I want is the only girl I can't have."

"You can have her...if you want her." I trembled. My heart successfully shattered a few ribs with its pounding.

"You know why I can't." He groaned and scrubbed his face. "Fuck, you shouldn't be in here. You can't keep visiting me like this. It's too hard."

Pain scattered down my back with awful goosebumps. "Do you want me to go?"

"Yes." He nodded firmly. "No." He groaned. "Fuck, I *should* want you to go."

"But you don't...not really?"

His chin tipped up; his dark eyes met mine. "No." He snarled as a rush of temper made him stiffen. "But say something. Do something. Anything to stop me from going out of my mind with—" He cut himself off and sucked in a deep breath. "Enough, Neri. This has to stop. Your parents hold my life in their hands. I love them as if they were my own. If I slip and give in, I not only lose you, but I lose them too. And I fucking refuse to lose any of you."

I rolled my shoulders, successfully scolded and chastised. "I'm sorry."

"Just give me what you came here to give and then go."

Without a word, I passed him the two boxes.

He took them silently, and my fingers strayed to my necklace. The necklace he'd secured around my throat after he'd rejected my kiss.

A full year and I'd never taken it off.

Every time I touched it, it was Aslan I touched. Aslan I spoke to. Aslan I wanted.

He laughed a little. His tone was strained and gravelly but his amusement genuine, shoving away his temper. "The Chronicles of Narnia."

I smiled as best I could, dropping my hand from my chain and charm. "I think my grandparents bought the boxed set for me when I was three. I have fond memories of my mum reading them to me. I know Rita, or was it Molly? I can't remember. Anyway, one of them mentioned that Aslan is the name of the lion. He's so protective and kind and...reminds me of you, in a way. And...well, I figured you might want to read them...especially if the research trip around Whitsundays gets boring."

His eyes glittered, already seeing my ulterior motives. "I've heard the Whitsunday Islands are stunning and are a tourist hot spot. I doubt I'll be bored."

I did my best not to pout or think about all the scantily-clad women sunbaking on gorgeous beaches. "They're okay, I guess."

He chuckled under his breath. "Don't worry, Neri. I don't think we have any time on shore."

I didn't reply, not quite trusting myself not to say something stupid or reveal the extent of my jealousy on hypothetical situations of him finding another girl who was trustworthy—a girl who wouldn't care that he was here illegally. A girl who could patch up the holes in his heart by touching him, loving him, protecting him.

Glancing at the other box I'd given him, his eyes snapped to mine. "You bought me a cell-phone?"

"The hand-me-down piece of crap that Dad gave you well and truly deserves to be retired. The calls drop out all the time, and its signal sucks."

Gathering my hair up, I twisted it into a rope over my shoulder, a nervous habit and one Aslan knew about, but I couldn't help it.

This meant so much to me.

Too much really.

If I couldn't have his body, then perhaps I could have his mind and heart…carefully gifted through the impersonal screens of technology.

"You want me to message you while I'm gone?" he asked quietly.

I want you to message me all the time. About everything. Anything. Always.

My cheeks heated at how pathetically high my heart leapt. "If you have the time. I mean…just so I know you haven't fallen overboard."

He sucked on his bottom lip and nodded. "I can do that. But I'm paying for the phone myself." His eyes strayed to the tallboy that'd seen better days and the bottom drawer where I knew he kept his money.

"It was a gift, Aslan—"

"I won't let you buy me something so expensive." Dropping the phone box on his pillow, he tossed the sheet away from his legs, revealing tight black boxer-briefs and an intoxicating bulge between his legs.

I leapt to my feet.

I shivered with lancing, breaking desperation.

It took everything I had not to throw myself at him.

I swayed toward him.

Selfishness to take what I wanted almost made me kiss him again.

But the idea of him being kicked out. Of him no longer living in the garden. Of no longer being so close.

I couldn't do it.

I wasn't strong enough to claim him, and I definitely wasn't strong enough to lose him.

Torturous agony burned through me as frustrated tears welled. "Oh, shit. Would you look at the time? I better go." Keeping my eyes firmly away from the one part of him I was breathless to touch, I collided into his door. "I, um…sleep well. Sorry I woke you. And eh, don't forget to message me. And, um….happy reading!"

I fell over his threshold, almost crashed into the pool, and barely made it back to my bed before I screamed into my pillow and gave in to the rush of hunger.

Being sixteen sucked.

Being in love sucked.

Being wet and desperate and head over fucking heels *sucked.*

It all welled inside me.

Tears fell.

My heart heaved.

And as my hand disappeared beneath my sheets and between my virgin legs, I made the awful decision to try to move on.

I couldn't keep doing this to myself.

I couldn't keep pretending that Aslan would one day drag me before my parents, plant a possessive kiss on my lips, and announce that he was breaking his promise to stay away from me.

As long as he was not permitted to live in this country, he had no choice but to obey.

Pity I could no longer do the same.

Chapter Twenty-Four

ASLAN

(*Moon in Swahili:* Mwezi)

ME: *HERE IS YOUR EVIDENCE THAT I have, in fact, not fallen overboard.*

I pressed send, along with a photo of the most stunning bay, beach, and palm trees where we'd been moored off, taking coral scrapings, water specimens, and drilling small core samples from the seabed.

The gathering of information had been requested and paid for by the Australian Institute of Marine Science for their yearly updates on the health of the reef and ecosystem. The Whitsundays attracted so many visitors with boats, pollution, diving, and water sports that it gave a good indication of what was working and what was not.

"Messaging Neri *again*, Aslan?" Jack asked as he carefully labelled, stowed, and secured the box with the latest samples we'd taken. He and Anna had spent most of the afternoon inspecting each sample under their expensive microscopes, making preliminary findings, and leaving the inputting of data into the laptop for me.

I nodded and shoved the phone Neri had bought me into the back pocket of my jean shorts. "She's jealous. If I don't keep her updated on what we're doing, she sends me streams of angry emoji."

"Jealous, huh? Not my passionate daughter, surely?" Jack snickered. "And I have no doubt she's jealous. This is one of her favourite places. But…her exams come first, and she'll soon be free of school and doing this for a living." Patting me on the shoulder, he padded toward the chiller where most of the ice had melted from a long day at sea.

It didn't matter how stunning this place was. How perfect the sun shone or how prettily the ocean glittered, I still couldn't get over that somewhere, beneath all that perfection, my family were now a pile of bones, most likely with coral growing through their ribcages and fish swimming through their eye sockets.

"Want a bevvy?" Jack asked, holding up an ice-dripping can.

"Sure. Thanks." I caught the ginger beer he tossed my way, and Anna smiled as he placed one for her beside the microscope where she continued to study a slide of coral scrapings.

"*Gratias tibi*," she said, smirking.

"You could just say cheers instead of some fancy Latin, you know." Jack planted an affectionate kiss on her upturned lips.

"But where would the fun be in that?" she asked, cracking open the can. "Almost all the creatures and plants we study have Latin names. I'm merely being polite by using their language."

"Showing off more like."

She stuck her tongue out at him. Their relationship was so playful and true, it made my gut twist for my dead parents.

"You might not get the thrill of speaking different tongues, but Aslan does, don't you, Aslan?" Anna pinned me with a stare so similar to Neri's, just darker.

I swallowed my mouthful of tart ginger beer. "Yeah, I get it." Lately, I'd been using the app Anna recommended instead of completing countless sudokus. Thanks to my new phone, I had numerous ways to keep my brain active, and learning new languages had become a worthy challenge. Mostly, I learned numbers, so I could practice math in Chinese, Latin, and French. "It feels good to stretch the mind."

Anna grinned. "See, husband? He gets it." Glancing at me, she added, "*Dilini çok güzel buluyorum ama çok kolay değil.*"

My eyebrows rose. A few mistakes but not bad. "Wow, Anna, you're getting very good. It's almost like I'm back home."

She laughed under her breath. "I've been practicing that one line for a while. I still have a long way to go."

"Next time, leave out the second *çok* and it's perfect."

"What did you say?" Jack asked.

I answered for her. "She said she finds Turkish beautiful but not easy."

"Seems I better learn too." Jack sniffed. "Otherwise, I'll be left out of the conversation if Neri keeps practicing too."

My heart skipped annoyingly at Neri's name; I took another drink. "She's too busy with schoolwork to progress quickly. We won't leave you out just yet, Jack."

He huffed with a roll of his eyes. "Well, if my daughter is anything like my wife, she'll learn it on the sly and then start using it to confound me."

"I do nothing of the sort." Anna threw me a smirk. "How do I say, 'but it's fun to annoy him', Aslan?"

I chuckled. "*Ama onu kızdırmak eğlenceli.*"

Anna laughed. "What he said, Jack. But don't worry, *wǒ ài nǐ.*"

"What was that now?" Jack scowled, his eyes dancing as he studied his intelligent wife. "Swahili?"

"Chinese." Anna blew him a kiss. "It means, I love you."

My mind soaked up those three little words. It was far simpler than the way my homeland said it but not as romantic as the French. Tonight, if I couldn't sleep, I'd learn how to say I love you in every language I could. Purely in the name of science, of course, not because I had anyone to whisper it to.

An image of Neri ghosted through my mind before I forcibly shut her out. Space between us was good.

At least out here, she couldn't creep into my bedroom and break my resolve night after night.

"Aslan, how do I say, 'I adore you'?" Jack asked.

I stiffened as a wave of jealousy crashed through me. Jealousy for what he and Anna had. Jealousy at love and family and togetherness. I would always be so grateful to them for giving me a home, but…no matter how welcome I felt or how deeply I grew to care for them, they weren't mine. And the one I wanted to be mine could never be.

Finishing my drink, I murmured, "*Sana bayılıyorum.*"

Jack blew Anna a kiss. "*Sana bayılıyorum.*" Throwing back his drink in one go, Jack burped, wiped his mouth with the back of his hand, then looked toward the horizon. "And on that note, I have a sudden hankering for a huge plate of ribs."

Anna broke into giggles. "You ate not long ago. You said those chicken sandwiches filled a gap."

"They did." Jack winked. "But that gap is back, and I want to fill it with ribs."

The fact that I'd literally just been thinking about crabs crawling through my mother's ribcage made me shudder.

Jack caught my gaze. "Not a rib fan?"

I schooled my face and swirling nausea. "I don't eat pork."

"Are you serious? How have I never noticed that? Jesus, just how unobservant am I?" Jack squeezed the back of his neck. "You don't have to stay so secretive all the time, you know. It's been years and we still don't know who you truly are."

I shrugged. "Not much to tell."

"Now that I don't believe." Giving me a smile, he added, "But stay cagey if you want. For now, you don't have to eat ribs, but you are coming to dinner with us. There's a place in Airlie Beach that does amazing food." Marching toward the captain's cabin, Jack tossed his empty drink can in the rubbish bin strapped to the wall. "Pack up, my love. We're finishing early tonight."

"It's only four o'clock," Anna grumbled, hastily packing away the box of fragile glass slides and screwing on lids of water samples.

"Clock off time." Jack grinned. "Besides, we're almost done anyway. One more morning and then we can hit the road for the long drive back home."

"Fine." Anna huffed but her eyes glittered with eagerness. "I could probably have my arm twisted into enjoying a cosmo or two."

"And just like that, it's a party." Jack laughed, starting the engine. "Let's go get tipsy and forget that we have a daughter and responsibilities."

"Poor Neri." Anna giggled.

"What she doesn't know won't hurt her." Jack shouted from the cabin. "Unless our little spy Aslan tattles on us."

I shook my head with a grin. "Whatever you get up to is your secret to tell, not mine."

"That's my boy." Jack paused with a raised eyebrow as I stood in the doorway of the cabin. "She's been behaving herself though, right? Each time I message her, she says she's doing her homework, staying out of the pool, and getting into bed by ten. Is she telling you the same thing or is she outright lying to her dear 'ole dad?"

I shoved my hands into my pockets, carefully keeping my smile in place. "She's said the same thing to me, Jack. She's behaving."

"Good." Turning around, he moved back to the helm and added power to the engine.

I braced myself for speed.

I'd told Jack the truth.

While we'd been gone, Neri had sent me photos of her homework spread over the dining room table, her bare feet as she watched a movie in the lounge, her bed covers as she read just before sleeping, and…a stunning selfie of herself, hair wet, eyelashes dripping, ice-blue eyes dancing as she swam in the pool.

She'd been warned about going in there alone while we were gone, but…with a nickname like little fish and more salt in her veins than blood, it was a given she'd break that rule.

All her messages had been friendly but not too friendly. They'd been funny and sarcastic and sent between classes as she darted from subject to subject.

But it was what she *didn't* send that had my hackles rising.

I didn't know if she thought I was an idiot when it came to technology. That she believed I'd come from a third-world country where I'd never had such things as laptops or cell-phones. And I supposed that was mostly my fault because I refused to talk about my past, my experiences, or my privileges.

Turkey was as metropolitan as Australia, and I knew how to use a damn phone.

I knew what apps came with factory hardware and which were manually installed.

And on the first night away, while I lay on the deck of *The Fluke* and watched a shooting star from my sleeping bag, I'd stumbled over an app called Sleuther.

As long as my GPS location was on, my whereabouts could be tracked.

The only person who could've installed that was Nerida, and my heart had raced at the thought of her tracking me. That she felt that strongly about me leaving, she'd gifted me a phone with a hidden agenda, all so she'd always know where I was.

A rush of anger had made me hot but then understanding made me pause.

I could rest easy at night knowing that Neri was back in Port Douglas, safe in the house she'd been raised in, doing what she was told.

But...if she was off somewhere else with people I didn't know...I couldn't deny I wouldn't worry. I wouldn't be able to stop myself from imagining a situation of her in danger or doing something she shouldn't be doing. Doing *someone* she shouldn't be doing.

Pity for her, I'd clicked on the app and stumbled over a two-way street. She'd downloaded the app to stalk me. But by doing so, I could stalk her. It was as simple as installing the mirroring app, entering her phone number, and boom. Her whereabouts appeared like an accusing red dot on the map of a country I'd been washed up on.

And it told a whole other story to the one she messaged me.

My phone vibrated, almost as if she could feel me thinking about her. *The Fluke* increased in speed. The boat was a far sight more graceful in the water than on the large trailer Jack had used to haul it down here with. Out of the ocean, it seemed so much bigger than what it felt like, and I hadn't minded sleeping on the deck while Anna and Jack took the cushions off the bench seats and made a bed below.

Stalking to the handrail to watch the sea churn behind us, I pulled out my phone and checked Neri's location.

I stiffened.

School had finished, but she wasn't at home.

She was in town, somewhere, doing who knew what. Unsupervised and terrifyingly free.

Bringing up her new message, I clenched my teeth.

Neri: *That picture is stunning! Here's my view. Wish you were here to help me with my breathwork. I really want to push for seven minutes retention. Kate Winslet did it, which means I can too!*

The photo she sent was of the Taylors' pool with its sandy bottom, man-made boulders, and ferns growing around the edges. Only problem was, the photo wasn't a snapshot of where she was at this very moment. And I couldn't call out her lie without exposing the fact that I was tracking her in return.

Me: *If I was there, I have a feeling you wouldn't be swimming.*

I pressed send before I could re-read it. I groaned as I did, cursing myself that it sounded so suggestive. I only meant if I was there then I could prove she wasn't by the pool at all.

Neri: *What exactly would I be doing if I wasn't swimming?*

Shit.

She'd seen the same undertones I had. Too perceptive on any hint of sexual tension.

And fuck me, there was a lot of that.

Enough to make me cross-eyed and rock hard, and it'd gotten to the point where I really, *really* needed to figure out a way to enjoy some female companionship without the very real terror of being deported.

After Neri gave me the books and phone the other night, I'd been in the worst fucking state of my life. The way she'd looked at me? The way her gaze locked between my legs and shot heated agony directly into my cock...

I'd fallen back on my bed and fought the urge for as long as I could.

But my heart had smoked, and my blood had boiled, and I'd had no choice but to yank my boxers down, swallow my thick shame, and fist myself in the dark.

I'd come from the memory of the way she'd studied me. The way she'd crashed into my door in her rush to get away from the agonising desperation between us.

It was wrong to think of Neri while touching myself, I knew that. It only kept me trapped in a situation that had no happy ending. But...I'd given up trying to picture anyone else the day she turned sixteen. I tried to console myself with a lie that Neri was literally the only girl I knew. Of course, she would be the most vibrant in my head. Of course, she would crowd my thoughts and make every day a thirsty misery.

But if I was stronger and a better man, I'd jerk off to pictures of Rita or Molly or the many girls parading downtown in their skimpy shorts and bikinis.

Not her.

It should never be Neri who I dreamed of.

Never Neri who I begged for as my cum coated my palm.

It could be literally anyone else.

Yet I was fucked because all my heart, my soul, and my body wanted...was her.

Fucking hell, I need help.

I needed to get over this infatuation so I didn't end up killing myself.

Because that would happen if I gave in.

If I made a mistake and actually thought I could have her, Jack and Anna would kick me out, I'd end up homeless, jobless, penniless, and be found by a heartless bureaucrat only to be shipped back to Turkey where a hoard of bloodthirsty bastards just waited for me to step foot on home soil. They'd take my blood, my bones, and my begs. Ripping all three out of me before they finally mutilated me so much, I was useless.

So yeah, even though every piece of me wanted to say fuck it and claim Neri as mine. To sneak behind Jack's back and defile his daughter, I didn't want to die.

Those days of wishing for death were over.

I liked this life, regardless of its restrictions.

And I liked being alive for *her*.

Even if it meant I would spend the rest of my days working on an ocean I despised and eventually have to watch Neri meet someone, fall in love, and move away to start her own family.

I pinched the bridge of my nose and sucked in a breath.

You need to do something soon. Otherwise, you're going to snap.

Paying heed to my own counsel, I dropped my hand and messaged Neri back.

Me: *Don't do anything stupid, dangerous, or illegal, Nerida. Your parents aren't there to save you.*

Her reply was quick.

Neri: *Why the sudden mood change?*

Me: *Long day, that's all.*

Neri: *What are the plans tonight?*

Me: *Your dad wants ribs. We're heading into Airlie Beach for dinner.*

Her reply wasn't as quick this time and when it finally did arrive, her tone had changed.

Despair sank like a rock in my belly.

Neri: *Airlie Beach is full of transient travellers. Who knows? You might find a fellow countryman…or woman. Enjoy your dinner, Aslan.*

I didn't message her back.

Chapter Twenty-Five

ASLAN

(*Moon in Italian:* Luna)

TEN FUCKING THIRTY P.M., AND NERI's LOCATION still showed her in some bar in Port Douglas.

What the fuck is she doing?

How could she lie to Jack when he called her after dinner, saying she was at home, doing a sketch of the latest whale calf, when she was definitely not at home and definitely not doing something as innocent as drawing.

"All done here?"

My head snapped up, and I shut off my phone screen.

The pretty waitress that'd served us all night gave me a wide smile. A smile that tipped upward with invitation and interest. A smile that said she liked the look of me and wasn't afraid to show it.

"I'm good. Jack? Anna?" I cocked my chin at the two giggling marine biologists. Considering they had a sixteen-year-old daughter at home, they'd flirted and drank as if they were newlyweds.

My temper soothed a little watching them. Watching their ease. Their love. Their desire.

My own parents came to mind again and the happy relationship they'd shared.

Nothing like these two, though. My father and mother were more reserved in their love. Meanwhile, Jack and Anna's had caught fire thanks to decadent food and a substantial amount of alcohol.

"Nah, think we'll get the check, please," Jack said, winking at the waitress as he brought Anna's knuckles to his mouth and kissed her.

The waitress laughed under her breath and leaned closer to me. "I have a feeling you're about to be dumped for the evening."

I caught her pretty green stare. Her accent hinted she was from Europe. Greece, perhaps. Spain, maybe. I was never good with accents but her honey-brown skin and striking black hair said wherever she was from, she was unique in her beauty.

"I disagree. We have an early start in the morning so they'll have to sleep it off." I helped her stack the dirty dishes and gave her an impressed smile as she balanced them all on her forearm.

"Well, if that changes, my shift ends in thirty minutes. We can go get a drink if you want."

I froze. "You're...you're asking me out?"

"For a drink, not marriage." She laughed. "I'm here on a twelve-month work visa. Gotta play hard while I work hard, you know?"

I nodded. "Right."

"You're not from around here either, though, are you?" Her ponytail swung over her shoulder as she cocked her hip.

"He's from Turkey," Jack piped up, winking again. "Best guy I know." Shifting in the booth where he and Anna had steadily worked their way through a few starters, mains, and drinks, he pulled his wallet out of his back pocket and tossed me his credit card. "You know the pin. Pay for us, will ya? Anna and I are going to get a hotel for the night." His voice lowered as he stood up and placed his hand on the curve of his wife's hip as she stood next to him. "Feel free to sleep below deck on *The Fluke*. Or...explore Airlie Beach and have a good night." He grinned. "Just be back at the pier by seven a.m."

Anna shook her head and hiccupped. "Be safe, Aslan." She waved. "I've never seen you have fun so...*have fun*." Blowing me a kiss, the two of them weaved their way through the many tables and vanished out of the busy restaurant.

"So..." The waitress laughed. "You've just been ditched. Told ya that would happen."

I chuckled and shook my head. "Guess you were right." Passing her the credit card, I said, "Can you charge everything to this card, minus the beef burger and beer that I had? I'll pay cash for those."

"Sure. Come up to the till with me, and I'll ring you up."

Nodding, I wiped my hands on my napkin, swallowed my last sip of beer, and followed her through the restaurant. The air swirled with heavy scents of grease and sugar. Laughter flowed and voices all blended together, loud thanks to the bare wooden floors and lack of soft furnishings. The ambience was a little lacking, but Jack had been right. The food had been amazing, and I was grateful I'd grown used to being in busy places like this to actually enjoy them.

Normal everyday people didn't have a clue that I wasn't papered or permitted. I was one of them. As long as I kept my origins hidden, I could pretend I belonged.

Placing the plates down on a sideboard, the girl guided me to a till where she pressed the screen, called up our table number, and subtracted my food from the Taylors' tally.

Tapping Jack's credit card, I put in his pin that I knew for when I ran errands to pick up things for the boat, then passed her a few twenty-dollar bills and accepted my change.

I'd stopped counting how much money Jack had paid me over the past four years. And I'd gotten over my aversion to spending it on myself, but I still didn't have many reasons to.

Apart from Neri's yearly birthday gift and a few odds and ends, I hardly went out for a meal and had no one else to spoil.

"Feel free to push off early, Rhea. Tomas just came in, and the kitchen has died down. Rest your feet for your big shift tomorrow." A large man with a bushy red beard and shaved head held out his hand. "Gimme your apron, and you're free."

The waitress shrugged, undid the bow of her black apron, and passed it to him. "Thanks, Charles. Guess I'll see you tomorrow, then."

"See ya!" He weaved his way back into the crowd, clicking his fingers at another waiter.

"Rhea, huh?" I shoved my hands into my pockets, wincing as I always did as the spikes of the spiny shell Neri had given me pressed against my thumb. "Pretty name."

"Thanks." Undoing her ponytail, she fanned out her hair and planted her hands on her hips. "What's yours, and what are we doing tonight?"

"Is that your way of saying you still want to get a drink with me?"

"Definitely." Her eyes narrowed with mock-seriousness. "Don't tell me you'd rather go and spend the night alone. Your work colleagues are getting lucky tonight. Pity to think of you all on your lonesome."

I stiffened a little.

Work colleagues?

Jack and Anna were so much more than that. They were the parents of the girl I was in love with. The people who, with one phone call, could change my life forever.

But tonight, I didn't have to be that person.

Tonight, I could just be…me.

Swallowing my discomfort, I forced a smile. "I suppose one drink couldn't hurt."

Neri: *How was dinner? Where did you go? Are you on* The Fluke?

I gritted my teeth as I waited outside the bar where Rhea and I had shared a drink for the past hour. She'd excused herself to go to the bathroom, and I'd stepped outside to wait for her.

I'd enjoyed the faint buzz I had going on, or I had until Neri's message pinged.

It pissed me off that she'd asked if I was on *The Fluke* when she knew damn well that I wasn't. Just like I knew, thanks to her blinking red dot, that she was still in Port Douglas township.

It took all my self-control not to tell her to get the fuck home. Not to ask what the hell she was doing out so late. But then she'd know I was tracking her. Just like she was tracking me.

Me: *Dinner was great. Went to a place called Fins. And no, I'm not on* The Fluke.

"As well you fucking know," I growled under my breath.

Neri: *It's late. I'm surprised Mum and Dad are still awake at this time, let alone out and about.*

Me: *Your parents decided to get a hotel for the night.*

Neri: *So…you're on your own?*

"Ready?" Rhea stepped out of the noisy bar, her cheeks pink from the hot night and her skin dewy from perspiration.

I looked up from the death grip on my phone. "Yeah, sorry."

I deliberated shoving it into my pocket without answering Neri, but…the four beers I'd had and the ocean of frustration in my heart made me do something I definitely shouldn't do. "Just give me one second."

Clicking reply, I typed.

Me: *No. I'm not alone.*

I sent it.

I shoved my phone deep into my pocket.

And the girl who'd happily chatted about herself all night and gave up asking about me when I deflected each question, placed her hand boldly on my chest. My heart pounded beneath my charcoal-coloured t-shirt.

"So…Aslan." Rhea licked her lips, her green eyes wide and eager. "We've shared a drink. Or three."

"We have."

"I've told you I'm unattached and nursing a broken heart from a bastard who didn't love me enough in Corinth."

"You did."

"I've asked you where you've come from, why you're here, and how long you're planning on being in Australia and all you've told me is: your name, your age, and the fact that you're unattached as well."

"I did."

"That leaves me with only one conclusion."

My lips twitched even as my phone vibrated in my pocket. Neri's reply. My heart clenched as I forced myself to focus on the girl before me and not the girl I couldn't have. "And what's that?"

Standing on tiptoes to reach my ear, she whispered loudly enough for the couple standing beside us vaping to hear, "I rent a studio apartment with another girl not far from here. She's working until six a.m."

"Sounds like your friend has a shit job."

She giggled. Her breath tickled my neck, making me shiver. "She does. But that's not the point."

I knew her point.

I'd known it since she'd smiled in the restaurant and Anna had told me to have some fun. This girl I was permitted to touch. Permitted to want. I could have *fun* with this girl.

Memories of Rita and Molly offering me a threesome last year popped into my head. They'd guessed I was a virgin because I was beyond sensitive when it came to touch.

I fucking hated that they'd guessed right.

I'd had a girlfriend back in Turkey. I'd kissed her. Touched her a little. And thought I was falling for her, until I met Neri and realised I'd never felt anything like it before.

And somehow, four fucking years had passed.

Four excruciating years of self-abuse and mental movies and aching frustration to be with a woman, all while knowing the one woman I wanted more than fucking anything could never be mine.

My phone vibrated again, ripping out my heart all while my temper made me reckless.

I was done torturing myself.

Done wanting what I couldn't have.

If I spent the night with Rhea, perhaps whatever hold Neri had over me would end, and we could finally be exactly what we ought to be.

Friends.

Confidants.

And nothing more.

"Come home with me?" Rhea asked, swallowing hard as if the invitation had cost her more than she wanted to admit.

For all the titbits she'd shared of her life. For all her confessions of running away from a boyfriend who hadn't valued her and landing in a country where no one knew her, she was still a total stranger.

A girl I'd spent two hours with.

A girl who didn't know my last name, my past, or a damn thing about me that could risk my future.

My heart screamed to refuse.

My cock begged to agree.

But it was my mind that made the decision.

Calculated and frankly rather cold, I knew what I wanted. And I wanted to get rid of my virginity before it drove me even more insane than it already had. Tomorrow, when we drove back to Port Douglas, I wanted to return to Neri with the knowledge that I'd been with someone else.

Therefore, I couldn't love her as much as I thought I did because how could I physically touch another, kiss another, fuck another…all while I was supposed to be head over fucking heels in love with her?

This was a test.

A perfect test and the perfect fucking cure.

Bending a little, I pressed my cheek to hers. "I'd be honoured to go back to your place."

Her sharp inhale made me harden and I steeled myself from checking my phone as she placed her hand in mine and guided me to her bed.

Chapter Twenty-Six

ASLAN

(*Moon in Swedish:* Måne)

"DO YOU WANT A DRINK?" RHEA ASKED as she shut the door to her tiny apartment.

I stood on the white-washed wooden flooring that did its best to freshen up the drab walls, unmade bed wedged in the corner, small table pressed against the wall, and dated kitchenette beneath the only window.

"Bathroom is through there if you need it." Rhea pointed at the only door in the entire place. I didn't need to go, but…my stomach hadn't stopped clenching as we'd walked here.

I'd put one foot in front of the other and did my best to leave Neri behind.

Yet she just kept haunting me, following everywhere I went.

Gripping my nape, I nodded. "Just water would be great. And I'll be back in a moment."

"Okay." Rhea gave me a shy smile as I opened the door and slipped into a bathroom the size of the one on *The Fluke*. At least *The Fluke* had a window and a view of the ocean. This was a black box with a flickering neon over a chipped mirror, a sorry excuse for a sink, a shower with a torn curtain, and a toilet that was clean but discoloured.

Grabbing the sink, I hung my head and fought myself.
Get it together.
She's super sweet. Super pretty. And super keen to get you naked.
I looked up and caught my eyes in the mirror.

I didn't often look at myself because my features reminded me too much of my father. I shared his straight nose, stern eyebrows, and distrusting black eyes. My hair was lighter these days from the sun and tussled over my forehead with no respect for neatness, and the oak leaf-shaped birthmark on my left ankle constantly reminded me of what I was.

Glowering into my stare, everything I'd been running from snarled and hurled itself at the walls inside my mind. I hated my height. My lips. My jaw. I looked just like my fucking father...*and that is not a good thing.*

The image in the mirror morphed into an image of Neri.

Her gorgeous mouth, her glacial eyes, her stunning eyebrows and cheekbones and smile. I hardened faster from a single glimpse of her than I did at the thought of fucking the lovely girl outside.

I groaned under my breath.

What would it take to stop being haunted by that girl?

I'd seen her as a twelve-year-old. I'd watched her parade around, flat-chested and gangly. Yet all I could seem to remember was the graceful curve of her spine, the perfect roundness of her chest and ass, and the indecent glimmer in her gaze whenever she looked at me when she thought I wasn't aware.

My cock twitched painfully.

I wanted to punch the mirror.

To shatter myself and her.

I want to stop feeling this way.

Spinning around, I yanked out my phone and opened the messages she'd sent.

Neri: *What do you mean you're not alone?*

Neri: *Who are you with? You don't know anyone.*

The last one was sent just a few minutes ago.

Neri: *Who is she?*

My heart hurt.

It physically ripped down the middle.

My fingers hovered over the keypad.

I typed.

Me: *She's not you—*

I deleted it without sending.

I waited for something appropriate to say, but in the end, I typed absolutely nothing.

There was nothing I *could* say.

Shoving my phone back into my pocket, I yanked open the door and slammed to a stop. "Fuck."

"Hi." Rhea tucked glossy black hair behind her ears, her hands shaking a little even while she stood naked in the middle of her tiny apartment. The bed behind her had been hastily made. A condom rested on the light pink blankets.

My eyes feasted on her flawless honey-brown skin. On the dark pucker of her nipples and the trimmed hair between her legs. She was shorter than Neri and curvier. Her complexion darker and lips slightly fuller.

Stop comparing them, you idiot.

"Wow." I breathed, drifting forward, wincing as my phone vibrated again.

"You're absolutely stunning."

Her nerves got the better of her, clasping her hands in front of her lower belly. "I thought I'd feel empowered to strip, but now? Now, I'm a little nervous."

"Don't be."

I wanted to be as brave as this girl.

It seemed women in this country weren't afraid to chase what they wanted. Rita and Molly had come on to me. They'd touched me brazenly. And this lovely Greek girl had offered herself to me in the most perfect of ways.

The least I could do was make her feel her risk had been rewarded.

Gritting my teeth and forcing every thought of Neri from my mind, I stepped into her and took her hand.

Our eyes locked as I tugged her forward, and with as much confidence as I could, I placed her palm over my hard cock.

She gasped.

I shuddered.

Regret mingled with desire, a sick recipe that made me shake.

My voice was strained as I whispered, "That's what seeing you naked has done to me."

Liar, that's what thinking about Neri has done.

Her eyes hooded. Her fingers gripped me. And the pain in my heart intensified until I feared I'd buckle to my knees and pass out.

Neri flashed through my mind; I shoved her out of it. If I stood any chance of surviving that girl, I had no choice but to do this. This was life or death…literally.

Not looking away, Rhea rubbed me through my shorts, then used her other hand to pop my button and pull down my zipper.

She didn't speak as she pushed my shorts down my legs; the sound of my phone hitting the floor sent another wrenching pain through my chest. Panic flickered that my shell might've snapped from landing on the hard wood, but rage flowed, and I forced myself to focus.

Neri doesn't exist.

Not tonight.

Not in my future.

She had somehow corrupted my every thought, and it was finally time I took back control.

I have to do this.

I'm going to do this.

Fisting the hem of my t-shirt, I yanked it over my head. It fluttered to the floor soundlessly.

Rhea sucked in a breath as she studied me. "Wow yourself." Her right hand kept stroking me through my boxer-briefs while her left trailed over the ridges of my abdomen.

Working with heavy scuba equipment and using my core to stay stable on the sea helped keep me in shape, but most of my strength came from the nightly torture I put myself through.

Nights were the hardest.

Nights were full of whispers to sneak into Neri's bedroom and torment *her* with a visit for a change.

Nights were when my self-control frayed to the point of non-existence.

Push-ups, crunches, and twenty-minute-long planks were my medicine against the sickness she'd given me.

Rhea's fingers hooked in my boxers, tugging them gently.

Her touch was confident but also wary, as if she expected me to shake my head and deny her.

Even though I battled with so many fucking things, I did what she wanted.

I stripped them off and kicked away my last piece of clothing, standing before her as bare as she stood before me.

Vulnerability shot down my back, followed by sadness I couldn't understand.

I wanted this.

I *needed* this.

I just didn't want it with her...

I grunted as her fingers wrapped around my bare cock.

My mind shot blank, giving me sanctuary from my agonising thoughts.

A bead of pre-cum welled as my balls tightened, and I schooled myself against the overwhelming intensity that touch always brought.

Instinct to run shot down my legs.

Despair to message Neri had fury tangling with lust.

Stop thinking about her!

Grabbing Rhea around the waist, I plucked her from the floor and carried her to the bed.

She laughed out loud as I tossed her down, her legs spreading, her breasts bouncing.

I crawled over her.

I slotted my hips between her thighs and hovered over her on my elbows.

If I was going to do this, I had to do it fast.

I had to lose what was keeping me trapped, and then...perhaps, when I was free, I could enjoy her again. Take my time and not have to fight the very crippling urge to run.

Lowering myself down, her eyes widened as she wriggled a little beneath my weight.

Her skin blazed against mine.

My heart *pounded.*

"You okay?" I strangled.

Funny how that word used to make me furious. It no longer did. I'd overcome that word. Just like I was about to overcome Neri.

The moment I thought of her, Neri's soft voice echoed in my ears and the electrical charge that I always pretended didn't exist when we touched shot through my blood, proving to me, in awful black and white, that I felt no chemistry when Rhea stroked me. No sting or spark or sharpness.

I groaned and fought for sanity.

My cock deflated a little, and I dropped my stare to Rhea's perfect breasts, forcing all thoughts of Neri away.

"Are *you* okay?" Rhea asked, her eyebrows knitting together. "You do…want to do this, right?"

I hated that I'd made her doubt.

That she'd seen how much I struggled.

I'd never been good at letting anyone down, let alone someone who'd been so nice to me.

"You have no idea how much I need to do this."

"Need?" she asked, her voice a little tight. "What does that mean?"

It means I'm breaking and doing my best not to.

I kissed her instead of answering her.

Need was the wrong word to use. The truth was the wrong thing to say. It revealed the dirty fact that I was using her. But then again, she was using me too: to forget about her ex who hurt her. To have a good time, a good night. As long as we both walked away pleasured, where was the harm in this?

You know where.

I winced at the thought of Neri ever finding out about this.

Just the thought of her doing this with another hurt more than anything.

I growled under my breath.

Fucking hell, stop it.

I had my mouth on a gorgeous girl.

Her lips were warm.

Her hot naked body willing to submit to me.

All I had to do was stay with her.

To have *fun* with her.

I opened my lips wider.

I forced myself to feel everything.

The slipperiness of her tongue as we tentatively licked.

The taste of her mouth from the sweet strawberry daiquiri I'd bought her.

The sound of her moan as she bit my bottom lip.

My spine snapped straight, revealing how reactive I was.

I flushed with shame as she smiled into my gasp. "You're sensitive."

Swallowing hard, doing my best to stay human, I hissed, "You have no idea."

Her nails scraped down my back.

I convulsed and choked on a groan.

She laughed. "I like it."

"I don't." I nipped at her bottom lip, pleased that her nails had distracted me enough that I wasn't running. I groaned again as she drew her fingernails down my ass and along the crease of my upper legs.

My body took control of my mind.

I sank gratefully into the rapidly building urge. "I'm sure I'll embarrass myself at some point."

"I highly doubt that." Her wet warmth rubbed against my hardness as I settled deeper into the V of her thighs.

Flashes of Neri came.

Her laughing on the boat when she'd stepped out of the sea from playing with the dolphins. Her running her fingers along my shoulders as she moved to her seat beside me at the dining table. Her smiling at me with her face alight and all her desires unhidden.

Fuck, not again.

I gulped and squeezed my eyes shut.

My body lost a little of its animalistic urgency, leaving me floundering.

Rhea's voice gave me an anchor as she whispered, "When I first saw you, I did wonder if you'd fit. I mean...I know it always does but...jeez."

I raised an eyebrow, doing my best to give her my full attention. "You're saying I'm—"

"Well endowed?" She grinned. "Yes, definitely saying that."

"Oh." I didn't know what to say. Never thought about it. Never had reason to compare, seeing as I had no friends to talk shit with or share sordid tales.

"You're really handsome, too," she whispered. "Are all men from Turkey as delicious as you?"

"You'll have to go and find out."

"I might just do that." She licked her lips, her shoulder rising as she slipped her hand between us and locked around my cock. "Especially if you'll be there."

I flinched.

My body jerked in her fingers—

'Seni seviyorum, Aslan. I love you as my friend. I love you for saving me. I love you for helping my mum and dad. I love you because you exist, and not a day goes by that I'm not super thankful to have you living with us."

The memory of Neri giving me the shell after I'd given her CPR filled my mind. A gift given by a girl who was sentimental and on some doomed crusade to fix me.

It was just a stupid shell.

Yet...it meant more to me than any other possession.

Priceless because she was the one who pressed it into my hand.

She was the one who stole my heart and in doing so stole everything else.

"Ah, shit." Trembling, I rolled off Rhea and threw an arm over my eyes, panting hard.

Stop it.

Get a goddamn grip.

"Aslan?" Rhea shifted beside me. Her hand trailed down my stomach and found me again. A growl echoed in my chest as she pumped me up and down, perfect pressure, perfect speed.

"Sorry, I just…"

"Let me help," she whispered, twisting and stroking.

And I let her.

I was desperate for her help.

Begging for her to free me.

"That feels really good," I murmured, unable to look at her but willing to feel what she did to me.

"Tell me how you like it." She added pressure.

I trembled. "Like that. I like it…hard."

"Like this?" She fisted me.

I convulsed again.

I could come from that.

I could let myself go and release before I was ever inside her.

I didn't have to fuck her.

Didn't have to free myself from Neri this way.

What if I can't…?

What if it doesn't work?

But what if I don't try?

What if I always felt this way and never learned how to be free? Doomed to always want what I couldn't have and never be happy?

Rhea suddenly scooted down the bed, her hair tickling my belly.

"Holy *fuuuck*—" I jack-knifed up and fell backward with a hiss as Rhea sucked me.

She wasn't shy like before.

Her mouth encircled me, her tongue speared the tip, and her hand slid down my length as she deep-throated me.

A stream of my native tongue filled my head.

A barrage of curses.

A storm of lust—

Her lips crashed hotly to mine.

Her breasts crushed firmly against my wet t-shirt.

Her hands yanked at my hair, sending bolts of pain and indescribable need.

She dove her tongue deliciously into my mouth.

I convulsed.

I drowned in her.
I lost myself in her.
I wanted and wanted and—
The vision of Neri kissing me on Noah Beach shattered.

Nausea pooled in my stomach as Rhea sucked me harder.

I ought to be out of my fucking mind with delirium. The sensation of Rhea's touch, the intoxication of her mouth…I'd never felt anything like it.

But…it paled in comparison to a forbidden kiss on a beach with a girl dripping in seawater. A girl giving me everything, all while knowing I couldn't take it.

With a fleeting kiss to my lower belly, Rhea grabbed the condom resting by my hip. With a tear, the packet revealed a lemony scent and the slippery sight of rubber.

My father had taught me how they worked.

My friend's mother—a nurse and keen to keep us sexually safe—gave us a bag of them when we were fourteen. We'd filled them with water, throwing them at each other, before taking a handful and not admitting that we'd sampled them on ourselves that night.

Rhea gave me a sexy smile and rolled the condom down my hard but quickly deflating length.

No matter what I did.

No matter how hard I tried.

My heart was with another, and my body refused to betray her.

Shit…

Her eyes caught mine with a worried inhale.

I gritted my teeth and cupped her cheek. "Rhea, I…"

I looked at her stunning breasts and dropped my hand from her cheek, over her chest, and down between her legs.

If I touched her, perhaps this nightmare could end.

Gritting my teeth, I lowered my fingers. I went to sink them inside her. She shifted a little, giving me access, revealing the glisten of her desire and the blatant invitation.

I touched her heat—

And I couldn't fucking do it.

Jerking my hand away, I fell backward. "*Kafamı sikeyim.*" I pinched the bridge of my nose and drowned beneath the sickness and regret I'd never be free from.

Rhea stopped rolling the condom on me.

With a sharp inhale, she jerked her legs up and hugged them, hiding her bareness. "If you didn't want to sleep with me, why the hell did you agree to come back here?" Her words were harsh, but her voice echoed with embarrassment.

Absolute rage rolled through me.

I wanted to punch myself.

I wanted to jump out the window and break into pieces.

I wanted to trade my heart for another.

I wanted to never have met Nerida fucking Taylor.

Sitting up slowly, I glowered at my semi-hard cock and tossed the blankets over my lap, hiding my shame. "I'm so sorry, Rhea. It's not you—"

"Oh, please. Save it." Anger painted her cheeks as her hands balled. "You're an asshole. A right prick of an asshole who doesn't give a rat's ass—"

"I'm in love with someone I can't have," I rushed. "I truly thought you could cure me…" I rubbed my hands over my face, unable to look at her. "I really, *really* hoped you could. Unfortunately, it seems as if I'm incurable."

Her shoulders lost a little of their tightness as I forced myself to glance up. "You're gorgeous and fun and *nice*. I'm the luckiest asshole in Australia to be here, in your bed, moments away from being with you, but…"

Silence fell thick between us before she murmured, "You can't keep it up because I'm not her."

I laughed coldly. "Appears that way."

"Can I ask you something?"

I nodded, bracing myself for a condemning question.

"If you could've stayed hard, would you have fucked me? Would you have been with me, all while imagining I was her?"

I gave her the respect of truly thinking about her question, coming face to face with stark truth. "No. Even if my body wasn't punishing me, I wouldn't have been able to do that to you. It wouldn't be fair to be with you when my heart is with another."

"Who is she?"

I jerked.

That was exactly what Neri had asked in her last text.

Urgency to grab my shorts and fish my phone from them gripped me. I wanted to text her, talk to her, tell her in every fucking language that I was hers even though she could never be mine.

"Just someone I know." I smiled sadly. "Someone I should never have met."

"You don't sound happy about loving her."

I snorted. "I'm not. I wish I could stop. One day, I'll have no choice but to stop."

"Why?"

"Because she'll fall for someone else."

"But what if she's fallen for you?"

I shook my head, more awful truth spilling free. "I'm pretty sure she already has."

"Okay, Dad, but don't get angry when I marry him."

The echo of Neri's conviction from when she was twelve fisted my heart.

Did she still feel that conviction? Did she still believe that fantasy even though I could never technically get married here?

Rhea sucked in a breath. "Then what's the problem?"

I smiled and swallowed back answers I could never tell her. "I hope you find someone who loves you and realises just how incredible you are, Rhea. I'm so sorry I turned out to be a disappointment."

"Don't do that." She grimaced a little. "And you're not a disappointment. Not really. I get it. I do. I tried to have a one-night stand a week after I broke up with Adrian, but I couldn't go through with it. You don't get to deflect, though. You can't use flattery to avoid not answering. Why can't you be with her?"

"To repeat a line that's often used by others: it's complicated." I scooted toward the end of the bed. As subtly as I could, I pulled the condom off, fisted it, and tossed away the blanket. With a self-conscious breath, I stood and walked across her small studio to my discarded clothes.

Goosebumps broke out down my spine as she watched me dress.

"Complicated doesn't mean it can't be done," she said quietly.

The weight of my phone and the spikiness of my shell settled my hammering heart as I zipped up my shorts and shrugged into my t-shirt. Slipping the unused condom into my pocket, wincing as it stuck to the same shell Neri had given me, I returned to Rhea, where she sat on the rumpled bed.

"I can't do complicated because complicated could cost me everything. But it turns out…I can't do simple either." Bending over her, I pressed a finger beneath her chin.

She looked up, obeying my pressure.

I pressed my mouth to hers.

I kissed her in apology, regret, and relief.

She kissed me back with a soft moan. "You sure you don't want to stay?"

"I'd love to stay. I'd love you to be the first girl I slept with. I'd love a great many things but—"

"Wait…you're a *virgin*?" Her mouth fell open, wet from our kiss.

Shit, I hadn't meant to say that.

"You're a twenty-year-old guy who looks the way you do and you're still a virgin?" She spluttered, "How…I mean…wow, that's…*wow*."

I chuckled under my breath, my cheeks hot. "If I'm still afflicted with it when I'm thirty, I'll come looking for you."

She laughed. "Do that. Definitely do that. Wait." Scrambling to her feet, she raced toward the small kitchenette and the notepad resting beside a dirty plate. Scribbling something down, she shot back to my side and passed me a piece of paper. "That's everything you need to find me. No matter where I'll be."

I scowled, recognising the Instagram handle. Neri had an account, posting photos of underwater shots, dolphin close-ups, and sharing ocean awareness to those who didn't get access to such worlds.

"Just DM me. If you decide you want to no longer be afflicted, then message me, and if I'm still around, we'll make it happen."

I shoved the paper into my back pocket. "You're being far too kind to me. Why?"

"Why?" She laughed softly. "Because…how did you word it? You're gorgeous and fun and *nice*. That's rare, Aslan. And even rarer for a guy who has a naked girl with her mouth on his cock—a guy who's never had sex—and is moral enough to be unable to go through with it, all because his heart loves another."

"His heart is a fucking idiot," I muttered.

"Possibly. But it's also loyal and true and that…" She pressed her naked, perfect body against my clothed one. "Is by far the most attractive thing about you." She kissed me softly. "She's a lucky girl. And I hope, for both your sakes, that one day you can figure out how to turn complicated into simple because it would be an absolute tragedy if you died a virgin."

I laughed.

A proper, relieved laugh.

This beautiful stranger had somehow turned one of the most embarrassing moments of my life into one of friendship and kindness.

I would never forget her for that.

"I'm grateful to have met you, Rhea."

"Likewise, Aslan. Now, get out of my apartment before I do my best to prove to you that your cock can work, despite your melancholy heart."

I grinned. "Pretty sure all of me is melancholy."

I'd meant it as a joke.

So why did it feel far too fucking real?

The grief I carried, the longing I festered, the fear I harboured—it didn't leave a lot of room for joy.

She gave me a pitying look. "Be happy, Aslan."

"You too." With a final kiss, I packed up my stupid heart, tucked my useless tail between my legs, and returned to *The Fluke* and the ocean that hated me.

Chapter Twenty-Seven

ASLAN

(*Moon in Filipino:* Buwan)

NERI: *I KNOW I HAVE NO RIGHT to ask who she is, but…it hurts, Aslan.*
Neri: *Message me back. Please…*
Neri: *All I can picture is Rita and Molly mauling you back in Daintree. It felt as if my heart splattered into the sand that night. But your silence now is like a thousand knives slicing into my stupid, stupid soul.*
Neri: *I forbid myself from messaging you for an hour. My self-imposed sentence is over, and…I can't help myself. It's been an hour and nothing, Aslan. I guess that means…I don't know what that means.*
Neri: *I hate that you're gone. I hate that I can't pop down to see you in the garden. I hate that I can't say any of this to your face. I know you think I'm young, but I'm not. Not anymore. I love you, Aslan. I…I want you. I want you to want me, and the fact that you don't…*
Neri: *Fuck, I'm sorry. I'll stop messaging. I'll stop visiting you at night. I'll stop making things so hard. Just please…message me back and let me know you're okay?*

My heart raced so fast I swore smoke curled through my veins.

I'd deliberately forbidden myself from checking her messages until I'd returned to the pier, climbed onboard *The Fluke*, tossed the unused condom deep into the bottom of the rubbish bin, washed my hands, stripped, and climbed into my sleeping bag.

The stars glittered in the cloudless black velvet above. The moon shone bright, refracting on the calm bay the same way it had the night Neri dived into the ocean and I thought a croc would tear her apart.

Her messages had successfully torn me apart better than any murderous reptile.

My hands trembled; I couldn't catch a proper breath. I was more alive, more *aware* from a simple message from Neri than I had been all night with Rhea.

My skin tingled from the night air. My belly clenched with need. And my cock was so hard, it throbbed with agony that I doubted I'd be able to ignore for long.

Sucking in a breath, I begged for wisdom on what to do.

This was dangerous.

This was complicated with a capital fucking C.

I should delete the messages Neri had sent, just in case her parents ever saw. I should pretend she never sent them. I should go to sleep without touching myself, and I should definitely deal with all the shit inside me that I still hadn't dealt with.

So why did I do none of that?

Another message came in from Neri, sending a painful flash through my entire body.

Neri: *I have a confession. I installed an app on your phone that lets me track you. I told myself it was just to watch you move about the ocean while I was stuck at school but…tonight, I watched where you went. I know you were in an apartment block. I expected that little red dot not to move all night. I'm not proud to admit that I drank some of Mum's lychee liquor because I needed something to dull the pain. To stop the images in my mind of what you were doing. But…you left. If the GPS isn't lying, then you're back on The Fluke. And now, somehow, my heart hurts even more.*

I *hated* the thought of her in pain.

I *hated* the thought of her alone.

I *hated* that I couldn't dash into the house and hug her.

I *hated* that I couldn't slip into her bed and fucking kiss her.

I *hated* everything that'd happened and everything that kept us apart.

But most of all, I hated myself because I was the one who'd done this. I was the weak one. The one who let Neri believe we could be anything more.

Bitter rage made my fingers fly.

Me: *I know about Sleuther. I've been tracking you too. Care to tell me why you were in a bar in Port Douglas until well past your bedtime? And stop drinking. You're alone. You're underage.*

I pressed send but then wrote more, unable to stop myself.

Me: *You asked me who she was? I wished I had the strength to tell you what I should tell you. I wish I could tell you that I slept with her. That whatever this thing is between us means nothing. I wish I could break your heart by breaking mine and prove to both of us that my fear of deportation and my loyalty to your parents will always win over how you make me feel. But…tonight, I can't. Tonight, I'll simply tell you the truth. Who was she, Nerida? She wasn't fucking you.*

My entire body thumped in time with my chaotic heartbeat. My fingers twitched with it. My toes clenched with it. I felt out of breath and manic and wild and when her text came in, I wanted to howl at the fucking moon for the awful mess we'd caused.

Neri: *I hate that there was anyone else. I hate that I'm not there with you. I hate that* even if I was, you probably wouldn't touch me. Put me out of my misery, Aslan. Did you sleep with her?*

I swallowed hard, clinging to honesty when all I wanted to do was lie.

Me: *I tried.*

Neri: *What does that mean?*

Me: *It means, I tried. And I failed.*

Neri: *Tell me I'm not crazy. Tell me you failed because she wasn't me. Tell me you don't feel this. Tell me something, Aslan, because I'm going insane feeling this on my own.*

This was the moment.

The last moment to stay safe.

Death cackled in the night, eager and ever watchful.

If I did this, I ran the risk of falling into its murderous embrace.

But I couldn't *not* do this.

I couldn't fight…not anymore. Not in this single moment beneath moonshine and starlight, floating on a sea I despised.

Me: *You're not crazy.*

Neri: *You feel it too?*

Me: *Fuck yes, I feel it. I dream of you. I ache for you. I'm so fucking wrapped up in you that it petrifies me because if I had to choose my life or yours…I'd choose you every time.*

Neri: *Come back and choose me then. We'll tell my parents and live happily ever after.*

Me: *Tell them what exactly? That the overstayer they've hidden in their garden for four years wants to fuck their daughter?*

Neri: *Is it wrong that I just got full-body chills? The thought of you doing that to me? The thought of you inside me…*

Me: *Neri…stop. I can't go there. I won't.*

Neri: *I think of you…when I touch myself. I watched online how to pleasure myself and now, I can't stop. Every time I do, I imagine you touching me, kissing me, fucking me…*

Fuck.

FUCK!

My cock rippled with a release, daring me to stroke just once.

She'd made me hypersensitive. Trigger-line reactive where I'd explode if she sent one more text, filling my mind with her writhing and coming and—

Neri: *I only want you. I want you to be my first and my last. I can wait. If you need me to wait for years, I can. I'll be patient. Just tell me what you want me to do, and I'll do it. Tell me that you want me the way I want you and I'll fight every day for you. We can try to get married. The moment I turn eighteen, we can apply for a family citizenship visa for you. You could stay here without any fear. You could stay here…with me…as my husband.*

My throbbing desire choked me.

All my need turned into horror.

I could see it so fucking clearly.

See us tangled in sheets and sweat.

See us obsessed and besotted.

See us sneaking around until she turned eighteen and then marching down to the courthouse for a marriage license.

See us being denied.

See a government official knocking on the door.

See them arresting me.

See Neri breaking into sobs as I was deported.

See her breaking into pieces as I died on Turkish soil.

I shot upright, the world swimming, nausea splashing my tongue.

Fucking hell, I wanted to be sick.

I wanted to snarl and tear apart *The Fluke* because as much as I wanted to pretend love could conquer all, it never worked out that way.

Neri had just shown me the depth of her heart, teased me with hope of claiming that heart, and proved just how fucked I was because I'd already given her my heart in return.

She was it for me.

I no longer cared if it was a curse from being saved by her or some sort of twisted fate.

No one else would do.

No one else would ever compare.

It didn't matter that we'd found each other so young.

It didn't matter our circumstances or complications.

All it would take was a single message.

A single word: YES.

A thousand times yes.

A thousand fucking times to the life and love she offered me.

But…I couldn't.

Because if I did?

If I agreed to her crazy plan and finally claimed her as mine, then I would lose her the moment the courts refused me asylum and the government got involved.

It wasn't just my refugee status.

It wasn't about betraying Jack and Anna.

It was the secret I hid even from myself.

The deep, dark truth of who I was, what I was running from, and just how far death would go to snatch me.

Eventually, it would catch me and the loss and grief I lived and breathed would land heavily on Neri's shoulders. She would feel that pain. She would live that loss. She would watch me die and leave her with nothing.

I'd break her.

Shatter her.

By loving her, I'd steal everything that made her Neri, and...*I can't*.

I would rather exist in heartbreak and watch her find happiness with another man than ever put her through that.

I crashed from aching lust to inconsolable love, and I gasped at the mistake I'd made.

I'd slipped and shown my truth.

I'd shown her how desperately I'd fallen.

And it made it so much harder to sell the lie.

But...I'd already told her how far I'd go. How I'd happily take the torture if it meant she remained safe. This was me...putting her first, above my dreams, my hopes, my *life*.

I swayed as I typed:

Me: *This was a mistake. You're young and fanciful, and...I'm sorry for leading you on. I'm drunk and got carried away, and in doing so, you proved that although I do have feelings for you, they aren't real. Not in the marrying way. It's just lust, and time will make those feelings fade.*

I couldn't breathe as I forced myself to send another. To slash at any hope she might hold. I couldn't leave her with any illusions that I didn't mean this.

I would never change my mind.

Me: *The night on the beach in Daintree, I told you I loved you and explained the reasons we could never be together. Those reasons were lies. I see that now. They gave you false hope that if we could overcome them, we could be together. But...there is no us. I don't want there to be an us. I want us to stay the way we are. I think the best thing to do is to delete this entire conversation. Let's delete everything, okay? I only want the best for you, Nerida. I always have. I always will. I love you. I'll keep saying that because it's true. But I'm not in love with you. And that's the part you have to believe.*

I bit my tongue to prevent snarling at the sky.

I waited for her reply with agonising breath.

And when it came, my entire soul shattered.

Neri: *Tell me...right now...Do. You. Want. Me? A simple question with a simple answer. Do you want me, Aslan? No lies. No spinning truths. This is your final chance. Your final moment to stop me from living a life without you in it.*

I read the words and heard what she meant.

She was done playing these games.

All it would take was an admittance that I would suffocate if she so much as looked at another guy, and it took every bit of strength to push her into that faceless bastard's arms.

I couldn't catch a proper breath. Tears stung like acid in my eyes. My heart stopped beating as I typed.

Me: *No. I don't want you. Find another.*

I tossed my phone away.

The stars continued twinkling.

The sea continued rocking.

And Neri accepted my lies.

I ought to be fucking grateful.

I'd freed her before I could hurt her far, far worse.

Instead, my bones ached as if they'd splinter.

My eyes stung as if they'd bleed.

And in the end, the sickness in my veins, the sickness of what my family had run from, and the sickness of wanting what I couldn't have all swelled to fever pitch.

I barely made it to the railing before I threw up.

Chapter Twenty-Eight
NERIDA

(Sea in Korean: Bada)

"NEEDLESS TO SAY, I DIDN'T BELIEVE him when he text me that night. I did what he asked and deleted the messages so my parents would never see, but I didn't delete what I knew was true between us.

"I let him believe I bought his lies. I didn't text him back. I waited until Aslan and my parents returned home, gave him a friendly smile and awkward hug, and pretended things were exactly like they always were.

"My parents were none the wiser. Aslan was utterly confused. And I hummed inside because, before he'd been an idiot and tried to convince me he wasn't in love with me, he'd already confessed his true feelings."

"By saying he ached for you?" Margot murmured.

"Exactly." I smiled sadly. "He *ached* for me." I shivered just as violently as I did the first time I'd read those words. "You can't say that to someone and hope to take it back. You can't say you dream of someone, ache for someone, and think you can rewind time and stop a heartsick girl from tripping into those words. It was already far too late.

"I had no idea, back then, of *why* he tried to push me away. Of course, I do now. I understand his reasonings and even pity him that he wasn't successful in convincing me that he wasn't in love with me because if he had, we both might've avoided unbearable pain. But back then...I was young, fanciful, and naïvely hopeful. In the short timeframe from telling me he ached for me, to then rushing to say he wasn't in love with me...well, I'd already planned our wedding and put on my boxing gloves to take on any bureaucrat who dared get in the way of me having the only boy I ever wanted."

Dylan cleared his throat, wrenching me from the past with a bone-jarring jolt. "You sound as if he eventually convinced you, though. That he made you believe he didn't want you."

"What makes you say that?" I raised an eyebrow.

"Your tone is tight again. Your eyes are dilated."

I laughed stiffly. "You are rather insightful. Annoyingly so."

He grinned. "I'm paid to sniff out the truth. I can see yours plain as day."

"Oh?" I cocked my head. "And what is my truth?"

Dylan glanced at Margot before lowering his voice and murmuring, "I think there's a lot more to come. I think...I think something happened to you that stole the rest of your childhood. And I think something happened to him. Something that changed both of you."

Goosebumps cloaked over my entire body. "Like I said. Insightful."

Dylan leaned back, rubbing his beard-covered jaw. "So...what happened?"

"Don't rush her," Margot snipped. "The story has to unfold the way she lived it, not leap forward."

I smiled at the eager girl, wishing I could pause my tale and live in that intense, skin-scratching newness of angst and want. Instead, the months had passed, the years had followed, and tragedy had come for both of us. And as much as I wanted to rewrite our history, I couldn't erase what I'd lived through, suffered through. I couldn't put out the fire that'd burned everything to the ground because then I wouldn't have risen from the ashes, even if I wasn't the same girl as before.

"I appreciate your commitment to the full events, Margot, but Dylan is right. Things happened. Things that irrevocably broke both of us. And they're just around the corner. The easy parts are over, unfortunately. I suppose I have to say goodbye to the light and tread deeper into the darkness that follows."

"Oh God, you're going to break my heart, aren't you?" Margot rubbed her nose. "Is it rude of me to ask for the easy version? The one where Aslan returned, realised he was being an ass and was ridiculously in love with you, took you to his bed, and then announced to the world to do its worst because you were together now and that was all that mattered?"

Dylan rolled his eyes. "There you go again. Making me worry that I should have you committed to some Romance Readers Anonymous. You need help, Margot."

"I need to know that this love story has a happy ending."

I gave her a smile that I hoped hid everything I had yet to share. "How about a drink? Something stronger than lemonade?"

"That would be great." Margot laughed, fanning herself. "A shot of alcohol would help steady my nerves."

Grabbing my phone from the rattan coffee table, I texted Tiffany to bring a selection of drinks down. I could do with some liquid courage too.

The moment I started this next chapter, I would find no peace until the end. I was condemning myself to living it all over again. Every harrowing and hopeful moment. Every ecstatic high and despairing low.

Was I strong enough?

I was barely strong enough to survive it the first time, let alone willingly reliving it.

Dylan fiddled with the microphone, and Margot swapped to a new page in her notebook. By the time Tiffany arrived with a tray of artisan beers and a few locally brewed liquors, the air crackled with anticipation.

"Thank you, Tiffany," I murmured. Taking the Mermaid Sea Salt Vodka that tasted like the ocean and was my poison of choice, I waited until Dylan had chosen a beer and Margot had selected a Scapegrace gin over ice.

With the sharp salty taste of liquor on my tongue, I began where everything started falling apart.

"My father was strict on chores. I loved him dearly, and he indulged me in many things, but he never backed down on chores and hard work. So that was how I found myself cleaning *The Fluke* one afternoon after school, a few days after they returned from their research trip in Whitsundays.

"Aslan hadn't pulled me aside to talk about our late-night messages. I forbid myself from asking him about the girl he'd tried to sleep with, and I bided my time. I had a plan, you see. I was going to wait until the next time my parents were away and then do something that Aslan couldn't refuse. I was going to seduce him. I was going to wait in his room and not let him say no.

"I was sick of him fighting it. I could see him hurting just as much as me, and I didn't understand why he wouldn't give in. I was done waiting…but of course, that all changed when I found the used condom in the rubbish bin."

Margot sucked in a breath, drinking her gin at record speed. "Oh no."

"Thank God I was alone because my legs gave out. I crumpled to the floor and remember just holding that slimy horrible thing, not caring about hygiene or where it'd been. I knew it wasn't my parents because my father had had a vasectomy. They had no need for birth control…but Aslan? He did.

"I came so close to throwing up that day. For the first time, I hated the gentle rock of the sea beneath the boat because I couldn't sit still. Couldn't breathe properly as I imagined a girl touching Aslan and him—"

I shuddered. "Anyway…. What I can tell you is, it wasn't Aslan's texts that finally forced me to face facts, it was that condom. I look back now and want to shake myself for not talking to him. Not having the courage to tell him I found it. He was under no obligation to tell me, of course. He could've lied when he'd said he failed to sleep with her and actually had. He could've been with multiple girls. He could've been telling the truth for all I knew that he truly *wasn't* in love with me and had let our connection get way out of hand.

"You see, Aslan was the type of guy who took others' expectations and dreams as his own personal quests. He would do absolutely anything to make you happy. He did it for my parents by not complaining a single day, working on the sea that killed his family. He did it for me by indulging my childhood convictions that he was mine and we were destined.

"He had a habit of putting all his wants and hopes on hold until he could deliver yours, and that sort of blind devotion made it extremely hard to stay normal. It was impossible not to lose sight of the fact that while he gave you everything, he was slowly losing himself.

"Giving every piece of himself until he had nothing left."

"He'd already given four years of his life to us, so who was I to expect the rest? Who was I to forbid him from being with others? Others that could make him happy instead of taking every shred of what he had left?

"I hated myself that day. I hated that I burned with jealousy just *thinking* of him with another girl. A girl who might have the power to make *him* happy for a change. And I felt sick to my stomach that *I* hadn't been that girl. That the only thing I'd ever given Aslan was my heart. And that heart came with so many complications.

"Forgive my rambling, but I suppose I'm trying to make it clear that my feelings for Aslan were what made me a better person but also made me the worst. I gave in to jealousy and possessiveness. And I also gave in to guilt. I felt guilty for pushing him, wanting him, cursing him for not confessing how he truly felt.

"That condom was a slap in the face. A slap of how he *did* feel. He might care for me, but he was obligated to if he wanted to stay hidden. He might dream of a different life with a different girl and was far too nice to tell me."

I swallowed another mouthful of vodka, gathering my self-control. "Kneeling on the boat, breaking with so many emotions, I grew up. I grew up…but in the wrong way. Instead of being wise enough to just *talk* to him, I allowed cynicism and fear to rule my decisions. I let hurt make me do stupid things. I let terror lead me down a path that only detoured from the truth."

"What truth?" Dylan asked.

"That no matter how much shit—excuse my French—I put us through. No matter the distance and misunderstandings, we would always be drawn back to one another."

"That sounds like fate to me." Margot sucked on an ice cube. "You both couldn't untangle yourselves because you were meant to be."

I rubbed at the aching in my heart. "I believe that now. I accept that even if we changed things and tried to be different, we would've ended up exactly where we are because there is no me without him and no him without me. And I can safely say that loving Aslan has been my biggest achievement. Not creating Lunamare. Not being nominated for a Nobel Peace Prize. Just him. Loving him through the worst pain and best euphoria."

"Can you tell us what the worst pain was?" Dylan angled the microphone a little closer, ensuring to catch my reply.

Tears stung, surprising me. Flashes of the worst day of my life filled my mind. I'd felt as if I was being flayed alive, burned alive, butchered into screaming still-alive pieces. I'd wanted to die. Yet I hadn't been given that salvation.

My voice was cool as I said, "Not yet. There are a few things to come before that day."

"Can you tell us now…please? I can't handle the suspense," Margot whispered.

"Soon. First, let me tell you what I stupidly did after I found that condom."

I sighed heavily, wishing I could reach through time and slap my sixteen-year-old self. "So many hurts coursed through me and the only medicine I could swallow was anger. Self-preserving anger that set in motion my first mistake.

"I couldn't stay on *The Fluke* after I'd found evidence of Aslan trying to move on from me. Instead, I cycled to Zara's house. She welcomed me in as she always did. We were best-friends growing up and in many of the same classes. She wanted to be a teacher and her older brother, Joel, wanted to shape surfboards for a living and travel the world on the surfing championship circuit.

"She never knew how I felt about Aslan, but she knew I'd had a crush on Joel and I used that to my advantage. I'm not proud of what I did. Like I said, I let hurt control my actions. But as I had dinner that night with Zara and her family, I rubbed my toes against Joel's bare ankle under the table and willingly went with him when he snuck outside later that night, waiting for me around the back of the house."

I flinched. "The one boy I wanted to kiss me was the only boy to refuse me, so…I made do with second best. I told Joel I'd made a mistake when I said I didn't want to be with him when we camped together in Daintree. I asked if he was still single. I asked if he still wanted me. And I felt sick because he was a nice boy and deserved a nice girl who didn't harbour feelings for another. He grinned and admitted he still had a huge crush on me, that he still wanted me, and wanted to make it official before I could change my mind again.

"He kissed me by the rubbish bins before proudly taking my hand and pulling me back inside. Unlike Aslan who did his utmost to hide how he felt about me from my parents, Joel wrapped his arms around me, revealed the extent of how much he liked me, and announced to his family that we were officially dating.

"Zara was ecstatic. She'd wanted me to be with her brother ever since that camping trip. She believed I'd become her sister one day. And Joel? Well, he was the best consolation prize I could've asked for. I still feel guilty for what I did to him. Still feel bad that while he was falling in love with me, I'd already fallen for someone else.

"I went home that night with two emotions. One of despair that Aslan might've lied to me about sleeping with someone and one of righteous rage that he might've been with someone, but now, so was I. Joel was my boyfriend, and it was only a matter of time before we slept together."

"Oh, no…so Aslan *wasn't* your first, after all? Please tell me he was your second and your last," Margot whispered sadly.

I swallowed another mouthful of chilled vodka, wincing. There wasn't an easy answer to that question, so I continued with the story. "The first time I invited Joel around to my house for dinner, Aslan looked like he'd die at the table. The second time, Joel came to watch a movie, and we snuggled on the couch. Poor Aslan only lasted a few minutes before marching out the door and vanishing into the garden. The third time, my mum sat me down and had 'the talk'. She'd already given me the main details, but this was different. This was her offering to take me to the doctor to go on the pill. It was her setting new rules for her rapidly growing daughter. I wasn't forbidden from having Joel around. In fact, Dad rather liked him and only had one strict rule that whenever Joel was in my bedroom, my door remained firmly open."

I blinked at the two reporters, not enjoying how this part of my life made me sound. "You have to understand, I didn't willingly do this to hurt Aslan. Of course, he was absolutely traumatised, and I wish I could go back and change things, but I truly did enjoy Joel's company. He was like a male version of Zara, and I loved her very much. So even though my relationship with Joel started off with lies on my part, I truly did grow to care for him."

"As much as you cared for Aslan?" Margot asked, her eyes sad and lips downturned.

I laughed quietly. "I could love any number of men or women. I could marry another. I could make a life with another. But there will never, not in a thousand years, ever be someone who will come close to the way I care for Aslan. Aslan is my other half. My mirroring piece. Life gave me my soulmate when I was just twelve, not caring that we weren't ready."

I gave Margot a smile right from my experience and my heart. "The only way I can describe it is: Aslan is Aslan. And everyone else…isn't."

"I can't lie and say that doesn't make me happy." Margot sniffed. "I'm so mad at you for being with someone else, but…you were young and hurt—"

"I was young and stupid. I should've just talked to him. But alas, that is what stupidity does to a person…it hides the clearest, most logical path. Instead of telling Aslan how hurt I was finding the condom and how much I wanted to believe he ached for me and only me, I didn't have the strength. What if he told me he'd been sleeping with half the town? What if he told me, to my face with no room for doubt, that he truly wasn't in love with me?

"I wouldn't have survived it. The depth of love I had for him terrified me. It still does. A single emotion has the power to twist my stomach, crack my bones, and rip out my heart. I honestly believed I'd die from how much I loved him, and I think he felt the same. That was why we clung to the shore a little longer. Why we played those stupid games. Because…the moment we let our love wash us away, we'd drown. Everything would change. Everything would come crashing down, and...we weren't ready."

I rubbed my chest and finished my drink. The alcohol didn't soothe my inner turmoil and I placed the goblet back on the tray before balling my hands. "I dated Joel for fourteen months. I celebrated my seventeenth birthday with him and inched ever closer to eighteen. I lost my virginity in his bed when his parents were away, all while Zara was in her room getting hot and heavy with Hadleigh. I waited for the lance of pain as he entered me, but the sharp sting from my body was nothing compared to the wrenching wound in my heart."

"That must've been so hard." Margot sighed. "To lose your innocence to someone who wasn't the boy you truly loved."

I spun my ring. Spinning, spinning, always spinning. "At the time, I thought it was the hardest thing I'd ever have to do. But it soon turned out to be one of the easiest."

Margot sucked in a breath. Dylan waved his hand for me to keep going, impatience in his gaze.

I looked away. "I was thankful Joel didn't know I choked on tears instead of lust. I closed my eyes and gave him my body, all while Aslan kept my heart firmly trapped in his aptly named lion paws. But then..."

I trailed off and looked up, once again surprised to find two reporters and not the burning black stare of my beloved.

The way Aslan would just *look* at me.

God.

It killed me every time.

I looked back now and could pinpoint what was different about him to every other boy.

It was the way he looked at me. Plain and simple.

No one else ever looked at me that way.

He looked at me as if he already knew how our story would end because it was how it always ended. It wasn't just fate but a strange kind of certainty that synced our hearts, merged our blood, and ensured we were born for each other. Over and over again.

It was his stare that undid me.

Every time I went home from sleeping with Joel, he seemed to know.

Every time he whispered hello and slipped from the house to the garden, his shoulders seemed a little more slouched.

Every time he caught my eyes and didn't guard himself in time, his soul literally snarled at mine with a guttural howl and feral despair.

I felt more from just a look with Aslan than I ever did with Joel thrusting inside me.

And the longer it went on, the more I had to be honest with myself. I loved Aslan singularly, senselessly, and nothing I could do could stop it.

Certainly not two teenagers fighting their hardest to pretend we hadn't tripped into destiny well before we were ready.

Gathering up my crying pieces, I murmured, "After fourteen months of being Joel's girlfriend, I could no longer pretend it was a fling. Joel whispered he was falling for me. Zara picked out her bridesmaid dress for our wedding. And even Joel's parents joked at the dinner table that they better start saving to help us with a house deposit.

"I biked home that night with tears streaming down my face because I knew I had to break up with him."

Settling back against the pillows, I smoothed down my dress and said as curtly as possible. "This is where things start getting hard…" I swallowed and braced myself. "I won't sugar-coat anything. I won't spare you a single moment of pain. Are you sure you want to continue?"

Dylan glanced at Margot.

Margot hunched and nodded. "Tell us."

I didn't pause.

I launched into the agony that I barely survived, needing to wade through it so I could breathe again. "The night I broke up with Joel was the single domino on a cascade of circumstances. One thing after another. One mistake leading to another and another…until they all crashed into the greatest mistake of all."

Chapter Twenty-Nine

NERIDA

AGE: 17 YRS OLD

(*Sea in German:* Meer)

MY LEGS BOUNCED WITH NERVES, MAKING ME fidget on the barstool. For a Thursday night, the Craypot bustled with customers ordering the famous mussel buckets and fresh sourdough bread.

I came here often with friends because the restaurant spilled out into a beer garden where the humid Australian air was kept at bay with freshwater misters and lush potted ferns, and the owner didn't care we were underage as long as we didn't drink. The décor with its craypots hanging from the ceiling and the lobster print uniforms gave off a homely vibe.

I wished I was in the beer garden where I could breathe a little easier. But I stayed where I'd told him I would be. At the bar, nursing a rapidly warming Sprite, begging him to appear so I could run.

"Neri?" Joel slipped through the crowd, his light brown hair tussled and bleached from being in the waves most of the day. A few eyes followed him appreciatively. At nineteen years old, Joel was starting to fill out in all the right places, leaving behind the lanky teenage stage and carving muscles into his trim physique.

Giving me a worried look, he pressed a kissed to my lips. "Everything okay? Your text sounded weird."

I gulped and looked down.

I'd had no one to discuss this upcoming conversation with. My mum and dad weren't options—as supportive as they were—and there was no *way* I'd ask Aslan for advice—not after the cold shoulder he'd been giving me for the past year. Ever since I'd turned seventeen, Aslan had withdrawn. I stopped visiting him in his room at night, and he stopped dangling his feet in the pool as I practiced my breathwork.

There was a strain between us that only grew worse, and that was the main reason I was doing this.

I'd tried to avoid doing this.

By doing this, I not only lost Joel, I lost Zara too.

She'd kill me. She'd never speak to me again. She was the reason I'd lasted fourteen months as Joel's girlfriend.

I loved Zara. I loved her like a sister. I loved hanging out with her and valued her friendship. We'd promised that we'd grow old and grey together, but after tonight…she'd hate me.

I should never have used her brother to get over my feelings for Aslan. I should've gone for any number of boys in school. If I had, I could go to my best-friend and tell her about this break-up. She would console me, and I could finally confess my feelings for the boy who lived in my garden.

But thanks to my idiocy, tonight she would break up with me forever, all because I broke up with her brother.

"Yeah, sorry, just been one of those days." I tried to smile, but nerves turned it into a grimace. Smoothing down my baby-blue sundress, I did my best to fight my trembling.

"What's up?" Joel's handsome face slipped into genuine concern. His black t-shirt strained as he sucked in a breath. "You're scaring me."

"I'm sorry." I hung my head, hating this. Hating myself. "I don't mean to."

A slow shadow filled his hazel stare. "What aren't you saying, Neri?"

My spine stiffened; I fought for strength. "Do you want to go into the beer garden? It won't be so crowded there."

I didn't think I could break up with him at the bar. That would be beyond tacky. If I was going to do it here, surrounded by tourists, I might as well just have texted him.

Joel sat next to me on an empty seat. Swinging my barstool to face his, he planted his hands on my upper thighs and stroked me with his thumbs. "Here is good. Just spit it out and then we can go and get something to eat. Did I do something wrong? I'm sorry I haven't been around as much lately. You know I'm training for the Rip Curl Cup. You said you understood that I have to chase the best waves and—"

"It's not that," I whispered.

If anything, I hadn't minded the long weeks he'd been away, hunting good sets and sending me snapchats of perfect sunsets on the beaches down the coast.

While he was gone, I could almost pretend that I hadn't ruined things between Aslan and I.

"What is it then?" He cupped my cheek. "Tell me."

I leaned into his palm, horribly taking comfort from him.

I'd grown used to how affectionate he was. How he always wrapped his arms around me, even with his family watching. How he'd kiss me for anything and everything. How he'd slip into a trance that made me feel both powerful and cruel whenever he undressed me.

Fourteen months.

And not one part of my heart had fallen for him.

If anything, my traitorous heart had fallen even deeper into Aslan.

And the more Aslan put up walls between us, the more I dreamed of him, cried out for him, desired him.

I couldn't do it anymore.

I couldn't keep lying.

This was my fault, and I had to fix it.

Are you sure?

Last chance, Neri.

If I did this, I would go to school tomorrow and be an outcast. I would spend my final months hated and whispered about, all because I hurt Zara's brother. It didn't matter that Joel had finished high school…he was well liked. People were tightknit in our town, and this would be such a betrayal.

But what was my alternative?

Marry the guy?

Allow another year to bind us together? Another decade to pass as I made a home with the wrong man and beared his children, all while I cried myself to sleep over another?

I couldn't.

I wouldn't.

It's now or never.

Inhaling a deep breath, I sat taller, took his hand from my cheek, and said, "Joel…I love you—"

"And I love you. I was thinking. When I've won a few more competitions, we should go away together. You finish high school at the end of the year. We could go travelling and maybe even get hitched in Bali—"

I clutched his fingers; my heart fisted. "Joel. You didn't let me finish."

He grinned. "Sorry. Go ahead."

I flinched.

God, this was so, *so* hard.

"I love you, Joel…but…I-I love you the way Zara loves you."

It took a moment for my message to sink in. The light in his eyes snapped to black. Disgust wrinkled his forehead as he slowly pulled his hand from mine. "What are you saying?"

"I'm saying…I…" I hunched in horror. "I love you as a friend. I love you as—"

"Fucking hell. You're saying you love me like a *brother*? What the fuck, Neri?" Leaping to his feet, he didn't care a few tourists looked our way. "What the *fuck* does that mean?"

My heart pounded, and sweat broke out down my spine. "I'm so sorry. I truly am. I didn't mean for this to happen. I never meant to hurt you. I hate that I—"

"Hold on." He raked a hand through his hair, shaking his head. "This can't be happening. Please fucking tell me you're not breaking up with me."

My shoulders slouched. "I didn't want to do it here. I wanted to go somewhere—"

"You could've done it at home. In my room. In the bed we've shared more times than I can count. You could've given me a chance to fix things before you—"

"I couldn't do this at your place." I swallowed tears. Tears at the thought of losing his sister, not him. God, if she overheard the pain in her brother's voice, she would've murdered me in her kitchen.

"Fuck *me*, I'm such an idiot!" He didn't lower his voice, and more eyes turned toward us. "You didn't want to do this at my place because you didn't want Zara to overhear us, right?"

I couldn't hide my wince.

"I knew it! I knew you two were close, but I figured that worked for all of us. We're already one big happy family, Nerida. I love you. She loves you. You love her, and I *stupidly* thought you loved me. We could've been so good together. We could've been *happy*."

"I'm so sorry."

"Stop saying that. If you were sorry, you wouldn't be doing this!"

"I didn't mean to hurt you, Joel."

"Bullshit! You knew exactly what you were doing." Pacing a little, knocking shoulders with a young guy trying to get the bartender's attention, he spun back to face me. "Wait…this is about him, isn't it?"

I narrowed my eyes, swiping at the few tears on my cheek. "Him? Him who?"

"Don't play games with me, Nerida." Shoving his face into mine, he spat. "Aslan. That bastard who never takes his fucking eyes off me whenever I come round to your place. That fucking asshole who looks at you as if you're his, and he's one decision away from punching me for touching you. That prick who grabbed me around the neck last year and said if I ever hurt you, he'd hunt me down and make me wish I was dead."

"What?" I gasped. "He did that?"

"*Wow*." Joel sneered. "You should see yourself. Your eyes just lit up at the thought of that cunt strangling me, yet you have nothing to say for yourself for the year we've been together. You've never once looked at me that way, Neri. Not once."

"And that's why you deserve someone who will." I wrung my hands. "I'm so sorry—"

"Say that one more time and I won't be responsible for what I'll do," he hissed. "You planned this well, didn't you. In a crowded place? Somewhere I can't get too irate or argue my side."

"There are no sides."

"Of course there are fucking sides. You didn't want to dump me at your place because Aslan would've heard. Then again, bet he'd be dancing for joy knowing you're done screwing me. And you didn't want to dump me at mine because Zara would've heard." He bared his teeth. "If you think you can keep my sister and get rid of me, you're gonna be sorely disappointed."

I sighed, sniffing back more falling tears. "I know. I know I've lost you both. Zara will hate me for this."

"Oh, I'll make sure she does more than just hate you," he spat. "I'll make sure she curses the very air you breathe. She'll never speak a single word to you again. She'll never even *look* at you. She'll make you realise the huge fucking mistake you just made."

"I truly am so sorr—"

His hand latched around my throat before I could blink. "I said *stop saying that*. You're not sorry. If you were, you would never have strung me along in the first place." He squeezed my neck just as a girl standing beside her boyfriend shifted toward us with wide eyes.

Letting me go, he shook out his hand as if he hadn't meant to do that. "I never want to see you again, Nerida. Ever, do you hear me? Don't come round. Don't call. Don't text. Don't even fucking *think* about me. I'm done. We're done. If I catch you trying to speak to Zara…" He wiped his mouth, swallowing back whatever threat he would've said. "Just stay the hell away from both of us."

Spinning on his heel, Joel barged through the crowd and vanished.

The girl who'd seen Joel touch me, wriggled her way out from under her boyfriend's arm and clicked in vibrant pink heels toward me. "Are you okay?"

My voice cracked as tears flowed. "Not really."

"Aw, sweetie." Wrapping me in her embrace, the shock of being hugged by a total stranger broke the dam of sadness within me.

I hugged her back and cried.

I let go for exactly ten seconds, and then I pushed her away and smiled the best I could. "I'm sorry for getting your pretty cami wet." Using a napkin from the bar, I sopped up my tears.

She waved her hand. "Don't worry about it. Do you want to talk? I'm a pretty good listener."

I sucked in a watery breath. I didn't know her name. She knew nothing about my life. But I suddenly had the strongest need for her validation.

"I just broke up with my boyfriend. We'd been going out for over a year—"

"Oh, that sucks—"

"But I'm not crying over him."

"Oh…you're not?" Her eyebrows rose. "Why are you crying then?"

"Because I just broke up with his sister too. She was my best-friend."

Her face fell. "Oh, girl, I totally get that. Those bonds are sometimes so much stronger."

"I used her brother because I've been in love with a boy since I was twelve. A boy who I'm pretty sure feels the same way about me."

"Jesus, this just keeps getting juicier." Her green eyes lit up, her dark-blonde curls shining from the craypot candelabra above. "Why aren't you with him, then?"

Because he's illegal and won't do anything to jeopardise his safety.
And I love him too much to run the risk of him being deported.

I shook my head and reached for her hand. Squeezing it, I murmured, "Long story." Slipping off my barstool, I pulled her in for another hug.

She giggled and squished me hard. Our breasts smooshed together. Our collarbones sharp against each other. Tears came hot at the thought of never having another bond like I'd shared with Zara.

I knew why I was so attached to her. It was because of Sophie. My childhood friend who'd been laughing one morning and then torn into pieces by a dog the next.

A part of me had never truly gotten over it and…I clung to girls out of fear that they'd be next. It wasn't healthy and I knew I needed to deal with it…but I couldn't help how I felt and it already hurt so, so much.

"You should message her," the girl whispered into my ear. "If you're as close as you say you are, she might one day understand and be able to forgive you for hurting her brother."

I pulled away. "Do you truly think so?"

"Worth a shot, right?"

"Definitely."

"Honey, ready to go? Our table's ready." Her boyfriend with his huge, broad shoulders and a thick Aussie twang appeared, smiling at us with questions in his brown stare. "Made a new friend, huh?"

The girl snickered. "Looks that way." She pulled out her phone, its pink rhinestone case blinding me as she opened up a new contact page. "What's your name and number? If you truly have lost your bestie, then you can have me to replace her."

My heart squeezed. "Do you live around here?"

"Nah, we're on holiday from Sydney but that doesn't mean we can't keep in touch."

"Sure." I took her phone and entered my number. "That sounds great."

"And you will never lose me as a friend for dating my brother. Know why?" She giggled. "Because he's as gay as they come and has been shacked up with his lover for years. They're gonna be buried together, that's how committed they are."

I snickered. "Good to know."

Taking her phone, she checked my details. "Nerida Taylor. That's a cool name."

"What's yours?" I asked.

"Honey Ross." She winked. "It's not a term of endearment. I'm literally called Honey. My parents live in a free-thinking commune in Perth. They're all about sustainable living and becoming one with nature."

"Sounds awesome."

"My brother, Teddy—short for Theodore—fully embraced their mission and has almost finished his university degree to be an architect. His dream is to create a community that's safe from every disaster imaginable. Drought, fire, floods, plagues…he has lofty aspirations."

Something slipped into place in my brain.

Something unfurled so swift, so right, it felt as if the seed had always been there, just waiting for a droplet of inspiration to make it bloom. "He won't find anywhere like that on earth," I said quietly. "His best bet is to build something beneath the sea."

Honey laughed. "Okay, I'll be sure to tell him. In fact, I'll pass on your number to him. That way, you can have two new best-friends."

"I'd like that. More than I should probably say." I smiled.

"Excellent." Grabbing her boyfriend's meaty arm, she smiled up at him. This pint-sized blonde sweetheart seemed at such odds with the man-mountain with his chequered shirt and baggy jeans. "Billy, can we invite my new friend to dinner, pretty please? Her heart is broken into teeny tiny pieces, and she needs a drink to cheer her up."

Billy looked me up and down with mock seriousness. "Three questions first."

"Oh, here we go." Honey rolled her eyes. "Don't take it personally. He does this to everyone."

I smiled despite myself. "Okay…"

"Do you own any crazy pets?" Billy asked deadpan.

I scowled and shook my head. "Does a dolphin count?"

"Oh my God, shut up!" Honey swatted my arm. "You do *not* have a pet dolphin."

"Not really, no, but my parents are marine biologists. I spend most of my spare time in the sea and have basically grown up with the same pod of dolphins. Sapphire is mine, but she's wild too."

"Okay, you're officially my most favourite person ever."

"Hey." Billy scowled. "What about me?"

"Okay, fine. Second most favourite."

"Better." Billy pinned me with his stare. "Question number two: if you could hook up with any person—alive or dead, famous or unknown—who would it be?"

I shivered as truth danced on my tongue.

What would be the harm?

"Aslan Avci."

"Oh...hot name." Honey grinned. "I have a thing for names."

"I'm the same." I shared a smile with her. "He's Turkish, and when he speaks his native tongue, good God in heaven."

"And moving right along." Billy chuckled. "If you could be famous for just one thing...what would it be?"

"Famous?" I shrugged. "I don't know. Not sure I want to be famous."

"But if you had to pick something. Would it be a film star? A writer? An evil scientist who blows up the world?"

The seed that'd bloomed in my head spread wider petals, merging a childhood fantasy with the very real concept of something tangible.

Would it be possible?

Could it be possible?

A chill ran down my spine that perhaps, just like finding Aslan was fate, meeting Honey was also destiny directing me on the path I was meant to follow. All those nudges that I used to follow so religiously when I was a child. All those inner knowings that'd faded as I'd grown older flared brightly, hotly, whispering that this was one of those moments that I would look back on and think...

That.

Right there.

That was the moment I became who I was meant to be.

Rubbing away my goosebumps, I whispered, "If I could be known for anything...I'd want to go down in history as the creator of underwater living. A town nestled in a reef. A sphere with whales for neighbours. A place where humans existed side by side with fins and gills instead of legs and lungs."

"Jesus, you really need to meet Teddy." Honey looped her arm through mine. "I think you two could do big things."

I shivered.

In a single chance encounter, I'd forgotten about the horror of breaking up with Joel and even the despair of losing Zara.

I buzzed with potential.

I hummed with possibility.

And all I wanted to do was run to Aslan and tell him everything.

Chapter Thirty
ASLAN

(Moon in Afrikaans: Maan)

"WHERE THE HELL ARE YOU, LITTLE FISH?" Jack growled.

I looked up from the laptop where I'd been inputting the final figures on the latest bathymetric map that Anna and Jack had been conducting. The topography of the seafloor was regularly rescanned as the rehab of the reef steadily expanded with more and more planted coral.

Jack paced in the kitchen, his hand buried in his silver-shot dark hair. "It's ten thirty on a Thursday, Nerida. You know your curfew is ten on a weeknight."

My hands stilled on the keyboard.

Where is she?

I'd just assumed she was at Joel and Zara's.

I assumed a lot these days because I didn't have the strength to ask.

I assumed she was fucking him.

I assumed she was in love with him.

I assumed she was over whatever infatuation she had with me.

I assumed she no longer cared.

I couldn't blame her for moving on after what I'd texted her that night.

I couldn't hate her for fucking someone else, all while I physically couldn't.

It wasn't as if I hadn't tried.

The day she brought Joel around, laughing at his jokes and holding his hand on the couch, something had snapped inside me that'd remained fractured ever since.

That night, as I skulked in the shadows and watched her kiss him goodbye, my heart wrenched from my chest, sickness splashed on my tongue, and I stumbled to my bedroom so drunkenly, so brokenly, that I'd slammed the door so hard, the latch didn't catch, and it shot wide open, hammering against the siding, announcing to anyone who heard that I couldn't fucking deal with the pain inside me.

I'd been so naïve.

So idiotic not to have seen how much Neri's affection meant to me.

I'd lost everyone who ever loved me.

I'd grown so used to Neri's assurances that she was mine even if I couldn't have her.

But now, I'd pushed away the one girl who cared. The one girl who actually wanted me and she left me spiralling into blackness, coming face to face with the nightmare that *I'd* done this.

I'd pushed her away, and now...she'd given me up.

I'd felt more alone that night than I had the day Neri found me and told me I was the only survivor.

I'd leaned on her too much.

I'd fallen for her too hard.

I'd fucked everything up and now the one place I was safe had become the one place I couldn't survive.

Once Joel left that night, I'd waited for Neri to come to me.

I trembled on my bed, doing my best to restrain myself, all while knowing that the moment she stepped foot in my room, I wouldn't be able to stop.

Not anymore.

I would've shoved her against the door and stuck my tongue down her throat, doing my best to replace that bastard's spit with my own, proving to her that a kiss from him was *nothing* compared to a kiss from me.

But she never came.

She hadn't visited me in the fourteen torturous months she was his.

And the morning I caught her popping a contraceptive pill before going out on *The Fluke* as a *family*, I'd known she was letting him inside her. He was coming inside her. He was touching her and kissing her and driving his fucking cock between her legs and—

Fuck, stop.

I'd hoped, after a year, that I would've begun the climb out of this sea of depression. That I could finally grab onto the shards of happiness that she'd once given me. She'd been my light while I floundered in the grief of losing my family. She'd been my smiles and laughter and hope.

And without her?

I forgot how to do any of that.

I acted around the Taylors.

I made sure to pull my weight and bent over backward for what they wanted, but my heart was dead. A useless piece of meat inside me, rotten and unwanted.

There was nothing for me here.

There was nothing for me back home.

I couldn't stay, but I couldn't go.

I was trapped and lost and hurting and so fucking sad that eventually, I would suffocate.

I longed for that day.

The day when I could just give in, give up, let go.

I fantasised about sinking beneath the waves that'd stolen everything and never coming back up.

And I hated myself because I wasn't that weak.

I wasn't supposed to be this way.

My father would have cuffed me around the head for a single notion of not coping.

But that was what Neri had done to me.

That was what not dealing with four years of grief had done.

That was what being stranded on a land that wasn't mine, existing with people who weren't mine, and longing after a life that could never be mine had done.

I supposed a therapist would call me depressed.

They'd say I'd reached critical burnout from refusing to deal with my past.

But…what was the fucking point?

How was I supposed to be happy when I was one phone call away from being deported and killed? How was I supposed to find joy when my dead heart remained so stubbornly loyal to those it'd lost? How was I supposed to chase after what I wanted, to build a life I desperately needed when it could all be taken away so easily?

Neri had no idea, but I'd installed a hook-up app on the phone she'd given me, desperate to find relief. The first few times the app matched me with someone, my chest tightened with hope that perhaps this time, I might be man enough to lose my virginity.

I might be lucky enough to find comfort in the arms of a total stranger.

But as I stole Neri's bike and cycled to meet Bethany or Claire or Tanya, I couldn't even touch them.

A single smile, a simple word, and my skin would break out in sweat. My stomach would twist, my heart would race, and my cock, which I wished would fucking cooperate, shrivelled with refusal.

It wanted one girl and one girl only.

Regardless that that one girl was off fucking another.

After the fourth shameful experience of apologising for wasting the girl's time, I stopped trying. I settled on sinking into hell and jerking off to daydreams of Neri finally realising that I was here, I was begging, I was on my fucking knees for her to come back to me.

At least I could come that way.

I could ease some of the frustration in my blood.

Pity that each time I came, I just felt evermore hollow. As if, with every release, I lost another piece of myself.

One day, I'd lose the final piece, and nothing would be left.

"What do you mean, you're at the Craypot? I thought you were with Joel." Jack scowled as he dropped his hand. "Right, stay there. I'll come get you."

He hung up before Neri could reply.

Looking at Anna who was watching a shark doco on TV, he growled, "Our no-good daughter is at a pub downtown. She sounds tipsy, for God's sake."

Anna turned and looked over her shoulder. "What on earth? Why would she be drunk? *How* would she? She's underage."

"She said she made some new friends. I'm guessing slightly *older* new friends." Jack marched to the side table where keys and junk lived. "I'll give her a piece of my mind as I drive her—" He cut himself off with a curse. "Dammit, I've had three beers. I'm over the limit."

"Shit, I've had two glasses of wine," Anna muttered.

Both their eyes landed on me.

"Have you drunk anything tonight, Aslan?" Jack's tone turned hopeful.

Sitting back, I saved the bathymetric map and closed the laptop. "Not a drop."

I hadn't drunk in months.

I found alcohol made my mood far too black.

The last time I'd had a few, I'd stood outside Neri's bedroom until dawn, wondering if I had the strength to sneak inside and confess everything. Tell her how much I was hurting. Tell her how much I wanted to let my family's death pass through me. How much I needed a friend.

I'd stood like a fucking stalker in the night, wishing I could cry like I had the first day she'd found me but only finding desiccated despair instead.

"Would you mind?" Jack jingled his keys. "I know we said that we should restrict your driving at night…just in case you get pulled over for whatever reason, but…she can't walk home on her own. Not at this time."

"It's fine, Jack."

At this point, the fear of being caught had dulled under the sadness of never having Neri creep into my bedroom again.

Slipping my bare feet into my discarded flip-flops under the table, I checked that my black shorts and grey t-shirt weren't filthy from a day at sea before striding toward Jack and grabbing his keys.

"I'll be back soon. With your drunk daughter."

Jack rolled his eyes. "She better not be. Otherwise, she's grounded for a month."

I forced a smile. "Good luck with that."

"Do you know where the Craypot is?"

"Yeah, I've been before." Once. On a failed hook-up.

"What would we do without you, huh?" Jack yanked me into a hug. "Thanks, mate. I don't tell you enough, but thanks. For all of it."

I froze.

Contact.

Human contact after so long with nothing.

The walls I hid behind. The chains I padlocked. The barriers I'd erected to protect me from pain all threatened to crash.

Extracting myself from his embrace, I kept my eyes down as I hurried out the door to find Neri.

Chapter Thirty-One
ASLAN

(Moon in Polish: Księżyc)

FLASHING LIGHTS UP AHEAD.

Blue and red, blue and red.

Men and women in uniform.

Barriers and road cones, funnelling the three cars in front of me to the curb.

Kahretsin!

Sweat broke out on my palms as I fisted the steering wheel.

SHIT!

Looking in the rear-view mirror, I deliberated pulling a U-turn, but a male cop waved at me, catching my eyes, and beckoning me past one of the cars already pulled over.

Nausea waked in my gut.

I waited for a panic attack. For the very real nightmare of cold cuffs to snap on my wrists and my borrowed time to be over.

I expected my heart rate to go through the roof as I slowly pulled over, threw the banged-up Jeep into park, and rolled down the window.

Instead, I turned cold inside.

Ice, ice cold as the depression fog wrapped me in thick terror and demoralizing grief.

I couldn't fight it.

I couldn't stop it sucking me down into the inevitability that I was a dead man. I had been for four years, and death had finally found me.

My pulse went dangerously slow.

I couldn't catch a proper breath.

This was it.

All my struggles. All my desires. All that wasted time.

I'd never see Neri again. Never find happiness with her or learn how to hide from this soul-sucking shadow that hunted me.

I was dead, and there was nothing I—

"Evening."

I jerked out of my bleak desolation and licked my dry lips. "Evening." Splinters of self-preservation made me rush, "Eh, did I do something wrong, officer?"

"Why? *Did* you do something wrong?" The youngish cop cocked his head, his police issued baseball cap catching the blue and red flashing lights. He might be young, but he was shrewd, and he studied me intently.

The first frissons of fear wracked down my spine.

I'd dealt with police before.

I knew their mind games and tricks to make you trip.

I might be already dead, but I wouldn't make it easy for him.

"Not at all. Just…just picking up a friend."

"Have you been drinking tonight?"

"No."

Holding up a black device with a tiny screen and funnel out the side, he commanded, "Count to ten directly into the breathalyser."

My hands shook as my heart finally got the fucking memo that I was one wrong answer away from never seeing Neri again. It took all my control to keep my voice stable as I did as he commanded. "One, two, three, four, five, six, seven, eight, nine, ten."

The many numbers I'd learned in different languages echoed in my head. Thanks to the app I'd been using, I'd mastered quite a few. But now it seemed I'd learned too many as my head swam with digits.

My mind felt crowded. Thick. Sick. Foggy.

Stark fear crawled through the blanket of my depression, feeding me images of Neri.

Of her smiling. Laughing. Swimming.

Of the way she used to touch me, watch me, want me.

My chest tightened. Agony lanced through my ribs.

I sucked in a thin breath as my heart stuttered and failed.

Could a twenty-one-year-old guy die of a heart attack?

If I ran from this cop before he could arrest me, was it better to die with a bullet in my back or die where Neri would never know what happened? Would Australia be a better tomb or Turkey?

The longer I sat there, the more I struggled with syrupy sadness and savage salvation.

I didn't want to die.

I didn't want to keep feeling this way.

I wanted to live.

I wanted Neri.

I want—

The little machine beeped, the cop glanced at it, then gave me a pleasant smile. "Have a good night. Safe travels." Stepping away from my window, he marched toward the next car that'd been pulled aside.

As suddenly as it'd happened, it was over.

I blinked.

No request for licenses. No arrest. No deportation.

The ice in my veins suddenly turned into an inferno.

I burned up.

I gulped down air.

I swerved back onto the road with single-minded determination.

Neri.

I have to find her...

My dead heart smoked with life.

I was done wasting time.

I was through letting fear win.

Neri…

My heart began to race.

I spotted her the moment I stepped foot into the Craypot.

She stood at the lobster-carved bar, her chocolate hair darker than usual thanks to the rainy season and more intense schoolwork. Her last year of study meant she hadn't been on *The Fluke* as much or spending as much time in the sun and salt.

My out-of-control heart raced even faster, burning through its shroud of decay, shocked alive thanks to the breath test and police.

I'd come face to face with law enforcement and was still free.

I'd been given a second chance.

A second chance to take what I wanted instead of lying and pushing it away.

I didn't care she was with Joel.

I didn't care that she'd chosen him over me.

I needed her.

Fuck, I *needed* her.

How long had it been since we'd been alone?

Since we'd talked? *Truly* talked?

The faintest stirrings of dark-shadowed happiness flickered in my belly. We would have time in the car. Just us. Away from eyes and ears and reality.

She'd be all mine, even if it was only ten minutes.

Marching toward her, I frowned as one of the guys beside her grabbed her elbow and pulled her into him. She struggled and shoved him away, shouting something I didn't catch. The guy didn't take no for an answer, touching her hair and laughing in her face.

I saw red.

Murderous fucking red.

My march became a jog, and I weaved through people drinking and mingling, coming to an explosive stop before them. "What the *fuck* do you think you're doing?" My snarl ripped through the drone of voices, stilling the guy's hand on Neri's shoulder.

Her eyes shot to mine, shock making them wide but then relief making them hood. "Aslan."

Shit, the way she said my name.

The way she *looked* at me.

It was a tsunami sweeping me off my feet.

But then…somehow, the heavy wave waked away. The depression I couldn't survive parted like a miraculous sea and I stood on earth again.

My spine straightened and I couldn't do it anymore.

I dropped all the guards I usually hid behind.

I didn't try to hide the depth of my feelings.

Whatever she saw in my gaze made her trip backward with a soft gasp, coming to a halt as the guy kept her pinned with his hand.

Tearing my eyes from Neri, I glowered at the bastard. "I suggest you let go of her before I break every single one of your fingers."

A few years ago, I would've cringed at saying such things. I'd cower from the memory of where I'd come from and the bloodline I carried, but not here, not tonight. Tonight, I would happily tear off his arm and feed it to him if he didn't let Neri go.

"Fuck off, mate. I was here first."

My nostrils flared.

Neri shoved his hand off her shoulder. "I told you, you idiot. I'm not interested."

"Wasn't what you said before. You batted those pretty eyelashes at me and—"

"I was being polite! You asked me if I was having a good night and instead of telling you I had a shitty one, I gave you a smile and moved out of your way."

"Bullshit, you pressed your tits against me—"

"I was pushed!" Neri waved her arms at the crowded bar with its craypots hanging from the ceiling and the seaweed draped candelabras above. "It's busy. You can clearly see that."

"I can see you making excuses. I bought you a drink."

"I didn't ask for it, nor do I want it."

"Well, you owe me. Fucking pay up. Give me your phone number. A drink for a date."

My hands balled. Power siphoned through my blood. I prepared to choose violence after running away from it all my life.

But then Neri shocked me stupid by coiling her arm through mine and hissing, "I can't go on a date with you because the truth is, I'm with him. This is my boyfriend. I already have one. See? So I suggest you give it a rest and—"

"Him?" The guy with his overgrown black hair looked me up and down. He was my height but heavier. I could win against him, but it wouldn't be easy. I'd get hurt.

Then again, I *wanted* to hurt.

I wanted to feel something, anything, so I wasn't so dependent on Neri for existing.

"Yes, him. We're together and—"

"I call bullshit." The guy crossed his arms. "He's just some guy trying to be a hero."

"Careful," I seethed. "I'm really fucking close to hitting you."

"Go ahead. I'll squash you like a fucking cockroach." Pinning his stare on Neri, he sniffed. "Give me your number. Stop lying. Admit that you want me and save this bloke a lot of pain—"

"I told you, he's my boyfriend. Not that it's any of your damn business," Neri hissed. "Now let us pass."

The guy laughed. "Gimme a kiss first."

I snapped.

I gave in to the red.

Yanking my arm out of Neri's hold, she gasped and tried to grab me.

"Aslan, don't—" Her eyes flared with fear that I'd punch the bastard. But she had me wrong. *I* had me wrong. All this time I'd chosen wrong, but right here, right now...I was choosing fucking right.

"See, I called it." The guy laughed. "He's not your fucking boyfriend—"

"You want proof?" I curled my arm possessively around her shoulders, jerked her into me, and grabbed her jaw with my other hand. "I'll give you fucking proof."

My mouth slammed down over Neri's before my mind caught up with my body.

Our lips crashed together.

Her moan tore through my ears.

And that was all it took for me to die.

I motherfucking died in her arms and was reborn again in a flash of burning fire.

Bone-breaking lust ricocheted through me.

I stumbled and shoved her against the bar.

Her hands dove into my hair.

My tongue speared into her mouth.

Everything vanished.

Nothing else existed.

Just her and me and this.

Fucking *this*.

I groaned as her tongue licked mine. Experienced and wet and hot.

I licked her back. Savage and raw and violent.

Our mouths opened wide, our kiss—our first official kiss—slipping straight into hell where we burned and mauled and scratched and bit.

A hand landed on my shoulder, wrenching me away from her. "Get the fuck off her, you animal!"

All the noise, all the lights, all the world that I no longer cared about came rushing back.

I blinked at the asshole who'd just ruined the best moment of my life.

And I didn't hold myself back this time.

I leaped headfirst into the darkness I'd inherited.

With a sharply aimed punch to his jaw, I spun on my heel and kicked him square in the chest.

He soared backward, landing with a loud grunt.

Eyes fell on me.

Eyes that saw everything I was.

Eyes that could steal me from Neri and everything I wanted.

I wouldn't let that happen.

Not now.

Snatching Neri by the wrist, I ran.

I pulled her tripping and gasping through the Craypot, fell out the door, and bolted down the street to where I'd parked her father's Jeep.

Chapter Thirty-Two

ASLAN

(*Moon in Hindi:* Chandrama)

"ASLAN...TALK TO ME." NERI SAT BESIDE me as I fisted the steering wheel and chose different streets to avoid the breath testing roadblock.

"Aslan...? What...what was that back in there? You...you kissed me." Rubbing her arms, she shook her head. "You kissed me and—" She cut herself off, touching her lips where I'd bruised her. "Did you kiss me just to stop that guy from being a dick? Did you mean to kiss me that roughly? Did you—"

"Not yet." My foot wanted to stomp on the accelerator, but I forced myself to drive below the speed limit. No way would I risk being pulled over. Not when I was so close to figuring out how to live.

"Not yet? What does that mean?"

"It means...I don't want to talk about it. Not yet."

"I hate to tell you, but you can't ignore this. You can't send me a text pretending that kiss didn't happen. You can't try to gaslight me into believing it meant nothing when every part of me says it was—"

"*Everything*. It was everything. I know that." I threw her a look before focusing back on the road. "It happened. I'm not going to deny it."

"You're not?" Her tone flirted with confused. "But...you haven't so much as touched me this past year—"

"You're with him."

"Joel?"

My teeth ground to dust, unable to picture her lips—lips that tangled my stomach and fisted my heart—on another guy's.

I nodded curtly.

A long pause before she whispered, "I broke up with him tonight."

"*What?*" I swerved into the other lane as I looked at her. "You did?"

She couldn't hold my stare, dropping her chin and twining her fingers together. "I couldn't do it anymore."

"Why?" I choked on those three little letters, heading back to the right side of the road.

"Why?" she whispered. "Do you really need to ask?"

I jerked and my heart lost all resemblance of pumping like normal. I was wired and jittery and so fucking wild, I couldn't stay human anymore.

Spying the first patch of darkness up ahead, I stomped on the gas.

Neri looked up. "Aslan, slow down. You don't want to be pulled over."

"Already have. On the way to you."

"You did?" Her mouth dropped open. "Oh my God. How did you…I mean…why didn't they—?"

"Take me?"

She swallowed hard. "Didn't they ask for identification?"

"I got lucky."

Placing her hand over her heart, her voice wobbled. "God, just the thought of you being taken. I don't think I could handle it." A single tear rolled down her cheek. "Promise me you'll find a way to stay here. Legally. So we don't have to fear—"

"I'm yours, Nerida." My gut wrenched in two as I reached across and swiped my thumb over her tear-wet cheekbone. "Here. There. Everywhere."

I'd never spoken such truer words.

Never thought I would allow myself.

I couldn't assure her that I'd never be deported.

I couldn't assure her that all her fantastical plans of getting married and gaining a visa would come true.

But I was done letting all of that keep us apart.

I was done fucking fighting.

Fighting every fibre in my being that screamed my one true path was her.

Sucking in a gasp, Neri turned her head and kissed my hand before I dropped it from her gorgeous face, placed it on the gearstick, and swerved into a local park.

A deserted park.

Driving beneath palm trees and cutting through the carpark to a shadowy spot beneath an ancient banyan, I slammed on the brakes, cut the engine, and hurled myself out the door.

Every step I took was jerky and manic, and Neri sucked in another gasp as I wrenched open her door, reached over to unhook her seatbelt, then dragged her unceremoniously outside.

She tripped a little.

I steadied her.

I slammed her door, fisted her hips, and trapped her firmly against the Jeep.

Our eyes locked.

Our breathing was wild.

All the familiar black dripping thoughts that usually filled my head were silent. I trembled and tingled, sparkling with energy so savage, so sharp, I couldn't stand up straight.

I had so many things to say, yet I couldn't remember a single one of them.

My eyes dropped to her glistening parted lips. I swallowed a groan. "Why? Tell me why."

Tears shot to her eyes again, knowing exactly what I asked. Her delicate hands that'd petted whales and played with octopus slipped deliciously through my hair.

I shivered.

The curse of oversensitivity shot through me, centring in my cock.

I *throbbed*.

"Neri…I—"

"He wasn't you, Aslan. No one will ever be you." Her gaze locked on my mouth. It was as if she touched me there. I grew hot and tight, and I sank my teeth into my bottom lip, fighting my true nature. Doing my best to stay the boy she knew and not give in to the monster I'd been hiding from.

"He wasn't you," she breathed, standing on tiptoe, offering herself to me, pulling my head down, drugging me. "And I'm so sick of wanting you. So sick of not being honest."

My mouth hovered over hers, so close, so near. Goosebumps scattered down my spine. My cock rippled with need. Restraining myself was the hardest thing I'd ever done, but it was also the most exhilarating.

To hover on that knife's edge.

To be so close to taking what I'd always wanted, tempting fate, dabbling with destiny. Dragging out the moment until we were both breathless and cross-eyed and seconds away from exploding.

I nudged her nose with mine. "So…be honest."

She laughed almost coldly, pulling away a little. "And if I am…what will you do? Will you run? Will you lie? Will you try to convince me it means nothing—"

"No."

"Why should I believe you?"

I caught her stare. I cupped her jaw. "Because I'm done, Neri. I can't do this anymore. I can't pretend you're not it for me. I can't lie that you aren't my very fucking air while I'm drowning beneath everything else."

I couldn't stop myself, my confession tart and sour. "I'm lost. I only feel alive when I'm with you. I shouldn't put that shit on you. I know that. I'm not being fair. I should work through my grief and fear without begging for your help. And I definitely shouldn't make you responsible for my happiness. But…I can't crawl out of the darkness without you. I feel nothing unless I'm with you. And…well, the honest truth is…I've been dying every fucking day seeing you with him."

She stiffened. "Why didn't you say anything—"

"This is me. Saying something."

"Aslan, I—"

"I'm willing to try, Neri. I have no choice. I can't survive without you. I want to be *happy*. I want to be free of my grief. I want to be with you without being terrified of losing you."

A tear rolled down her cheek. "I'm yours, Aslan." She repeated what I'd said to her in the car. "Here. There. Everywhere."

My forehead crashed on hers as my knees threatened to give out. "And that's what petrifies me because if I'm deported. I…I won't survive, Neri. And you'll be alone. I'll take your heart and leave you as broken as I am."

"If you're deported, I'll come with you."

True panic roared through me, just like on the beach when she was fifteen. "Vow to me that you will *never* do that. You will never step foot in Turkey or mention my name—"

"Why? What are you hiding?"

"*Promise* me."

She scowled. "I can't promise that. I can't promise I won't follow you because I know I always will."

I exhaled with a snarl. "Then this can't happen." It took superhuman strength to release her and step back.

I swayed on the spot.

My cock pounded behind my zipper.

I could barely see straight with how desperate she made me.

"It's already too late to stop." Pushing off from the Jeep, she stalked me as I backed deeper into the trees. "It was too late the moment we met."

"Don't say that. If I keep my hands to myself, you will find another. You'll meet another Joel and—"

"Be miserable."

"Did you fuck him?" The question fell from my tongue before I could bite it back.

She froze.

Fury coated my vision as answers clouded her face. Lies. Truths. Until she finally just gave me a simple. "Yes."

My eyes snapped shut.

It shouldn't hurt as much as it did.

I'd guessed. I'd assumed. I'd tortured myself with images of her with him. Yet having her admit it?

Anger had me striding forward and planting a fist between her breasts. Marching her backward to the Jeep, she gasped as I shoved her against the door. "Aren't you going to ask me if I fucked anyone?"

She winced; pain coated her voice. "Have you? Did you—?"

"I tried." My fingers spread over her chest, my thumb on the top of one breast, my pinkie on the top of the other. "I tried multiple times. And you know what happened?"

She sucked in a breath, pushing more of her flesh into my control. "Tell me."

I'd dreamed of touching her like this.

I'd convinced myself, late at night while I jerked off to fantasies of her, that if I could just steal a single kiss, a passing touch, I would be satisfied.

Lies.

This wasn't enough.

Nothing would ever be enough when it came to her.

And in that, it seemed I was doomed.

She could find comfort with another, all while I suffered impotence.

If I was a better man, I would find solace in that. I would be relieved that if anything did happen to me, she would eventually move on with another.

But that would mean I'd have to be willing to share her, and I could *never* do that. I could never be that honourable. That decent. I wanted her to want me as desperately, as manically, as suicidally as I wanted her.

And that showed me how twisted I truly was. How unhealthy my obsession with her had become—

"I slept with him, but I never found pleasure," Neri breathed, freezing me. "Every time I was with him, it was you I wanted. It's your name I breathe as I make myself come. It's you who I dream of. It's you who has me so wrapped up in need that the mere thought of being with anyone else makes me want to scream and fight and tell the whole world that you are mine. You and only you."

Tears ran down her face as her voice cracked. "I wanted you to be my first, Aslan. I wanted you to take that because it was always yours to take—"

"Fuck." My temper gathered at my helplessness. At all the tragic and tormenting shame I'd carried for not being able to be with someone who wasn't Neri.

But...standing there, with her tears glistening in the moonlight, I was glad.

Glad my body had betrayed me.

Glad my heart had bound me in every tangible way to this incredible girl, this matching piece of my soul.

"I don't care that I wasn't your first, Neri. But if I have my way...I'll damn well be your last."

She moaned. "Do you mean that? Truly, truly mean that?"

My lips pulled back as I fisted myself through my shorts with my free hand. I hissed at my reaction. At the way I jerked for more. I'd never been so fucking hard. So ready to come with a single stroke. "Just the mere thought of being with someone who isn't you turns me as useless as a eunuch. Your father used that word the night he told you to stop fantasising about marrying me. I looked it up because I didn't know what it meant. All my power. All my virility…it just vanishes. I can't keep it up. I go soft—"

"You mean…you've never—"

"Never. I'm twenty-fucking-one years old and I've never been with a—"

Her lips shut me up.

She threw herself on me…

…and…

I snapped.

Shoving her against the car door, the metal twang of its protest rang around us as our mouths crashed and our tongues hunted. As quickly as our kiss back in the bar had gone straight to hell, this one went far past it.

This one drove us into the depths of brimstone and perversion.

I forgot who I was.

I forgot to be gentle and respectful and kind.

I grabbed fistfuls of her hair and held her tight, plunging my tongue into her mouth, swallowing her moans, drinking her gasps.

She fought me just as wildly.

Her teeth nipped at my lips, her leg came up and wrapped around my thigh.

It wasn't enough.

Dropping my hands from her hair, I grabbed her waist and shoved her up the car. When she matched my height, I slammed her against the door again, panting as her legs locked around my hips, shoving her sundress up, and giving me access to her heat.

I saw stars.

I saw death.

I thrust my denim-clad cock against her, unable to stop.

Her hands shot up my t-shirt.

Her fingernails scraped along my spine.

Her head tipped back as she gasped for air, and I fell on her neck.

I licked and bit. I sucked and claimed.

And my hips never stopped thrusting.

Driven by five years of desperation.

Unhinged from years of denial.

"God, Aslan. Fuck…" She moaned as I ground my aching cock against her wet underwear.

A guttural groan escaped me as an explosive ripple cracked down my back and up my legs.

"Take me. Right here—" Her pleas drove me straight into depravity.

Her hand burrowed between us, crushed and bruised as we writhed and fought.

I hissed as she found my button and undid it. The sound of my zipper coming down screeched through the night.

And when her fingers found my length for the first time, my world shot white, my body took control, and I buckled.

"*Fuccckkk!*"

I came.

Spurt after spurt, I coated her wrist. Wave after wave of the best fucking release of my godforsaken life. It went on forever, draining me, reincarnating me. But unlike all the other self-given releases, this one didn't leave me hollow. It filled me up. It made me glow, and when the last ripple quaked through me, I opened my eyes and froze.

Neri bit her bottom lip, her ice-blue eyes dancing. A snicker escaped before she gave up, exploding with quiet laughter. "Wow, I had no idea you were that hung up over me."

My cheeks burned.

The back of my neck prickled.

Her laughter coated me in self-consciousness but also...tugged at my mouth with mirth.

The crazy level of my need for her. The way my body had chosen her and only her...it was ridiculous, really.

I was probably the only guy alive who couldn't just fuck someone. A guy who'd blown the moment the love of his life merely touched him.

A half-chuckle, half-groan fell from me. "I'm sorry. I—"

"Don't you dare say you're sorry. You have no idea the power rush you've just given me." She held up her cum-roped hand. "Knowing you wanted me this badly?" She smiled with overwhelming love in her eyes. "It gives me permission to stop hiding. To stop pretending. It gives me everything I didn't know I needed, and I can finally admit to your face that I love you, Aslan. I love every single thing about you. I've said that before. I've hidden behind the ruse that I love you like a friend, like a family member. But the truth is, I'm *in love* with you. God, I'm so madly in love with you that I can't believe this is happening. I'm head over heels, and I think...I always have been. And the fact that you seem to love me—"

"I do." I held her stare, hoping she saw everything in my soul. Every secret I no longer needed to hide. "I love you with every fibre of my being, *canım benim. Sana aşığım, Nerida. Sana o kadar aşığım ki, seni güvende tutmak ve benim kalman için ne kadar ileri gidebileceğimden korkuyorum.*" I went to put her feet back on the ground, but she wrapped her arms around my neck and kissed me. "What does that mean?"

I kissed her back and fed the translation directly into her mouth. "I said I'm in love with you. I'm so in love with you, I'm afraid of how far I'd go to keep you safe and mine."

She moaned and threw herself into me.

She kissed me like I needed to be kissed. Deeply, devotedly, full of hunger, acceptance, and love.

I sank into her.

I kissed her back as deeply and as devotedly as she kissed me.

I didn't think about the future.

I didn't think about what would happen when Jack and Anna found out.

All I thought about was *her*.

We lost time as we let the kiss sweep us away like a tide, ebbing and flowing, licking and tasting. By the time I pulled away, her lips were red from my five-o'clock shadow and my cock swelled for a second round.

All it would take was to pull her underwear to the side, shove down my shorts, and I could be free of the affliction that'd haunted me for years. I could give her all of me. She could be my first *and* my last.

But...I wanted more than a quick fuck against a car door. Her *father's* car door. When I finally sank inside her, I wanted her to know exactly who took her because I would never let her go once she was mine.

Breathing hard, I lowered her slowly to the ground.

"Are you always that...sensitive?" she asked quietly, wiping the mess I'd covered her with on her pretty blue sundress.

I winced at the wet patch left behind and chuckled under my breath. "Let's just say, I don't need much to go out of my mind."

"And even with such sensitivity, you couldn't...with someone...ever?"

"The minute someone touched me, it was over."

She giggled, and it made my heart fucking burst. "You're right about that. I touched you, and...it was over."

Gathering her tight, I whispered against her mouth. "You're the only one who has ever made me do that. Not counting myself of course."

She trembled. "I want to watch that one night."

"What? Watch me jerking off?"

She nodded, licking her lips. "I want to see how many strokes it takes."

"If I'm thinking of you, not many."

"I'm the same," she whispered. "I suppose you could say I'm sensitive too—or at least, I am on my own."

I didn't want to ask, but a part of the desolate darkness inside me needed reassurance. "And you never...with him?"

"Not even close."

An idea sparked in my head. For the first time since I'd screeched into this park and yanked her out of the Jeep, I looked at our surroundings. Trees did their best to hide the moon. Stars did their best to shine through the silhouette of their branches. The soft *hish-hish* of waves on a beach somewhere close by battled for supremacy with the drone of night instincts.

Life existed all around us but no people.

No one to report public indecency or have me arrested for what I was about to do.

Stepping into Neri, I didn't say a word as I ducked a little and feathered my hand up her dress.

She froze.

Her breath hitched. "What...what are you doing?"

"I want to know how sensitive you are. Are we the same, Neri? Can I make you come as quickly as you made me?" I traced a finger over her drenched underwear. "You're certainly wet enough. As wet as the sea you love so much."

"Because of you." She shivered as I drew my touch up and hooked my fingers in her lacy waistband. Tugging her knickers down, I waited for her to kick them away before our eyes locked, and she brazenly stepped a little wider.

I wanted to drop to my knees and worship her for that.

I wanted to taste and devour.

I wanted to learn every inch.

But for now...I had to be patient.

I couldn't even see her.

But I could feel her.

And that first touch...*fuck me*.

Looping her arms over my shoulders, she whispered, "I can't promise I'll come..."

"And I can't promise I know what I'm doing." I kissed her perfect mouth. "But I want to touch you. I've wanted to touch you for years."

"Then touch me."

Her head fell back as I accepted her invitation.

I cupped her core.

I hissed at the heat pumping from between her legs.

And I shuddered as I pressed a single finger inside her.

My cock rippled with warning, hinting that I might not even need touching this time to come. Just having my finger inside Neri blew my ever-loving mind.

She sucked in a breath as I pushed my entire finger inside her. Her heat burned. Her wetness welcomed. And the strength of her inner body sucked me deeper as if desperate to claim me.

Rocking my wrist, I focused on everything about her.

I never took my eyes off the way her lips parted as she panted. How her shoulders tensed, and her eyes squeezed tight as I withdrew, then pushed back in.

I might not have any experience in this, but instinct roared through me. I inserted a second finger and rubbed my thumb against her clit.

She spasmed in my arms, her legs buckling. "Jesus, Aslan..."

I caught her with a chuckle. "Still think you won't come for me?"

She struggled to speak. An unintelligible mumble was my reward.

I lost myself to giving her pleasure. I wanted tonight to be a night of firsts for both of us. I wanted to be the only one to make her unravel. I wanted to give her the same euphoria that she'd given me.

With every rock of my wrist and pulse of my fingers, I read her.

With every thrust and withdrawal, I did my best to find her perfect rhythm.

And she spoke loud and clear.

She whimpered as I increased my pace.

She clawed at my back as I pressed her against the car and kissed her.

She cried out as I thrust my tongue into her mouth in time with my fingers in her body.

And she trembled as I gave up trying to keep my own pleasure out of it and pressed my throbbing length against her hip.

I gave over to our mutual writhing.

Her hips thrust forward to meet my fingers.

Mine rocked hard, forcing her to feel what she did to me.

We lost control.

We lost our breath.

We thrust and humped and panted and clawed.

And as I drove my hand hard between her legs, she stopped breathing completely.

Her eyes flared wide.

We fell into a stare.

I had the absolute fucking pleasure of watching her break apart.

Her chin tipped down, and her cheeks flushed pink, and I fucked her with my hand as fiercely and as possessively as I wanted to do with every part of me.

The first clench of her release took me by surprise. The second broke me. By her third, I gave up everything I was as I ripped my hand from her heat, snatched her from the ground, and wedged my undone shorts against her pussy.

She cried out as I thrust against her. Just a simple piece of clothing stopped us from joining and it drove me wild. My mouth smashed to hers as I rode her hard and fast, driving her against the car door, wringing out the rest of her orgasm, all while I gave in to another.

Our tongues were messy and wet.

Our groans full of ecstasy.

Our pleasure seemed to go on forever before we finally stopped shuddering and gave a heavy sigh.

Our eyes opened.

Our lips twitched into satisfied smirks.

We didn't speak.

What was there to say?

We'd chosen each other, despite everything that could go wrong.

I'd claimed her as mine, regardless that I could never truly be hers.

And as we kissed gently and cleaned up the best we could, we refused to look into the darkness surrounding us. The night that lashed around us, keeping us safe…for now.

Pity we didn't.

What a shame we thought we were free.

If only we'd looked into that darkness…

…we might have seen the nightmare that was coming for us.

Chapter Thirty-Three

ASLAN

(Moon in Icelandic: Tungl)

"DAD, CAN YOU PASS THE PEANUT BUTTER, please?" Neri held out her hand, wriggling her fingers.

My gaze locked on her elegant wrist.

I'd always found every inch of her stunning…but now?

Now everything about her turned me the fuck on.

My cock swelled.

I shifted in my seat, schooling my face into bored normalcy, all while my body became determined to blare all my secrets.

Neri flicked me a glance. She wore no make-up and had secured her hair in a high ponytail. Fresh-faced, newly washed, and dressed in her school uniform of blue shirt and black skirt, she looked utterly innocent yet somehow completely corruptible.

My heart skipped.

I looked away. Focusing on Anna as she poured us all grapefruit juice, I did my best to get myself under control.

This was bad.

This was our very first morning after our confessions and stolen touches last night.

If I was one heartbeat away from launching over the table and dragging her onto my lap, how the fuck was I going to survive months of secrecy before we could tell her parents?

Months that we'd agreed to last night.

"Did you sleep well, Aslan?" Anna smiled, splashing juice into my glass.

"Yeah—" My voice broke as another wake of lust for her teenage daughter clutched me around the throat.

Get a fucking grip.

Locking eyes with Anna, I did my best to distract myself and her by slipping into my mother tongue. "*Peki ya sen? İyi uyudun mu?*"

Her face lit up, and she bit her bottom lip, remembering what to reply. "*Teşekkürler, evet iyi uyudum.*" She wrinkled her nose, looking so much like Neri, I balled my hands under the table as my eyes shot to her daughter, and I suffered a full-blown bolt of love.

"Did I say that right?" Anna asked.

Swallowing hard, I nodded. "Perfectly. You said you did sleep well and thank you."

"Phew." Sitting down, she took a bite of her honeyed toast with banana.

"Dad. Jeez, come on." Neri clenched her fingers. "Peanut butter."

Jack grunted something and waggled his phone, reading the local news like every morning. "Impatient, little fish." Without looking up from whatever article he read, he fumbled around on the table for the tub.

Neri rolled her eyes, standing in her chair. "I'll just get it." Her buttoned shirt gaped open a little, revealing a tight white sports bra beneath. The nymph and sea lion necklace I'd bought her—that never left her neck—swung and glittered in the morning sun.

My cock stood to full mast, making me wince as my zipper stabbed me. *Fuck, I'm in trouble.*

How could something as familiar as sharing breakfast with these people suddenly turn into one of the most erotic moments of my life?

The table hadn't changed.

The garden and deck where we sat outside hadn't changed.

The only thing that had was me.

I now knew, in explicit detail, what Neri's fingers felt like around me, and I knew what mine felt like deep inside her.

My cheeks heated, and I grabbed the peanut butter, passing it to her.

Our fingers grazed.

We froze.

My skin erupted in goosebumps.

Flashbacks of last night worked through me.

She'd promised that we'd be civil and act no differently around her parents. We'd sat outside the front door in the idling Jeep, formulating rules on how this would work.

Rules that I'd hastily come up with as she'd tried to kiss me goodnight. I'd planted my hand over her lips in horror, glancing at the windows where Jack could be peeking. "Anyone could be watching, Nerida. What happens between us, stays between us. Okay? You can't tell anyone. Not yet."

She'd scowled and licked my very sensitive palm.

I'd jerked away and fisted the steering wheel. "I mean it. You're seventeen. You're still in school. Jack and Anna will never forgive me for this."

"I'm of legal age for sexual consent, Aslan. They can't stop us."

"They can kick me out."

"They won't when they realise you're in love with me."

"It was their one stipulation, Neri. They kept me safe and hidden, lying on my behalf, supporting me and giving me a job...as long as I kept my distance from you." I glowered at the slightly-run-down, very well-loved house that'd been my prison and sanctuary for the past five years.

The very real threat of being kicked out of it made my stomach tangle.

"That made sense when I was twelve and you were sixteen. Those four years between us mean nothing now."

"I've still gone behind their back."

"No, you finally followed your heart." She smiled softly. "And I followed mine."

"We won't tell them until after you graduate." I rubbed at the tightness in my chest. "We'll pretend nothing is going on until then."

"What does that have to do with anything?"

"You'll be almost eighteen. You'll start your degree in marine science. We can maybe get our own place." I pinched the bridge of my nose, seeing all the complications that would unfold from choosing this. Choosing us. "You'd have to sign a lease on your own, of course, and we'd have to make sure I wasn't listed on any bills, but...I think we could live together. At least, I hope."

"We could just stay here."

I threw her a look. "You expect me to live in your parents' garden even when I'm forty?"

She smiled. "I can't wait to see you forty."

"Have a fetish for older men?"

She shivered. "I have a fetish for you."

I groaned and readjusted my swollen flesh. "Fuck, you have to stop. Go inside and go to bed." I narrowed my eyes. "And before you ask...you're going to bed. *Alone.*"

"Spoilsport." She pouted deliciously. "If we're honest and tell Mum and Dad that feelings are involved and not just fucking, they won't kick you out."

I stiffened as my heart hammered. "I'm not fucking you."

"Not yet you're not." She leaned across the gearstick and cupped my still-hard cock. "But you're going to. Regularly, I might add. In fact, I can safely say, we might as well stay naked, Aslan, because I'm never going to want to stop." She laughed under her breath. "Perhaps when I'm eighty, I might finally have my fill of you, but until then, be prepared to be ravished nightly, daily, and very, *very* frequently."

I was literally one stroke from coming again.

Pushing her hand back to her side of the car, I groaned and looked at the ceiling. "*Bana ne yaptığını biliyor musun?*"

"What did you say?"

I squeezed my eyes closed, desperately trying to remind myself why I couldn't drag her into the backseat of Jack's Jeep right in front of her family home. "I said what the hell are you doing to me?"

Her face softened with affection. "I could ask you the same question." Her hand sneaked toward me again, rubbing against my straining zipper. "Let's find out, shall we?"

I jolted and saw fucking stars.

Panic filled me that Jack might wonder why Neri hadn't gone inside yet and come to investigate. My hips rocked into her hold, all while I forced myself to grab her wrist and pull her electrifying hand away. Fear that I'd lose her before I'd even claimed her made my voice colder than I meant. "Promise me that we won't…go that far…not until we have your parents blessing."

"What?" Her eyebrows shot into her chocolate hair. "After what we just did in the park? After how much I want to do it again? No." She crossed her arms. "No way. I'm not waiting, Aslan. I've waited long enough."

"I'm not saying I won't touch you…when they're not around. I'm not saying that I won't kiss you, but…" I growled under my breath. "I won't be able to trust myself around you if I fuck you, Nerida."

"Why?" she breathed.

"Because just having my fingers inside you has made me insane. Once my cock has been inside you…" I winced. "I won't be able to function doing anything else."

Her cheeks pinked. "I'll come to your room tonight. We'll finish what we started—"

"No. Absolutely not. You're forbidden from coming to see me. Ever."

"Now that's just ridiculous. I've come to see you many times."

"And each one of those times you had no fucking idea how close I was to shoving you against the door and burying myself inside you." I wiped my mouth as a wave of sickness crested. "Obviously not when you were twelve but…the past couple of years. You've not made my life easy. Or my nights."

She stilled. "Would you find a release on your own after I left?"

I swallowed hard. "Most of the time, I wouldn't have a choice."

"Me too," she whispered. "I'd burn so badly after visiting you that I'd slip into my bed, open my legs, and—"

I slapped my hand over her mouth again. "Finish telling me that story when I'm free to touch you. Not here. Not in full view of whoever might be watching." Dropping my hand slowly, I murmured, "Please, Neri. Just…give me time. We'll figure this out, okay? We have to do the right thing. We've already admitted how we feel…the rest can wait."

She moaned and squeezed her legs together. "Speak for yourself. I can barely breathe with how much I want you."

"*Seni seviyorum*, Neri."

Her eyes glowed in the night. "I love you too."

"Now get inside and pretend this never happened."

She'd obeyed me and had gone to bed, but neither of us was very good at pretending. The very air sparkled between us. It was both thick and foggy, sharp and slicing. Just being around her made my entire body hum to her frequency, begging me to touch, to kiss, to fuck.

Thank God Jack was absorbed with his news this morning, Anna had her headphones on learning a new phrase, and Neri was minutes away from going to school.

If I could get through today working on *The Fluke* and not give away just how fundamentally I'd changed, then we might be able to do this. We might be able to sneak around for a few months. We might be able to be together and not ruin the generosity, friendship, and kindness that Jack and Anna had given me.

Because when I told them that I'd broken my promise, I wanted it to be on bended fucking knee with a ring in my hand. I wanted Jack to know that I was in love, heart and fucking soul, and I wasn't breaking his rules by loving Neri; I was begging him for the chance to keep her in this life and the next.

Neri: *You're on one of my favourite parts of the reef. I'm highly jealous.*

Swiping back my sweaty hair and adjusting my sunglasses, I smiled and hit reply.

Me: *Stop stalking me.*

Neri: *If you cared, you would've deleted the app.*

Me: *I like being able to see where you are. Least I can ensure you're still where you're meant to be. How's school?*

Neri: *Boring. I love science. I'm in love with biology. But chemistry can kiss my ass.*

Me: *I'd like to bite your ass.*

Neri: *Only if I get to bite yours.*

Fucking hell.

My mouth went dry as I did my best to keep our texts respectable and not swerve straight into pornography.

Me: *No more talking of biting and behave yourself, Nerida Taylor. Don't set your class curtains on fire again.*

Neri: *That was an accident. The Bunsen burner was totally at fault.*

Me: *Only because you put it on the windowsill instead of blowing it out.*

Neri: *I'm never telling you my secrets again.*

Me: *I have a pretty big secret…want to hear it?*

I glanced around the sun-sparkling deck of *The Fluke*. Jack and Anna were about to appear from down below, ready for the last tray of lab-grown coral that they were planting. Sapphire and her pod of dolphins had played in our wake and even a shark had cruised on by, its fins slicing silently through the water.

Five years, and I still hadn't forgiven the sea, but I had learned to appreciate its merciless beauty.

Neri: *Oh, tell me. Better yet…show me.*
Me: *I'm not sending you a picture.*
Neri: *Why? Is it a picture of how hard you are for me?*
Me: *We're deleting these messages the moment we're done here, but yes, if you must know.*
Neri: *Now who's misbehaving?*
Me: *You're a bad influence on me.*
Neri: *Pretty sure you're the one who started this. The moment you kissed me at the bar….*
Me: *You're fully to blame for calling me your boyfriend…I liked it far too much.*
Neri: *Do you want to be my boyfriend, Aslan?*
Me: *No.*
Neri: *No? What the hell is that supposed to mean?*
Me: *It means I want far, far more.*
Neri: *God, if I was there, I'd show you how far you could have me.*

Fuck.

I shuddered.

Pain flashed through my cock as it bruised itself against my zipper.

My shorts had been a torture device all day. Every inch of this boat carried memories of Neri, and I couldn't stop thinking about her. Couldn't stop remembering her in skimpy bikinis. Couldn't stop myself fantasising about smearing her perfect skin with suncream or the way she'd glitter with seawater as she climbed from the sea.

Biting my bottom lip, I shoved my palm over my painful erection. Fuck, if it didn't deflate before Jack and Anna resurfaced, I'd have to wrap a hoodie around my waist.

Neri: SENT A PHOTO

I swallowed hard as I stared at the most gorgeous girl I'd ever seen. Taken quickly, probably as the teacher had their back to the class, the focus was a little blurry, but Neri's smile made my stomach hurt with just how much I fucking loved her. Students milled behind her on long desks, beakers and test-tubes littered the tables, and she blew me a kiss, her shirt slightly gaping, her necklace twinkling.

Fuck.
Me.
I shouldn't be this obsessed.
I shouldn't feel this level of need.
I was destroyed at twenty-one.
Utterly ruined by an Australian girl in a country where I wasn't permitted.
The sound of bubbles and the woosh of oxygen escaping a mouthpiece

wrenched my gaze to the side of the boat. Jack shoved his mask to his forehead, staying afloat with well-practiced kicks of his fins. "Hey, mate. Got that final tray of coral for me?"

Shit.

"Yep, of course." Keeping my hips averted as much as I could, I marched to the table where the specialised tray of baby coral waited. Spiky ivory, subtle pink, and soft greens of new coral looked so innocent in their carefully sealed seawater capsules.

Neri would've loved to have been here, helping.

Stop thinking about her. For once in your damn life.

Doing my best to keep my hands steady, I secured the main lid so they wouldn't float away, then carried the coral to Jack. Dropping to my knees, I passed the tray carefully, my hands dipping into the ocean before he claimed it.

"Cheers." He grinned but then studied me a little closer. "You okay? You're a little flushed."

"Am I? I feel fine. No problems." I sat back on my heels, hiding what his damn daughter had done to me. "Everything all good down there?"

"Yep, going swimmingly." Studying me a little more, he frowned. "Get in the shade, Aslan. You don't look so good." Yanking down his mask, he balanced the tray on one hand, inserted his oxygen mouthpiece, and sank beneath the surface.

I fell back onto my ass, breathing hard.

Pulling my phone from my pocket, I typed.

Me: *Delete this thread as soon as you read this and stop sending me photos. I was seconds away from coming in my shorts, and your bloody father appeared. I must look insane. He told me I'm flushed. That's your fault, Nerida. Your fucking fault that I really, really need to come. Your fault that I'm going out of my mind with lust for you.*

Neri: *So come. They won't know.*

Me: *I am not jerking off over the side of the boat. With my luck, your parents would see my goddamn sperm floating past them.*

Neri: *OMG, you just made me laugh out loud in class. How about this...next time we're on the boat together, I'll get on my knees and you can come on my tongue. I'll swallow all your evidence and lick my lips while doing it.*

Me: *Holy fucking hell. How did I not know you were this dirty?*

Neri: *Because you refused to see me. But now you do. And I'm free to give you everything.*

My heart collided with my ribs, making me trip into the shade and fall into the chair.

Me: *When you get home from school come to my room, unsuspiciously.*

Neri: *Oh, I'm actually being given permission to step inside your domain now, am I?*

Me: *Come to me, Neri. I'm going to show you just how hard that photo made me and you're going to put me out of my misery.*

Neri: *Your wish is my command. See you soon, Aslan.*

With trembling hands, I deleted the thread of messages, saved the innocent-enough photo, and threw myself into work.

Chapter Thirty-Four

ASLAN

(*Moon in Bulgarian:* Luna)

SHE DIDN'T KNOCK.

Why would she?

She'd never knocked in the past. She'd always marched in as if she owned me, not caring I'd be scribbling in my sudoku books or later playing with numbers in different languages. That felt normal. Familiar.

This felt taboo and deliciously new.

Launching off my bed, I stalked to her as she turned and closed the door.

She gasped as I grabbed her shoulders, spun her to face me, then slammed her against the same door she'd just closed. The only barrier between us and her parents who were laughing in the garden, sharing a twilight drink before heading inside to eat dinner.

"Don't move," I whispered. "They can't see us through the Perspex windows if we stay here."

She opened her mouth to reply, but I planted my hand over her lips. "And don't make a fucking sound, do you hear me? Not one cry. Not one moan. You do, and I stop. Immediately."

Her eyes flared as her nostrils widened for breath. The innocence of her school uniform added another layer of sin.

I stared into her, drinking her in, allowing my body to flash with all the heat and hardness that I'd battled today.

Slowly, her eyes darkened, and she nodded.

Dropping my hold, I collapsed on her.

My mouth slammed to hers.

She sucked in a breath as her arms looped over my neck, and her hands fisted my wind-tangled hair.

I groaned—breaking my own rule—as she pulled hard, yanking me into her, forcing me to kiss her brutally hard.

Our lips bruised.

Our teeth clacked.

Our tongues fought and hunted, licked and slipped.

I was fucking starving for her; it seemed she felt the same hunger. She attacked me as violently as I attacked her. Our kiss utterly savage and out of control.

We'd gone from hello to almost climaxing in a heartbeat. But I couldn't slow it down. I couldn't stop. I didn't *want* to stop.

Her leg hooked over my hip.

I hoisted her a little higher, wedging my cock in that perfect wet spot between her legs.

Her hips pulsed against mine.

Mine replied with a torturous rock that had lust dripping down my spine.

"More," she whispered into my mouth. "I want to come like this."

"How? With me dry-humping you like a dog?" I wrinkled my nose. "I can do better than that—"

"I want us to come together. I want to feel you come against me. Wait…" Pushing me away a little, she unbuttoned my denim shorts, unzipped me, and palmed my raging cock. My black boxer-briefs strained; the waistband pulling away from my skin as my painful erection did its best to escape.

Without a word, she shoved my shorts to mid-thigh. Leaving my boxers on, she dug her fingers into my hipbones then pulled me forward, slotting me right back where I'd been.

Only this time…

The only obstruction between us were two feeble pieces of cotton.

Both damp with desire.

Both steaming with need.

I felt every fucking part of her.

My world swam. "*Fuck*, Neri." I kissed her hard. I licked her and worshipped her, growing utterly drunk on the musky scent of her arousal. "I wish you'd changed before coming to see me."

Her kiss-bitten lips quirked up. "You don't like my school uniform, Aslan?"

"You've made my life a living hell because how can I hug you chastely now? How am I supposed to ever forget how you look, pinned against my door, your nipples poking through your shirt, and your pussy begging for me?"

"And you say I'm the dirty one."

I grinned. "I did tell you, you're a bad influence."

"I'll have you know I'm forcing myself to obey your rules. I'm doing my best to behave."

My hips pulsed into hers, making her eyes roll back. "How is this you behaving?"

"I didn't shove your boxers down. If I had my way, you'd be inside me right now. And I'm not talking about your fingers."

"Neri—"

"Enough words, Aslan." She rocked her hips forward, stroking me with every inch of her. "Didn't you say I had to put you out of your misery? Well...put me out of mine."

I lost the ability to breathe as I looked down at where we were joined.

The white of her underwear had turned translucent with her desire, revealing the dark shadow of her pubic hair and the utter drenching of her need.

How was I supposed to survive this girl?

She would kill me.

Of that I was absolutely certain.

"You sure?" I kissed her nose. "I could use my hand—"

"Like this." Her eyes hooded as I rocked upward. "God, *exactly* like that."

My heart hammered a tribal rhythm as I gave in and let instinct ride both of us.

It wasn't a conscious decision.

It was primal.

I thrust into her.

She rocked over me.

We dry-humped like two crazy creatures, trying to climb inside one another, doing our best to reach that pinnacle with just the friction of clothes and desperation.

I kissed her harder, deeper.

The door creaked a little as we fought to get closer.

We kissed because we couldn't not kiss but also to gag us from every explicit roar, every shivering moan, and every guttural cry swelling inside us.

Our warring tongues kept us silent.

Our kiss seduced and drugged us. I lost every thought, every fear as I rode Neri against the door that her father had installed for me.

Grabbing both her wrists, I shoved them above her head, trapping her with one hand while my other dropped to her chest.

Her back bowed as I cupped her.

Her heart charged beneath my touch as I pinched her nipple.

Her lips slipped under mine, tingling with connection.

I'd always felt a unique kind of power between us. An awareness that crackled in the air whenever we were too close; a sixth sense that made my blood burn whenever we touched.

But this was on a whole new fucking level.

The magnetic pull I felt toward her exploded from its soft suggestion to blistering belonging. I was hers. Fuck, everything about me was hers. I couldn't have fought it if I tried.

The moment she'd found me on that broken piece of boat, this was inevitable.

Just like she'd said.

I hadn't just drowned in her, I'd inhaled her, and what I'd told her last night was terrifyingly true.

She was my air in a world full of oceans.

She was my dream in a nightmare full of death.

She was my sun in a night full of fear.

And I kissed her as if I'd collapse to her feet and stop breathing. Because I would. I wouldn't survive if I lost her. If they found out where I was hiding and took me...*fuck*.

Riding her harder, my thoughts scrambled.

I gave in to the burn.

Crackling power crashed down my spine, centred between my legs, and made my toes curl. "I need...I can't stop—"

"Me too." She tried to get free from my wrist lock, but I held her tight.

I pumped against her pussy.

Her quiet cry of absolute surrender made my heart smoke, bones melt, and a rip-roaring release to spurt up my cock and drench my boxers.

I shuddered as I came.

I choked her with my tongue, silencing her moans as she jerked against me, again and again, her release lasting longer than mine. I opened my eyes, watching the final throes of delirium wring her dry.

My chest swelled with love.

I tripped evermore harder for her.

So beautiful in body and soul. So strong and brave and good.

I couldn't stop wave after wave of absolute adoration filling me to the brim.

There were so many things I could say. So many things I *should* say. But the only words that came to mind were: "*Benimle evlen.*"

I froze.

Shit.

"I didn't mean that. Fuck, I only meant—"

"What did you say?" She blinked with a sated smile. She trembled and quivered as I released her wrists and pressed my forehead to hers. I could lie, but I wouldn't. I'd spoken those words because I was so full of love. I meant those words because I never wanted anyone else, and I didn't need time to tell me that.

I'd had time.

I'd had five years.

I *knew*.

Pressing my lips to hers softly, sweetly, I kissed her like I hadn't kissed her before. Nothing fast, nothing fierce. I did my best to show her how much I cared and cherished her.

"I said…" I kissed the tip of her nose, catching her dilated eyes. "Marry me."

For a moment, she didn't move.

A horrible chill gusted down my spine.

But then her knees buckled, and she fell into my arms, pressing her cheek to my pounding chest. "You don't have to ask me, Aslan. I already did. The very first moment I saw you, my heart said yes. I've just been waiting for you to catch up."

My arms lashed brutally hard around her.

She hugged me back.

We stood glued together until our breathing evened and the shared wet patches of our release became sticky.

"Aslan, Neri! Dinner's ready." Anna's kind voice sailed through the door, making me blush.

Shame for what I'd done and fear of how this would end made my pulse skyrocket.

Pulling away, I ran my fingers through her hair. "You look like you just got fucked against a door."

"I got dry-humped against a door. But next time…I think we should get rid of the underwear."

I shook my head and let her go. "Not until you've finished school and I can tell Jack just how much you mean to me."

Glancing down at my semi-hard cock and the very obvious stain, I suffered a sudden wave of shyness. "Because if he knew what I just did to his daughter, he wouldn't just kick me out, he'd turn me into the authorities himself."

Brushing down her uniform skirt, Neri smiled and opened the door.

I flung myself onto my bed, tossing the blanket over my lap. "Shit, Neri."

"Don't be late to dinner. You know how that irks Dad. Oh, and I expect you to give me a well-deserved dessert afterward." With a sexy, evil little grin, she dashed around the pool and vanished into the house.

I collapsed onto my pillow with her scent in my nose and a stupid smile on my lips.

Chapter Thirty-five

NERIDA

(Sea in Welsh: Môr)

"AND THAT WAS HOW THE SNEAKING AROUND started. For all Aslan's rules that he wouldn't touch me unless my parents were away; for all our promises that we wouldn't be stupid, we were stupid."

I smiled, my heart so full and light in my chest.

God, I'd give *anything* to go back to that brief moment in time when we tripped and crashed into each other. It was as if the past five years of emotionally falling meant our bodies had a lot of catching up to do.

I caught Margot's wide-eyed stare.

I smiled with all the smug satisfaction I'd floated on back then. "We literally couldn't keep our hands off each other. He was all I could think about, dream about. When he touched me, I knew bliss for the first time. I'd never experienced the exquisite joy of feeling another's soul before."

"What do you mean?" she asked softly.

"I mean…that raw spark between us. That stinging hum whenever we hovered our hands close but didn't touch was more than just our bodies connecting, it was *us*. The part of us that exists within our bodies and our minds. The part that's immortal and destined to find its missing half, no matter what shell it wears in this life."

"Forgive me for saying this, Nerida, but you're nothing like what I expected." Dylan cleared his throat, looking slightly uncomfortable.

"How so?" I asked.

"Well…you come from a science background. You are trained in facts and tangible data. You created Lunamare out of sheer determination and mastered technology that exists thanks to brilliant leaps in building innovation—thanks to what *you* envisioned. Yet you seem…"

When he didn't go on, I sat forward a little, interested to see where he was going with this. "I seem?"

"Well…*opposite* of that, if I had to choose a word. You seem…spiritual instead of scientific."

"Aren't all achievements in this world created by spirit? Van Gogh often said he dreamed his paintings and painted his dreams. That is what I did, Dylan. Nothing in this world has been created without first being a thought, a spark, a hope."

"Forgive me if I overstepped." Dylan spread his hands. "I'm merely trying to understand how you created something that no one else has, yet can speak of Aslan as if he was your—"

"Soulmate?"

"Well...yes. As a woman of science, surely you don't believe such phenomena exist."

I leaned back and linked my hands. "I was wondering when this question would arise. So allow me to put it frankly. I believe the world we see is not the only world that exists. To believe so is to believe in our own egoic importance. I believe there are many worlds and many paths, and we only have to *listen* to know that. I'm proud to sit here and tell you that yes, I do. I do believe in soulmates and intuition. I've always felt there was something bigger than me. I don't believe you can free-dive under the sea with creatures that look so alien to our land-dwelling eyes and not realise there are so many different realms in one. We are merely animals, Dylan. As a race, that was where we went wrong. The day we removed ourselves from the animal kingdom was the day we believed we were better.

"And we're not. For example, to a dolphin, I am deformed. To a crab, my pink skin is unprotected. To me, the mere concept that I could exist in this world and not find my other half is unthinkable...and because I believed that...I made it true."

My voice softened. "The day I fished Aslan from the sea and knew he was irreversibly mine, it wasn't childish whimsy. It was the strongest knowing I'd ever had. I used to be very intuitive as a little girl. I would follow nudges that felt so real, only for life to dull those nudges. It took effort to learn how to listen again, but I can honestly tell you, with as much scientific proof and assurances as I can, that Aslan just felt different.

"His kisses made me vibrate inside, and I often felt as if I could fly out of my body and explode into light. His whispers of how much he loved me, how much he'd longed for me, had the power to make me sink into a velvety kind of darkness where everything became achingly intense. And when he touched me...truly touched me as a lover would...nothing was between us. Not flesh, not blood, not bone. We were linked on a level that frankly terrified me.

"After all, I was seventeen. I'd slept with one other boy who had no gift at making me feel such things. I cared for Joel, but I never truly understood how sex between two people could erase who I was and make me become something so much more. And...for all my passionate promises that I knew what I was getting into by falling into Aslan's arms...I didn't. Not really."

"Did that scare you?" Dylan asked gently. "That depth of connection?"

"Oh dear God, yes." I chuckled. "I'd lie awake at night with my heart suffocating at the thought of losing him. I couldn't concentrate in class without wondering what he was doing. I could barely hold a conversation with my parents at the dining room table without shouting how deeply I was in love and how desperate I was to make him mine."

"And he asked you to marry him." Margot sighed. "On the second day you finally began your romance."

I chuckled again. "Some would say that was far too soon."

"I wouldn't." Margot clutched her pen. "I'd say love was speaking, not societal expectations."

"I'd say the same thing."

"So...what happened next?" She bounced in her chair. "Did your parents find your texts? Did they walk in on you with his hand up your skirt?"

I grinned, reliving those dangerous days. "We were diligent about deleting our texts and did try our best not to be entirely stupid. However, those first two weeks were the hardest. I wasn't lying when I said we literally couldn't keep our hands off each other. We teased each other by day with texts and innocent-enough photos, exploded in each other's arms the moment I was home from school, and then spent the rest of the evening with my parents as if nothing ever happened.

"I look back now and honestly don't know how my parents never noticed. Sure, we thought we were being sly. That the barest of hand holds or lingering looks went unseen. We thought we were invisible whenever Aslan would take the rubbish out, and I'd follow under the ruse of helping. We wouldn't return to the house for ten minutes, flustered and red-lipped, unable to wipe the satisfied smirks off our faces."

"How on earth did they not call you out on it?" Dylan asked. "I have a son. He's fifteen and just learning about girls, but I can already pick out his horny face from his innocent one."

I laughed. "It helped that Aslan wasn't a new addition to our household. He'd laid a well-planned siege on gaining their trust with every plate he washed and every chore he completed. If he was spotted going down the corridor to my room, it was probably to place the freshly folded laundry on my bed, not to ravish me against my door. If he lingered in the lounge after my mother and father had gone to bed, it was because he was watching TV, not because he threw a blanket over my lap and sent me to heaven with his fingers.

"You see, the day Aslan saved me from drowning was the day he was given the ultimate faith and trust from both my parents. He could do no wrong in their eyes. I knew my dad kept trying to pay him extra for all his help around the house, and it only increased Aslan's mystical worth when he refused."

My face fell as my heart fisted. "I truly wish we'd just told them after those first few weeks. I knew in my gut that my parents would've come around after the initial shock had worn off. They would've seen how deeply Aslan cared for me. How tenderly he touched me. How his words would dry up and his body would sway as I walked past him.

"It wasn't just teenage lust driving our midnight fumbling and hastily snatched kisses. It was true love. Everlasting love. A love that lasted their entire lifetime. A love that allowed me to read their epitaphs at their funerals with the wisdom of what they had shared themselves."

"When did your parents pass away?" Margot asked gently.

I sighed with a twinge of sadness, but it was long enough ago now that I'd accepted they'd had an amazing life, shared most of it together, and got to see all my successes before they went on their next adventure.

"My father passed when he was eighty-nine. My mother a year after…almost as if she didn't want to stay without him."

My thoughts turned inward, mulling over my own life and mortality.

I understood my mother.

I understood her more than she'd ever know.

Swallowing away the quick pinch of heartache, I smiled at the reporters and threw myself into the last few months of joy before facing the coming despair. "After those first few weeks of drowning beneath years' worth of denial and copious amounts of desperation, we managed to restrain ourselves…just a little. We'd fall into each other's arms when I came home from school and again before we went to bed. If it was raining, I'd pretend Aslan was helping me with my math homework in my room—my parents were fully aware of how gifted he was when it came to numbers. If the stars were shining, I'd slip into the pool and practice my breathing. Aslan was a permanent feature on one of the boulders as he sat with a stopwatch, timing me, coaching me, and my parents saw nothing unusual that he now slipped into the pool with me instead. With the underwater lights turned off, they couldn't see where he touched me underwater. They didn't know how hard it was to keep from crying out as he pushed aside my bikini and—"

I cut myself off with a chuckle. "You can fill in those blanks yourself. This is an autobiography, not an erotic memoir."

Margot giggled. "Don't stop on my account. I'm loving every second."

Dylan rolled his eyes. "I think I should've left you two ladies to it. I have a feeling the content on this recorder would've been a lot raunchier if I wasn't here to rein you in."

Margot nudged his shoulder with hers. "I can always come back for the bonus chapters once Neri has given you the skeleton story. Can't I, Nerida?" Her eyes glowed with eagerness, so much so that I couldn't spoil her fun.

"Of course. If you want to know where Aslan's very skilled fingers went, I'm not shy in telling you. We're all sexual creatures, after all."

"Oh, goodie." She smoothed down her dress. "It's a date."

Sadness did its best to seep over this gift of remembering, and I clung to the past a little harder. "So…there we were, two very turned on, two very eager young lovers, doing our best to stay sane even though each encounter and every release left us more and more frustrated.

"No matter how much I begged or how much I teased, Aslan refused to sleep with me until I finished school. He wanted time to figure out how best to tell my parents. He was annoyingly loyal to them. I think he believed that finishing school would mean I'd left behind my childhood, and it wouldn't seem so twisted that the boy who'd been living in our garden was doing his best not to defile their very innocent, very virgin daughter.

"Which was silly, of course, because my mother knew I'd slept with Joel. I'd told her. She was the one who regularly checked on me to make sure I took my pill and drilled me on the importance of condoms. In a way, I was more worldly than Aslan. He was twenty-one going on forty, but his body was stuck as an oversensitive sixteen-year-old."

"Ah, I wanted to ask about that." Margot's cheeks pinked. "Did he…um, you know. Was he always sensitive? Even as he got older?"

I winced a little, trying to cover my reaction. His sensitivity had made me love him all the more, yet I wished he hadn't been cursed with such awareness. It only made what he went through that much worse.

"He remained who he was." I left it at that. I didn't tell her why a single stroke to his skin from me was the best thing in the world to him, but a single touch from another was the worst nightmare he'd ever endured.

That part would come later.

For now, enough darkness crept on the horizon without jumping straight into the horrors ahead.

Just for a moment, one tiny precious moment, I let memories sweep me away, indulging in secrets I couldn't share with the reporters. The way Aslan dropped to his knees one night when my parents were down the road at the neighbours. He'd laid me on the couch, then used his tongue to make me come. Joel had never done that, and I was as inexperienced as him as he whispered against my centre how to pleasure me. His eyes had burned me from between my legs as I'd run my hands through his bronze-frosted hair, whispering the words 'harder, slower, deeper' until those words slipped into moans, and my cries of ecstasy were silenced by his arousal-wet fingers over my mouth.

That was the first time he gave me more than his hand or his clothing-clad body against the door. It drove us into another realm of insanity, and I grinned as I recalled the first time I repaid the favour.

"What are you thinking about?" Margot asked with a huff. "It looks like something delicious, and you're not sharing."

I chuckled and relaxed against the pillows. "Oh, it was delicious alright."

"No fair."

"Don't worry, I'll share the rest." I glanced at Dylan, and the light in my heart dimmed. "I'll share everything but…" I struggled to find the right thing to say. "What I'm about to share won't be easy to hear."

Margot froze. "What? Why?"

Dylan understood, giving me a terse nod. "We're entering the territory of bad things."

"We are. I understand if you'll eventually edit out what I'm about to tell you, but I promised I'd tell you the truth, and this is a part of it."

Dylan reached for the microphone. "Do you want me to turn it off? I can just take notes."

I deliberated for a second before shaking my head. "To be honest, if you can't handle the next part, then you definitely won't be able to handle the rest, so it's probably best to keep recording. That way you can make the choice if you want to stay and hear the end or leave and finish early."

"You have my word that we will stay and listen…for all of it." Dylan gave me a sad smile. For the first time, I wondered what grief he had in his life to commiserate with the very mentioning of mine.

A connection grew between us that wasn't there before, and I smiled. "Thank you, Dylan."

Pulling out a fresh notepad from his satchel, he clicked a pen and quirked an eyebrow. "Ready whenever you are, Nerida."

"I suppose I'll begin by saying, please see me as I am now. See the successes I've had with Lunamare. See me sitting here, old and weathered with so many blessed memories. And take comfort that I survived, I thrived, I triumphed."

"Oh, God…my heart is already hurting," Margot whispered.

And that was the last thing I heard as I gave myself over to the past and prepared to survive all over again…

Chapter Thirty-Six

NERIDA

AGE: 17 YRS OLD

(Sea in Vietnamese: Biển*)*

"WHAT'S THE WORD FOR SEA AGAIN?" I glanced at Aslan behind my sunglasses, bubbling with joy to be on the water with him and not in a stuffy classroom.

Four months.

Four long, frustrating months of his hands and his mouth but nothing else.

School was almost over.

I'd already applied and been accepted to the James Cook University for my Bachelor of Marine Science. I didn't let myself think that it was almost six hours away and would require me to stay in Townsville for three years.

I'd miss my home, my reef, my dolphins, and my parents.

But most of all, I'd miss Aslan.

Unless he comes with me.

I couldn't see him *not* coming with me.

We'd get a place together, just like he said. We'd use the money he'd saved from working for my parents, and I'd get a part-time job between studies. If and when he ran out of funds, then…?

Who knows…perhaps he can get a job where they don't ask questions and pay under the table.

I hated that the deeper I fell into Aslan and daydreamed of our future together, the more scared I became as my eyes opened to adult things. We needed somewhere to live, a career to sustain ourselves, healthcare if we got sick, and documentation to get married.

We were so lucky that Aslan very rarely got sick. I had a sneaking suspicion it was from all the vitamin D and sunlight we received as a family on the open water. Apart from a couple of colds during the rainy season and a bout of stomach flu, he'd been healthy and happy for years.

But it just takes that one time…

A broken bone.

A serious illness.

And then he'd end up in the hospital, not able to provide a name, a Medicare number, or give any explanation on how he came to be here or where he'd been staying.

Stop thinking about what can go wrong and focus on what's right.

I shook myself out of my funk and blinked at the stunning day before me. The ocean glittered turquoise. The sun beamed gold. The scent of salt and squawk of seagulls made my heart overflow as Aslan caught my gaze and murmured, *"Deniz."*

"And because no one asked me, the word for sea is *mare* in Latin, *hǎi* in Chinese, *laut* in Indonesian, and *meer* in German." Mum finished yanking up her wetsuit, kissing my dad on his cheek as he came over and zipped her up.

"Show-off," he muttered, slapping her neoprene-covered butt.

"Give me another one." Mum laughed.

Aslan chuckled where he sat at the table beneath the shade sail, tapping in whatever data the sonar pinged from where my father had placed it below. "You're going to run out of languages soon, Anna."

"Oh, I don't know. I'm still getting the hang of yours."

"You're almost fluent." Aslan gave her a genuine smile, and my heart burst. "I'm beyond impressed."

"Can't have you living with us and be ignorant of your culture, can I?" My mum blew him a kiss. "Your language is now our language because you are one of us."

Aslan stiffened. He blushed. "You have no idea what that means to me."

God, I did.

For so long, Aslan had held back his love as if he was being disloyal to his true family. But over the years, he'd fallen for my parents as much as he'd fallen for me, and as I stood there, with my father and mother and love of my life, I fought tears at how perfect it all was.

My parents adored him.

He was already practically their son.

Why couldn't I tell them? Right now? Tell them that Aslan would be mine for the rest of my life. That we were fooling around directly beneath their noses, not because we were horny and stupid, but because we were happy and finally found.

My feet moved of my own accord, and I wrapped my arms around Aslan from behind.

He froze in the chair, shooting a wide-eyed look at my parents.

"Seni seviyorum," I whispered into his ear, giving up one of the few phrases I knew in Turkish. *I love you. I love you. I love you.*

Standing quickly, Aslan laughed as if I'd said something unimportant and headed toward the cabinet where litmus test strips and beakers lived. "*Ay.* That's the word for—"

"Moon," my mum jumped in. "*Luna* in Latin, *yuèliàng* in Chinese, *bulan* in Indonesian, and…damn, I forgot what it is in German." She didn't look at us oddly. She didn't narrow her eyes at me hugging Aslan because it wasn't anything out of the ordinary. Even Dad hadn't raised an eyebrow because it was familiar, acceptable, *right.*

Frowning at Aslan, I put my hands on my hips. The strings from my black bikini tickled my fingers. "I didn't ask what moon was in Turkish."

"Yes, you did." He shot me daggers with his stare. "That was what you whispered just now, remember? You said without the moon and the sea, we would never have met."

My heart hiccupped.

Just like I'd had a slightly out-of-body experience when I'd first met Honey and she'd mentioned her brother, the gay architect, and how he wanted to create a community safe from all disasters, and I'd said he'd have to live beneath the sea for that, I had another one.

He's right.

Without the moon guiding the people-smuggler to shore and the storm that knocked them off course and the sea that carried Aslan to me…we would never have met.

My knees almost buckled at the thought.

To think he might've stayed in Turkey, and I would have grown up in Australia, and we would've existed our entire lives without ever knowing who we belonged to.

"Thank goodness for the *ay* and the *deniz* then," I murmured.

"For the *luna* and the *mare*," he whispered, his eyes locking onto mine and making the world drop away. "I'm not grateful it took away my past, but I am grateful it gave me you." He cleared his throat, looking worriedly at my parents. "All of you. I'm grateful for all of you. Not just Neri."

"Ah, Aslan." My dad strode over to him and scooped him up in the biggest bear hug. "You're gonna make me cry, mate."

Aslan tolerated the hug before forcing a smile as Dad let him go. "You all set?"

"All set. We're just going to investigate the report of illegal spearfishing. Apparently, some punks have been shooting starfish all over this reef and leaving them to rot."

"Assholes." Aslan crossed his arms.

"I would've used a stronger word, but that one works too, I guess." Striding toward the cage where scuba tanks and gear remained safe on voyages out to sea, I watched in silence as Dad shrugged into his tank, tightened his weight belt, and then carried Mum's to her and strapped her in.

Once they were ready, Dad gave me a stern look. "Do we need to go over the rules again, little fish? No freediving with that monofin. Not on the reef. No trying to cut up loose nets and save any doomed turtles until we return. And no giving Aslan a heart attack by holding your breath for days. If you must swim, stay on the surface where he can keep an eye on you."

I rolled my eyes. "I'm not twelve anymore, Dad."

"No, you're much worse because you're seventeen and think you're invincible." Mum laughed under her breath. "Anyway, be good. We shouldn't be too long."

Not looking at Aslan, I smiled as innocently as I could. "I'm not planning on swimming today, anyway. Might sunbathe for a bit. I've lost my tan with all this 'being trapped in a classroom' nonsense."

"Put cream on then. Byeeee." Mum secured her mask and her regulator, then fell backward off the side of the boat. Dad followed her, their bubbles dispersing as they sank below the crystal water and became black blobs on the sea floor.

Only once I was sure their equipment worked correctly and they had no reason to resurface for a while, did I push away from the side, and stride with as much sensuality and invitation as I could toward Aslan.

"Neri…" He jerked where he sat on the plastic chair. His eyes hooded as he drank in my barely covered body, lingering on my breasts and the necklace he'd given me twinkling in the sun.

"Behave. I beg you with every bone in my body…please fucking behave."

"Oh, I'll behave. I'm going to be such a good girl. So very, *very* good."

He scrambled upright and backed into the scuba cage. "Your parents are only a few metres away."

"With a wall of water between us. They can't see or hear us."

"They could come back at any moment."

"Guess we better be quick then."

He gulped and held up his hand as I stopped within touching distance. The cage rattled behind him, blocking any chance of escape. "Don't."

My fingers toyed with the strings on my hips. "Don't what?"

For all our fumbling and touching and coming and licking, he'd never seen me fully naked. Never stripped me to nothing, just in case we got walked in on.

And there'd been plenty of those close calls.

Frantic kisses cut short because my dad called us. Illicit touches wiped hastily on clothing because Mum's footsteps sounded down the corridor. We'd been playing with fire these past four months, and I was wound up, frustrated, and beyond fucking ready to take the next step.

"You know what."

"I do." I shivered as lust made my skin prickle. "I do know what. But I don't think you do."

He swallowed hard again, his voice strangled. "What don't I know?"

"Well, I have a little problem."

"What problem?" His eyes changed from trapped to worried. The depth of his concern and caring for me made me suck in a breath and fall all over again. "Are you okay?"

"I have a little debt. A debt that I'd very much like to pay back. Right now." I licked my lips, deliberately running my tongue slowly, ensuring he became transfixed by my mouth. "It shouldn't take long…in fact, I'm guessing you're going to rather like this favour and will finish fairly quickly."

He groaned. "Stop trying to embarrass me. I can't help that you twist me inside out and turn me all the way on. I've gotten better. I can ride you into two orgasms now before I give in—"

"Oh yes. You're very, *very* generous."

His eyebrows knitted together. "I don't like your tone or how close you are." Planting his hand on my sternum, carefully keeping his fingers off my tingling breasts, he tried to push me back.

I refused to budge, keeping him imprisoned by the scuba cage.

"Damn you, Neri." He breathed hard, sweat glistening on his temples that had nothing to do with the sun. "I'm begging you, *aşkım*. Keep your damn bikini on, cover yourself in suncream, then go and jump overboard."

I snickered. "That's a first. Encouraging me *into* the sea instead of out of it."

"If it means I can survive today without screwing everything up, then I'm all for it."

"Would you come in with me?"

His eyes shot black. "I'd love nothing more than to come *in* you." He groaned, then pinched the bridge of his nose, doing his best to behave. "But coming in anything else? No chance."

"Well, then…I suppose I don't have a choice but to refuse your command." Dropping to my knees, I blinked up at him as my hands landed on his waistband. "In fact, I have no choice but to submit myself entirely to you in another way."

The groan that fell from his lips made my toes curl and wetness gush between my legs. "Fucking *hell*, Nerida."

His hands landed on mine as I popped his button and tried to unzip him. "We *can't*."

"We can. If we're quick."

"But what if they appear and see?" His eyes darkened and he bent over me, fisting my loose hair. "What if your father returns and sees his daughter with her mouth on my cock and me pumping like a maniac down her throat?"

I trembled. "God, Aslan. Just let me—"

"No."

My breasts ached. My clit throbbed. There was no possible way this was not happening. "I text you that I wanted to do this, remember? The day you told me how hard I made you and how close you came to jerking off. I said I'd suck you dry and swallow every drop."

His guttural snarl had my heart stopping then leaping headfirst into a fire.

Dropping his head, he smashed his mouth to mine.

Tugging on my hair, he dove his tongue past my lips and practically choked me with how savagely he kissed.

I relished in the position. In the power he had over me. The way I bowed at his feet and he curled over me as if he'd protect me from everything. Everything but himself. His hands yanked and his mouth devoured; I unzipped his shorts and pulled his hard cock out from his tight boxer-briefs before he had enough restraint to break away and haul me to my feet.

"Not here."

I panted quickly. "You can't stop this now. Look at the state you're in."

"I'm not saying no to your mouth, *canım*."

I melted all over again at the term of endearment. He'd been slipping a lot lately. Using Turkish words that meant my love, my beauty, my angel, and of course, the one he said had lost all meaning yet still meant my life, my soul. Mum had overheard him last week as we'd pulled bags of groceries out the back of her car. I'd caught her stare and prepared to blurt the truth, but she just squeezed my hand on the way past, cupped Aslan's cheek as if hearing him say such an adoring word made her happy, then vanished into the house.

Aslan and I had finished taking in the groceries and then 'happened' to need to run an errand in town. He'd snatched Dad's Jeep keys, given me the hottest look of my life, then driven me to the same park where he'd fingered me for the first time and dragged me into the thickest part of the trees.

He'd swallowed my cries as he made me release all over his hand.

I'd gagged him with my tongue as he came all over my leg, jerking himself off to the racing speed of our very horny hearts.

"You're saying yes?" I whispered, desire flushing every part of me.

Not replying, he took my hand and dragged me tripping and skipping into the captain's cabin. He didn't stop. Pulling me down the steps to the small kitchenette, table, and bench seating where he'd been placed, unconscious and broken when he was sixteen.

Letting me go, he paced the small space, his chest rising and falling, his cock spearing out the top of his tight shorts.

He looked like a caged lion fighting his true nature.

"Aslan...relax." I went to him.

He leaped away from my touch. "We better hurry...if we're gonna do this."

"Do you *want* to do this?" I asked, sudden worry clenching my heart. I'd thought he'd worship me for this. I wanted to blow his mind and make him realise he could never live without me.

He laughed tormentedly, then looked at the ceiling. He muttered something in Turkish, his tone riddled with the temper I knew so well. Marching into me, he clamped shaking hands on my shoulders. "Are you seriously asking me if I want you to give me a blowjob?"

I blushed but nodded. "Yes. You don't seem all that keen."

"I wonder why that is." He smirked. "Your father and mother are—"

"Away. That's all we need to know. And you're the one who wants to keep sneaking around. They'd be fine with us. I know they would be."

"Dammit, not this again, Neri. You finish school next month. Just…wait. Okay?"

"Fine." I kissed him and cupped his cock. "Only if you shut up and let me suck you."

"You are seriously going to fucking kill me." He hissed between his teeth as I pressed my thumb on the tip, making him jerk like he always did.

"What…what should I do?" His voice turned gruff and gravelly. "Should I stand, should I—"

"Sit on the bench, push your shorts down, spread your legs, and stop talking."

"Fucking hell, *hayatım*." He shuddered on the spot, pressing his hand over mine where I fisted him. "You're going to make me come just with your commands."

"Do you like being told what to do?"

A black look settled over his face. "I'd rather tell *you* what to do."

"Oh yeah?" I blinked and licked my lips. "What do you want me to do, Aslan Avci?"

His gaze shot with darkest lust as he palmed my breast and shoved his thumb beneath my bikini. Toying with my nipple, he pulled me forward and whispered in my ear. "I want you on your knees. I want you to open wide. I want you to suck me like I'm the best fucking ice-cream you've ever had, and then I want to watch my cum dribble out of your lips so I can smear it…right here." He ducked and kissed my cleavage.

"*Fuck.*" My knees buckled.

He chuckled and caught me. "Not here, Neri. Kneel at my feet over there." Sweeping me into his strong arms, he carried me to the bench. Putting me back on the floor, he hooked his thumbs into his boxer-briefs and shorts, then with a delicious glower, pushed them down to mid-thigh. With a worried but desire-demented look at the staircase, he sat down, spread his legs the best he could, then pointed at his pre-cum glistening cock.

It stood to full attention. Thick, roped with veins, far bigger and girthier than any ice-cream I'd ever had.

"Suck me. Please fucking suck me before my heart stops."

Praying to everything holy that I'd hear the clunk of fins and scuba tanks on the deck above, I pulled my bikini top to the side, exposing my nipples to him, then collapsed to my knees.

His jaw clenched and his growl echoed like a snarling beast in the small cabin. "This right here. I will never forget how you look, Neri. I'm going to dream of this moment. Worship this moment. Realise that this was the moment that, even if I never earn the freedom to truly marry you, my soulmate got on her knees and—FUCCCKK."

My tongue shut him up.

I fisted his hard, hot length and opened wide.

I sucked him down.

I licked him hard.

And Aslan lost every ounce of his sanity.

With every inch I swallowed, he became more and more animal.

He forgot to be silent or that he'd begged me not to do this.

His hips drove up, his mouth opened wide, and his heart hammered so hard, I heard it over the thundering of my own.

A thrill of power shot down my spine.

My blood exploded with supernovas.

I gave him everything I was. All my inexperience and eagerness. All my desire and obsession.

And he gave me everything of his.

I didn't care that I'd done this once before.

I didn't think about sucking Joel or that I'd merely done it because that was what girlfriends were expected to do.

This was incomparable.

I hadn't swallowed with Joel.

I'd hidden the fact that I'd found it rather gross.

But there was nothing gross about sucking Aslan.

And I knew why.

I knew why I sucked Aslan as deeply and as wildly as a porn star. Why I twisted my wrist and stuck my tongue in his slit, all while my other hand dove between his legs to cup his balls that always went so tight and hard just before he came.

Every gasp he strangled made me thrill.

Every grunt he gave made me shiver.

The warning ripple of his cock and the faintest taste of salt only made me suck him harder.

I *adored* making him unravel.

I wanted to do this again and again because this was Aslan. And he made me feel so seen, so cherished, and so fucking *wanted*. The way his fingers clenched and unclenched in my hair as if he was a beast with claws. The way his hips drove up to meet me, forcing his length down my throat, gasping for air as I hummed around him. The way he trembled and quivered, and his hands fumbled at my chest, fisting my breasts, bruising me with his lust.

I wanted to touch myself.

I needed to come as badly as him.

I threw myself into making him explode so he could repay the favour.

Rising higher on my knees, I positioned myself directly above him, held the base of his pulsing cock, then sucked up and down, up and down. I fucked him with my mouth, and he didn't stand a chance.

"Fuck. Ah, fucking *fuck*—" He writhed beneath my control. His thighs bunched. He fisted the bench cushion on either side of his legs. He held on as I pumped him into my mouth. His breathing rattled and sweat poured down his face.

"I'm gonna—I can't. Fuck, I'm—" His hands landed on my head, shoving me down, holding me deep as wave after salty wave splashed onto my tongue.

He didn't stop holding me down as he drove his length past my lips again and again, forcing me to drink every drop, doing my best not to gag.

As suddenly as he'd snatched me and held me down, he released me. "Ah, shit. Neri. I didn't mean…fuck, what did I do?" Pulling me off him, our eyes locked.

His were wild. Stars sparkled in his black depths. Volcanoes freshly erupted in his soul, bleeding lava and brimstone, etching his face with pleasure.

Never looking away from me, he ran his thumb over my burning bottom lip, scooping the remainders of his release from the corner of my mouth.

I shivered as he captured the white fluid, staring at it as if he couldn't quite believe what we'd done. And then he did exactly as he promised. Pressing his thumb to my exposed nipple, he smeared it over me. Branding me with his cum. Wedding me in the most perfect primal way.

"Neri…I…" Plucking me from the floor, he dragged me onto his lap. "Fuck, I love you. I loved you when I couldn't have you and now that I've been lucky enough to touch you, I'm so fucking terrified. How am I supposed to survive without you?"

His cock still stood to full mast; I whimpered as it rubbed against my clit. I hated my bikini. I couldn't catch a proper breath. My skin scratched, and my heart smoked, and I couldn't focus on him, drowning, drowning, *drowning* beneath agonising desire.

I wriggled on his lap, rubbing myself with a keening noise against his cock.

"Ah, *meleğim*. That oversensitivity you're feeling? That's how you make me feel with a single touch." Pressing the softest kiss on my swollen mouth, he reached between my legs and pulled aside the crotch of my bikini.

I moaned, waiting for his fingers to sink inside me. To put me out of my aching, burning misery.

But he froze as he stared at how wet I was, drinking in my folds. His gaze dropped to his glistening cock and his gorgeous face turned hard. Without a word, he wrapped an arm around my hips and pulled me up.

My wetness smeared along his cock.

My mouth parted in shock. "Aslan…?"

"Sit on me. Fuck me as hard as you want. I'm done. I'm so fucking done."

My heart smashed through my ribs and flew into the sky. I could barely kneel over him as he reached down, angled his length, and gasped.

Finally.

Finally.

I trembled as I sat down.

I cried out as the first breach of him blew my soul apart.

I turned to liquid. Burning, churning liquid as I went to sit and—

"*Fuck!*" Aslan ripped me off him, tripped upright, then stumbled across the small cabin with his shorts down, cock out, and me in his arms. Shoving me in the tiny bathroom, he yanked up his shorts, ran a manic hand through his hair, then spun to face the stairs. "Hi, Jack."

"Aslan, hey."

With a cry, I closed the bathroom door as quickly and as quietly as I could. My father's voice sailed through the thin wood. "Neri swimming?"

"Upset tummy, I think. Just came to check on her." Aslan's footsteps moved away from the door, his voice strained. "How are the starfish?"

"Worse than we thought. Just came back to grab the bags to clean up. Bastards slaughtered thousands."

"If Neri is up to it, I'll see if she'll swim down and help."

"Thanks. That would be great. See you soon."

My father's splash as he fell back into the ocean didn't settle my heart.

My straying hand between my legs didn't help.

Even as I brought myself to a very unsatisfactory orgasm, tears ran down my cheeks because I'd been so close. *We'd* been so close. We could've slept together, and if we had, there would've been no more sneaking. No more hiding. The day Aslan fucked me was the day he'd have no choice but to tell my parents about us because I *knew* him.

He wouldn't sully me without confessing how he felt.

He would be honest with them that we were together.

Everything would be out in the open, and we could move on…

Yet the way he hid me so quickly…

I hated that a twinge of shame and something dirty coiled insidiously through me. He'd hid me so fast…almost as if he never expected to face the consequences of what we'd been doing.

Don't…

Don't go there.

That's not true.

So why did those nasty thoughts grow louder, tangling and tormenting worse and worse, trailing behind us in the water like toxic oil all the way home?

Chapter Thirty-Seven

ASLAN

(*Moon in Ukrainian:* Misyats')

I PACED MY SMALL SALA-BEDROOM.

Images of Neri on her knees, her lips stretched around my cock, her grunts as she took me as deep as she could manage—

Fucking hell...

Dragging my hands down my face, I gritted my teeth.

Think!

The way Neri licked her lips after I came—

Not about that.

About what you're going to do about her parents.

We'd been *so* close today.

So close to having sex.

So close to being caught.

I was surprised we'd lasted four months with just a few close calls. I was even more surprised we'd both lasted four months without snapping and giving in to sex, regardless of my strict rules not to fully cross that line until I had Jack's permission.

But today...when she'd swallowed and I'd smeared her with the last droplet of my desire, and she'd looked at me with that aching, breaking darkness that I knew so well, I couldn't help it.

My body had had no intention of deflating. It'd been inside her mouth. It knew what it'd been missing now and desperately wanted to be in other parts of her. And, *fuck me,* that first tight, wet, insanely hot sensation of her as she sank over my tip had blown my ever-loving mind.

But then I'd heard a heavy thump.

Followed by a grunt of effort.

I'd moved before I fully understood it was Jack back on the boat.

And thank hell, I did. Otherwise, I doubted the rest of the day would've been as smooth. We wouldn't have all sat down for Nemo burger takeaways or been as calm and chatty around the outdoor dining table.

The entire time we ate dinner, my skin prickled with the electrical current constantly arcing between me and Neri. She'd done her best to avert her eyes from mine because every time she caught my gaze, we both froze. Both sucked in a breath. Both *burned*.

Not that Anna or Jack noticed.

Poor Neri was hovered over by her mother for the white lie I'd told of her stomach being off. And Neri had vanished into her room after dinner, almost as if she couldn't wait to get away from me.

I stopped pacing, looking at my door.

I want to see her.

We needed to talk about what *almost happened,* but…I didn't have the strength.

I couldn't get my cock under control and the rip-roaring lust between us was making everything so fucking dangerous.

I needed to tell her parents.

I needed to figure out how to march up to Jack and tell them…

Tell them what, exactly?

That I've been fingering their daughter for months? That I've had my tongue inside her? That she undoes me in ways no one else ever has, and she's mine now, not theirs?

How the hell was I supposed to say she now belonged to an illegal immigrant who had nothing to his name, no prospects, and no way of keeping her safe? In their eyes, I was taking their daughter from them for no valid reason whatsoever. I could just imagine myself confessing that I couldn't live without her. That I *needed* her.

Those reasons just made me sound so fucking selfish.

Even if Jack believed I was truly in love with Neri, and it wasn't a silly teenage fling, he'd still believe I had ulterior motives. Still harbour suspicions, even if he didn't say them out loud. He'd never look at me the same way again, and all that trust he'd given me would be ruined because, in his eyes, I let lust drive me into fucking the only girl available to me. I'd chosen the easy way by choosing Neri because I literally couldn't choose anyone else.

He'd throw all my own fears into my face because why *wouldn't* he think that? Why would he believe me that Neri was always meant to be mine? Why would he believe in fate—when I'd been fighting that same fate all along.

It'd taken me five years to admit that I was hers.

He'd be expected to accept it in five minutes.

And he'd most likely only see the obviousness: I'd pursued the only girl I could in this country, purely to get laid without being caught. Neri had proven she was good at keeping my status a secret. What was one more secret compared to that?

He'd think I'd strung her along to fuck her, and it fucking sucked that I felt that scorn myself. That even though I knew how Neri truly felt about me.

That I trusted what we had was *real*, it didn't stop my nightmares from whispering filth inside my head that I'd taken advantage of convenience.

He'll hate me.

Grabbing fistfuls of my hair, I yanked. Hard.

Sitting heavily on my bed, I bit my bottom lip and forced my mind to stop spiralling. If it took me all night to come up with a reasonable way to tell Jack why I'd broken my promise and touched his daughter, then so be it.

I'd find a way for him to see—

Show him…don't tell him.

I froze, my thoughts colliding.

My fear of his reaction came from him thinking I defiled his daughter, when every touch affirmed that I was hers in every way. I was a slave to her every desire and wish. A protector to her every terror and tragedy. A partner to her every hope and dream.

If he could see how much I cared. If he knew how much I would *always* fucking care, then he'd have no choice but to see past my shame and forget any concept that I'd stolen her for selfish reasons.

Propose.

I could propose to her, right in front of her parents. I could show them how much I loved their daughter, show them how much she owned me, body and soul, and let a ring speak far louder than words ever could.

But you can't marry her…not really. Not here.

My shoulders deflated, and I wedged my elbows on my knees, cradling my head. By showing Jack and Anna the depth of how deeply I needed Neri, I put them all in a terrible situation. In a declaration of love, I'd be binding Neri's fate to mine, ensuring she'd be the one interrogated for harbouring a refugee if I was ever caught. She'd be the one dragged through paperwork and fines and…*fuck, I can't do that.*

I could never take more from the Taylors than I already had.

My heart cracked and fissured down the middle.

So…where does that leave me then?

An awful whisper wriggled through my head. A whisper I wanted to tear into shreds before it could say…

Leave.

I groaned and pressed my knuckles against my eyes.

If I was honourable—if I wanted to do right by Neri…I would stop putting her in harm's way and—

"Aslan?"

My head shot up. Black stars exploded over my eyes from pressing my knuckles so hard into them. "Neri. What…?" I shook my head, willing my vision to settle. "What are you doing in here? I thought we said—"

"I told Mum and Dad that I wanted to practice my breathwork in the pool. I have water withdrawals." She wrinkled her nose. "They've been overprotective of me tonight after someone, not saying who, but *someone* said I had a tummy upset and that's why I stayed in the bathroom most of the day on *The Fluke*."

"It was better than telling them the truth."

"Was it?" She hugged herself, dragging my gaze down her pink beach-towel wrapped body. The strings of her silver bikini snaked around her elegant neck. "If we were just honest with them, we wouldn't have to sneak around. I wouldn't have to make up excuses about why I'm in the garden at nine p.m. visiting you. I wouldn't have to bite my tongue at the dinner table when I want to tell you how much I adore you. I wouldn't have to wonder that you're hiding us from them because you keep thinking it will end eventually, and if they don't know what happened right beneath their very noses, then you'll be able to continue working for them and living in their garden, even if you decide to break up with me."

"Fuck, Nerida." Leaping off my bed, I shot across the small space and yanked her into my embrace. "That's what keeps you up at night?" I chuckled, thinking of how different our thoughts were. I feared trapping her with all my instability. And she feared me breaking up with her...

I stiffened as the whisper that'd broken my heart came again.

You should leave.

You should *break up with her.*

To keep her safe.

My arms banded excruciatingly hard around her.

Never.

That was as impossible as suddenly breathing seawater.

And yet...

The entire reason I didn't want to be with her was because I didn't want the bone-deep knowledge that no matter how much I cherished her, I was the one person on this planet that could hurt her the most.

I could tear out the heart she'd so freely given me.

I could snuff out her life all because we were now one.

I would never do that intentionally but my situation...

I hugged her so hard, my biceps twitched with pressure.

Burying my nose into her hair, I breathed every salty, frangipani scent of her into my lungs.

She moaned and shimmied closer, feeling my anxiousness but not asking what caused it. She knew. She could read me so easily, with or without her knowing little nudges that always seemed to guide her right.

"Come swim with me?" she whispered.

I moaned into her hair. "I don't think I should be around you at the moment, especially when you're half naked."

"Please?" She pulled away, her ice-blue eyes welling with tears.

"Hey...don't cry."

"Sorry, I—" Stepping out of my arms, she sniffed and rubbed at her eyelashes. "I'm just tired." Her voice was sharp enough to make me wince.

"Are you angry with me about today?"

She went to shake her head but then nodded slightly. "I know I shouldn't be. I have no right to be. You did the only thing you could by shoving me in the bathroom but…"

"You're still unsatisfied."

She gritted her teeth and nodded. "I feel as if my bones are glass and my blood is on fire. I can't stop thinking about how you felt inside me. How the barest part of you felt more intense than anything I've ever known."

I wanted to ask if that was how Joel had felt when she fucked him. Out of the two of us, she was the one who'd been there, done that. But I didn't want to know. Didn't want her to have to lie to me and say I was different.

"We almost went too far today," I whispered. "We can't do that again."

Her eyes shot to mine. "What do you mean?"

"I mean…" *What do I mean?* "We got carried away."

"We're moving to the next step, Aslan. We're in a relationship. That's what happens in a relationship. Hearts get entwined. Minds get knotted. Bodies want to become tangled and—"

"We're not in a relationship, Neri."

She froze. "What on earth do you call this, then?"

I glanced through my hazy plastic windows at the house across the lawn. Jack and Anna were inside the lounge, the faint glow of the side lamp and TV revealing a relaxing Saturday evening. The windows were open, catching the faint muggy breeze.

They could hear…

"Keep your voice down." I pointed behind her to the door. "Let's go to the pool after all. I'll help time your breath hold and—"

"No. I think we should talk about this. Actually, properly talk. We've done everything else but that lately." Crossing her arms, she raised her chin. "So…talk, Aslan. If we're not in a relationship, what the hell are we?"

I braced myself against her rapidly building anger. "I don't think there are words for what we are."

"Bullshit."

"Neri…I don't want to fight with you."

"Then agree that this has grown into something we can't hide anymore. We need to tell my mum and dad and then we're free, Aslan."

"*Free?*" I laughed coldly, my own temper sparking. "How the hell are we free? Do you think I can magically conjure a visa to stay here? I'm not free, Neri. I haven't been free since my father boarded us on that godforsaken boat."

She trembled on the spot. "By your tone, you almost sound like you're blaming me for that."

"I'm not." I sighed with annoyance. "Of course, I'm not. I'm just saying—"

"That you want to keep fooling around and not tell anyone."

"I didn't say that. I merely think we've reached a point of no return, and before we step over that line—"

"The point of no return line." Her voice was deceptively soft. "The point that your entire future is hinged on."

My temper twitched into anger. "Well yes, when you put it that way. That point. It's a pretty big point, Neri."

"And you're now wondering if I'm worth stepping over that line for, is that it? You can either fuck me and deal with the consequences of what my parents think…or pretend nothing is going on. That we aren't in a *relationship*, and you can go on believing that you can exist this way—this hidden, non-happy way—for the rest of your life."

I glowered at her. "Once again, I didn't say that."

"I hate to tell you, Aslan, but regardless of us and what my parents will say, you can't keep living this way. You have no life of your own. You haven't left this garden in months. You work all hours. You say you're content with your language apps and math puzzles, but really…I think you're just scared."

"Scared?" My hands balled. "Of *course* I'm fucking scared. I'm *terrified*. I've told you that. I've told you why. I won't survive losing you, and all it would take would be an anonymous phone call to immigration—"

"I think your fear runs deeper than that." She huffed and raised her chin, her temper making a full ugly appearance. "You've never given yourself permission to *live*. Ever since you lost your family at sea, you've punished yourself for surviving when they didn't."

My heart stopped beating. "Careful, Nerida."

"You can't see what I do, Aslan," she seethed. "You don't know how much I watch you. How much I *understand* you. You've never dealt with your grief. You've never said goodbye. You carry their ghosts around with you so much, their darkness has infected—"

"Neri…I'd stop if I were you."

"Stop? Why would I? I think it's time someone forced you to see the truth."

"The truth?" I marched into her, clamping my hands on her bare shoulders. My fingertips stung from touching her. The undercurrent of awareness and need between us flowed faster than the tide. "The truth is—"

"The truth is you're stuck, Aslan. You let yourself have me only after you lost control. You made the *choice* to be with me, but when it came to you, I *never* had a choice." Her eyes dimmed a little. "And yet…even as I say that, I actually don't think you had a choice either. I think you felt that same inevitability. That same unfightable fate."

Felt?

Why is she using past tense?

"I do feel that way, Neri. I'm in love with you. You know that."

"But is it enough?" She sucked in a shaky breath as tears ran down her cheeks. "Is it enough to overcome the sadness inside you?"

"What the hell are you talking about? I'm fine—"

"I sense it, Aslan. Even when you're happy with me, a deeper part of you still doesn't believe you're worthy of happiness. You use this sala and our garden as a prison but really, it's your own heart trapping you."

I fought the urge to shout, keeping my voice at a harsh whisper. "You don't know what you're talking about."

"All of this talk of not wanting to cross the line with me…it's because you don't know how to cross that line with your own family. They're *dead*, Aslan. You're alive. You're letting the past steal your future and—"

I tore my hands from her and speared them through my hair. "I suggest you go before we say things—"

"No, I think I'll stay right here. Say what you want to say. Tell me what you really think in that depressed, despairing heart of yours."

My eyes shot to hers, hating that she'd sensed that no matter the happiness I found with her, it wasn't enough to fill me completely with light. I felt as if a part of my soul was still with my parents, sister, and cousin, rotten and tumbling over the seafloor, crushed by millions of litres of seawater, and kept trapped by the moon and storms.

"Why are you saying all of this?" I asked tightly. "What changed from this afternoon. We were—"

"What *changed* is that the moment you shoved me into the bathroom—"

"For your own protection!"

"The moment I stared at myself in the mirror—after making myself come from needing you so much, I might add—I had an awful epiphany. An awful epiphany that…I'm willing to fight for this. For us. I'm willing to tell my parents something they might not approve of. I'm willing to put everything on the line *for us*. I'm willing to be there for you if you're found out for overstaying. I'm willing to fight beside you to get you citizenship. I'm willing to move to your beloved Turkey with you if it means we can be together and…" She swiped at her quickly falling tears. "I don't know if you're willing to do the same for me."

Of *course*, I was.

Fuck.

"That hurts, Nerida. You know I'd do absolutely *anything* for you."

"Anything but tell my parents about us."

"I will. I was thinking up a way to tell them tonight before you barged in here and started yelling at me."

She narrowed her eyes. "If that's true, let's go tell them together. Right now. Hand in hand. Heart with heart. Let's tell them that we've been in love for years and have no intention of ever being separated."

"Just because we have no intention of being separated, Neri, doesn't mean it won't happen."

"Nope." She shook her head with violent denial. "When and *if* you get found out, I'll just come with you. They can't stop me from going to Turkey with you."

"*I* would stop you." I looked at her from beneath my brows. "I've told you before and I'll tell you again. You are *never* stepping foot in that country. You will never see the beauty of my homeland or experience the gorgeous people or the relics and vast history. *Never*, do you hear me?"

She scoffed. "Why? Because your parents thought Australia would offer you a better life? I've researched İstanbul, Aslan. I've been in forums online with people who love living in İzmir and Ankara and—"

"My home is stunning; I am not denying that. The culture, the people, the cities, and history…I miss it with every fucking part of me. But my parents weren't running from Turkey. They were running from—" I snapped my lips together.

Despite breaking one promise to Jack that I'd never touch Neri, I hadn't broken my other one. The very first one I'd made when he'd offered me homemade pizza and a chance at survival. He'd made me vow I would never tell Neri why I couldn't go home. That I would be tortured and butchered. He'd never asked me for details, and like most things about me, we swept my past and what I was running from under the proverbial rug.

But he knew I would die.

And I had no intention of scaring Neri with that awful truth.

It was enough that I had to carry that fear. The worry that deportation didn't just mean our life would be moved to a different country together…it would mean my death and her becoming a widow.

Her forehead furrowed as a dangerous spark appeared in her stare. "What are you running from? Finish what you were going to say."

"I can't." I crossed my arms. "All you need to know is, I need to stay here. With you. Under any and all circumstances."

"Any circumstances being, you're willing to live your entire life working for my parents, never rocking the boat, and putting all your dreams on hold?"

"You. You are my dream, Nerida. I don't need anything else."

"But you do!" she cried. "That's what this is all about, Aslan! You're sad. You're most likely depressed from not dealing with what happened. I can love you all I want. I can shower you with all my affection, but it won't heal you in the way you need to heal."

"Don't worry about me. I'll be fine—"

"But I *do* worry! Are you not listening! I worry that you might never tell my parents. That you think this is just a fling for me. Perhaps you're just biding your time until I go to university, and then you'll let me go as if we were just childhood friends who grew apart."

"I would never do that. I'll come with you—"

"And do what, huh? How will you earn a living? How will we get a joint lease? How will you buy a car or even *drive* that car, or go to the damn dentist for a check-up? How will you buy a TV that isn't with cash under the table?"

My anger turned to sickness. None of those questions were new to me. I worried over each of them like *tespih* beads in the dark. "I don't know, *aşkım*. All I know is I love you—"

"If that's true, then let's go. Right now." She held out her hand, her towel slipping to her waist and revealing perfect breasts barely hidden beneath silver Lycra.

I pinched the bridge of my nose and groaned. "Don't push me. Not tonight. I think we should let tempers cool and—"

"You came down my throat today."

My eyes shot to hers as I dropped my hand. "What...what are you saying?"

Fuck, she wouldn't tell Jack that...would she?

"Are you...are you *threatening* me?" I breathed coldly.

"I'm saying you've already come inside me and..." She suddenly sighed and looked at the exposed rafter and plywood ceiling. "God, I don't know what I'm saying."

"Like I said, tempers are high. We should calm down before we do something rash." Stepping into her, I tried to wrap her in a hug, but she backed away from me.

I sighed heavily. "Let's just go for a swim and—"

"Just tell me one thing." Looking up, she snared my eyes with hers. "One thing and I'll leave you alone. I know I need to sleep this off. I'll feel better in the morning, and I'll be mortified for how I've acted, but...I can't help feeling that something is wrong. A shadow that I can't banish until I hear from you that I'm imagining it."

My stomach churned, terrified of what her question would be. I nodded despite myself, needing to give her comfort when all I'd done was cause her pain. "Ask and I'll be honest."

"Did you want this, *us*, to happen?"

I winced, not prepared for such a direct, agonising question.

"Did you want to be with me, Aslan, or did you make a mistake kissing me at the Craypot that night?"

I froze.

I scrambled for the truth.

How could I tell her that I'd just been stopped by the police for a routine breath test and had come face to face with my terror of law enforcement and deportation? The thought of never seeing her again had done things to me I hadn't even acknowledged. And then I'd driven to her as a free man (for as long as that lasted) and watched her being hit on. And the moment she touched me, the moment she called me hers...all the fear I had of being taken and all the horror I had at her falling for someone else became a war I couldn't fight.

I'd tried to stop myself.

Even as I went to kiss her, my head had been screaming not to.

But my heart and body had taken the reins, and when our lips touched...that was it. That was it for the rest of my godforsaken life.

Stepping away from me, she shook her head with a soft gasp. "It was, wasn't it? A mistake?"

"It's not what you think. I never meant to kiss you, but it happened and—"

"And you wish it never did so my parents would never have to know."

"Stop putting words in my mouth. It was a mistake, Neri. I admit that. It was a mistake because I couldn't fight how I felt...I couldn't fight *you* anymore. But I don't regret it. Not for a single moment. I should. I should hate that I couldn't stop myself. By falling for you, I've condemned you to a life of misery."

I grabbed her elbows, holding her as she tried to escape. "If I get deported, that's it for us. There is no happy ending where you live in Turkey with me, do you understand? There are no second chances. This is our *one* chance. Here. In this country. And it fucking petrifies me because you're so brave and willing to fight for me, but you can't. I forbid it. You can't get your family tangled in the mess that I brought to your door, do you hear me? The only way we can have this is by staying hidden. I want to keep you, Nerida. But every damn day, I'm so incredibly aware of how easy it would be to lose you. How easily I could hurt you. How easily I could destroy you. And...that kills me because as much as I want you to love me as deeply as I love you, I'm only sentencing you to a worse fate the moment I'm caught and—"

"So you're saying all this—all this sneaking around and refusing to tell my parents—is for *my* sake...not yours?"

"No, I'm saying—"

"That you would change what happened, if you could."

"What? *No.* That isn't true."

"Isn't it?" Her nostrils flared as her gaze turned to a raging blizzard. "Look me in the eye and tell me that if you had the choice, if you had the self-control not to kiss me that night, you wouldn't have."

"Neri...I—"

"*Tell me.* Tell me the truth because that's the only truth I can see. You speak of love and forever, Aslan, but really, you're just waiting for reality to swoop in and steal everything. Just like what happened with your family. You expect that to happen again. You keep thinking I'm going to end up like them—"

"You *will* end up like them," I roared, shaking her and digging my fingers into her arms. "If I die, I'll take all the good pieces of you with me, Nerida, and I can't...I can't stomach that. I can't be responsible for making you feel the way I do every damn day. Feeling so lost and black and afraid."

Dragging her into me, I shook her. "You want the truth? Fine, the truth is, I wish I didn't have this need for you. I wish you didn't have this need for me. I wish we could've stayed safe and *apart* because now that we're together, nothing is safe, and I hate that I'm the one who caused it. I want to keep you protected, Neri. I want to love you until my dying fucking day but how am I supposed to do that when I'm the one putting you at risk of so much hurt, so much pain, so much grief?"

"You're not going to die, Aslan. Stop thinking you're being hunted by death just because it came for your family!"

My head rushed with images of my mother being struck by men. Of my sister screaming. Of my father on his knees begging for our lives. Of my uncle's mutilated body—

It would be so much easier to tell her. To make her understand that yes, I was afraid of death, but for a very good fucking reason. Instead, I grazed my nose against hers. "*Seni seviyorum—*"

"Let *go* of me." Shoving her arms down, she broke my hold on her and spun to the door.

"Where are you going?" I tried to snatch her wrist. "Don't go—"

"Don't worry, I'm not running to tell my parents. Our dirty, dangerous little secret is still hidden."

"Don't do that. Don't make it sound as if I wish we weren't together."

"Oh, so *now* you agree we're in a relationship? You tell me you love me and expect all of this to be forgotten?" She snorted and ran her hands down her face. When she glanced back up, her anger was pinched with pain. "Look, I'm sorry, okay? I need...I just need some space. Before I say or do something else I'll regret." Ripping open the door, she looked back, and I fell into her agony.

I winced at the way she looked at me. At the hurt I'd given her with the truth. The hope I'd crushed by refusing to tell Jack and Anna.

"I'm sorry, Aslan."

With that final whisper, she bolted down the three steps to the garden, flew over the steppingstones ringing the pool, and vanished into the house.

Every part of me screamed to go after her.

My heart flopped pathetically in my chest to *fix* this.

But...she'd asked for space.

I couldn't give her much of anything...but I could give her that.

For an hour or so at least.

With a trembling hand and a snarling heart, I closed the door and fell face first onto my bed.

Chapter Thirty-Eight

NERIDA

AGE: 17 YRS OLD

(Sea in Greek: Thálassa)

"MUM? DAD?" I FORCED MY LIPS into a smile, begging all my heartache to stay hidden. "You okay if I go see Zara?"

That question was a damn sight better than the statement I really wanted to say:

By the way, I gave Aslan a blowjob today. But don't worry. He didn't take advantage of me. We're in love...or at least, I think we are. He loves me, but he's not happy about it. Fun fact...he called me a mistake. Oh, don't kill him, Dad. I'm more than capable of doing that.

Biting back those confessions, I stayed stiff and aching on the threshold.

Dad twisted on the couch and looked at me standing in the doorway to the lounge. The potted ponytail palms, dotted around the white-tiled space, granted the perfect splash of green against the dark grey walls and weathered tan couches. "I thought you guys had a falling out when you broke up with Joel?"

"We did." I did my best not to fidget. "But...she's come around."

Oh, how I wish that were true.

I needed a female friend more than anything.

Mum shifted onto her knees and laid her arms and chin on the back of the couch, eyeing me up with her keen intelligence. "You sure you're not just using her name so we'll let you go gallivanting around town with another boy?"

I hid my wince. The only boy I wanted to go gallivanting with had just admitted everything between us was a *mistake*.

"No. I'm truly going to see Zara. I miss her, and I need her back in my life."

Mum's eyes softened like I knew they would. "You still think about

Sophie, don't you?"

Sophie.

My friend who I'd known was dying on the street, thanks to the strangest nightmare of fangs and claw. My friend who'd left a permanent mark on me.

"She's gone, Mum. I'm well aware of that."

"You don't still talk to her?" She raised an eyebrow, hinting she knew more about my little chats with a ghost than I thought.

"Not in a while." Those chats had helped me move on. I'd kept her close and denied her passing, but with each year and every conversation, I found it easier to accept she was gone, and eventually, I'd let her go.

Unlike someone I know...

Perhaps I could teach Aslan how to talk to ghosts because it was obvious he needed help. Help he couldn't ask for, and therapy he couldn't pay for.

"So...can I go?" I glanced at the large reef-inspired clock on the wall by the TV. Each number had a pretty anemone swaying through the digits. "It's only 9.00 p.m. I can bike to her house, hang out for a bit—"

I was going to say 'and be home before curfew' but...I didn't.

I didn't have the strength to stay here tonight. I needed a break. I needed to be far away from Aslan because I honestly didn't know what I'd do if he came to find me in the night. I'd probably either kill him or fuck him, and neither of those options was permitted.

I'd rather sleep on the beach with the waves whispering nice things and the stars keeping me company.

Smiling brighter, I lied, "She asked if I could stay the night."

"She did, really?" Dad frowned. "What about Joel? Won't he have a problem bumping into you in the dead of night when he gets up for a pee?"

"He's not living at home anymore." I crossed my arms and leaned against the wall. "His socials say he's in Indo training for the Billabong Pro Teahupoo in Tahiti next month."

"Oh, well, that's good, I guess. No awkward midnight oopsie-daisies."

"Yep. Phew." I laughed. It sounded strained to my ears, but Dad bought it.

With a grin, he ran his hand through my mum's hair, casually touching her like he always did, being affectionate without realising it. "In that case, go have fun. Spend the night, get your friend back, and as long as you're home by ten p.m. tomorrow night, I won't send out the search party."

"Gee, thanks."

"You okay, love?" Mum asked quietly. "You don't seem quite yourself."

"I'm fine, Mum. Honest. Bit nervous about seeing her, after everything that's happened, but I'm also super excited to have her back in my life."

"Well, I hope you slip right back where you left off."

"Night, little fish. Keep your phone on so we can call you if needed," Dad muttered, his attention already back on whatever Netflix program they'd chosen.

Mum studied me for another terrifying second before she blew me a kiss and waved. "Bye, sweetheart. Have fun."

"I will."

Darting back to my room, I quickly changed from the slouchy grey jumper I'd thrown on over my bikini after I left Aslan and slipped on a slinky ombre maxi dress that looked like a sunset. Vibrant orange on the chest before bleeding to blue, navy, purple, and black by my toes.

Running a brush through my wind-swept hair, I nodded approval in the mirror as my naturally dark hair shimmered with gold highlights from the sun's bleaching. The salt always gave it volume and wildness, giving me the perfect boho chic that took no time at all. A chic that Zara always fought so hard to achieve with hairspray and teasing.

My heart clenched.

Zara.

She had no idea I was going to see her.

Why would she? We hadn't spoken since the week I broke up with Joel and I tried to talk to her at school. She'd thrown her Coke bottle at me and screamed in my face. She'd yelled at everyone listening that I'd broken her brother's heart and was now a whore and a pariah.

I'd kept my distance after that.

But...then Aslan happened.

Falling in love happened.

Being told I was a *mistake* happened.

I needed to talk to someone. *Anyone*. But when I stalked her on Facebook, intending to send her a message begging for her forgiveness, I'd noticed she was having a house party. Her parents were overseas again, which meant...she was free to play.

She'd be happy on vodka.

She'd be high on hosting a great party.

A face-to-face meeting would be better than an impersonal message. If I grovelled hard enough, surely, she would let me be her friend again?

Catching my eyes in the mirror, I straightened my shoulders, applied a liberal amount of mascara, then grabbed my house keys and phone, and slipped out the front door.

My ears rang with how loud the music was.

If she didn't turn the songs down, the police would soon visit for noise control.

Clutching my phone, I weaved around the familiar large house that I'd practically grown up in the past few years.

A lot bigger and grander than mine, Zara's parents had prided themselves on renovating a two-story brick monstrosity into something super fancy with openable skylights, large glass windows, sliders onto wraparound balconies, and white carpet in the bedrooms.

For all the size and pristineness of their home, I preferred mine with its shabby loved exterior, natural pool, and walking distance to the beach. This house was trapped in the maze of suburbia, perched on its patch of manicured grass, not permitted to weather or decay.

Teenagers spilled on the front lawn and every room downstairs. Their chaos gave me access to Zara's house without having to announce myself.

Slipping through the front door, I followed the open plan living from lounge to movie room to another lounge before entering the cabinet-glossy kitchen. I searched for the gorgeous tanned skin and blonde hair of my friend. I recognised a few people from school but no one paid me any mind. No one asked why I was there or offered me a drink.

I skirted gossiping groups and narrowly avoided being squashed by a drunk dancing couple.

But still no Zara.

Stepping outside, the air clogged with sweet-smelling vape clouds. The glass roof and open-sided conservatory was my favourite part of Zara's home, and it seemed her guests agreed, all congregating en masse.

So many boys and girls. So loud with laughter and voices.

I weaved and ducked, finally finding who I was looking for.

My heart skipped, and a hopeful smile painted my lips as I drifted toward where she sat on the stone wall, cutting the grass from the flagstone pavers, providing a patio for the many strewn colourful beanbags.

She didn't look up as I held my floaty dress, careful not to get it close to the vaping teens or the ones playing a drinking game. Zara sat with a group of older-looking boys. Older than even Aslan at first guess.

A guy with shaggy dark-blond hair—perched beside Zara on the stone wall—was the first to catch my eyes. He did a double take and looked me up and down, running his tongue slowly over his bottom lip. His navy-coloured eyes twinkled with mischief.

I looked away.

I wasn't here for that.

I wasn't here for anyone but Zara.

Gathering all my courage, I sucked in a breath, and whispered, "Zara…"

She didn't hear me.

Of course, she didn't hear me.

Even out here, the drum and bass music made my teeth ache and ears ring.

The guy watching me chuckled and rubbed his palms on his faded jeans.

His grey button-down had some sort of Celtic design on the left breast pocket. Even sitting next to Zara, I could tell he was tall and well-built.

Looking past him, I once again focused on my friend.

She threw her head back, giggling dramatically at something the guy on her other side said. A guy with darker skin and black hair. She swatted at his arm in a flirt, her legs unfolding to turn more toward him.

The guy laid a possessive hand on her upper thigh. She licked her lips suggestively.

My chest tightened.

She had a boyfriend.

The way she swayed into him and whispered into his ear revealed intimacy that didn't come from strangers meeting at a party.

She had an older boyfriend and had moved on with her life...*without telling me any of it.*

A familiar giggle ripped my head up; my eyes landed on Maggie. A fiery redhead who'd always disliked me for being with Joel and had done her best to get close to Zara but never quite managed it. She stood with the group of girls that Zara and I often sat with at lunch and studied with for exams.

Seemed when I was kicked out, she was invited in.

With my stomach churning, I stepped closer to the two guys flanking Zara and dropped the hem of my dress. The vibrant sunset colours clashed with the outdoor beanbags and vape clouds, but I stood as bravely as I could, balled my hands, and said, "Zara."

Her head ripped up; her hazel eyes landing on mine.

Somewhere in the house, the drum and bass track finished, sliding into a more sensual trance song, giving a much-needed reprieve to my ears.

Crossing her arms and legs, Zara's body language went straight into defensive. She looked me up and down and sniffed. "What the hell are you doing here?" Her white teeth glistened in the fairy lights around the patio. "If you're looking to screw over my brother again, he's not here."

"I know." I kept my chin down and stayed as submissive as I could be. "I didn't come to see Joel. I came to see you."

"Why? What on earth makes you think you'd be welcome here after what you did?"

My eyes prickled with sadness, but I kept my voice steady. "I know I hurt Joel. And by hurting him, I hurt you. But—"

"You didn't just hurt him, you cow. You ripped out his fucking heart. Did you know he was planning on proposing to you next year? He asked me for advice on what ring you'd prefer and how he should do it. He wasn't joking about getting hitched, you know. It was real for him."

I froze. "I...I had no idea."

"Of course, you didn't. He wanted it to be a surprise. And you were too busy stringing him along and fucking someone else."

"What? I never—"

"Don't lie to me, Nee. You were caught kissing a guy the very night you dumped my brother at the Craypot! You were spied, red-fucking-handed with your tongue down some other prick's throat mere minutes after you kicked my brother to the curb."

"It isn't what you think. It wasn't just anyone. It was…" I bit my lip. Should I tell her?

Was it wise to tell my oldest, dearest friend—who was now my mortal enemy—about Aslan? But that was why I'd come. I wanted to tell her everything. I wanted her advice on what I should do next. I needed some outside perspective, and she was the only girl I trusted.

"It was who?" She snarled. "Spit it out. Go on."

Balling my hands, hoping to God I wasn't making a massive mistake, I murmured, "It was Aslan. The guy I kissed…was Aslan."

She cupped her ear dramatically. "Sorry, didn't hear that. You'll have to speak a little louder."

The shaggy blond-haired guy snickered. His stare never left me. He was far too intense and enjoyed my squirming far too much.

Stepping a little closer so everyone at the party wouldn't hear my sins, I repeated, "It was Aslan. He kissed me and—"

"Hold up." Zara stood, her manicured hand strangling the strawberry vodka bottle she was drinking. "You mean to tell me…you made my brother, me, and my whole bloody family believe you were in love with us—that you were going to be part of our future as my sister-in-law and Joel's wife—all while you were fucking the guy living in your garden *shed*?"

"No…that's not it at all. Aslan never touched me. Not until that night—"

"The night you dumped my brother. The night you had the *audacity* to drag him into a public place to shit on his heart instead of doing it privately at home?"

"I know I should've chosen somewhere else, but—"

"You were spineless." Her eyes narrowed with hate. "Don't tell me you were afraid of him, Nee. That you dumped him in public so he wouldn't hit you. Because if you even *whisper* a slander like that, I will bitch slap you so fucking hard you'll wake up in the neighbour's fire pit."

Tears stung my eyes. "Never. I would never say such things. Joel was kind and sweet and—"

"And far too good for you."

"He was. I agree. I know I didn't deserve him just like I know I didn't deserve you. I'll never stop feeling awful for what I did, but the pain I feel for hurting Joel is nothing compared to the pain I feel from losing you."

Zara stiffened.

The dark-skinned handsome guy beside her snaked his arm around her waist. "You making a play for my girl now? You changing teams, slut?"

I winced.

I looked at Zara, begging her to defend me.

But Zara merely smiled coldly. "So *that's* what this is about? You came here thinking I'd take you back?"

"I miss you."

"And you can continue missing me for the rest of your life for all I care."

I glanced around at the gathering crowd. The drinking games had stopped, the music had quietened; all eyes were on my public shaming as Zara smiled cruelly.

"Tell you what, Nee. If you miss having a friend so much, how about you go screw someone else's brother and see if they'll like you."

"I'm sorry!" I exploded, splaying my hands in surrender. "I'm truly, endlessly sorry. I know I broke your trust and I hurt Joel, but I need you, Zara. This thing with Aslan...I need your advice. I want things to be good between us again. I want to be able to call you at dawn and text you in the dead of night. I want—"

"You can't have everything you want." Zara marched right into me, stabbing her vodka bottle into my chest. "You hurt my brother. You lied to my face. Every time we laughed in the dark about how we'd grow old together and have our babies together and they'd all grow up with cousins in a happy, perfect life was a *lie*." Tears glittered in her gaze, hiding her hurt beneath her rage. "A lie you let me keep believing, all while you were fucking your family's hired help."

Her face twisted with a mixture of betrayal and fury. "I will *never* forgive you. You weren't there to pick up the pieces. You weren't the one who had to console your brother all while wishing you could pick up the phone to talk to your best-friend. You weren't the one who had to listen to your brother saying how in love he was and how excited he was for our future, all while the girl he was in love with was cheating—"

"I *never* cheated. Not once."

"Didn't you, though?" Her eyes narrowed. "The camping trip in Daintree. The first night when Aslan chased you down the beach after Rita kissed him and you kissed Joel...what happened, huh? You said he didn't touch you, but I don't believe you. Tell me the truth. Right here. Right now. Tell me what happened on that beach and who knows...you might earn my forgiveness."

I searched her face, my heart breaking at the hate glowing in her eyes.

If I gave her the truth, I'd lose her forever.

But I couldn't lie.

I'd never been good at lying.

Clasping my hands to stop them trembling, I said, "I kissed Aslan."

"Ah see! I fucking knew it—"

"I kissed him, but he didn't kiss me back. He said he'd never be with me in that way and—"

"And you used my brother as second best. I *knew* it. I knew you had reservations after that trip because Joel said you didn't kiss him again. So when you chased him a year later, I worried you were using him. But then he seemed so happy, and you seemed so happy, and we were all so fucking happy that I figured I was wrong. But it was all a lie. All of it."

"No." I licked at a salty tear as it ran down my cheek. "I love you, Zara. That isn't a lie—"

"You can keep your love, brother fucker." Her chin rose and she bared her teeth, her words like a dagger in my belly. "Now leave me alone, you whore. Go find another girl to befriend or a boy to fuck because we're done here."

With a fierce pirouette, she whacked me in the face with her hair and stormed into the house. Her boyfriend looked me up and down with scorn, clucked his tongue, then chased after her.

I hiccupped on a breath. Everything that'd happened today with Aslan. All my feelings and fears churned and crested until my knees trembled to run. Turning on my heel, I swallowed down a sob and went to bolt—

Only…

A strong hand clamped around my wrist.

I froze, blinking back tears as I glowered at the blond-haired guy. "Let go of me."

He pouted. "You're crying. Let's go get a drink."

"No. I'm going home."

"Not until you've calmed down. Come on." Not giving me an option, he dragged me around the beanbags and vapers and back into the house. The trance music had switched to another drum and bass track, making my blood pound in my veins.

My head hurt.

My eyes stung.

I wanted to leave so badly.

But he didn't let me go and dragged me into the kitchen, pushing aside some lingering people around the sink and yanking open the fridge.

Pulling out a bottle of Coke, he let me go long enough to head to the cupboard above the range, grab a mug, and pour some Coke into it. He knew his way around which hinted he'd been here before with Zara and her boyfriend. His back flexed beneath his shirt while he poured. Screwing the lid back on, his fingers disappeared into his front pocket for a split second before he spun, and his face cracked into a commiserating smile.

"Here." He passed me the coffee mug with a picture of a cat hanging off a branch. "A bit of sugar and caffeine will knock the shock right out of you." He shrugged. "Being called a whore and a brother fucker by your ex-bestie has got to hurt."

I took the mug automatically, my well-bred manners not giving me a choice. "Thanks."

"No worries." He shoved both hands into his back pockets and leaned against the countertop, his eyes never leaving mine. "Name's Ethan."

I looked at the fizzy Coke hissing in the mug. I wasn't in the mood for soda, and I definitely wasn't in the mood to talk to a total stranger.

The sea was calling my name.

A steady ebb and flow of the tide tugged on the salt in my blood, begging me to go for a moonlit swim where there were no boys, no girls, and no heartache.

Sapphire...

Dad would never know if I took *The Fluke* out and went to visit the dolphins. She'd listen to all my woes and make me feel better. Dad wasn't expecting me home until this time tomorrow.

The sudden sense of freedom—knowing I could go anywhere and do whatever I wanted for the next twenty-four hours—buoyed me enough to give a half-smile of thanks and raise the mug to my lips.

Ethan never took his eyes off me as I drank.

My skin prickled as a slow smile curled his lips.

He was handsome in a true-blue Aussie kinda way, but my skin didn't prickle, and my heart didn't flutter. He was light whereas Aslan was dark. He was broader whereas Aslan was lean and strong. He was young in the eyes, while Aslan carried centuries of hardship.

Lowering the mug, I went to place it on the countertop.

Ethan crowded me, pressing gently beneath my hand and raising it back to my lips. "Finish it. You need the pick-me-up."

A scared little nudge kicked my stomach, and I pushed my hand against his. "I'm fine." I looked at the dark popping liquid in the mug. "I drank half. That's all I need. I'm going to go home now."

"Ah, really? But we just met." He smiled so wide, I could've counted all his perfect white teeth. "Don't you want to party? My buddy Cooper is fucking your friend right about now. They're pretty wrapped up in each other, and I bet I could put in a good word for you. Better yet, if you spend the night with me, then she'd see it wasn't just her brother you were interested in and could drop her guard that you were gonna hurt him again."

I scowled and backed away. Placing the half-drunk mug down, I shook my head. "Thanks for the offer, but I'm just gonna go." Without waiting for his reply, I spun on my heel and weaved around the party-goers behind me. More people had arrived; the living room was tight with bodies.

I got to the dining room before fingers locked around my wrist again.

"Hey...where're you going?"

Pinpricks of fear. I turned to face Ethan. He grinned his huge grin, and his eyes sparkled with something I didn't like. "I told you. I'm going home."

"You should just stay here. It's safer than walking the streets alone."

"I know those streets like the back of my hand. I'll be home in ten minutes. I'll be fine."

"I could walk you—"

"I'm good." Yanking my arm out of his grip, I raised my chin. "Goodnight, Ethan. Go find Zara and your friend."

He sniffed and crossed his arms. He didn't speak as I left him in the dining room and cut through the snug. My heart hurt as my eyes fell on the slouchy linen couch. How many movie nights had I spent curled up with Zara under a blanket, watching rom-coms? It was those nights I remembered and wanted back. The nights of whispers and secrets and giggles. I wanted those rather than the nights when Joel started joining us and touched me under the blanket right beside his sister.

Sucking in a deep breath, my balance switched to sudden lightheadedness and I swayed into the coffee table. The small bronze elephant that Zara's mum had bought in Africa wobbled.

My hands shot out to steady it.

The bronze felt strange. Not cold like I imagined but fuzzy and—

My left knee gave out, dropping me to the thick cream rug. "Whoa...what the hell—?"

I swallowed, wincing at the sour aftertaste on my tongue.

I blinked, and the TV wobbled on the wall.

Get up.

Gritting my teeth, I pushed off from the rug, suddenly fascinated with how silky and soft the strands were. I accidentally stood on the hem of my sunset dress, sending me down again.

My head swam, and the music became excruciatingly loud in my ears.

Get up.

You need to go home.

Now.

Groaning under my breath, it took all my energy to clamber to my feet and stay upright. Keeping my eyes locked on the front door in the distance, I balled my hands and fought against the sick dizziness in my blood.

"Ouch..." I rubbed my shoulder as I bashed into the doorway of the snug. The barn door hanging on its black slider rattled, making me trip into the marble tiled foyer and—

"I've got you." Arms circled my waist, pulling me against hard muscle. "You're okay."

I blinked and struggled against someone tall and strong. The hazy swirl of a face looked semi-familiar. A guy I just met. A guy my instincts screamed to run from. My breathing became shallow, and I felt like I did when I'd held my breath too long. My stomach ached. My heart palpitated. My head swam and—

"I don't feel so well—"

"Let's get you somewhere quieter, huh?" Ethan slung his arm around my shoulder and took my hand with his free one.

"No…I need—"

"What you need is to lie down. Relax. I've got you." Clutching me to him, he gave me support as he guided me toward the sweeping grand staircase with its thousand shell chandelier that me and Zara had made. Months and months of beachcombing to find the shells and then months of hand drilling holes in each for the electrician to thread into a dripping LED masterpiece.

I struggled as he guided me up the first few steps. "No…I-I want to go home."

"I'll take you home when you can walk unassisted." He chuckled directly in my ear. "You're drunk."

"No. I-I didn't drink anything—"

"Yes, you did, remember? When Zara called you a brother fucker and a whore? You downed six tequila shots." His arm dropped from my shoulders to around my waist, practically picking me up and hoisting me up the thickly carpeted stairs. "You were a beast. Put them away like a maniac."

"No." I shook my head, my tongue smacking against the horrid aftertaste in my mouth. Wait…*was* that tequila? Had I done that? I hated tequila. I'd hated it ever since the night Zara and I raided her parents' stash and then threw up the following morning.

"It's okay, I won't tell anyone." His hand clutched mine as we reached the top landing. He pulled me to the left, toward Joel's and Zara's bedrooms.

I squirmed and shook my head, my feet tripping and stumbling, my heart racing and skipping. "Wait. I don't want to be up here. I'm not allowed up here anymore."

"It's fine. Zara's fucking Cooper in her room, which means…" Propping me against the silver-wallpapered wall, he opened Joel's door and grinned. "Your ex isn't here. You can lie down and sleep it off."

"No. I don't want to. I want to go home." I fumbled for my phone. "Call my dad…he'll…he'll—" I forgot what I was going to say, my mind skipping. I patted my dress, searching for my phone.

Gone.

Where…where is it?

"Joel will never know you were in his bed. You're fine." Dragging me inside, he closed the door and locked it.

The snick of the lock had always sent my heart racing when Joel brought me up here. He'd kiss me sweetly, then pull back his covers and wait until I'd snuggled in and removed my jeans and knickers before crawling in beside me and wedging himself on top.

I shuddered as memories fogged my brain. Being with Joel had been okay. But being with Aslan was thermonuclear.

The way I felt about him. The way the world caught fire whenever we touched.

He was incomparable.

Aslan.

My eyes welled as his gorgeous face with his bronze-streaked hair, achingly deep-dark eyes, and stern sexy expression popped into my head.

God, I should never have picked that fight.

What was I thinking?

I'd give anything to be with him right now.

"Please…" Tears beaded and rolled down my face. "I just…I just want to go home."

"You will. I promise. I'm just gonna take care of you, and then you can go home."

Dragging me toward Joel's neatly made bed, he threw me down.

The room spun. Nausea crawled up my throat. I bounced off the mattress and landed on my knees on the black rug. I moaned as the room spun; I very nearly threw up.

A hand landed in my unbound hair, yanking me upright.

I cried out, scratching at his wrists and bending backward from his yank. "Stop, *ow*—"

"You should've drunk the whole thing, you know. This would've been so much easier for you."

Letting my hair go, Ethan bent down and grabbed my elbows. Plucking me from the ground as if I weighed nothing, he tossed me back on the bed.

The familiar sights of Joel's room with his ocean bedspread, desk in the corner, and posters of surf champions on the wall, spun and dipped as stark, icy fear slammed through me.

The dizziness vanished for a moment.

My mind roared with self-preservation.

Run!

Launching myself off the bed, I bolted for the door. My hand connected with the knob; I fumbled with the lock—

I cried out as Ethan drove his hand against the back of my head, smashing my forehead against the wood.

My legs buckled.

The world went black.

I came to a second later, sprawled on the floor.

Pain.

Pain ricocheted through my skull; I crawled onto my knees. Pressing shaking fingers to my forehead, a single tear rolled down my cheek as I touched a throbbing bruise.

"Ah, see? Now look what you made me do," Ethan whispered, dropping to his haunches and brushing my hair back. "I didn't want to hurt you, you know."

I recoiled away from him, bumping into the side table where Joel kept his junk and surfing magazines. "What do you want? Why are you doing this?"

He didn't follow me.

His eyes crinkled as he smiled. He shrugged good-naturedly. "You're really fucking beautiful."

A full-body shiver rolled down my spine. The way his tongue caressed the awful compliment made me *terrified*.

"You really shouldn't tease a guy looking the way you do. This is as much your fault as it is mine, you know."

I bared my teeth. "You're a sociopath."

"Possibly." He nodded with a laugh. "I admit, I've even googled that shit 'cause I don't seem to work like the others. But…you know what? I don't care. All I care about right now is I'm hard as fuck, and you're not leaving this room until you help me out with my little—well, not little, I'm actually bigger than average—problem."

He sighed and pouted as if I was a bad puppy who'd peed on the rug. "Ah, oops. Guess my secret is out, huh?" His lips turned up. "You're not leaving until you spread those pretty legs, brother fucker."

I flinched. "Unlock the door and—"

"I'll be the perfect gentleman and give you a choice, how about that? You can finish the Coke I made for you. You can fly off into dreamland and enjoy it…or…you can just accept this is happening and get on the bed." He scratched his jaw. "If you'd just drunk all of it, you would've been asleep by now and wouldn't even know what happened."

I dry-retched and fought to stay conscious, all while black spots grew bigger and stars sparkled brighter. "Y-you drugged me?"

His smile hardened. His eyes turned sinister. "Well…you have to understand, my friend is with Zara now. I came to visit him from Adelaide, and he's all obsessed and shit. Says he's not coming home now that he's met 'the one'. I'm merely looking after his girl—doing something nice for him." He chuckled. "And the fact that I get to fuck you is just a bonus."

My heart ripped itself apart.

Aslan…

His face crowded my swimming thoughts.

Tears shot up my spine.

Why didn't I stay home tonight? Why did I think Zara would forgive me? Why had I picked a fight with Aslan when the truth was, I would do whatever he wanted as long as he loved me—

"I'm doing you a favour, really." Ethan laughed. "You gotta move on from your ex, after all. They say fucking someone else is key to getting over them." He pointed at his tented crotch. "Happy to be of service."

My insides shrivelled. My heart screamed for the boy I'd always loved. The boy I was born for. The boy the sea had given me.

Aslan!

Please...

Swallowing back my tears and my fears, I snarled, "I won't let you touch me."

He clucked his tongue. "Ah, see, that's a bit silly. I'd rather you didn't say that because I'd hate to prove you wrong." He narrowed his eyes, evil shining in them. "Regardless that you didn't have the full dose, you won't be able to fight me off, so I suggest you don't even try."

My vision greyed; my skin turned slippery with sweat.

Every part of me throbbed and scratched. My bones were put together wrong. My blood fuzzy and weak, terrified and woozy.

Ethan murmured, "Now, while you're conscious enough, stand up and get on the bed."

My heart grabbed an axe and hacked through my ribs. Scrambling to my feet, I forced my knees to stay strong and my vision to stay focused. "Let me go or I'll scream."

He laughed and extended from his crouch. "Do you honestly think anyone will hear you over the music below?"

"The poliice will co-come." My tongue tied itself into knots. "The poliwice—"

My own body betrayed me, tripping deeper into the drugs. Fear shot through me again, keeping me clear-headed for another second. "A noise commmplaind will be fil-filed and—"

"I better hurry then." With a smirk, his hands went to his jeans. With practiced fingers, he undid his belt, yanked it from the loops, and smacked the leather against his palm. "Now...seeing as I'm in a happy mood, I'll once again give you two choices."

My heart stopped pounding; I went deathly still.

The room turned upside down.

I couldn't catch a proper breath.

I stumbled and caught myself on Joel's side table, sending a stack of glossy magazines to splat against the carpet. "Plwease...just let me go."

"Choice number one." He advanced, making me dart toward the bed, stumbling to my knees as the walls became the floor. "You spread those pretty legs for me and enjoy it. I'll be nice, I promise. Option number two is—"

"Fuck you!" Scrambling back up, I tripped to the other side of Joel's bed. Ripping open his bedside table, my hands dove inside the messy drawer.

A knife.

A letter opener.

Something...please!

Ethan threw himself over the bed, knocking off pillows and bumping into me.

I went flying as my balance turned into bubbles, and I popped into nothing.

"Fuck it. You don't get a choice anymore." Wrapping his arms around me, he picked me up and tossed me onto the bed.

I fought for the edge.

I kicked as he landed over me.

I screamed as his knees imprisoned my waist and his hands grabbed my wrists.

I groaned as the room went black.

I clawed at my consciousness to stay sane, but sanity slipped through my fingers. Like water. Like air.

I blinked, and the moment had changed.

How many moments have passed?

My wrists were tightly bound.

I tried to bring my arms down.

Rip-roaring *panic* as they refused.

I looked above my head at the belt wrapped around my wrists and looped around the wrought-iron headboard.

I screamed.

Fuck, I screamed.

He didn't even try to stop me.

He let me scream until I gasped for breath and passed in and out of awareness.

Pockets of moments. Snippets of heartbeats. I was here and there. This world and another. I was sick and horrified. Cold and terrified.

Aslan!

ASLAN!

"Easy there. Don't give yourself a heart attack." Ethan shifted off me, his hands once again going to his jeans. This time, he unbuttoned and unzipped, and with a smirk, shoved down his jeans and boxers to mid-thigh.

"Fuck you. Fuck you. *Fuck you*!" I snarled.

"I think you'll find *I'll* be fucking *you*." He laughed as his cock sprang out, thick and hard.

I screamed so hard, I passed out for a moment.

I came to with his palm tapping my cheek and my dress shoved up to my stomach.

Something broke inside me as I noticed he'd removed my white cotton knickers.

He spun them around his finger. "You gonna stay awake for this or fall asleep? Either way is fine with me. I still get to fuck ya." Reaching into his jeans pocket, he pulled out a condom.

My heart smoked, blazed; it burned me into cinders.

"Zara!" I screeched. "Zara. ZARA!"

"She can't hear you. Cooper likes to tie her up. He told me that she loves it when he steals all her senses. She begs for a blindfold and headphones so she can fully focus on his dick inside her." He winked. "Should we do that with you? So you can feel every inch of me?"

A keening noise rose in my throat.

I couldn't help it.

I'd never made such a noise before.

A helpless, suffocating noise that reminded me of dying animals and broken things.

"Please…"

"Patience. Just gotta wrap it up." Tearing at the packet with his teeth, he rolled the condom on his erection. "Can't have any tiny Ethans running around, can we?"

Or leave evidence of rape.

Who would believe me?

Who could I tell?

Aslan…

God, what would he think—

Tears dripped out of my eyes as I jerked my legs together—

Only, they wouldn't obey.

No…please, no—

Not wanting to look but unable to stop myself, I raised my chin and looked down my spread and naked lower half. Joel's empty pillowcases were wrapped around my ankles and tied to the lower framework of his bed.

I lost all shreds of my humanity.

I kicked and screamed.

I squirmed and fought.

The belt bit into my wrists.

The pillowcases burned my ankles.

My vision spluttered in and out, in and out.

"Help! Someone! **Help**!" I panted and tripped, awake and dead, awake and dead.

Everything spun.

Everything bled.

"Hey!" Ethan crawled over me. "Stop that. If you die that's on you, not me. Now…ready for the best fuck of your life?"

Kneeling between my bound legs, he planted his fists on either side of my head.

I tried to bite his arm.

He laughed.

I tried to buck my hips.

He clucked his tongue.

I tried to scream.

He kissed me.
I bit him.
He slapped me.
I sank into pain, drugged by oblivion, gagged by despair.
His hips dropped.
His condom-slick erection slid over me.
I turned hysterical.

My terror blew through the drugs in my system, bulldozed through the spacey, sickening weakness, and I fought with every single part of me.

"Get the FUCK off me!"
But it was no use.

With the softest kiss to my cheek, Ethan reached between us, positioned himself at my entrance, and caught my tear-running eyes. "You look really pretty all tied up." Nuzzling into my throat, he murmured, "Fuck, I'm gonna enjoy this."

I screamed—
He thrust.
My back bowed.
My entire body shattered.
I imploded in on myself.
A collapsing.
A crashing.
My entire soul folding into nothing.
As inconsequential as paper.
A dirty and torn, used and abused, stupid piece of paper.
Soaking into the sea.
Dissolving into the salt.
Vanishing
and tearing,
fraying and fading…
into
n
o
t
h
i
n
g.

Chapter Thirty-Nine

ASLAN

(*Moon in Spanish:* Luna)

"ASLAN...EVERYTHING ALRIGHT?"
I froze.
Shit.
I'd hoped Jack and Anna wouldn't hear me as I sneaked past the lounge, heading toward the corridor and Neri's bedroom.
I needed to see her.
I'd given her enough space.
Fuck space.
Every minute I let tick between us filled my chest with awful pressure. My heart kept stuttering, my blood kept burning...urging me to go to her, almost as if I could hear her soul screaming for mine.
Crazy, I knew.
Probably meant I was going mad, but I couldn't shake the feeling that...something wasn't right.
Catching Jack's eyes, I replied, "Just gonna check on Neri. Make sure her tummy is okay."
"Oh, she's fine." Jack grinned, stretching his arms above his head as Anna snuggled deeper against him on the couch. "She left about an hour ago."
"Wait, what?" Everything inside me stilled. "She left?"
"Yeah, apparently she and Zara have made up?" Anna wrinkled her nose. "Not sure if that's Neri's wishful thinking or real. Last time I spoke to Zara's mother, it sounded terminal between them."
My hands shook a little as I stepped over the threshold into the lounge. "She's there, right now? At Joel's?"
Jack scowled, looking at me a little funny.
Did he hear the thick jealousy in my tone? The sudden punch of despair in my chest at the thought of Neri running to her ex the moment we had a sort-

of fight?

"According to Neri, Joel's in Indonesia training." Jack reached for his beer bottle on the mango wood coffee table. "I believe my daughter when she said she wants Zara back. And...if Zara is anything like me, she won't be able to last against Neri on a mission." Taking a drink, he toasted me. "Mark my words. Those two girls will be thick as thieves again and most likely sitting in the garden on those stupid beanbags of theirs, gossiping about who knows what."

A twinge in my chest.

A tugging in my heart.

Neri had been at Zara's and Joel's countless of times. So why did my gut beg me to go over there? To see for myself that she was safe?

"She said she was staying the night." Anna smiled, accepting her glass of wine that Jack handed her. "I'm afraid you'll have to wait until tomorrow evening to talk to her."

"Tomorrow evening?"

Why so long?

So, so much can go wrong in that length of time.

"Once those two make up, they'll be inseparable again." Jack grinned. "A sleepover will turn into brunch, which will turn into lunch, and swimming, and sunbathing, and God knows what else. As long as she walks back through the door before ten p.m., I'm not gonna stress."

Doing my best to keep my face from blaring all my worries, I smiled. "Awesome. In that case, do you mind if I borrow your truck? Just gonna go to the supermarket and get a few things before they close."

"Sure. You know you don't have to ask. Keys are in the bowl by the door."

"Cheers." I rocked on the balls of my feet. "Okay, then...enjoy your movie."

"Sleep well, Aslan." Anna blew me a kiss before snuggling back into Jack's embrace.

The moment they both looked back at the TV, I dropped all pretence that I wasn't burning up with unexplainable fear, marched through the house, grabbed the keys from their usual spot, and bolted out the door.

A party.

She'd lied to her parents yet again. Just like she lied about the camping trip in Daintree having parental supervision, she'd lied and said she was spending a quiet night with Zara.

Quiet?

Fuck, my poor ears were about to fall off from the noise.

No one questioned me walking through the front door and prowling through the rooms. Teenagers and young adults shared drinks, jokes, saliva, and vapes. The house reeked of booze and artificially sweet smoke, riddled with cheap perfume and sickly aftershave.

Cutting through the crowd, I scanned for the one girl I would know blindfolded. I followed that strange nudge in my gut. The constant hum of worry. The niggle of panic that I couldn't shut up even though I had no reason to be concerned.

Just because Neri and I were together now didn't mean she was in danger whenever we were apart. I didn't have this sickening feeling whenever she was at school. My palms didn't sweat and my skin didn't itch when she went out for dinner with her friends.

So why now?

Why tonight?

Why—

"Neri." I caught sight of her slipping through the crowd. With a flick of her wrist, she grabbed a black cardigan resting on the back of a chair, then scurried out the front door.

She didn't hear me. Didn't stop.

Her shoulders braced and head down, she threw the cardigan on and buttoned it tight over her dress.

Her hair looked a little tangled, and the dress she wore was one of my favourites. I always loved when she wore it. The vibrant orange set off the tan of her skin and depth of her sun-streaked hair. But it was the way the brightness bled into darkness that I loved. I liked to think it was us. She was the Australian sun, and I was the Turkish night. Blending together in seamless perfection.

My heart eased, and the fear I'd harboured faded just a little.

She's fine.

Ignoring a girl smiling at me and side-stepping a drunk guy who almost splashed me with his beer, I followed Neri out the door and broke into a jog as she darted across the front lawn, beelining for her bike leaning against the frangipani tree in the front yard.

"Neri. Wait up." I balled my hands, adding a burst of speed.

She didn't stop.

I frowned as she reached for her bike.

I touched her elbow.

She jumped so fucking high, she tripped over the front wheel and tumbled into the flowerbed.

"Shit, Neri…are you okay?" I bent down to gather her up, but she scurried away from me, her eyes as wide as moons, her face drawn and white.

The fear that'd swirled in my stomach amplified. Dropping to my haunches, I whispered, "It's me. Just me."

Her eyes met mine.

Something filled them.

Something I'd never seen before.

A strange kind of tide, full of secrets and pain.

But then she blinked, and it was gone. Dipping her chin, her tangled hair swung around her face, cutting me off. With a quiet gasp, she dug her hands into the soil, crushing pretty flowers, not caring she got her dress filthy.

Pushing upright, she swayed and almost fell again.

I caught her.

She made a noise that clenched my heart.

A noise I'd never heard before.

A noise that sounded as if she was fucking petrified of me.

Pushing me away, she groaned, "I need too gwesh away from hereee."

I turned stone cold.

Kafami sikeyim.

My forehead furrowed as anger filled me. "You're drunk."

She kept her chin down, not meeting my eyes.

Now I knew why.

Why she'd run and why she didn't want to make eye contact.

She was pissed as a fucking sailor.

Bloody hell, Jack would kill her for this. He'd been far too lenient on her. He hadn't set enough boundaries.

With trembling hands, I reached for her. "What the hell were you thinking?"

She cried out as I grabbed her elbows and shook her a little. "Do you have any idea what danger you could've been in? And you were going to bike home? Drunk? Fuck, Nerida. Anything could've happened. A guy could've kidnapped you. You could've fallen off and hurt yourself. You could've been run over, for fuck's sake!"

She sucked in a shaky breath.

A single tear rolled down her cheek.

Grabbing her chin, I forced her to look at me.

Truly look at me.

And what I saw made all my fear churn thickly inside.

I'd sensed this.

As much as I didn't understand how or why, I'd felt her needing me. I'd come for her because she'd put herself in harm's way. All that protectiveness I felt toward her had urged me here. At least I wasn't too late. At least I was here before she could put herself in any more danger.

But...how had I known?

How were we so linked that I'd *felt* her?

My pulse raced, and the depth of what I felt for her surged through me. I wanted to shake her, kiss her, scold her, embrace her.

I wanted to be gentle with her.

But...fuck, I was livid.

Beyond livid.

I was terrified.

What if I hadn't found her in time?

What if she'd ended up in a ditch or smuggled to a different country?

What if I never saw her again?

My heart stopped, and I pinched her chin, keeping her head tipped back.

She moaned and tried to push me away, but I didn't let her. "How much did you drink?" Her stare was overly dilated. She couldn't stay focused on me. Her nostrils flared as if she couldn't catch a proper breath, and her lips looked slightly swollen.

Another gush of cold fear filled me.

"Are you high?" I grabbed her cheeks with both hands, forcing her to stand still, all while she wobbled. "Fucking hell, you're stoned, aren't you? You mixed alcohol and drugs? Fuck's sake, Neri."

Curling into herself, she hugged the cardigan tighter around her body as I let her go. I scowled. Something was off about that piece of clothing... "That's not yours. I've never seen that jumper before."

Neri hunched even deeper into herself.

I dragged both hands through my hair. "Wait...I saw you grab it from a chair. Did you...did you *steal* that? Fucking hell, this night just keeps getting worse. Now you're a thief as well as a drunk and stoner? What the *hell* is going on with you?"

"I-I'll bwring it ba-back...tomorrwow." Her shoulders rolled, and she swayed into the tree.

My stomach lurched to catch her. My heart begged me to be kind.

But if her parents saw her in this condition, she'd be grounded for a month. How much of this could I hide from Jack and Anna? My mind raced with damage control. "Is Zara as drunk as you? Are her parents here? Stupid question. 'Course they're not here. Chances are both of you have alcohol poisoning and—"

"Zara didn't do..." Her voice cracked. "Zara didn't help—"

"Didn't help with what? Give you more booze? More drugs? You should be ashamed, Neri. You know better than this. You—"

"Aslan..." She hiccupped and brushed at the tears falling down her face. "Please...don't—"

"Don't what? Tell you what you need to hear?" Fear from seeing my cousin falling in with the wrong crowd back in Turkey raged through me. She'd been so close to being raped one night. She'd been so lucky my uncle found her in time. And it was her fault my uncle was dead the next night. I loved my cousin, but because of her reckless endangerment, she'd marked my entire family for death.

I won't let Neri fall down the same slippery slope.

"Please…I just need to…" Spinning around, she hugged the tree and vomited violently into the flowers.

Instinct made me shoot forward and grab her hair, gathering the silky softness at her nape while her body retched and purged.

"That's it. Better out than in. It's okay," I soothed, rubbing between her shoulder blades. She shivered and moaned as another retch worked through her. "It's okay, *aşkım benim*. I'm here. I'll take care of you."

A sob broke through her lips, her entire ribcage cracking at the sound. "You…I…I begged. And you…didn't—" She convulsed with another sob.

The keening noises coming from her brought fucking tears to my eyes.

"Neri." Horror sliced through me. "Hey, it's okay…" Gathering her up, I turned her to face me. Her face shot white and sweaty, her lips tinged with grey. "You're alright. I've got you. I'm so sorry I yelled. I didn't mean to, okay? I just…I'm so worried about you, and I got caught up in all the things that could've gone wrong—"

She cried harder, falling into my arms.

She was so loose and heavy, so intoxicated and hurting. All my anger washed away, leaving me trembling with need to keep her close and make her the same happy, wonderfully perfect girl I'd fallen head over heels for.

She felt both icy and sweaty in my arms. Both shaky and small.

Fury for how I'd treated her roared through my blood. I cracked beneath the knowledge that I was responsible for this. *If we hadn't fought…*

My arms turned into vises around her. "I'm so sorry, Nerida. I didn't mean to be so hard on you. This is my fault, isn't it? You came here because of me…" I whispered into her knotty hair. "You drank because of what I said? That kissing you was a mistake?"

She flinched and doubled over in my arms.

My heart twisted into two as I clutched her so damn hard. "I'm so sorry. *Ben çok üzgünüm.* I *hate* that we fought. I fucking hate it. I love you, *hayatım*. You weren't a mistake. Fuck, you could *never* be a mistake. You're the only thing that makes sense in my life. The only thing I live for."

Pulling away a little, I cupped her cheeks again.

Her eyes managed to stay on mine this time, haunted and darker than usual. Her tears kept raining as I nuzzled her nose with mine. "*Seni seviyorum.* So fucking much, Nerida. I love you more than I thought capable. You have my word we'll tell your parents. We'll tell them together and—"

"Aslan." She bit her bottom lip, her entire body trembling. "Please…t-take me away from here."

Her voice still wavered, but at least her words were stable. I probably didn't have to take her to the hospital to get her stomach pumped, thank everything holy. But I couldn't take her home. Jack and Anna would see. I was responsible for this; I didn't want her to pay for the consequences.

"Do you want to go home?" I asked softly.

She shook her head violently, moaning as she swayed.

I narrowed my eyes, that flutter of fear sparking up again. "What...what aren't you telling me, Neri?"

She sucked in a tattered breath. "Take me to *The Fluke*. Please, Aslan. I need...I need the sea."

A pang of jealousy shot through me.

Stupidly. Crazily.

I suffered a quick slice of jealousy at the very ocean that'd brought me nothing but despair yet granted Neri such salvation.

"You sure?" I kissed her forehead, tucking her into me.

She sighed and slumped in my arms, giving up everything she was. "Please...I need a swim." She choked on the last word as if slipping into the water would wash away all the sins of tonight.

I'd been born for this girl.

If I didn't believe it before, I had no choice but to believe it after tonight.

I'd come because she'd summoned me.

My heart was synced with hers.

No matter what the future held, she was mine, I was hers, and if she wanted to spend the night on the sea...then I'd spend all my nights giving her exactly what she wanted.

"Okay, *canim*. Let's go find the sea."

Chapter Forty

ASLAN

(*Moon in Galician:* Lúa)

NERI DIDN'T SAY A WORD ON THE drive to the pier.

She stayed hunched and pressed against the door as if trying to crawl into a shell and hide from me.

My hand itched to reach across the agonising distance between us and touch her.

I longed to touch her.

My heart *begged* to touch her.

Yet everything about her screamed to leave her the hell alone.

She was still so angry with me about what I'd said. So hurt that I'd confessed I'd never meant to kiss her. But what about what I'd said afterward? Why couldn't she remember that part? Why couldn't she trust me when I said that no matter how we'd fallen together, we were together now. In sickness and in health. In secret and in sight. I wouldn't change any of it. Even knowing I stood the risk of hurting her the day I got deported. Even knowing I'd doomed her to feeling the same grief I knew so well, haunted by ghosts I couldn't say goodbye to.

I'd decided to be selfish and keep her.

And having her hide from me was one of the worst things I'd endured because I wanted things to be right between us. I needed her smile like I needed air. I needed her love before I fucking suffocated.

Pulling into the parking lot reserved for boat owners permanently moored at the pier, I turned off the engine and switched off the lights. Twisting, I opened the centre console and pulled out the keys for *The Fluke*. The small plastic bauble full of air—to keep the keys afloat if they fell overboard—filled my palm as I clutched them tight.

"Ready?" I whispered. My voice was far too loud.

She flinched but nodded. Her hands trembled as she unbuckled her safety belt and opened the door. She didn't give me a chance to scoot around to her side and help her down. With her arms wrapped tight around her middle, she met me on the footpath, and we walked in slow silence to the boat.

I offered her my hand to walk up the small gangway.

She refused, not catching my eyes, making my heart pound with another awful wave of worry.

Kicking off her jewelled flip-flops the moment she was onboard, she padded softly to the front of the boat and stood staring at the full moon above.

I stood there like an idiot, not sure what to do.

Had she come here to sleep off the rest of her intoxication? Did she want to finish what we started today? I wouldn't be able to tell her no tonight. If she dropped to her knees like she had today and gave me a blowjob, I'd be inside her before she even opened her mouth.

Even as the images of us finally writhing together filled my head, I didn't step toward her with arousal. I didn't get hard. I didn't expect certain things.

My heart was still awfully wary, still picking up on signals I could feel but not see, energies that swirled around her that tasted dark and full of sorrow.

Silently, I joined her at the railing.

I didn't press against her. I kept a foot between us, hoping she'd come to me but accepting if she didn't. I'd never seen her drunk. I didn't know if she'd be melancholy or mean or just slip downstairs and go to sleep.

"Do you want anything to drink?" I murmured. "They won't be cold, but I stocked up on drinks yesterday. Sprite and Coke—"

"No." She gasped and shook her head. "I'll never have another Coke as long as I live."

I frowned. "Why? Did you mix it with bourbon or something?"

Her lips twisted as yet more tears tumbled down her cheeks, silver in the moonlight, etching her face with painful edges.

My heart once again fisted, feeding off her, ready to fight off her enemies but not able to see where they were coming from. "Nerida…"

Biting her bottom lip, she shook her head, refusing to make eye contact.

Words tangled on my tongue; I looked around the boat. "Do you want me to go and pick up some food? I'm sure a doner kebab place would still be open."

She inhaled sharply as if each time I talked, I sliced open her veins and made her bleed.

My heart pounded. My pulse throbbed in every finger and toe. Sweat slicked down my back from nerves, and I lasted as long as I could before I turned to face her and whispered, *"Bana ne olduğunu anlat. Buna dayanamıyorum. Senin bu kadar acı çekmen bana dayanılmaz geliyor. Nasıl durdurabileceğimi söyle. Neri, bunu durdurmalıyım çünkü seni böyle görmek beni çıldırtıyor."*

I froze, noticing my slip of languages.

Her eyes snapped closed, and she clutched the railing with white-knuckled fists.

Repeating myself in English, I murmured, "Tell me what happened. I can't stand this. Can't stand you hurting like this. Tell me how I can make it stop. I need to make it stop, Neri, because I'm going out of my mind seeing you this way."

Slowly, ever so slowly, she turned to face me.

Tears ran down her cheeks.

Clouds churned in her harrowed stare.

Licking her lips, she said ever so quietly, "If you commit a crime here…the worst thing they can do is deport you…right?"

I froze. My back snapped straight.

Deport me to my death.

I swallowed that truth and murmured, "I don't know. I'm not sure how the criminal system works. Why? Why are you asking me that?"

Her face twisted with more sadness. She wrung her fingers and asked again. "If I asked you to hurt someone…would you?"

"*What?*" My stomach sank even as my heart turned to ice. That damn link between us. That series of nudges and knowings fed me things I didn't want to hear, didn't want to see. Sickness swelled in my belly as I shook my head. "Neri…wh-what are you saying?"

Her lips thinned as she grimaced. She wedged both hands against her belly. She shuddered as if she couldn't bear to stand up, to talk, to live, but then she stood taller and looked me dead in the eye. "If I asked you to kill someone…would you?"

My knees locked to prevent me from dropping before her. I balled my fists to prevent me from touching her. I swayed on the spot as horror bled through me, pore by pore, cell by cell.

And I knew.

I knew before she reached for the buttons of her cardigan and slowly undid them.

I knew before she pulled the stolen clothing off her shoulders and shrugged it to the floor.

I knew before she raised her wrists and angled them in the moonlight.

And my heart motherfucking *broke*.

Stepping into her, I grabbed her wrists and studied the bruises, the blood. Tears stung my eyes. I groaned with murderous fury and despairing grief. "No…" I choked. "*No…*"

She cried silently as I raised her bruise-smudged and blood-coated wrists to my mouth. I trembled as rage surged through me.

Rage.

RAGE.

I couldn't contain it.

It cracked my bones.

It snapped my veins.

I kissed her wounds, I tasted her pain, and I lost myself.

"Fuck. *FUCK*!" My knees gave out.

I collapsed before her.

And the moonglow beamed on her perfect feet.

I couldn't breathe.

No.

Fucking hell, no…

She cried out as I ran my fingers over the bruises around her ankles. At the burns in her skin. At the ligature marks of imprisonment.

And I broke again.

I kissed her feet.

I gave in to my fury.

Tears bled down my face, burning like acid, corroding like poison.

Her hands landed in my hair as I bowed over her. My back retching. My entire body jerking with rabid violence, savage revenge, and merciless, relentless cruelty.

He'd pay.

Fucking *fuck*, he'd pay.

Bone by bone, blood by blood, he'd be in motherfucking pieces before I was through.

Standing with strength I didn't feel, my tears dried up, and my fury settled like a glacier within me.

With aching tenderness, I cupped the love of my life's cheek. I smudged away her tears with my thumb. And I pressed my mortal promise to her lips.

I would murder for her.

I would accept death for her.

I would kill whoever she needed so I never, *never* had to see her hurting like this again.

"Who is he?"

She choked on a sob as our eyes met but then she straightened her shoulders and whispered too quiet for the sea to hear. "His name's Ethan. He's friends with Zara's new boyfriend."

"What does he look like?"

"Blond, shaggy hair. Tall. A grey shirt with a Celtic emblem on the breast pocket."

Her words seared into my brain.

I finally had an enemy.

She opened her mouth to tell me more, but I had everything I needed.

I stalked away from her.

I vanished into the captain's cabin and ripped open the cabinet holding diving knives and a speargun. Grabbing the biggest blade and the harpoon, I marched to the side of the boat.

Leaping over the railing, I bolted up the pier and didn't look back.

Chapter Forty-One

ASLAN

(Moon in Galician: Lúa*)*

HE STOOD PISSING ON SOME WEEDS AROUND the side of the house.

The party was even more chaotic. The music louder. The guests drunker. No one noticed me stalking through their midst with the diving knife hidden in the waistband of my jeans. I didn't bring the speargun. I didn't trust myself not to shoot him in the fucking face the moment I found him.

The entire drive here, my heart had resembled an earthquake, rumbling with revenge, cracking with fury, creating craters and crevices where evil things sprang from.

Every part of me burned with rage I couldn't control.

He would die tonight.

Of that, I had no doubt…but I wanted to make him scream first.

I wanted him to feel a tenth of the pain he'd caused Neri.

I'd spoon out his eyes for daring to look at her. I'd break off his fingers for daring to touch her. I'd rip out his tongue for daring to taste her. I'd flay his cock into ribbons and feed it to him for fucking *daring* to be inside her.

Only once he was begging and pissing through a bleeding hole in his body would I put him out of his misery.

A black thought wriggled through my brain.

For all my upbringing as the son of a professor and all my attempts at being good, it turned out I couldn't run from who I truly was. Who I'd been hiding from since I was born. Who my very parents had tried to protect me from.

Pulling the knife from my waistband, I kept my breathing shallow and quiet as I prowled toward the shaggy blond-haired guy wearing a grey shirt with a tribal emblem on the pocket. I'd followed him from the kitchen where he'd joked with a dark-skinned guy and Zara.

I'd buckled beneath fury, waiting to hear his name. Needing to know I'd found the right bastard.

Zara laughed at something he said.

He'd whispered in her ear.

And then she'd said his name. "Oh, Ethan. You're freaking hilarious."

My insides turned to ice. My blood to frost. My rage to a funnelling blizzard.

I'd almost thrown myself across the room to strangle Neri's so-called best friend. Had she heard Neri screaming? Did she know that she was laughing with a motherfucking *rapist?*

My anger spiralled out of control again.

I inhaled hard, bringing my attention back to the guy holding his dick as he watered the garden beds. The same dick that'd been inside Neri. The same dick that'd raped—

FUCK!

My vision went red. I backed into the shadows by the rubbish bins.

Calm down.

If I didn't, I'd kill him.

Right here.

I'd slice open his throat until his blood sprayed the entire utility side of the house and then I'd gut him, rip out the ribbons of his intestines, and—

"Ah, shit! Cops!" a girl screamed.

"Time to go!" a guy laughed.

The music inside the house screeched into silence. Chaos ruled as people fled Zara's house like ants escaping a fire.

Ethan looked over his shoulder, past me in the shadows, to the stampeding feet of people fleeing from the garden. Stuffing his dick back in his pants, he stumbled in my direction.

I had to make a decision.

A very quick decision.

The police were here.

I couldn't be arrested but I also couldn't let Ethan leave.

He tripped a little and muttered like a drunk as he skirted the rubbish bins and then…

Dropped stone-cold unconscious by my feet.

I blinked at my outstretched arm. At the butt of the knife I'd used to strike him in the back of the skull. At the twanging vibration shooting up my forearm from hitting him before I'd even made the decision.

Lowering my arm, I nudged the rapist with the toe of my flip-flops.

He didn't move. Didn't even mumble.

Shit…now what?

"Everyone, go home. Anyone found loitering on the streets will be taken into custody. Any underage drinking will be firmly dealt with. Anyone found driving under the influence will spend the night in jail and have a date with a judge." The echoes of a male police officer's warnings drifted out the open kitchen window beside me.

I froze, waiting until the sound of heavy boots disappeared into the house, chasing the last tipsy stragglers.

Move.

Now.

Move!

Stabbing the knife back into the waistband of my jeans and yanking down my black t-shirt to cover it, I ducked and grabbed Ethan's shirt. With a grunt, I wrenched him off the ground, shoved him against the fence, then slung his arm around my shoulders.

I slapped his cheek. Hard. "Wake up. Cops are here. I'm getting you out before they arrest you."

He groaned and blinked. "Ow…fuck…" He struggled, but I kept my arm around his waist.

"Walk with me, and I'll get you away from here."

"Who-who are you, man?" His head tipped forward as he lurched with wobbly legs. He winced as he touched the back of his skull where I'd hit him. He slurred, "What the fuck schhappened?"

"Doesn't matter. Trust me and I'll take you back to your friend."

"Ah…that's nice—" He hiccupped and passed out again. His knees buckled.

Kafami sikeyim.

Why had I hit him so hard?

Why did the police have to fucking show up?

Couldn't they have waited ten more minutes?

"Whherre's Coop?" His eyes feathered open.

Coop?

My skin crawled from touching him. "I'm taking you to Coop."

"Okay, sweet…" His eyes closed again.

"Don't pass out. One foot in front of the other." I jiggled him and slapped his cheek again. He inhaled and shook his head as if trying to shake away the fuzz in his brain.

Keeping my hand locked around his waistband, I used all my strength to keep him standing as he faded in and out of consciousness.

Closing my eyes briefly, I begged the stars that'd witnessed my attack to help me get him out of there without being arrested.

Gritting my teeth, I opened the side gate and marched across the front lawn, dragging Ethan with me.

Two police officers had detained a small group of teenagers, scribbling down notes and glowering at them. The lawn looked as if it'd been trampled by a herd of deer, the grass pockmarked with a few shoes scattered and forgotten.

Not making eye contact with anyone, I walked as fast as I could with Ethan tripping and lurching beside me. The Jeep was right there. Parked innocently on the street, just waiting for me to drive away.

Just a few more metres…

Come on.

Hurry—

"Hold up."

My heart flew into my throat; I jerked to a stop.

Shit. *Shit!*

"Where do you think you're going?" A male cop stepped into my path, blocking the Jeep and my escape. His dark eyes narrowed on Ethan muttering nonsense in my arms. "He have a lot to drink?"

"Yeah. I'm taking him home." My mind raced with lies. "I'm sober. He's my younger brother. And—"

"Brother?" The cop raised his eyebrows, looking at my darker complexion and the blond bastard beside me.

Fuck.

I grinned with gritted teeth. "Adopted. Obviously."

"Obviously." The cop frowned. "What's your name? Have you been drinking tonight?" Ripping out his offending notebook, he yanked a pen free from his breast pocket. His uniform glittered with buttons and buckles, weapons and authority. "Name?"

My face stayed smooth and calm as I said, "Riley Cooper."

"And his name?"

"Ethan Cooper."

"And where do you live?"

"Nautilus Street."

The cop looked up. "That's just a street over."

"Yep. Our parents made me come get him when he called saying he'd had too many. I've been studying all night. I haven't been drinking."

"Studying?" the cop asked, his tone more curious than accusing. "What are you studying?"

"Marine biology."

"Oh yeah?" He gave me half a smile. "Like with whales and stuff?"

I nodded. At least this lie I would be fluent in. He could ask me absolutely anything about that profession, and I'd be able to answer every single one.

Holding my stare, he sighed and put away his notebook. "Count to ten for me and rouse your brother to confirm what you said, and I'll let you drive him home. Only home, mind you. It's late."

Smiling with as much innocence as I could, I reeled off the numbers he wanted then jiggled Ethan and pinched him in the side. "Wake up, brother. This nice cop wants to talk to you."

"Wha—why?" His eyes cracked open and true fear flashed over his face. Fear from raping Neri? Fear that he'd been caught?

What a shame he didn't know that being caught by the police would end far better for him than with me. He hung in the arms of his murderer, and he didn't even know it.

"Officer..." He smacked his lips and stood a little taller, giving me a break from his weight. "What...?"

"What's your name?"

"Ethan."

"Are you feeling okay, Ethan?"

"Yeah...drank too—too much."

"Do you just need to sleep it off or do you need a hospital?"

Ethan recoiled and shook his head. "Nah, no hospital. Just bed, mate."

The officer watched him for a moment then nodded and stepped out of my way. "Have a good night, gentlemen." He marched away without another word.

Relief almost buckled my legs.

Two run-ins with the law and I'd remained a free man.

I took that as a sign that I was doing the right thing.

That I was allowed to kill this bastard.

That I was supposed to do this for Neri.

Dragging Ethan to the Jeep, I opened the back door and shoved him face first inside.

He tried to sit up, glaring at me. "What the fuck? I don't know you. What the hell is going—"

I punched him square in the jaw all while my eyes shot to the cop to make sure he hadn't seen. No one looked my way. No one cared I kidnapped a rapist right beneath their lawful noses.

Ethan's eyes rolled back.

He collapsed against the seats.

I slammed the door, climbed into the driver's side, smiled at the cop who waved farewell, then drove away to kill him.

Chapter Forty-Two
ASLAN

(*Moon in Romanian:* Lună)

WAVES SLAPPED AGAINST THE HULL AS I pushed *The Fluke* to its limits.

Ethan lay slumped at the front of the boat, his arms and legs bound with plastic ties from the tackle box, his head nodding on his chest as we rode the ocean.

He hadn't woken up.

I'd hoisted him and the speargun over my shoulder from the back of the Jeep, hauling him down the pier like a sack of fish guts. I hoped to hell no cameras had recorded me carrying him aboard and no automatic logs knew we'd untethered from the mooring and cast off into the dark.

Neri.

My heart clenched as my eyes found her through the salt-streaked window. She stood at the side of the boat, her hair snapping in the wind, my favourite dress in her hands, destroyed by the knife that she used, ribbons of it flying behind us as we sailed.

I'd found her cutting up her dress when I'd tossed Ethan on board.

She'd changed into a red bikini and one of Jack's hoodies from the box of spare clothes below. Her hands white in the night as she hacked away at the pretty dress with single-minded determination.

I hadn't stopped her.

I'd barely talked to her.

I understood that her pain would manifest in different ways and make her do whatever she needed to cope.

She'd padded after me as I secured Ethan and propped him against the front of the boat, glowered at him with memories I wished she didn't have, then drifted back to her spot to continue shredding her dress.

I'd disappeared into the captain's cabin, unable to be near her without breaking apart.

I didn't trust myself not to burst into tears for what she'd endured or tear into Ethan like a beast. Using my teeth and fingernails, ripping him apart until nothing was left.

I wanted to be far out to sea before that happened.

The Fluke had bleach for washing away his blood. I could toss his remains overboard. His body would be eaten, just like my family had been.

No one would know.

Neri's nightmares would be over.

And there would be one less monster in the world.

I added more speed.

The boat complained.

Dropping my stare from the black horizon, I fiddled with the controls, raising the engine a little to skim faster over the water.

"What the *fuck* is going on?"

My head ripped up as Ethan exploded into awareness, fighting his binds, glowering at Neri who stood over him. In her hand rested the knife she'd been using to cut her dress, the tip glinting red.

Shit.

Cutting the engine, I didn't bother dropping anchor. Darting through the door, I skidded on the deck and grabbed the speargun I'd placed by the railing.

Breathing hard, I stopped beside Neri.

She glanced at me, her ice-blue eyes churning with torment.

"*İyi misin?*"

She nodded with a wince, knowing that phrase. "I'm okay."

The ocean rocked beneath our feet as *The Fluke* bobbed untethered. In the dark, I had no idea if we were close to an island or about to scrape over a reef. But we were far enough away…

"*Ona ne yapmamı istiyorsun? Söyle bana, yapacağım.*" My native tongue came freely, almost as if by embracing the darkness inside me, I became the man I'd been running from all this time. Cursing myself a little, I repeated, "What do you want me to do to him, *aşkım*? Name it and I'll do it."

"What? What the fuck?" Ethan spat. A streak of blood where Neri had cut his cheek with the knife glistened in the solar light from the cabin. Starlight and moonlight fought with the yellow glow, casting everything monochrome and merciless.

Ethan glared at both of us. "Where the hell am I? Where the fuck is Cooper?" He squirmed in his plastic tie-binds. "Why the fuck am I tied up?"

Something switched inside me.

The control I'd clung to over my temper.

The smothering of my rumbling rage.

It all snapped.

Red mist.

Vicious hate.

Without a thought, I brought the speargun up, aimed, and pressed the trigger.

Ethan *howled* as the harpoon shot through the meaty part of his calf. The string from the harpoon and the gun dangled between us, swaying in the night.

He bent forward, clutching at his bleeding leg, his bound hands quickly becoming a massacre. "What the fuck, you stupid cunt! *Fuck*!"

Neri hadn't even jumped.

Hadn't looked away.

Didn't react like she normally would.

And that broke yet another piece of me because the innocent girl, with her heart full of purity and goodness, had been shattered. She clutched her knife as if she was moments away from driving it into her rapist's heart.

Dropping the speargun, I stepped into her and wrapped my hand around her much smaller one.

Ethan continued to howl and curse.

I tuned him out.

My entire attention locked on the girl I loved more than anything.

She flinched at the contact.

Her eyes met mine.

And a crack appeared. A single crack in her façade as tears welled. Tumbling into my arms, she let me catch her, cradle her. Her spine rippled with sobs, and I hugged her hard enough to suffocate all the bad things inside her.

Pressing kisses to her wind-whipped hair, I murmured, "I've got you, *canım*. I'll always have you. Forever. What happened is done. But I vow on my life, it will never happen again. By anyone. You have my absolute vow."

Her arms slinked around my waist.

I buried my face into the delicious curve of her shoulder and neck. My back bowed, my knees had to duck, and I inhaled her scent of salt and ocean, desperately trying to stay human, all while my vision coated everything red and my tongue watered for blood. "*Sen benimsin*, Nerida Taylor. That means you're mine. To protect. To avenge. To love. To worship. *Sen benimsin*."

Pulling away, I thumbed away her tears and stared into the soul of the girl who'd captured me when she was just twelve years old. I'd wanted her to stay that innocent. That happy. But shadows existed in her now. Shadows that answered my own and I stared at my equal in every way.

I was no longer afraid that my darkness would destroy her. She carried her own darkness and survived.

Letting her go, I palmed the knife she'd been holding and twisted it until the blade caught moonlight. "How do you want me to do it, *hayatım*? Give me any command and it'll be done."

"Listen, you cunt! Let me the fuck go. Whatever you think happened didn't—"

"*Quiet.*" A snowy cloud of control cloaked over me. Fisting the blade, I turned to face him. Neri slipped by my side, her hands balled and jaw clenched.

"You raped her," I hissed.

"*What?*" His eyebrows shot up his pain-sweating face. His blood dripped on the deck from the harpoon in his leg. "I didn't touch her—"

"You tied her up, you fuck." I growled. "You—"

"Drugged me," Neri said coldly. "You drugged me and bound me and took me against my will."

"You liked it!" Ethan snarled. "You moaned as I slid right in—"

I kicked him right in the balls.

I stomped right on his dick.

He jack-knifed into a trembling huddle and collapsed to his side, gasping. The string in his leg from the harpoon jerked against the gun, making him howl all over again.

Panting hard, he shook his head, choking on pain. "I let you go after. I told you I would, didn't I? I didn't hurt you—"

My fist collided with his jaw, pummelling his cheekbone against the deck. "What do you call the bruises and blood on her wrists and ankles?" I punched him in the temple. "What do you call the bruise on her forehead?" I kicked him right in the nose. "What do you call the fucking trauma you've caused her?" I kicked him in the kidneys, my toes bellowing with agony. "You trapped her. You hurt her. You *raped* her—"

"It was her fault!" Ethan gasped, spitting out a mouthful of frothy blood.

A black nightmare rolled through me.

Stepping off him, I embraced the icy power. "*What* did you say?" My voice was a sword, glinting and sharp, singing with thirst to slice.

"She flirted with me!" he shouted. "She went to that party dressed to fuck. She knew what she was doing."

I could barely talk.

My jaw cracked.

My knuckles popped.

"And what was she doing?" I murmured with sleeting snow.

"She was trawling for a fuck. Even her friend called her a whore!"

And that was it.

That was the moment I became an animal.

With a roar, I threw myself on him. I kicked and punched. Kicked and punched. I wanted to break every fucking bone in his body. I wanted to drain every drop of blood from his veins.

My elbows smashed against his face. My knees buried into his gut.

He howled and cried, begged and gasped.
I lost who I was.
I embraced the breeding I'd always run from.
I brought up the knife.
I grabbed his bound hands.
And I hacked off one of his disgusting fingers.
A finger that had dared to touch what wasn't his to fucking touch.
His howl tore through the night.
It fed me.
Pleased me.
I hacked off another.
His howl became wet, wracking sobs, and I relished them.

I dragged the knife to his streaming eyes, piercing his cheekbone with a wrathful detachment that made my heart barely beat and my humanity drown beneath the devil freed inside me. "You don't deserve to look at her, you fuck." Angling the tip, I went to scoop out his eyeball, but then…I stopped.

Ethan gagged and groaned, choking on his tears. "Please. Please, don't! *Please!*"

Dragging the knife down his throat, his chest, and his heaving belly, I stopped above his jeans-clad cock. With a flick of the blade, I popped his button, yanked down his zipper, and inserted the pointy end directly over him.

"You can keep your eyes while I cut this off."

"No! Fuck, no. *Don't*—"

I pressed down on the blade over the soft meaty part of him that'd done something so un-fucking-forgivable.

He screamed.
I smiled.
I went to impale the knife, to castrate and mutilate—
"Aslan…stop." Neri's hands landed on my shoulders, tugging feebly.
I could ignore her.
She had no strength to pull me off.

It would be so easy to slice Ethan's cock from stem to root and tear off his balls, one by one. Only once he was neutered would I drag the blade from navel to nose, revealing the rottenness inside him. His insides would spill out. He'd be reduced to a pile of meat. A pile of stinking, bloody meat for the sharks below to dine on.

The darkness sank over my vision again.
I pressed a little harder.

Neri fell on top of Ethan, shoving her face into mine. Her hands captured my cheeks and her flawless skin smeared with Ethan's blood. Her breath came fast as her eyes locked with mine, and she whispered, "Enough. *Enough*, Aslan. I don't want you to kill him. I changed my mind."

"*What?*" I hissed. "But. He. *Hurt.* You."

"And you hurt him."

"Not nearly enough."

"It *is* enough." She ran her fingers through my hair, making me jerk. "We're even. You've delivered enough revenge. I'm okay, Aslan. I'm okay with this. I can't ask you to kill him. I don't want you to live with that."

"You're not asking me." I pressed a little harder on the knife.

Ethan's legs spasmed, and he sobbed like a child. He tried to wriggle away from my impalement, but with Neri's weight on top of him and the wounds I'd already given, he barely clung to consciousness.

"I'll happily do it. I *want* to do it." My stare dropped to her mouth. "I'd kill him a thousand times if it would take away what he did to you."

She smiled sadly. "And that's enough for me. That's more than enough. To know you care that much. To know how far you'd go."

"I'd go to the depths of hell for you."

"Don't kill him," she breathed. "I made a mistake asking you to. And I'm asking you now…please. Don't kill him." She pushed me back, firmly, resolutely.

My rage faded a little, leaving me jittery and confused.

Sitting on my ass, I brought my knees up and fingered the knife. The hilt was heavy teak with brass detailing down the sides. I'd seen Jack rinse it every time he used it in the sea so the saltwater wouldn't eat its way through metal and wood.

It gleamed with crimson and moonlight, angry at being denied.

It needed blood.

It wanted to taste every drop of Ethan's contaminated blood.

Shaking my head, I refocused.

He has to die…

Neri kneeled before me.

Ethan lay on his side, barely breathing.

His nose looked broken.

He moaned with every breath as if his ribs were cracked.

Two fingers were missing, pumping blood as quickly as the spear hole in his leg.

He didn't look like a monster anymore. He looked chewed up and spat back out by an even bigger one.

I shivered as humanity slithered back through me.

I'd done that.

I would flay him bone by bone if Neri asked me to.

I would do whatever it took to take away what she endured.

I'd kill fucking *everyone.*

The knife suddenly fell from my icy fingers, clattering against the deck.

I'm worse than him…

Trembles caught me unaware.

I'm my father's son…

Neri crawled into me, laying her hands on my quaking knees. "I don't want you to kill him."

Shoving away the nightmares swirling inside me, I glared at her. "But why? After what he did to you. He deserves—"

"He deserves to live with what he did."

"But what if he does it to others?"

"He won't. Not after this."

"But how do you know?" I balled my hands. "I couldn't survive if he hurt another girl like you. I wouldn't forgive myself if I could've prevented her pain and her family's agony at letting it happen."

"You didn't let this happen. It was just…bad luck."

"*Bad luck?*" I snarled. "It was my fault you went looking for Zara in the first place. I should never have said what I did. I should never have made you doubt how much I feel for you." My stomach cramped, and hot tears burned my eyes. "Fuck, I should *never* have yelled at you thinking you were drunk. I should've known. I should've felt you…" I groaned and buried my head in my bloody hands. "I *did* feel you. Fuck, I felt you so strongly, Neri. I knew something was wrong, but I didn't listen until it was too late. If I had come for you just a little sooner—"

"You'll drive yourself mad with those thoughts." Her voice threaded into a whisper. "Believe me, I know."

Our eyes caught and held.

I drowned in all her pain.

I choked on all the things that'd gone wrong.

And I made a promise. Right there. Painted in blood and cursed by fate, that no matter what happened in the future. No matter who tried to keep us apart or what circumstances got in our way, I would always, *always* find her. Always go to her. Protect her. Love her.

"*Ruhun benimkine sesleniyor,*" I breathed. "It always has. That's why you were there. That day on the water after we'd capsized. You felt it too." Cupping her beautiful cheek, I repeated, "*Ruhun benimkine sesleniyor.* It means your soul calls to mine, Neri. Whatever you ask of me, I'll do. Whatever you need of me, I'll provide. *Always.*"

Tears rained down her cheeks. She swallowed hard as she nodded and accepted my vow. "I want this to be over. I don't want to fear you being deported. I don't want to layer you with more death. I don't want to be responsible for bringing a shadow between us when all I want to do is forget."

She wiped her cheeks, her eyelashes sparkling with crystal tears in the moonlight. "I should *never* have asked you to do this. It was wrong. Wrong to fall to his level just because of what he did. Wrong to jeopardise our future…knowing how fragile it is."

"But, *canım*—"

"Please, Aslan." Standing on stronger legs than before, she collected the knife I'd dropped and stepped into Ethan. With two vicious slices, she cut off the plastic ties around his wrists and ankles.

Ethan mumbled something as Neri moved his shot leg, nudging his ankle so the thin harpoon was easily reachable. Wrapping her fingers around it, she sucked in a breath, then yanked it clean out of him. The small barbs tore through his muscle, shredding it.

He roared and woke up.

His eyes flared wide, pain making him hyperaware and lucid.

Spying Neri holding the blood-drenched spear, he rushed, "Please, no more. I'm sorry, okay? So fucking sorry." His face scrunched into tears. "Please don't hurt me anymore. I'll never do it again. I promise. Please…just…*please* don't hurt me."

His lips had turned blue from blood loss. Adrenaline kept him awake, all while his body slowly perished from the wounds I'd given.

I couldn't move as Neri tossed the bloody spear beside the gun and moved toward the chiller by the scuba cage. Opening the lid, she yanked out a can of Coke. Carrying it back to Ethan, she tossed it at him.

The guy sobbed and sniffled, his reflexes too broken and his hands missing too many fingers to catch it.

It landed heavily on his lap as Neri bared her teeth. "If you *ever* drug another girl or believe she's asking for you to fuck her, even when she *clearly* screams no, I will find you. I'll let Aslan chop off your cock, and I'll feed it to the sharks. Do you hear me?"

Ethan nodded furiously. "I promise. I promise on my life. Never. Never again. I promise."

Spinning on her heel, Neri headed into the captain's cabin.

A second later, the whir of the engine vibrated through the boat and the aimless drifting turned into an arrow of direction, shooting us forward back to shore.

Standing slowly, I braced myself against the rock and slap of waves, unable to take my eyes off Ethan.

How had this happened?

Why had Neri changed her mind?

He deserved to die.

I was prepared to do it—regardless of the consequences.

I tried to catch her attention through the window, but she stared resolutely ahead, pushing *The Fluke* toward the lights glittering on the shore in the distance.

My heart pounded with unfinished business.

How was I supposed to be okay with this?

This bastard had *raped* her.

He'd irrevocably broken a piece of her.

To let him live?

No.

Just...*no*.

She could hate me all she wanted.

She could curse me and call me names and never talk to me again, but this wasn't how this ended. This wasn't how I kept her safe or slayed her nightmares. This was me doing what needed to be done.

Tripping a little as a wave sent us higher than expected, I lurched toward Ethan.

His face shocked white. The can of Coke Neri had given him—that I supposed was symbolic if the bastard had drugged her that way—rolled away as Neri brought *The Fluke* into a graceful curve.

Every moment, Port Douglas came closer.

Every moment, my window of opportunity closed.

"No. Don't touch me. Don't—" Ethan threw up his bloody, misshapen hands as if to ward me off.

I merely fisted his ugly shirt and hauled him to his feet. He cried out as I pressed against his wounds. He trembled in my hold.

"Look, man...I get it." He snivelled. "I did a bad thing. You taught me that. I've learned my lesson, okay? I know I fucked up. I promise I'll never—"

"Shut up," I hissed, pressing him against the railing and letting him get his balance. He wasn't injured enough that he couldn't stand. I doubted I'd broken anything too important, minus the missing digits.

This retribution was nothing compared to what he'd done, what he'd *taken*.

My hands balled as fresh rage poured through me. "You made the biggest mistake of your life touching her," I seethed. "And the fact that you think you'll walk away from that..." I grinned.

He gulped and looked at Neri skippering the boat. With raw, feral panic, he went to scream for help. To scream for help from the very same girl who'd no doubt screamed that word, over and over again, as he bound her, stripped her, took her.

That sickening red mist was back.

I embraced it.

Sank into it.

Primal savagery rushed up my throat, and I clamped my hand over his mouth. "Scream and I'll gut you right here. You'll slip on your innards as they splash at your motherfucking feet."

He went white.

Silent.

Still.

While cloaked in that misty icy detachment, I dropped my hand, wiped my blood-sticky palm on his hideous shirt, and turned to face Neri.

She narrowed her eyes at us, suspicious and wary. Ethan clung to the railing, his back to the sea, his hands behind him as he kept all his focus on me. "What do you want? Money? I-I have some. I can—"

"*Quiet*," I whispered, never taking my gaze away from the girl who would always own me, body and soul.

I mouthed the words, *"I love you."*

Neri flinched as if what I'd done here tonight had opened her eyes to what I truly was.

And then…with strength and power that hummed in my tarnished blood, I round-housed the motherfucker in the upper chest. "Scream all you want. Scream where no one can hear you."

His breath exploded.

His face crumpled.

He tumbled backward and vanished overboard.

His splash was entirely satisfying.

His disappearance into the depths totally justified.

Neri cut the engine.

The Fluke groaned as it sank back into the sea, swallowed up by the very waves it'd just been surfing. We rocked and rolled as our wake caught up to us.

On bare feet with her father's hoodie hanging to her mid-thighs, Neri bolted toward me and looked over the railing.

Nothing.

No sound of gasping. No splash of swimming.

If Ethan survived the fall, he'd have to fight to survive.

His blood would ring the dinner bell; the scent of his suffering bringing predators slinking from the deep.

Neri's eyes searched the moon-glowing ocean. Her shoulders slouched as she turned toward me. "Why?"

I shrugged. "There was no other way."

"But I asked you—"

"To kill him. You only changed your mind because you didn't want me to wear that sin. You didn't want me to carry what I did. You were thinking of me, Neri…not yourself."

"But you'd already hurt him so much—"

"Does that sicken you? Seeing what I'm capable of?"

She didn't answer.

It killed me that she didn't answer.

Her voice was quiet as she asked another question. "What if he drowns?"

"What if he survives?"

Stepping into her, I placed my stained hands over her shoulders.

She flinched.

My heart spasmed.

"Are you afraid of me, Neri?" I breathed. "Do you hate me now?"

It took an endless moment before the tension in her spine faded and she sucked on her bottom lip. "I'm not afraid of you, Aslan."

"Are you sure? Do I repulse you? Standing here, covered in blood, struggling to remember how to be a man and not a monster?"

Her hand came up and cupped my cheek, shaking a little. "I love that man…and that monster."

A guttural groan of stark relief escaped me. My chin dipped to my chest; my forehead kissed hers. "I'm so sorry, Neri. For all of it. For what he did…and for what I did in return."

The fear in her eyes faded, burning up in the fire of surviving. "Thank you. For coming for me."

"Always." I nudged her nose with mine. "I'll *always* come for you. I'm just so sorry I was too late." Running my thumbs over the delicate lines of her collarbones, I murmured, "I hope he dies tonight. I hope his flesh is torn from his bones by a thousand hungry teeth, but at least this way…his fate isn't up to us to decide." I pulled away a little, staring into her crystal eyes. "It's the sea's."

"The sea might choose to save him," she whispered.

"It could. Just like it saved me and devoured my family." My voice hardened. "The ocean claimed good, honest people and left me alone, all when it should've been me in their place instead."

"What—?"

"The sea looked into my heart and mocked me by keeping me alive. Ethan can pass the same test. He merely has to swim to shore."

"But he's hurt."

"He is. But so was I. I was broken and bleeding when you found me."

Her eyes welled with tears. "I was always going to find you."

"I know." I kissed her gently, expecting her to recoil but grateful that she didn't. "This, *us*, is the reason the sea spat me out. You were what I was searching for without even knowing it. And now that I've found you? Nothing can keep us apart because…I need you. I need you to stay human. I need you to stay good. I need you to stop this curse and—"

"Curse? What curse?"

I sighed, struggling with the truth and so many lies.

I'd hidden from the truth for five years.

I wanted to keep hiding.

I'd never breathed a word of it to anyone.

But after tonight, I owed her.

I owed her the truth about who I truly was.

"There are things about me that I haven't told you, Neri. Things that I didn't know until the night my family boarded that smuggler's boat."

"What things?" she whispered.

"Bad things." I flinched. "I'm not who you think I am. I'm not…good."

"You're the best man I know."

"The fact that you can say that…after what I just did makes me want to drop to my knees before you and never let you go." I kissed her again, a fleeting worshipping press.

She sucked in a breath. Her lips slowly parted beneath mine.

And when we pulled apart, her eyes were aglow with ferocity. Ferocity that sang to the ferocity inside me, full of fangs and fate.

"I don't care who you are or why you believe the ocean should've chosen you instead of your family to die that day. All I know is…I need you. I need you to help me forget him. I need you to erase him from my thoughts like you erased him from my life." Her voice wavered but she forced herself to say, "I-I don't want a single night to pass where he exists inside me."

I went deathly cold. "What…what are you saying?"

"I'm saying I don't want him in my mind anymore. I don't want him in my body. I never want to think of him again or remember a single moment when I was his. Take those memories away from me. Burn them to dust and cut them into tiny pieces. Be with me, Aslan. Be with me so I never have to remember being with him."

My heart thundered.

I knew.

I knew what she asked of me and part of me recoiled at the thought. To be with her in that way after what she'd endured? To think I had any power whatsoever to heal her from what that bastard had done?

"Neri…I—"

"*Please*, Aslan." Her jaw worked, hiding the depth of her torment. She stood so strong, so brave, so forgiving. She'd wanted Ethan to live. She was so much better than him. So much better than me. She'd been willing to let him keep his life, even after he'd stolen such a vital piece of hers.

I was in awe of her.

In absolute fucking awe and if I was honest, I didn't deserve her.

Not tonight.

Nor any night.

And yet…

She flinched as she swallowed on a silent sob, revealing just how much she wasn't okay. Just how much her strength would eventually break, and I needed to be there to pick up her pieces.

If this was what she needed from me.

She could have me.

All of me.

Forever.

Kissing her forehead, I murmured, "Okay, *aşkım benim*. I'll do whatever you want me to do."

She shattered a little. Her composure fractured. Fresh grief wracked through her.

But then she sucked in a breath.

She kissed me on the mouth, then strode without a word back into the captain's cabin.

Chapter Forty-Three
NERIDA

AGE: 17 YRS OLD

(*Sea in Zulu:* Ulwandle)

I KEPT MY EYES GLUED TO THE bright screen.

The ridges and valleys of the reef below ghosted in the night.

The contours of another world where coral replaced trees and fins replaced legs. The water world was as familiar to me as the one above, and I followed the canyons and undersea hillsides as if they knew the way to happiness. As if they could heal me, revive me, and guide me to an existence where evil didn't exist, where stress and worry, violence and rape didn't happen.

Gritting my teeth so hard, bottling up the torrenting emotions inside me, I focused on navigating by the ocean floor.

The night sky enveloped us.

The faint lights of the town faded the longer we sailed.

No birds. No people.

Just me and Aslan, riding the sea beneath a gleaming moon.

The conversation from earlier today—*God, it feels like decades ago*—echoed in my mind.

"*You said without the moon and the sea, we would never have met.*" He narrowed his eyes.

"*Thank goodness for the* ay *and the* deniz *then,*" I murmured.

"*For the* luna *and the* mare," he whispered, his gaze locking onto mine and making the world drop away.

Those two Latin words swirled in my head, a mantra that I clung to as other memories stalked and scratched.

Occasionally, I checked the moon's location, using the compass to affirm I followed the right path. As long as I focused on the picture of the reef beneath my fragile feet, I could pretend I was okay.

I could convince myself that I would survive this.

I could lie and say I was fine—

I turned my head and stared at Joel's grey curtains as Ethan jerked and came. His repulsive body rippled and released in mine, filling the condom. My mind had fractured. Before I was light and bright and brave. Now, I had boxes. Neat and tidy boxes where all my goodness had fled and hidden. All my hopes had scurried and died. All my faith in people crushed into dust.

He rutted into me a final time, and there was absolutely nothing I could do about it. I'd gone quiet. Still. Shut down.

My instincts had switched into self-preservation, and I blocked it out. I pretended it never happened. I stared at those damn curtains and lied to myself that this was a nightmare, and when I woke up…it wouldn't be real.

Withdrawing, Ethan sat on his knees between my spread and bound legs. With a grunt, he yanked the condom off.

Tears leaked from my eyes.

A strange new part of me—a sharp and savage, meek and mauled part—flushed with gratitude that he'd worn protection. The thinnest piece of latex had kept me clean, kept me safe.

I hyper-focused on that condom.

It made everything seem a little less…worse.

Shaking my head, I dragged myself back to the starlit sea.

Aslan clung to the railing at the front, his back to me, his face toward the darkness. He trusted me to take him wherever I wanted. He hadn't come to ask where we were going. He hadn't tried to take me home. He didn't speak of police or hospitals or parents.

He trusted me.

He gave me everything he was, and as he stood beneath the moon with Ethan's blood painting him, I accepted every last shred of the soul he'd given.

He'd turned into a beast for me.

He'd mutilated and tortured for me.

He'd turned to me with quaking fear, terrified that his violence would make me run.

I would *never* run.

How could I ever run from a man who would do anything, absolutely *anything*, to keep me safe?

He wore blood for me.

He snapped bones for me.

With his heartless savagery, he proved, once and for all, that he was mine, and I was his, and all of this…meant nothing.

Only he made sense.

Only him.

Covered in blood.

Cast in moonlight.

Prepared to fight the devil himself to protect me.

Tears rolled silently down my cheeks.

The headache that'd grown worse the more the drugs wore off pounded in my skull.

Aslan.

My soulmate.

Without him, I wouldn't be standing here.

Without his dedication and devotion, I might not have the power to go on.

But the way he watched me.

The way he cried when he saw my bruises.

The way he fought for me and killed for me and bound himself to me...I evolved beneath the cloak of his everlasting care.

He would help me.

He would heal me.

He would take it all away—

I cried out as the belt unravelled from my wrists and the pillowcases fell away from my ankles.

"See?" Ethan tapped my cheek. "Told you I wouldn't hurt you." *Looming over me, he smiled as if we'd shared a consensual evening.* "You were so good, baby. I'll put in a good word for you with your bestie, okay? Perhaps we can all double date."

I didn't shake.

I didn't cry.

I just wanted to run.

Rubbing at the wounds on my wrists, I swung my legs over the bed, smoothed down my dress—my hated, awful dress. A dress that no longer looked like a pretty sunset but like evil suffocating light. I wanted it off me. I wanted his sweat off me. I wanted his kisses and touch and defilement **off me.**

My nostrils flared as he ruffled my tangle-thrashed hair.

"Obviously, we don't need to have the chat not to tell anyone, huh? I mean...we had a good time. I let you go. You're free."

Marching to the door, he zipped up his jeans and rethreaded his belt through the loops. "See ya 'round, baby girl."

My hands trembled as I pulled on the accelerator, slowing our cruise.

Stars twinkled a little brighter as silhouettes of palm trees and the golden glitter of sand welcomed me home.

Low Isles.

A place where I'd dreamed of as a child, wishing it could become my home. I had visions of sleeping on the beach, living off coconuts, and swimming with Sapphire and her pod every day.

I begrudged having a bed. Having a table and food and family.

A part of me felt so solitary when I was young. As if I was being called back to somewhere I used to belong but no longer did. Of course, it was nothing more than a wild imagination. I'd always lived in stories when I was young. Always fantasised about living underwater and having a pet turtle. Of running away and being stranded on an atoll where I turned into a fish and never breathed air again.

I needed those wishes to be real tonight.

I needed a fantasy because I could no longer survive in reality.

Aslan twisted to look at me as I slowed *The Fluke* even more. I followed the picture of the reef, bouncing from echolocation waves into tangible pictures, steering the boat carefully through the channels in the reef.

When I'd sailed as shallow as *The Fluke* could go, I cut the engine, dropped the anchor, and...cried.

I pressed my forehead against the helm and let go of the filthy mess inside me. All those neat little boxes that my mind had compartmentalized threatened to tumble and spill. The implosion would be impossible to clean up...so I fortified their stacks. I let my light glow from one and allowed my newly formed shadows to churn in another.

One day, I could unpack and be free.

But not tonight.

Raising my head, I swiped at my tears and turned to face the love of my life as Aslan padded into the captain's cabin and gathered me in his strong arms.

I didn't break down again.

I didn't cling.

I merely soaked up the comforting energy and tingling hum of home.

Had Ethan survived the fall into the sea?

Was he swimming, even now, to shore?

Or was he already dead? Floating to the bottom of the ocean where crabs would crawl, starfish would smother, and sharks would tear into his skin.

I waited for guilt.

I paused for the awful feeling of wrong.

But...nothing.

Ethan had made a choice to rape me.

I'd made the choice to tell Aslan.

And Aslan had given his choice to the sea...survive or die...it wasn't up to us. It was up to the ocean I loved so much.

Pulling away a little, Aslan caught my stare. "*Iyi misin?*"

I smiled as much as I could and nodded. I loved that he slipped more and more into his own language. It made me feel privy to the parts of him that he kept hidden. I'd been learning on the same app that my mum had. I'd mastered simple sentences and questions like the one he'd just asked. But I wasn't fluent enough to keep up with him when he spoke with such ferocity and passion. His voice thick. His depth of feeling turning every vowel into a weapon.

"I'm okay," I whispered.

And in some small way, I was.

I'd reclaimed some of the power Ethan had stolen when I'd cut off his wrist and leg ties. I'd released him…just like he'd released me. I'd given him the same kindness after being brutally hurt. He knew what it felt like to be given freedom after pain.

"You brought us to Low Isles?" Aslan asked quietly. "It's a tourist trap. I thought you wanted to go somewhere private and…" His cheeks pinked, swelling my heart with just how perfect he was.

He'd done things tonight that would paint him as a monster. Yet the mere mention of sleeping with me…? He suddenly looked so shy.

I'll be his first.

And he'll…he'll be my last.

Never again would I be with another.

Tonight was the first night of all our nights.

The night where no other nights existed.

"Only a skeleton staff sleep on the island to man the lighthouse and other facilities," I replied. "They won't see us. We'll be alone."

"You want to go ashore?"

I nodded. "I want…I need to feel the sand. I need to wash away what he did."

Fury mixed with agony in his dark stare. "Lead the way. I'll follow wherever you go."

Taking his hand, I led him to the side of the boat and opened the small partition where the staircase unfolded and slipped into the black sea. Grabbing the hem of my father's baggy hoodie, I tore it over my head.

Moonlight kissed my skin and turned my red bikini a darker shade of blood. I shivered as the warm night air caressed me. I waited for fear at being so bare. I braced myself for the freedom I'd always felt in my own body to be taken from me after what Ethan did.

But…Aslan made me feel so safe.

He didn't touch me, almost as if he waited for me to break. He kept his eyes on my face as I turned to look at him. His gaze didn't linger on my breasts or drop between my legs. His stare gleamed with moonlight, and it was *my* choice to step into him. *My* choice to stand on tiptoe. *My* choice to press my mouth to his.

He sucked in a harsh breath as I kissed him.

He shivered as I licked his bottom lip.

And when I pulled away, his chest rose and fell with feeling. His face twisted with tightly restrained affection. "I love you, Neri."

"I know. I feel it. All around me. In me. Through me." I tapped my heart and laid my other hand over his. "I feel it. Right here."

"Me too," he breathed. "I think I always have."

Standing beneath the spritz of stars and listening to the gentle *hish-hish* of lazy waves on island sand in the distance, I could almost believe Ethan hadn't happened.

He didn't exist.

Only we did.

I threw myself into the fantasy and stepped toward the edge of the boat. I stared at the inviting blackness. "The salt will rinse away tonight. And after it does…" I met his eyes. "I want you to kiss me. I want you to touch me. I want…" My throat dried up as my heart raced.

What if I couldn't?

What if Ethan had broken me so badly, I panicked the moment Aslan slid inside? What if I was never free to—

"Hey. I'm here. You're safe." Aslan stepped into me and slinked his fingers through my hair, tender and soft. "Don't think about what might happen, Nerida. Only what is." His fingers feathered to my chin, pushing gently to raise my head and kiss me.

His lips claimed mine.

Harder than before.

Possessive and familiar.

I let him sweep me away. I teetered on falling into the ocean.

He spoke into our kiss, "If I have to wait a thousand years to be with you, I'll wait. We don't have to do this. Not tonight. Not any night. My body is yours, Neri. Just like my soul and heart. You don't ever have to fear my reaction if you decide not to—"

I threw my arms around him, pressing my breasts to his black, bloody t-shirt. I pushed my tongue into his mouth, shutting him up, kissing him deep, reclaiming another piece of my power.

I'd wanted this boy since I'd found him clinging to a shipwreck. I needed this boy with all my being.

Breaking the kiss, I reached for the hem of his t-shirt and pushed it over his head.

He didn't stop me.

His bare chest gleamed silver, etching the contours and shadows of muscle. His belly flexed as I drank him in, drawing my eyes to the darker trail of hair running down the middle of the V of stomach muscles before disappearing into his jeans.

Swallowing hard, I dropped his t-shirt to the deck, then reached with both hands to his button and zipper.

He let me do whatever I wanted to him.

He swallowed a soft moan as his jeans opened and fell down his legs. His black boxer-briefs did their best to contain him, but his erection speared out the top. The tip glistened wetly in the moonlight.

"I'm sorry. I can't…I can't help it," he groaned. "The moment you asked me to be with you, I can't stop thinking about anything else." He growled with self-repulsion. "Which makes me as bad as *him* because how can I be hard after what you went through? How can I even think of sleeping with you after what you've endured?"

Laying my palm over his hardness, I never took my eyes off his face.

At the way his eyes snapped shut. His throat constricted. His head fell back.

With one touch, I owned him.

And it was because of that, that I knew I was doing the right thing.

I wanted good to replace evil. Love to erase hate.

Because of the way Aslan reacted to me, because of the sensitive awareness we shared, because our lust came from love…I was free.

If I asked him to, he'd kneel before me and give me whatever I wanted. I could take whatever I needed, and he'd never, not once, try to take anything from me that I didn't want to give.

And that…

That gave me another smidgen of my power back.

The power of my sexuality.

The power of my consent.

"Come swim with—" I cut myself off, glancing at the sea. *Oh God. How could I have been so stupid?* I'd been so wrapped up in my own tragedy, I'd forgotten all about his.

He can't step foot in the ocean.

My shoulders rolled.

He wouldn't jump in.

We couldn't go to the island.

The fantasy of forgetting who we were and spending a night beneath the stars was gone—

"Finish what you were going to say," he whispered. "Ask me."

I met his eyes. I saw true fear shining there. Unresolved ghosts haunting his mind.

I shouldn't ask this of him.

I should honour his wishes about the sea.

Just because I'd endured something that'd irrevocably changed me didn't mean—

"Ask me, Neri." He smiled, but it didn't reach his stare. His smile was tight and stern but given with all the love he held. "Ask."

Inhaling hard, I licked my lips and whispered, "Come swim with me, Aslan Avci. Swim to shore with me."

For the longest moment, he didn't reply.

His eyes closed as if he was saying goodbye to a part of himself that he still couldn't bury or get free from. But then he nodded, placed his hand over mine, pressing my palm against his erection, and murmured, "For you, Nerida

Taylor, I'll swim in every sea."

He kicked his jeans away, sending something spinning in the starlight.

He grabbed my hand, tucked his hardness back into his boxers, and positioned us by the open side.

I tugged on his hold. "Wait."

He immediately let me go. "It's okay. I'm sorry. I didn't mean to make you feel trapped."

"It wasn't that." I gave him a grateful smile. "Something fell out of your pocket."

"Did it?" He shrugged. "Ah well, it will be here when we get back."

"What is it?"

His gaze skated away; a fib tumbled from his lips. "Nothing important."

I scowled. "You just lied."

"No, I—"

"Tell me." Marching away from him, stepping over our discarded flip-flops, I collected the small secret thing.

The instant my fingers cupped it, I swayed under the onslaught of bone-deep, soul-slicing emotions.

The shell.

The spiny frog shell that I'd clung to, all while he'd brought me back to life when I was fourteen. Three years since he'd saved me. Three *years*.

Turning on trembling legs, I held up the peach and cream shell. "You kept it?"

He rubbed bloody hands over his face, streaking the ribbons of blood already on his cheek. Dropping his arms, he gave me a despairing smile. "Of course, I kept it. It was from you."

"Do you use it? Do you speak to your family through it?"

"No."

"Then—?"

"I speak to you." Stepping toward me, he stroked the shell that wasn't nearly as spiky now, after three years in pockets and palms. The edges were dull. The spines worn. "On the nights when I couldn't bear how much I wanted you, I'd confess my darkest desires. On the nights I dreamed of you, I'd admit how much I loved you. On the nights when I feared being taken from you, I begged it to keep me hidden so I could stay here with you."

He laughed under his breath, slightly unhappy, slightly angry. "The idea of losing you is repellent. The very concept of being away from you is so abhorrent, I literally can't sleep sometimes. I can't let go of the past, but I also can't grasp the future. Partly because my existence in this country is out of my control but mostly because...I'm so fucking afraid that you'll see me for who I truly am. That if I tell you the truth, you won't want me anymore."

"Why?" My fingers closed over his and the shell. "Why would you ever think that?"

He sighed heavily. "Because I haven't told you a single thing about who I am. The man you think you know isn't real."

"You're as real as I am."

"I'm a product of my past."

"Tell me. Tell me so I can prove to you that nothing else matters but this." Squeezing his hand, wincing as the shell dug into my palm, I urged, "Tell me whatever secrets you think will drive me away so I can prove to you that they will only bring us closer."

His gaze caught mine. No moonlight shone in them. Only darkness.

I expected him to refuse, but he slowly nodded. "I'll tell you anything you want to know. I'll tell you who I truly am...before we sleep together. That way, you can decide if you still want me before I make you mine."

Pulling the shell out of my hand, he dropped it onto his discarded jeans. "Let's swim, *canim*. I'm so sick of fucking hiding."

Without another word, he grabbed my wrist and pulled me overboard.

Chapter Forty-Four

ASLAN

(*Moon in Javanese:* Rembulan)

SEAWATER CRASHED OVER MY HEAD.

My present life split down the middle, allowing space for the past to haunt.

"You need to know something, Aslan." My father shifted closer to me on the tight bench of the rickety boat. He looked older. Drained from the year of hiding, running, and endless flights. His eyes were black with terror for this voyage.

"What do I need to know?" I hugged my baby sister closer. She'd fallen asleep the moment we cast off. Afet, my cousin, whispered to my mother, their heads tipped together. All around us, other people who'd signed up to be smuggled out of Indonesia kept to themselves, watching each other with wariness.

"I don't quite know how to say this," my father whispered. "But if anything happens to me...you need to know why you can't ever go back to Turkey."

I stilled. "You sound as if I'm the only one who can't go back."

He chewed on his cheeks before replying, "If any of us go back, we're dead. But if you go back..." His hand landed on my shoulder, squeezing hard. "If you go back, Aslan...you'll suffer a far, far worse fate—"

My burning lungs sliced through the memory.

My fingers unwrapped from Neri's wrist, needing all limbs free to swim. Kicking to the surface, I sucked in air as ocean flowed over my face. Jerking my head back, I flopped wet hair away, leaving my eyes free.

Neri popped up beside me, her face so young and pretty, the gleam of the moon making her hair silver-black. "You okay?" she asked quietly, her arms fanning in the water as she swam.

I kicked and forced myself not to think about what stalked below. I didn't let images of rotting corpses and the tiny skeleton of Melike haunt me. I'd lived with my adversity for years. It was nothing compared to Nerida's.

Tonight was about her.

Not me.

I'd survived thanks to her.

It was my turn to repay her kindness.

"I'm fine." I gave her a tight smile. "It's colder than the pool."

"Not by much."

"It's deeper too."

"It's about three metres right here, but it will be shallow enough to touch the bottom soon." She swam around me effortlessly. "Ready?"

Clenching my jaw, I nodded. "Lead the way."

Kicking off, she kept her head above the water, performing a swift and powerful breaststroke. I swam after her, not nearly as graceful but able to keep up well enough.

The lighthouse on Low Isles shimmered on the other side of the island, providing the faintest glow. The beach welcomed us the closer we swam, and by the time Neri dropped her legs and hovered vertically, my heart had stopped trying to hyperventilate at the memory of that night.

Of the storm.

The cracking of wood.

The screams of dying.

I flinched as my toes touched sand and broken pieces of coral below. Dangerous creatures dwelled on the bottom. Things with barbs and poisonous spines. Yanking my legs back up, I swam a little closer to shore, following Neri.

A little farther and Neri suddenly stood.

Water sluiced down her back, lapping at her waist as she turned to face me and ran her hands over her hair, squeezing out raining saltwater. "You can drop your feet, Aslan. The bottom is mostly sand here."

"What about stonefish?"

"They prefer rocks and reefs. We should be fine."

"Should? But not guaranteed?"

Her eyes turned sad. "Is anything guaranteed?"

Her pain echoed all around us. I couldn't reply. I had no words that could take away what she was going through. Taking a deep breath, I let my legs sink and pushed up. Gravity grabbed a hold of me again, making me feel heavy and cumbersome after floating in the sea.

I wanted to get out.

I looked at the shore only a couple of metres away and longed to keep going.

But I didn't move as Neri stepped into me and kissed me softly.

I bent my head so she could reach me easier. I let her control how deep and hard she wanted. I followed her lead but didn't attempt to take control. I willed her to feel safe with me, protected by me. I was a perfect gentleman, even though my cock hadn't deflated and the discomfort of swimming with a hard-on had been an interesting experience.

Would a fish nibble it?

What the hell would I do if something aquatic decided it looked like a tasty snack?

An image of a nasty fish attaching itself to my cock made a horrified shiver and an amused snort work through me.

I snickered under my breath as Neri broke the kiss and quirked an eyebrow. "What on earth are you laughing about? Did I kiss you wrong?"

My humour faded instantly. "No. God, no. Every kiss you give me drives me out of my mind." I chuckled quietly again. "I-It wasn't you. I just…" I pinched the bridge of my nose, my hand dripping seawater. "I just had an image of a fish deep-throating me by accident."

Her eyes popped wide.

For a moment, I didn't know if she'd have me committed to an insane asylum or find the humour that I had. But then her lips tipped up and a healing peel of laughter tumbled from her.

Laughter that made my heart stop because I'd honestly feared I'd never hear it again.

"I know I shouldn't laugh but…your aversion to the sea and all its wonderful creatures always surprises me…even after five years. We're so similar in so many ways, but when it comes to the ocean, we couldn't be any more different."

I didn't remind her why that was. I wasn't offended or annoyed. It was the truth and really, if I'd jumped into the sea the day Jack had removed my cast, I could've gotten over my hate toward the ocean and enjoyed it instead of cursed it. I might even have found a resemblance of acceptance and peace.

But I was a stubborn bastard, and I wasn't ready to say goodbye. Wasn't ready to accept that Melike was dead. That they'd died because of me.

She tapped her chin, doing her best to stay light-hearted when such heavy tragedy swirled around us. Death and violence, abuse and loss. At least the darkness swallowed those sinister shadows, giving us space to pretend they weren't there.

"What would you do if a fever of stingrays surrounded us? Would you panic?"

"Fuck yes, I'd panic," I said. "I'd leapfrog over them and get the hell out of here."

I scowled as her laughter turned into giggles. "They're not aggressive. They're like giant sea kites. Like paper planes floating in the ocean."

"Sea kites that harpooned Steve Irwin."

Her laughter faded. "Good point. I suppose everything is dangerous if not given the right respect."

I nodded.

"Just like you," she murmured. "To me, you are the kindest, sweetest person I know. You prefer math over mayhem. You love to read and study. I've never even seen you kill a mosquito…and yet, when you launched yourself at Ethan?" She shook her head with a wince. "You were wild, Aslan. I've never seen you that way. That…fierce. That—"

"Violent?" I muttered.

"Yes."

"I know I already asked, but…did I scare you?"

"Scare me?" She jerked back. "Why would that scare me?"

"Because of how much I wanted to kill him. How much I enjoyed it."

"I only saw my soulmate avenging me." She ducked her chin, drawing circles on the water's surface with her fingertips. "Watching you attack him gave me power. Power in the way you defended me. I wasn't afraid. I'll *never* be afraid of you."

"You might not say that once you know who I truly am."

She stilled, her hands sinking into the black sea. "Then tell me. Tell me who you truly are."

I gulped.

I thought I wanted to do this. To cure myself of my debilitating fear that the day Neri found out about me, she'd run and never look back. But…words lodged like rocks in my throat, and I couldn't speak.

Her hands went to the ruby strings around her neck. With a single tug, she undid the bow; the bikini fell away from her breasts.

I braced myself for more bruises.

I forced myself to stay standing and not go feral with despair at failing her.

But her perfect, pale skin glowed in the moonlight. No other marks. No other evidence of what he'd done. Reaching to her back, she undid the final bow and balled up the wet bikini and tossed it to the shore. It splattered on the sand. Without looking away from me, she undid the bows on her hips and tossed away the second and final piece.

I couldn't see below the waterline, but I could see her breasts. See the way her nipples pebbled, and her skin puckered with goosebumps. My cock crawled up my stomach, escaping my boxers again and throbbing painfully.

"Are you sure?" I balled my hands. "Are you truly sure you want me…after what you've gone through?"

"It's because of what he did that I need you to do this. I need you to replace him. I want to only think of you. I need you to turn the worst night of my life into the best, Aslan."

Her words struck me.

Profoundly.

Deeply.

The night seemed heavier, holier.

I suddenly felt the presence of those I'd lost and all the years that'd been stolen from them. A clawing, slicing pain rose from my belly and centred in my heart. I gasped under the onslaught. I trembled as the sensation of them standing behind me made my nape prickle and instincts hiss to turn around.

I finally understood what Neri had been saying.

How this ocean was now my sanctuary.

A place of serenity and sanctity. Where I could whisper to my dead family, and they would hear me. They were a part of the sea now. They existed in every droplet of salt and in every flick of a fish's tail.

They were dead, but standing there in the moonlight, they were not gone.

Tears burned my eyes as I silently spoke to my father and mother for the first time since that awful night. The worst night of my life. *Benim yüzümden burada olamadığınız için üzgünüm.* (I'm sorry you're not here because of me).

A low groan escaped me as I closed my eyes and drowned beneath everything I'd bottled up for five years. *Keşke sizin yerinize ben ölebilseydim. Keşke kader, sizin yerinize beni seçmeseydi. Keşke hayatta olup bu kızla tanışabilseydiniz. Bana yeniden yaşamayı öğreten bu inanılmaz kızla.* (I wish I could've died in your place. I wish fate hadn't chosen me over you. I wish you were alive to meet this girl. This incredible girl who taught me how to live again).

I swear the ocean swirled warmer around my feet. The stars sparkled a little brighter. And I drifted forward, drawn by forces I couldn't control, guided by fate as I cupped Neri's cheek in my ocean-wet hand and pressed my forehead to hers. "You turned the worst night of my life into the best thing that's ever happened to me. I'd be honoured to do the same for you, *hayatım*."

Kissing her gently, I murmured, "But first, I'm going to tell you what you need to know so I can rinse myself free from this darkness. And while I talk, I want you to wash. Use the ocean you love so much to scrub away what he did to you. Pretend this is a new beginning, for both of us. No more hiding. No more secrets. Tonight is the first night of all our nights."

She shivered as if she felt the same magic in the air, the same power and connection of life and death, beast and mortal.

Her eyes shimmered with moonglow-blue. "You...you literally just used the same words I thought before."

"I did?"

"When I cut the engine, my head was full of thoughts. Of decisions and dreams and—"

"Like what?" I whispered.

"I'll be your first, Aslan." Her hand cupped my cheek, mirroring me. "And you...you will be my last."

"You will be my first *and* my last." I kissed her. A fleeting but full of feeling kiss. "We do this, and there is no one else. Ever."

"No one else." She nodded. "*Ever.* Tonight is the first night of all our nights. The night where no other nights exist."

"Exactly," I groaned, embracing the full-body tremble she caused. "And if you can still stand to touch me once you know who I am, I'm going to carry you to that beach. I'm going to lay you down, kiss you, and do what I've wanted to do ever since the day I realised I was stupidly in love with you."

"Stupidly?"

"Crazily, madly, dangerously…*completely*."

The pain in her eyes softened a little. She found healing in my love, which only made me want to give her more. To shower her in it, bathe her in it, make her swim in it night and day so she never had to reach the shore again.

It took effort, monumental effort, but I let her go.

Taking a step back, doing my best not to fear what lived in the sand beneath my feet, I kept my eyes locked on hers and confessed, "My name is not Aslan Avci."

"Wait…what?"

"It's Aslan Kara. And I'm not the son of a kind math professor but am the one and only heir to Cem Kara…the biggest crime lord in Turkey."

Chapter Forty-Five

ASLAN

(*Moon in Russian:* Luna)

NERI DIDN'T MOVE.

She blinked but that was it.

"Wash, *canım*. Wash and I'll talk."

In a daze, her hands came up, sluicing seawater over her breasts.

Ignoring my pounding cock, I allowed all my secrets to claw me back into their midst.

"Why would I suffer a fate far worse than death?" I whispered, keeping my voice down so I didn't wake Melike or summon my mother's and Afet's attention.

"Because…you aren't one of us." My father winced. "That came out wrong. You are one of us. You are my son. You are ours, Aslan. You always have been. You proved that the day you solved those math problems better than any student. You might not share our blood, but you share everything else."

I froze. "I'm not…I'm not yours by blood? I wasn't born to you?"

He shook his head.

I struggled to breathe. I wanted to leap to my feet and pace. To shout and scream. But the captain glowered at us, ensuring we obeyed his rules of staying quiet and calm, shoved into too small a boat, slipping through the night and into open seas.

"What are you saying?"

"I'm saying we left behind our names, our homes, our very way of life because it was the only way to keep you safe. We forged your birth certificate to get you a passport. I used contacts to get us out. I've done everything I can to make you completely untraceable because…your true father is hunting for you. And he won't stop."

My voice blended past with present, spilling everything I'd learned on that fateful voyage. "My family has always been gifted with numbers. My father with his teaching and his brother with accounting. They earned a reputation for being so talented that Cem Kara approached them. My father and uncle declined his offer, but…over the course of two years, Kara managed to feed enough of his business—through nameless companies and shell outfits—through my uncle's firm, that he didn't have a clue he'd become his main accountant.

"Once Kara told him, that was it. My uncle knew too much. He was his for life and there was nothing he could do about it.

"Of course, Kara paid him well. My uncle bought a new house, new car…he got a little flashy. My father didn't agree with any part of it and put distance between them. It hurt because he and his brother were close, but my father didn't like what Cem Kara did, and he lost respect for his brother. At the time, my father and mother had been trying for kids but couldn't get pregnant. They refused to take money from my uncle for medical help but then…one night, my uncle pitched up with a baby. He told my mother—my adoptive mother—that I'd been the product of a drug deal gone wrong and belonged to no one. No one alive, that is. He said he'd found me alone and screaming. He gave my parents the option of keeping me as theirs or…hand me into the police and let the system have me.

"They chose to make me an Avci. I was loved and adored for years, and when my mother fell pregnant with Melike, we all believed we were blessed. I never questioned that my cheekbones and nose were different to both my parents. Never thought to enquire why I was taller than my father even at thirteen. I believed wholeheartedly they were mine and I was theirs."

Neri kept bathing, ducking into the ocean, covering her shoulders as her hands roamed down her body. "But you weren't a drug deal gone wrong? You were the leader's son…"

I sighed and looked away. "It was Afet who told. She went to a party. Got drunk. She was so close to being raped that night, all because she kept laughing that she had a secret. Taunting dangerous men about a secret of the stolen baby of Cem Kara."

"Oh no…"

"She was only fourteen. She probably overheard her father confessing to his wife one night about my true origins. She fell in with the wrong crowd at an early age and used family secrets to stupidly win friends. Unfortunately, everyone knows the Kara family. And tongues started wagging.

"It only took a single night. One night for Cem himself to pay a visit to his favourite accountant. He asked where his son was. My uncle lied that he didn't know. He didn't admit that the night he'd gone to help with an overseas transaction, laundering money into different accounts, he'd seen four young girls being dragged into Cem's mansion. Girls of similar age to Afet. You have to understand, my uncle was a good man. A family man who merely had smarts for numbers. He didn't want to be in a world of murder, child trafficking, drugs, and violence.

"He hated that he was in too deep and, as he left that night when Kara was called away to deal with something urgent, he didn't go to his car like normal. He snuck into the estate and tried to find those smuggled girls. He didn't find them, but he found me. Sleeping in a crib, innocent as can be. He had no idea I was the biological son of one of the most dangerous men in all of Turkey. He just saw another child about to disappear into a world of monsters. So…he took me."

"What a brave but terribly stupid idea," Neri breathed.

I nodded and drew patterns through the water. "No one found out. No one suspected my uncle for my disappearance. Apparently, Cem tortured most of his men, trying to find out who stole me. They put it down to a rival gang and obliterated them.

"So much blood was spilled in my name, yet Cem never stopped looking for me. Never lost hope that I was alive. His reach doesn't just end in the underbelly of society but has infiltrated politics too. He has politicians on his payroll. He's personally done things for high-ranking leaders, placing them in his debt. He has spies everywhere, so no wonder my parents put as much distance between us as possible. No wonder my father burned our passports—even though mine wasn't entirely legal—before we headed to the dock in Indonesia. Cem Kara has the power to find me anywhere, so I had to end up nowhere with nothing."

Wiping my mouth with a slightly shaking hand, I continued, "According to my father, I was wearing a jumpsuit covered in lions when I was first given to them. They didn't think anything of it. It was just a silly baby print. They used it for inspiration and called me Aslan. They named me after a brave beast, not realising that the very reason I wore a jumpsuit covered in lions was because that was my real name."

"Oh my God," Neri gasped.

"Unfortunately for my uncle, Afet shared this with her drunk friends. Who shared it around town. Who brought the devil knocking on our door. They killed my uncle and aunt. They tried to kill Afet, but she was too quick. She ran to our house. She arrived just before Cem's men did. I hid with Melike, not knowing then that it was me they were after. If I'd known…I would've walked right up to them and given myself up. I would've done anything to keep my family safe. I might not have been born to them, but I *loved* them. So damn much. They were good. They were kind. They weren't murderers like Cem Kara. They weren't rapists or child traffickers. They were decent, hard-working people who donated time and money to the less fortunate.

"And because of me—because they kept me and gave me a good life—they had no choice but to abandon their world and run."

"So that's why they left Turkey?"

"It's my fault. If I'd just gone to Cem myself, they might've been spared. But my father never told me why we ran. He never told me who I was or how I could protect them. He only told me when it was too late to do anything...on a boat bobbing out to sea."

"He was protecting you."

"And by doing so, he earned the wrath of a monster." My heart fisted at the thought of Melike falling into his grasp.

"A monster who is still looking for you," Neri murmured, her hands bathing, washing.

I flinched. "That's why I can't ever go back. Everyone knows my face. Every police. Every criminal. Every politician. Cem made sure that the entirety of Turkey knows what I look like." I laughed coldly. "Doesn't help that I look exactly like him."

"But...he wouldn't kill you. You're his son."

"I'm his pawn. He only wants to control me."

"Did he have any more children?"

"No. According to my father, he was shot in his groin not long after I went missing. Not sure if the bullet tore off his cock or if it was just fate refusing him another child. Either way, he never had another. I'm his one and only. Heir to his blood-soaked fortune and murderous empire."

I shivered at how similar I'd turned out to be. How the violent urges within me were the product of being the offspring of a killer. Why I'd gone out of my way to never embrace them. Always chose calm over anger. Acceptance over fury. It was why I'd never let myself mourn my dead parents because whenever I thought of them...decomposing on the seafloor...the surge of absolute *rage* terrified me. Rage directed at my loved ones. At Cem Kara. At myself.

If I let go...truly let go...who the fuck knew what I was capable of.

"That's why you don't want me stepping foot there? Because you think he'd kill me for loving you?" Neri asked quietly.

I watched her as she rinsed between her legs, a flicker of memory and pain casting shadows over her face.

"I never want you stepping foot there because Kara still has men searching for me. He's desperate to find me, not to welcome me into the family business but to tear me apart. He knows I'll never be what he wants. He lost his heir the day I became an Avci, and right now, I'm his biggest enemy. I'm his greatest threat. And until he's eliminated that threat, his empire isn't safe."

"But you wouldn't go after his business. You want nothing to do with it." Standing on one leg, Neri finished her bath with a quick scrub of her feet.

"Doesn't matter. I'm alive. And that is not permitted."

A cloud covered her face as she suddenly stood upright. Pieces fell into place in her horrified stare. "God, Aslan...y-you willingly hurt Ethan for me, all while knowing you'll die if you're deported back to Turkey?!"

"I'd kill anyone who ever laid a finger on you without your permission, *aşkım*."

"But you can't!" Her face twisted into fear. "You can't, Aslan. *Ever.* Do you hear me? You can't ever be caught. You can't ever go back there."

"I don't plan on going back."

"But if you ever feel the need to defend me. If you ever try to help—" She clamped both hands over her mouth before whispering, "The night you came to get me when I broke up with Joel and we kissed…you said you were stopped for a breath test."

"I was."

"You could've been arrested!"

"They didn't ask for ID. And I wasn't drinking. It was just routine."

I didn't tell her about the cop tonight. When I'd carried a semi-comatose Ethan in my arms. I'd been an illegal immigrant plotting a murder. The fact that I was still free showed fate was on my side.

For now.

"But still…." Tearing her hands through her hair, she waded through the sea. "God, how have you lived with this for so long? I've been so *stupid*. All along, I figured you were just being dramatic when you said I couldn't follow you to Turkey. I was so sure I'd just go with you if you were ever caught. As long as I'm with you, I don't care where we live—"

"And I love you for that but—"

"But now you're telling me that if you get caught, that's *it* for us? That it's over because you'll be *killed*?" She shook her head, her eyes brimming with fresh tears. "No. I can't…*no!* That can't happen. How are we supposed to live with that? How are we supposed to go anywhere? God, Aslan, how do you even leave the house without panicking? How are you so calm about this?"

I smiled gently, stepping into her to brush away her tears. "Now you know why I'm perfectly content in your garden. Why I don't go out unless it's necessary. Why I'm so fucking loyal to Jack and Anna because without them, I would've died years ago. They're the reason I've survived this long. And to go behind their backs and fall in love with you makes me sick because…they are as good as the people who kept me as their own. Twice I've been lucky enough to be cared for by parents who aren't mine by blood. That's why I need to do this right, Neri. Why I need time to ensure Jack knows I didn't have a choice when it came to you. That I can't exist without you. That I didn't intend for this to happen but—"

"We'll get married. That will show them."

"I wish I could. Don't you think I haven't thought that? It was what I was thinking about when you came into my room tonight before you went to Zara's." I winced and swallowed a growl, cursing fucking Ethan all over again. "I was so close to marching into town and buying you a ring and dropping to one knee in front of your parents."

"You were?" Her forehead furrowed as more pain carved its way over her beautiful face. "Then why did you say kissing me was a mistake?"

"Because I also thought about leaving. I pictured myself running and never coming back. I never want you to know the agony of grief. I don't want to steal any more of your life, and I'll steal all of it if I get caught. I'll take the soul you've so wonderfully given me, and a piece of you will die with me, Neri. Just like I would die if anything ever happened to you. That's how this works. A heart for a heart. A life for a life. It was a mistake kissing you because it was the most selfish thing I've ever done...but if I had to go back and make the choice all over again, I would probably kiss you that first night I escaped from the hospital when the nurse told me agents were coming to question me. You found me eating a carrot from your veggie garden. You were twelve. So fucking young, yet I knew. Even then. I should've just given in right there because there was no other path for us. I know that now. I accept it. And, even though I can't legally marry you, I still have a question to ask. A very important question that I really shouldn't ask. A question that demands an answer. An answer that can never be changed once you give it."

She froze.

Her eyes searched mine.

"Ask," she breathed, trembling and causing wakes to feather out in the water around her.

Cupping her face, I ran my thumbs over her cheekbones. "Do you promise me, absolutely fucking swear, that if we ever get separated, you will never come searching for me? That you will let me go. Trust that, if I'm able to, I will return to you. I will come back to you. And if I don't...it's not because I don't love you, but because I can't."

She flinched. "That wasn't the question I was expecting."

"Answer it. Vow to me, here and now."

Looping her fingers around my wrists, she held on to me as tightly as I held onto her. "I swear." Tears glittered on her eyelashes as she murmured, "I will never stop loving you, Aslan Avci. I will never stop hoping that we will find a way to keep you here legally. But...if something happens, I promise I won't go to Turkey."

"In that case, Nerida Taylor..." I stepped into her, our legs kissing in the sea, warmer eddies from our bodies swirling around us. "*Benimle evlenir misin?*"

A smile lifted her lips. "I bet you think I don't understand, but...I have a little secret of my own." Her voice dropped to a whisper, "After you said a similar phrase to me four months ago, I've been learning. I'm my mother's daughter, after all. I can't have her talking to you in Turkish and not be able to eavesdrop."

I chuckled, so grateful she was still Neri. Still pure and strong and brilliant. "And what did I ask you?"

She leaned in and kissed me ever so softly. "You asked me to marry you. Again."

"And?" My belly flipped. "What's your answer this time? Bearing in mind you can never change it."

"*Seninle evlenmeyi çok isterim.*"

My knees buckled. Her words were a vicious punch to the chest. She made a few mistakes. Her tongue didn't quite master the dialect, but...*fuck me*...hearing her speak my language did things to me. Dark things. Light things. Wonderous things.

My fingers slinked from her cheeks and through her hair, dragging her into me.

I didn't think about what she'd endured.

I forgot about what she'd survived.

I lost myself as I pressed my mouth to hers and kissed her.

Kissed her as if she was the only reason I was alive because that was the truth.

Her arms shot around my waist and our legs tangled beneath the surface. Her hips ground against my upper thigh, and my hard cock wedged against her belly. She shuddered in my arms as I plunged my tongue into her mouth.

A small part of me that still contained common sense had just enough strength to pull away. Panting hard, I gasped, "Is this okay? Too fast? Too hard? Tell me how I should touch you and—"

"Forget about what happened, Aslan. I have. Or at least...I'm trying. Don't let him steal us. I love how rough you are with me. I love how desperately you need me. Don't touch me as if I'm breakable because I'm not."

I fell on her again.

I didn't hold myself back.

I kissed and kissed her. Deeper, harder, I forced her to kiss me back. Stroke for stroke, bite for bite.

She'd said yes.

She'd said 'I'd love to marry you'.

Euphoria made me high, but reality made me sink.

Marriage in the eyes of Australian law could never happen.

But...why couldn't it happen right here? In the very sea where we met, beneath the very moon that guided me to her?

Desire suffocated me, and the ever-growing desperation that I'd never been able to outrun slammed into my heart and made me blurt, "Marry me. Right now."

She blinked. "What?"

I had no idea what they said at wedding ceremonies. I had no idea what made them binding. But...before our bodies joined...I wanted us to be official.

Screw age and race and circumstance. Fuck fate and fear and law.

Call me old-fashioned but the moment I entered Neri, I wanted it to be as man and wife. A consummation witnessed by the stars, even if that was all we could ever be.

"Do you, Nerida Taylor, take me, Aslan Avci…previously named Aslan Kara…as your husband? Do you promise to trust me, love me, challenge me, frustrate me? Do you vow to give me your heart in return for mine? Do you promise to let me slay your demons, fight your nightmares, and keep you safe in my arms? Do you accept that you are mine until your dying day, just like I am yours, and trust that we will find each other again and again, always together and never apart?"

Tears rolled down her cheeks, but these seemed different.

They didn't gleam with sadness but glittered with healing. These were the tears of my terribly young wife as she gave me everything that she was, letting me shoulder her shadows and her light, knowing I accepted her for exactly who she was.

"Yes. A thousand times, yes."

I kissed her, my heart racing faster than it ever had before.

Pulling away, she whispered, "Do you, Aslan Avci…previously named Aslan Kara…take me, Nerida Taylor, as your wife? Do you promise to trust me, love me, push me, protect me? Do you vow to give me your heart in return for mine? Do you promise to let me stay by your side, hide you in plain sight, and do whatever it takes to keep you alive? Do you accept that you are mine until your dying day, just like I am yours, and trust that we will find each other again and again, always together and never apart?"

"*Evet, aşkım*," I whispered. "It means, yes, my love. A million times yes."

She laughed softly. "A million yeses are a lot."

"And somehow not nearly enough."

Our lips touched. Our breaths mingled. And I whispered into her mouth, "By the power of the *luna* and the *mare*, the *ay* and the *deniz*, the moon and the sea, I pronounce us man and wife. And seeing as I'm already kissing the bride, I think it's about time I fucked her…just so there's no confusion on the legalities of this union."

Her laughter made me whole.

Her kisses made me ache.

And her trust in me, as I plucked her from the seafloor and carried her to shore, made my heart burst with everlasting fate.

Chapter Forty-Six
NERIDA

AGE: 17 YRS OLD

(Sea in Finnish: Meri)

ASLAN HADN'T JUST BEEN NAMED AFTER A lion. He didn't just share the title of a creature in a children's book: a creature loved by generations and graced with the symbolism of being a king and God. He also shared that magic. That epic evil-defeating power where just being with him made me heal.

Beneath his touch, I could forget.

Beneath his kisses, I could move on.

I'd asked him to replace the memories of what Ethan had done. I'd fallen into his arms, hoping to enjoy it but fearing that I wouldn't. That it would be too soon. That I'd suffer flashbacks and ruin this incredibly important connection, this soul-stitching bond by forcing my body to do something it wasn't ready to do.

But all those fears vanished the moment Aslan wed me beneath the moon. Standing in the sea that'd brought us together, he gave me a new life. He ripped me from the one I'd been living as a young girl with only herself to rely on and gave me everything that he was. His past, his future—he put me above himself in every way.

And that sort of blind devotion cracked open my last remaining shell of teenage-hood, and I grew up. I accepted that this was my mate in life, soul, and heart. This was the man who would take my potential and make me soar—all because he believed in me, supported me, and gave me exactly what I needed to be *me*.

His lips crashed against mine as he waded onto the shore with me in his arms, heading up the beach. Our lips tangled and tongues touched; I'd never felt so exquisitely safe.

During the day, the sand was pockmarked with tourist's feet as they explored around the tiny island. But tonight, it was just us. No signs of humankind. Just the soft hissing of the sea, the bright sparkle of the stars, and the bone-deep knowledge that Aslan hadn't just married me with words but with his very essence.

I felt it in the way he touched me.

It sang in the energy arcing between us.

I tasted it on his tongue as he lowered me gently to my feet and planted his hands on my hipbones.

I swallowed all his promises and made some of my own.

His needs were now my needs, his wants were now my wants.

My allegiance switched from myself to him, knowing he'd done the same for me.

This wasn't just a silly wedding ceremony, committed by two young lovers after a night of horror. This was a rebirth, a baptism, and the beginning of our truth. I had the son of a crime lord to watch over me, secure in the knowledge he would do absolutely *anything* to protect me. And in return, I vowed on my life that I would keep him hidden. He was *mine*, and heaven help anyone who tried to take him from me. This wedding, this marriage, this star-fated union didn't just bind us together, it merged us into one.

One heart. One body. One life.

And as he swept me into his strong arms and placed me gently on my back in the sand, I gave in. I let moonlight flood through me. I let every cell blaze bright and true.

Ethan was nothing. Nothing more than something I'd endured and survived.

Aslan's true heritage was nothing. Nothing more than an origin that didn't define him.

The shadows in our past had no sway on our future and we threw ourselves into the light.

Coiling my arms around his powerful shoulders, I dragged him down on top of me.

He grunted as his erection pressed against my belly, and his chest rose and fell with lust.

He shuddered as I dug my fingernails into his nape, pulling his mouth to mine.

Our kiss was deep and slow, erotic and romantic. Our tongues danced. Our breath mingled. Our blood heated until every inch of me *burned*.

Running my hands down the rippling strength of his back, I slipped my fingers into the wet material of his boxer-briefs. His firm ass was cool to touch and damp with seawater.

He groaned as I squeezed, pulling his hips harder against my belly, grinding him against me.

"Neri…" he breathed, falling over me. "We can go slow…"

I kissed him hard, panting into his mouth. "I don't want to go slow. I want you. I want you inside me."

Digging his elbow into the sand, he hovered over me. The moon glowed behind him, granting a halo and scribing him as a looming silhouette.

My heart kicked.

I ran my hand through his hair.

And then I froze as my gaze shot to the dark horizon.

Only faint. Barely noticeable. But there. Like colour dusted straight from the heavens.

Pink and green.

Green and pink.

Dazzling, flashing, blanketing.

"Oh my God." I sat up, pushing Aslan off me. He rolled onto his side, getting sand stuck all over him.

"What? What is it?" He went to leap to his feet, looking for a threat, but I grabbed his hand and pointed at the sky. "Aurora Australis." Tears filled my eyes in awe. I'd only seen the stunning display a few times in my life. Normally far out to sea, away from light pollution and people, but having them appear tonight of all nights? The night when I'd suffered something unimaginable only to stand taller than I ever had before was...symbolic. It reminded me that I was so much *more*. So powerful, invincible, and strong.

My heart skipped and tripped and *glowed*.

"Wow..." Aslan flopped onto his back.

Faint flamingo pink flickered above, followed by a wash of faded emerald green.

"It's brighter the farther south you go," I whispered. "Tasmania is said to have the best light shows in Australia."

"Better than this?" he choked, his delicious baritone thick with amazement. Another flash of pink, bleeding into midnight purple. "This is insane."

The catch in his voice made my eyes drop to him instead of the perfect sky. His lips parted as his gaze flickered from one subtle splash to another. The moon cast him in silver, and his entire face went slack with wonder.

For a boy of twenty-one, he seemed so wise, so present. He lived with the daily threat of death, yet he never became numb to that fact. Instead, he existed as if each day was his last, aware and perceptive, experiencing with as many senses as possible.

He whispered something in awed Turkish as his eyes mirrored the pink and green magic from above.

And I couldn't help myself.

I tripped even deeper into love.

I wanted him.

Right now.

With the sky raining colours and the stars giving us their blessing.

Without a word, I sat up, brushed off as much sand as I could, then kneeled and straddled him.

His eyes shot to mine.

Questions filled them, worry for my state of mind, questions of what I would do, but then, with a sigh of surrender, he dropped his hands to my hips and swirled his thumbs along the paper-skin fragility of my lower belly.

"I'm yours, Neri. Take whatever you want from me."

Biting my lip, I hooked my fingers in his boxer-briefs. The tip of his cock glistened above the waistband, trapped and angry. How many times had I touched him in the past four months? How many times had I brought him to a release? How many times had I wanted more than just a fumble in the dark or a rushed grind against the door?

Tonight, I got my wish.

There was nothing to stop us.

No one to see.

Ever so slowly, he raised his hips just enough for me to pull the wet material down to mid-thigh. His hands flexed on my hips as I sat slowly…pressing my hot wetness against the base of his erection.

He shuddered and clenched his teeth. "Now is probably a good time to remind you of how sensitive I am. Be kind to me, *aşkım*. Understand that this…having you so near. Being bare against you, I've never been so close to coming in my entire life."

Rocking my hips, I dragged my wetness over him.

He almost jack-knifed up. "I mean it, Neri. If you want me inside you, you can't tease me tonight. Tomorrow, sure. A week from now, I'll have better control. But right now…fuck, *boşalmamak için elimden geleni yapıyorum*."

Grabbing his hands, I threaded our fingers together. Our palms tight. Our grip almost painful. "What did you say?" I rocked again, feeling a rush of power as his thighs bunched beneath me, turning into rocks.

His eyes rolled back as I found the tip of him, sitting still and heavy.

His cock rippled beneath me as he fought for control.

"Fucking *hell*, Nerida. I said, it's taking everything I have not to come. I'm going to embarrass myself. I know I am." His eyes opened, blazing with anger and desperation. "Only you have this magic over me, wife."

That word echoed between us.

"*Fuck*," he groaned. "Wife…"

Everything stopped.

Our fingernails dug into each other as we clasped hands so hard.

"Wife…" he murmured again. "You're my wife. *Karıcığım*." He licked his lips, choking on a guttural groan. "How can a single word make me fall even deeper into love with you?" Untangling one of his hands from mine, he reached up and cupped my cheek. So tender. So pure. So *real*. "When will the falling end, *karıcığım*? Where's the bottom of this feeling? Because I honestly won't survive if I keep falling."

My heartrate blew through crazed and went straight into manic. My entire body broke out in goosebumps. "Never. We keep falling for the rest of our lives."

"In that case, I better learn how to fly." He chuckled darkly. "So I can keep us falling without fear of what will happen when we crash."

"God, I love you, Aslan. Or should I say…*kocam*."

His groan this time echoed in the palm trees and swirled across the sand. "You called me your husband. When did you…how did you…*why* did you learn that?"

I bent over him, my core sliding over his hardness, my lips connecting with his.

He trembled and broke out in a sweat as I kissed him deep and hard.

His mouth opened wide, he sucked on my tongue, his hips bucked upward as he lost himself in me. I could break him with a single roll of my hips. I could make him shatter against his control. And that knowledge, that authority over a man who was so much stronger, so much bigger than me, gave me back the final piece of what Ethan had stolen.

Aslan unwittingly made me whole again, all by breaking in my hold.

"I learned the word because I knew that's what you were," I whispered, breaking the kiss and using the link of our left hands to sit upright. I planted my right palm on his heaving chest, all while his fingers tightened against my cheek.

He stiffened and gritted his teeth. "You make me feel so guilty, Neri. So fucking guilty because…instead of cursing the storm that stole my family, I find myself being so damn grateful it gave me you." His gaze fell from my lips, to my nipples, to the trimmed hair between my legs.

Shyness overcame me, but his hand on my cheek trembled as he caught my eyes again and murmured, "You are the most beautiful creature I have ever seen. I'm honoured that you chose me, Nerida Taylor."

"I didn't choose you," I whispered. "I just found you again…that's all."

Tears glossed his eyes, all while his lips twisted into a snarl. "If you're still planning on consummating this marriage, I suggest you do it before you destroy me entirely."

I laughed under my breath. "You don't mind…me taking control?"

"Mind?" He bared his teeth. "It's a fucking pleasure." A dark gleam replaced the overwhelming love in his eyes. "I'm yours to play with. Yours to touch. Yours to ride. You have my word that I won't take control…unless you want me to." His gaze dropped between my spread legs again. "You're driving me insane. You have me wrapped around every piece of you so tightly, you only have to ask and I'd tear down the fucking sky for you."

He made me feel like a queen.

Like a goddess full of unimaginable power.

I hadn't planned on being the one to take him. But there, sitting above him, holding him at my mercy, a heavy wash of gratefulness filled me.

He gave me that mercy out of respect and love. He could overpower me in a second. He could prove that, for all of society's conditioning that females and males were equal, when it came to brute force, most of us…weren't.

In a way, we were stronger.

Stronger because we held the hearts of beasts and men. We could make them kneel for a kiss and beg for a single word. With his heart-given submission, Aslan gave me back my trust in *myself* and my hips drifted forward and back, forward and back. Stroking him, tormenting him, sending me headfirst into the drunken power he'd given me.

He groaned long and low, the tendons in his neck standing out starkly, his face etched with restraint. "You're going to break me…aren't you, *karıcığım*?"

I grinned, embracing the thrilling sensation of ruling him. "Would that be so bad?"

"Yes. Bad. Very bad." He squirmed a little beneath me. "Give me time to get myself together. Let me pleasure you, Neri. Come higher." His eyes glinted with wicked welcome. "Sit on my face and let me break you apart before you break me."

Running my hand down his carved chest, I sat a little taller and wrapped my fingers around his cock.

He flinched as a stream of curses tumbled from his lips. "*Neri*—"

"Yes?"

"You do this, and I'm done. I'll be the worst husband in the world because I'll blow as—*FUCK*." He snarled like a savage as I angled his rock-hard cock and inserted him an inch inside me.

His entire body broke out in trembles. "Please, Neri…wait—"

I sank over him.

His vicious growl made my hair stand on end and nipples pucker into stones.

"Fucking *hell,* wife." His hand dropped from my cheek to my hip, digging his fingernails into me. "Never imagined. Never dreamed you'd feel like this—"

"Like what?" I whispered as I sat inch by delicious inch.

My body had no memory of being abused by Ethan. The bruises on my wrists didn't ache. The burns on my ankles didn't sting. Every part of me was here. With Aslan. Humming and thrumming, coming alive in ways it never had before.

"Like fucking *everything*," he gasped. "You are everything to me. My air. My blood. My bones. I-I can't breathe. I can't think. I can't—" Another stream of curses cut him off as my body adjusted to his impressive size, and I kept sinking.

I took him piece by piece. I took him deep. I claimed him forever as mine.

And when my clit rubbed against the base of him, I let out a cry full of healing.

By claiming him, I claimed myself.

I was free.

His hand pulsed like a lion's paw on my hipbone, his claws unsheathed and branding me. Our linked fingers sweated and cramped with how strongly we held each other.

Seeing Aslan gasping and sweaty beneath me made my heart grow wings and soar.

Bracing myself against his hand, I let instinct roll through me, giving myself to the primal dance of fucking.

Aslan's chest shot off the sand as I rocked once. His face scrunched up with agony as sweat beaded on his temples. "Neri…I can't. You're too much. You feel too good. I can't hold—"

"It's okay," I whispered.

"It's not fucking okay," he strangled as my thighs tightened against his hips.

I kneeled up, then sat back down.

"*Fuck!*" His mouth fell wide as he rode through the spasms working through his entire body.

I shivered at how full I was, how much he stretched me, filled me. He hadn't touched me, yet I was almost as close as him. Stars coiled in my lower belly. That delicious warning-tightness of a release gathered like a supernova between my legs.

I rode him again, moaning at the friction.

He stiffened beneath me; his jaw clenched so tight.

When he could speak again, he choked, "Get off me, Neri. Let me take a cold swim. I'd never live with myself if the consummation of our marriage lasted two fucking seconds."

I laughed under my breath, so grateful to find humour, so honoured to feel his love. "Watching you struggle makes me wet."

His groan was feral. "You're truly determined to break me."

"I am."

"And *I* want to make you feel a tenth of what you're making me feel. So get off and—"

"You are. Your every twitch. Your every snarl…it drives me wild." I bent and licked his cheek, tasting seawater and sweat. "Want to know why, husband?"

His eyes flashed open, epically dark and glowing like the devil. "If you're going to mock me for being stupidly sensitive, I—"

"Having you so close to losing your mind makes me feel so terribly powerful. Knowing you want me this much—"

"Don't you get it, Nerida? I've wanted you for years. And to finally be inside you?" His chin tipped down and his gaze locked on where we were joined. His groan swallowed the entire island as he bared his teeth and thrust up. "Seeing *me* inside you? Feeling your heat, your incredible searing heat…it's more than I can bear."

"I want you to let go, Aslan."

"Not until you—"

"Let go."

"I *can't*."

"I won't give you a choice." Rocking upright, I sat down heavily, driving him exquisitely deep.

He roared.

His back bowed.

I rose up and sank back down, and something snapped inside him.

Bolting upright, he tore his hand from mine and wrapped both arms around my back. They coiled beneath my underarms, and I cried out as his hands landed heavily on my shoulders. He clung to me, pushing me possessively down onto his cock. The angle of his penetration deepened as my legs kicked out behind him.

"I'm sorry," he groaned, thrusting deep.

"I'm not." I bounced in his lap. "Let go…show me how much you need me."

"*Fuck.*"

Keeping me tightly pinned with his hands on my shoulders, he lost control. He pounded into me, driving upright, riding deep, he became the beast I'd witnessed as he delivered such ruthless revenge for me.

He did exactly what I wanted and let go.

No thoughts. No words.

We were animals, clawing and thrusting, grunting and groaning, fighting with violent desire.

My eyes closed as sensations exploded through me. The rocking, the thrusting, the way he took everything I offered and then demanded more. He shoved me headfirst into a place of core-clenching need.

"Neri. Fuck. *Fuck*—"

He drove unapologetically into me.

He bruised me, used me, and forced my body to forget everyone but him.

He wasn't gentle.

He wasn't slow.

He rutted.

He fucked.

And the first ripple of his cock warned he'd lost the battle.

"I can't—" His growl pushed him over the edge.

He took me even harder, trying to merge us into one.

His hand dove between us, spangled with sand and coloured by moonlight as he found my clit and touched me. He knew my body. After four months of touching me, he knew what I needed better than myself.

I didn't stand a chance.

The abrasiveness of sand. The possessiveness of his stroking. The way he pistoned unforgivingly into me made me break, just like he had.

I cried out as the first wave clenched through me.

His mouth crashed over mine, drinking down my moans, making me give him everything.

I jerked and spasmed in his hold as he continued to ride me, dragging out our pleasure until we flinched with oversensitivity, our bodies singing, our souls raw, our hearts flayed wide and bleeding.

His cock twitched deep inside me. His kiss turned tender from being almost cruel.

He couldn't catch his breath as his forehead pressed to mine, and we just hovered there. Hovered in that perfect moment of shared pleasure and blown apart existence.

Dropping his chin, he kissed my shoulder. He kissed me again and again, schooling his breath all while his cock remained buried deep within me. "I didn't mean to do that."

I chuckled. "I liked it."

"I didn't scare you? You didn't feel trapped—?"

"Never."

I expected him to push me away. To withdraw and end this fragile, aching moment.

Instead, he wrapped his strong, protective arms around me, and pulled me even deeper onto his cock.

Shivering, he whispered, "I shouldn't confess this. I don't know what I'm thinking telling you this, but…knowing my cum is inside you. Knowing a part of my body is inside yours, just like your soul is inside mine is one of the biggest turn-ons of my life."

I snuggled deeper into his arms. "I feel the same way."

Lifting his head, his nostrils flared as his breathing remained fast. "Should I have used a condom? I know your mother took you to get the pill—"

"What?" I frowned. "You know about that?"

"I know everything about you." He gave me a lopsided smile. "Is that creepy? To know that I'm aware of everything you do?"

I twirled his hair around my finger. "Not as creepy as me admitting that I went on the pill, hoping you'd have your wicked way with me."

He chuckled, making his cock twitch deep inside. "My wicked way, huh?"

Pressing my breasts against his naked, sand-sticky chest, I whispered in his ear, "I have a lot of fantasies where you're concerned, Aslan. But my favourite is…" My cheeks heated as I gathered up courage to tell him what I pictured late at night.

"Go on." He nipped my collarbone. "You can't stop now."

"I imagine I'm doing the dishes."

He burst out laughing, jostling me on his lap. "You have some strange fetishes, *canim.*"

"You didn't let me finish." I chuckled. "You always do the dishes. I blame this fantasy on watching you doing chores even when you were sixteen. It's always bugged me that you did so much and never let me help you."

"I could barely breathe having you near. I needed as many excuses as I could to put some distance between us."

"Well, that was pointless." I grinned, squeezing my internal muscles, making him flinch with surprise. "There's no distance between us now."

"Fuck…do that again."

I clenched.

He groaned.

I whispered, "Wanting to help you morphed into a different kind of help as I grew older."

His heart thundered against mine as he licked his lips. "You have me sufficiently intrigued." He smirked. "Do I fuck you while you're vacuuming? How about when you're begrudgingly hanging out the washing? I could use a couple of pegs on your nipples—" He froze as my entire body involuntarily clenched around his again.

Cocking his head, a sly, sexy look glowed in his gaze. "You'd like that? You'd like me to use toys on you?"

My skin prickled with heat. "I-I wouldn't be opposed."

"Fuck, Neri." His burning eyes dropped to my mouth. "Just how hot do you run, my little nymph? Perhaps you're not named after a sea-sprite but a siren."

"If you'd let me finish telling you about the dishes…you'd find out."

His smile was brighter than the moon and aurora lights combined. "Sorry. I'll stop interrupting. Please, put me out of my misery and tell me how a chore like doing the dishes can turn into a full-blown fetish."

Pressing a fleeting kiss to his mouth, I loved how effortless it was between us. So grateful that our togetherness hadn't changed, now that we'd slept together. Our connection had only strengthened, inked in flesh as well as spirit.

"Well…you finally let me help. You're giving me orders on how best to get them clean and…I don't do it right. You get angry with me. Tell me I need a lesson. You move behind me and…punish me."

He groaned, his cock swelling inside me. "Go on."

"You push up my skirt, shove aside my knickers, and take me hard. Soapy bubbles fly from the sink as you ride me. Plates smash as you make me come. And we crash to the floor once you've filled me, unable to stand from the intensity."

He didn't say anything for the longest moment. Self-consciousness filled me, and I leaned back, needing to see his face.

What I saw made my heart crack with overwhelming affection.

He looked at me as if I was the most precious thing he'd ever touched. The most wonderous. Even more wonderous than the pink and green light above us and all the stars in the sky. "Next time your parents are away for the night, you're doing the dishes." He kissed me with a sharp nip. "And then I'm going to fuck you as hard as you want against the kitchen sink."

I shivered. "Promise?"

Seriousness filled his deep dark eyes. "I promise I'll bring all your desires to life…but, I just need to know one thing. Answer me honestly, Neri. And you have my word, I won't ask again. I'll trust you to tell me if you ever need my help."

The air thickened around us. I held his stare. "What do you need to know?"

"Are you okay?" He brushed aside my salt-tangled hair, caressing my cheek with his knuckles. "Was *this* okay? That bastard is dealt with, and I hope to God he's dead, but I can't stop the surges of rage, wanting to find him and hurt him all over again. I want to tear him apart for what he did to you. I want to tear myself apart for not being there for you. I know it's going to take time for me to get over what happened, which makes me hate myself because how can I admit that when it was you who—"

"I give you my word, Aslan. Right here, right now, I'm okay. I'm more than okay. I'm married to the best man in the world, and I feel so cherished and cared for. I can't promise that I won't have moments. That I won't have nightmares of what he did, but…I vow to you, I'll talk to you if I need to, and I'll seek help if it gets too much."

I touched his mouth with trembling fingers. "And in return, you need to talk to me. You can't keep running from what happened that night in the storm. You have to forgive yourself for your family's death. I understand now why that's so hard. I get the depth of guilt you carry. But…I can't stand to see you sad, Aslan."

"I'm not sad. Not anymore. I have you."

"And you can lean on me. You can tell me things. Just like I know I can lean on you. I want to know who you are. I want to know what you loved about Turkey before everything went so wrong."

Nuzzling his nose with mine, he whispered, "Okay, Neri. Next time the darkness comes for me, I'll find you. You have my word. As long as you come to me in return." Kissing me deep, his tongue stroked mine with lazy possession.

Words fled from my head as I drowned in his eternal affection.

His hips rocked up, his body hard and ready.

His arms banded around me in the tightest embrace, and I gave myself over to him.

We sealed our bargain with another release, another magical moment…

Another perfect consummation.

Chapter Forty-Seven

ASLAN

(*Moon in Samoan:* Masina)

IT WAS OFFICIAL.

Neri had collared, leashed, and made me hers to the point of embarrassing domestication. I couldn't imagine living a single moment without her by my side. I didn't want to be apart from her. I slept on a damn beach for her, covered in horrible sand, and highly aware that as dawn crept closer, people would encroach on our little slice of paradise, and our wedding night would be over.

She'd not just broken me last night, she'd broken me all over again this morning when she cuddled into my side, kissed me good morning, and murmured, "You turned the worst night of my life into the best, Aslan. No nightmares. Only dreams come true."

I'd rolled on top of her.

I'd been so fucking close to slipping inside her, sand be damned.

But then the sound of a boat engine growled in the distance, and I reached my limit of beach tolerance.

As much as I still despised the sea, I yanked her to her feet, snatched up her discarded bikini, and dragged her into the ocean.

We didn't speak as we rinsed away the night and swam side by side to *The Fluke*. It welcomed us back onboard with an innocent rock as if it hadn't been an accessory to attempted murder last night. Streaks of Ethan's blood clung to the side where he'd sprawled. Puddles of darkened crimson hadn't fully dried from where I'd shot him in the leg, and two morbid fingers floated in a sad ruby puddle.

The plastic ties Neri had cut off his wrists and ankles rested unwanted, and the can of Coke had rolled through another bloody mess, painting its way across the deck before coming to a stop against the opposite railing.

Jack would kill me if he saw.

Then again, he'd never know.

Never know what happened to his daughter or what I'd done in her name.

All it'd taken was a shared look, a raid of the spare clothing box below so we both weren't naked, and Neri and I got to work. I hauled buckets of seawater to do the initial rinse down while she put on rubber gloves and scrubbed with bleach.

I tossed the fingers overboard.

I tried to take the brush off her.

She shouldn't have to clean up the blood of her rapist, but she merely pecked me on the cheek, gave me a stern look that gave no room for arguments, and we continued working side by side.

Tourists crawled all over Low Isles by the time *The Fluke* sparkled, and occasionally a kid would wave at us where we moored off the reef, never knowing what we'd done the night before.

Once all evidence was gone and we'd eaten a couple of muesli bars and a banana from the cooler, I turned to Neri, ready to suggest returning to Port Douglas.

But she'd already unlocked the scuba cage, pulled out one of the smaller tanks, a regulator, mask, and weight belt, then marched toward me.

And that was how I found myself three metres below the surface, sucking on pressurised gas, struggling with the extra effort it took to breathe. Neri had given me a basic lesson. Rushed through the explanations of how to equalise my ears and what to expect when breathing using a regulator. I'd tried to tell her I knew all that. I'd learned from the best, even if all my knowledge was theory instead of practical. But she didn't stop chattering, keeping me distracted long enough to strap me into the gear, march me to the side of the boat, and push me overboard.

I honestly didn't know how she got me down here.

But I knew how she stopped me from leaving.

I'd never seen anything so….spellbinding.

This place.

This world.

This hidden incredible existence…

I'd been so fucking blind to it. So coloured by my hate and what the ocean had stolen from me that I flatly refused to see its beauty.

I couldn't unsee it now.

Couldn't look away.

All my hate dissolved as colour burst around me.

Death didn't reign here…life did.

Abundant, swift, *vibrant* life and my heart ached at the thought of Melike becoming part of this world. She'd love it. She'd love all the jewelled colours and sparkling prettiness. She'd never want to leave after finding this brilliant city of coral with its treasure trove of gemstone fish.

No wonder she didn't find shore.

Why would anyone want to live in concrete and brick when this existed right below our feet?

I sank to the seafloor, dragged by weights, and did my best not to panic. Reminiscent fear whispered not to trust the beauty. To see danger beneath its façade. To see past the gleaming colours to the dull rocks beneath. Rocks that hid stonefish, eels, and urchins.

But even as I looked for danger, I couldn't help but be seduced by the shoals of fish flittering in the spangling sunlight.

It was like a forest.

A living, breathing, swaying forest full of blinding bright pigment all around me.

The shadows of the deep sea cradled it, protected it, most likely hiding sharks and stingrays and so many other nasty beasts.

But here…on this reef, it was sublime.

Neri dived in, arrowing toward me on the seafloor like a minnow.

Dressed in her red bikini, only wearing the monofin she got for her fifteenth birthday, she moved so seamlessly, so effortlessly, I forgot about the enchanted reef and became utterly enchanted by her instead.

The design on her fin mimicked fish scales, shimmering and opalescent, making her seem like a fucking mermaid. She wore no tank, no mask, no belt. Air bubbles occasionally escaped her nose as she sank beside me, touched my cheek, then tore open a banana that she held in her hand.

Her hair clouded above her, lazy in the current.

And I finally understood.

Understood why she adored this place. Why she had the nickname little fish.

She belonged here.

She was as much a part of this reef as the clownfish and the turtles.

Breaking off a piece of banana, she raised an eyebrow, and let it go.

Instantly, a rainbow swarmed us.

I jerked as my vision clotted with fins of every colour.

Fish that I'd studied and knew so intimately thanks to all the papers and research I'd helped Jack and Anna with. Angelfish, parrotfish, gobies, cardinalfish, butterflyfish, and damsels. They flitted and fought, moving like quicksilver as Neri broke off pieces of banana and let the fruit hover in the sea.

The sound of clicking and snapping filled my ears, giving noise to the feeding frenzy before us. The quick feathers of fins against my bare chest and legs made me flinch as more hungry fish mobbed us.

I struggled to breathe through the regulator as a giant grouper fish lumbered from the hazy distance, sailing through the manic crowd of colour, swallowing a piece of banana before ambling away again.

I suddenly knew what Jack meant.

What he'd warned me about this job.

It would always remain a job while I sat onboard and stuck to facts and figures. I could learn that there were one thousand, six hundred, and twenty-five known species of fish on the Great Barrier Reef, over six hundred corals, and three thousand molluscs but until I saw them with my own eyes...their wonder didn't affect me.

It was just a job, not a calling.

A job I was grateful for as it kept me hidden and let me help those who saved me.

But this...

Fuck me...this was life-changing.

She was life-changing.

She made my chest burst, and my entire body tingled with energy as she took my hand, squeezed my fingers in farewell, then kicked toward the surface.

I stayed on the bottom, kneeling in my little sand shallow—the only bare piece of reef that wasn't swallowed by vibrant purple and blue coral, two-toned swaying anemone, or blood-red seafans.

Neri swam lazy and strong above me, leaving a trail of bubbles as she broke the surface. She spent a few moments catching her breath, before descending to me with a powerful kick, a beaming smile, and her hair streaming wildly behind her.

My heart fisted as she reached for me.

I held out my hand.

Her cool fingers threaded through mine, and she tugged me to my feet. Pointing at a crowded boulder, overgrown with staghorn coral and anemones of neon green, she cocked her head. Clownfish darted in clouds of yellow poisonous fronds, glaring at me as Neri pulled me closer, then pointed at a shadowy crevice.

I grabbed her wrist as she went to insert her hand.

Cutting my fingers across my throat, I shook my head, willing her to see the dangers, trying to speak in a world where air and speech weren't permitted. *Don't put your hand in there, are you crazy? There's probably a damn sea-snake.*

She grinned as if she'd heard me and untangled my fingers from her wrist with firm pressure. Slowly, she dipped her hand into the hole, sending my pulse skyrocketing.

I froze as she gracefully pulled her hand back out, revealing the tiniest gold seahorse bobbing in her palm, its tail looped tightly around her thumb.

A rush of bubbles escaped my regulator as I fell yet again.

I thought I'd reached the bottom of my love for her last night, but this...this was yet another level. A level of absolute enchantment and out-of-control obsession. A level that made Neri otherworldly to me.

The seahorse happily clung to her thumb. She didn't offer it any banana but held it in a shimmering patch of seawater. I watched in absolute awe as the tiny thing ate something I couldn't see.

Thanks to a study Jack had made me type up, I knew seahorses were carnivores and preferred plankton, shrimp, and copepods. The males carried the babies, and most species mated for life.

On paper, they were strange little beasts, yet here, in their element, they were magical.

Neri tapped my shoulder, wrenching my attention from the seahorse to her face. She pointed at the surface and gently unwound the seahorse's spiny tail from around her thumb. Passing it to me on a buffet of water, she kicked off with a flex of her powerful core, leaving me on the reef while she caught another breath.

I'd never been more in awe of her.

I'd spent hours timing her breath holds in the pool, yet I hadn't appreciated the freedom it gave her out here. To swim unencumbered. To be just like the fish who belonged here. The fish she believed she was.

While waiting for her to return, I placed the seahorse back near its crevice. I didn't have the guts to put my hand into its home, but the creature fanned the fins on its back and vanished without a trace.

I lost myself to the chaos.

All around me life bloomed. Luminous prawns and cheeky crabs, flounder fish burying themselves in sand, and a shoal of yellowfin goatfish spiralled in the distance. A drifting piece of seaweed tangled itself on some coral, revealing a seadragon hiding in its folds.

I wished I had a camera.

I wanted to capture this insane day, this insane world.

Neri tapped me on the shoulder, making me flinch.

Twisting to catch her eyes, I frowned.

She'd put on a mask.

Her eyes blinked behind the clear covering, and the strap around her head did its best to trap her dancing seaweed hair.

My pulse crept higher as she waved the diving knife I'd used on Ethan in my face.

Why the hell does she have a knife?

Bubbles rushed from my regulator as I fought with questions I couldn't ask. Cursing the lack of ability, I shrugged. *What?*

Twisting, she used her monofin to spiral on the spot, pointing toward the edge of the reef in the blue-hazy distance.

A flicker of something grey.

Is it Sapphire?

I had no idea what the hand gesture was for a dolphin. Had her pod come to see her? Did they know *The Fluke's* engine? Perhaps they'd been waiting just off the reef since last night, patiently waiting to see Neri.

Giving me a come-hither wave, Neri kicked her fin and cut through the water. I jumped off the bottom and swam behind her. Without flippers of my own, I wasn't nearly as fast, but I focused on my breathing. On the effort it took to inhale and exhale, following her path through the reef, keeping my legs far away from stinging coral and my feet from venomous stonefish.

When we reached another sandy area, I sank to the bottom and shrugged again.

Neri hovered above me.

Holding up her finger, she kicked toward the surface. She broke the water above, her fin swaying backward and forth as her head remained in the world where humans were meant to exist.

She stayed up there longer than I expected and another flicker of grey whipped my attention to the murky depths beyond the atoll.

Shit.

Every muscle in my body froze.

I went rigid.

I forgot how to breathe.

Every instinct told me to fight for the surface, but Jack's lessons echoed loudly in my ears. *"If you see a shark, hold your ground. They're most likely just curious. You have a much better chance of surviving if you make eye contact, stay head on, and punch it square in the nose if it charges."*

The shark twisted in the water, its fins slicing effortlessly. Rows upon rows of jagged teeth glittered in the sunlight spearing through the water. Scars branded its side and part of its gills looked torn, but the wounds were old, not new. They spoke of a vicious war that it had won.

Its tail never quickened, but it changed direction, swimming directly for me.

Fuck.

FUCK!

I glanced at Neri still hovering on the surface.

At least it wasn't going after her.

At least she was safe and—

Shit.

The shark picked up its pace.

Its powerful grey body undulated and weaved.

Three metres, two metres, one—

Neri shot in front of me, blocking my vision and placing herself in harm's way.

Instinct roared through me.

Grabbing her around the waist, I shoved her to the side, desperate to put her behind me.

She fought and struggled, elbowing me in the stomach.

I doubled over, losing my regulator and sending a tornado of bubbles flying.

The shark baulked and swam around us.

I grabbed the mouthpiece and shoved it back between my teeth. Neri cupped my cheeks and studied me. She mouthed, "*I'm sorry*", then took off after the damn shark.

What the actual fuck—?

Spinning in place, I almost lost my regulator again as Neri swam alongside the shark, gently touched its dorsal fin, then cut in front of it.

My heart tried to leap into the sea.

I swam after her, panic and fury pouring through me.

How *dare* she put herself in such danger?

How *dare* she try to protect me, then swim after the same monster she protected me from!?

How fucking dare—

My mind went blank as Neri folded her legs and descended to the sandy floor in front of the shark. She sat on her heels, her monofin wafting up grit. The knife in her hands glinted, and I braced myself for a fight.

What the hell is she doing?

She wouldn't hurt the shark…she'd never do that.

So why does she have the knife?

The shark slowed its cruise and circled her. It wasn't the biggest predator I'd ever seen, but it could still rip off her arm as it bumped her shoulder, then slowed to a coast. Its eyes stayed locked on Neri as it hovered over her lap, sinking down and down until its head rested on her knees.

I couldn't fucking move.

If I wasn't sucking on air, my mouth would be hanging wide and my eyes popping out of their damn sockets.

What the hell is going on?

I couldn't believe what I saw. Couldn't believe this girl. This insanely incredible, recklessly crazy girl. This girl who I'd loved since she was twelve and somehow been lucky enough to make my wife…a girl showing me an entirely different side to her.

The siren side.

The siren currently sitting on the seafloor with a pet fucking shark!

Catching my eyes, Neri shook her head once. Her hair shifted left and right then bloomed upward as she tipped her head and stabbed the knife into the sand.

The shark didn't move. Its gills ebbing and flowing with breath, sending fresh seawater through its system, siphoning the minuscule amounts of oxygen from the brine.

I shot forward as Neri's hands touched its jaw.

Neri!

A cloud of bubbles shot around my face. Swiping them away so I could see, Neri held up her hand as I stumble-swam closer.

The shark shifted a little on her lap, but she laid her free hand on its nose and shook her head angrily at me.

Angry with me?

Kafami sikeyim, I was *ropable* with her.

What the hell are you doing?

She tapped her chest as if to say she was running out of air and gave me an okay signal with her forefinger and thumb. She threw the signal at me again, obviously trying to get me to accept.

It went against every instinct and took every inch of control, but I nodded reluctantly.

She narrowed her eyes, daring me to move.

Crossing my arms over the vest holding my tank, I stayed where I was. I trusted that she knew this world far better than me. It drove me insane having her sit so calmly with a fucking shark in her lap, but…what else could I do?

If she gets bitten…

That shark is fucking sushi.

Once she knew I'd obey, her attention returned entirely to the grey-skinned monster.

Her forehead furrowed as she ducked her head, her fingers diving into the corner of its mouth.

Fuck me.

It took every inch of control not to go to her. Not to punch that beast in its gills and tear her back to the surface.

Her fingers dived deeper.

My gut churned with nerves.

It felt like it took an eternity but it was only a few awful breaths before she extracted something sharp and curved, stroked the shark's nose, and pulled her hands away as the aquatic beast swam lazily off her knees.

The moment it was gone, she fisted whatever she'd pulled from the jaws of death, grabbed the knife, then kicked toward me.

Pointing toward the surface, she smiled and raised her hands above her head.

The sleek lines of her belly made me hard.

The curves of her breasts made me desperate.

I couldn't move as she kicked toward the surface with the knife cutting through the salt, moving as gracefully as the shark she'd just stroked.

Chapter Forty-Eight
ASLAN

(Moon in Arabic: Qamar)

"WHAT THE FUCK WAS THAT DOWN THERE?" I demanded, hauling myself onto *The Fluke* and hooking my mask on the staircase. Seawater dripped off me as I fought against the buckles and straps wrapped around my waist.

Neri had already removed her mask and monofin and stood in a puddle of her own making, wringing out her hair with both hands. Nudging her chin at the table, she said, "It had a hook in its mouth."

My eyes narrowed. "How could you possibly know that? It looked like it was ready to eat you."

Tossing her hair over her shoulder, she padded toward me and unbuckled my weight belt with practiced fingers. Placing the cumbersome thing on the table beside the large rusty hook she'd salvaged, she went behind me and turned off the oxygen, grabbed the tank, and waited for me to shrug it off before stowing the scuba gear against the table leg.

Turning back to face me, she gave me a shy smile. "Would you believe me if I told you I knew why it'd appeared and that's why I went to get the knife?"

"To protect yourself?"

"No, to cut any twine that might've been caught it its gills. I've had a few sharks where the hook gets lodged in their jaw but the line goes through them. It's a delicate operation to remove it all."

"You mean to tell me you've done this *before*?" I raked both hands through my hair, raining ocean. "Fucking hell, Neri."

"Of course." She shrugged. "That's how the sharks know to find us."

"What?" I laughed under my breath. "That's insane. They're an apex predator. They don't seek out human company, just like we don't—"

"They're not violent, Aslan. They're mostly gentle and super intelligent." Linking her hands, she murmured, "There's a woman who's been diving with sharks her entire life. She noticed so many had hooks that one day, she decided to remove one. After the initial shock wore off for the shark, it came back for pets and to say thank you. Without fail, that shark always turns up whenever she dives, visiting her and showing its gratitude, and…it also told others what she did. Just like the ones I've helped have told others on this reef."

I paced in front of her, my mind racing. "I don't believe this. I thought—"

"Sharks seek out remora fish to eat the parasites off their skin. This is the same thing. Is it so hard to believe that they know the sound of the boats that help them? That they'll come for help, knowing we'll give it?"

I stopped pacing, glowering at her. "How many hooks have you removed?"

She grinned. "Only twenty-two so far but the other woman, Cristina Zenato, has removed over three hundred."

"Twenty-two—" My voice caught. "Twenty-two times you've put your hands in a monster's mouth." Stalking into her, I grabbed her wrists and looked at her hands. Such delicate, fragile hands. "You expect me to believe that your parents allow you to do that? That they don't dress you in chainmail and forbid you from going near a shark?"

"It was Mum who helped me with the first one," Neri whispered, her ice-blue eyes darkening. "I'm fine, Aslan. I know you were worried, and I probably should've waited until you were back onboard before doing it, but…I wanted to share it with you." Her voice turned husky. "Having you dive with me…I never thought that would happen. I know I didn't really give you an option to say no this morning but…I want to tell you how much it meant to me. To share that world with you. The world where I most belong. To show you that your family is safe down there, amongst all that magic and colour."

"Neri, I—"

The air suddenly crackled around us. My heart beat thickly.

It was a mistake to touch her while my rage flowed. I shouldn't have grabbed her when all instincts screamed to protect her…from herself.

Having her sway toward me. Having her eyes scream an invitation. My anger quickly exploded into lust.

Pulling her into me, I pressed her hands against my bare stomach. My wet black boxer-briefs clung to my cock, revealing how hard I was, how fucking desperate I'd become to prove to myself that she was okay. She wasn't hurt. She wasn't gone.

"You have no idea what you do to me, *aşkım.*"

Her fingers flexed against my belly as her gaze locked on my straining erection. "Oh, I think I have some idea."

"No." I shook my head, my heart swimming with black desire. "You don't."

Her gaze lingered on my mouth.

She sucked in a thin breath.

Electricity flared painfully between us.

"Show me then," she whispered.

I stiffened. I did my best to let go of her wrists. "Not here. Not with the tourists so close and so soon after last night."

"Last night was our wedding."

"You were also rape—"

"*Don't*," she seethed. "Don't ever utter that word again. Nothing happened to me last night apart from the most incredible thing." Stepping into me, she coiled her arms around my waist, pressing her belly against my hardness.

I flinched and sucked in a groan. "Nerida...I'm warning you. I'm not in the right headspace to be gentle. You've infuriated me by putting yourself in harm's way. You made me watch while you put your hand inside a horror show of teeth. You pushed me overboard for fuck's sake—"

"So take that anger out on me. Show me how I made you feel."

"Neri...don't push me."

"Aslan, give in."

"Not today—"

"Yes, today." Her hand wriggled between us and wrapped around my cock.

"Shit." I buckled over, fisting her wrist again, trying to stop her but traitorously pressing her palm harder against me. "You drive me insane."

"Show me."

"I can't. I refuse to hurt you."

"You won't hurt me."

"In my current state, I can't guarantee that."

She trembled and bit her bottom lip. "Don't you see what that does to me, Aslan? If you touched me, you'd know how wet I am."

A stream of Turkish curses escaped me as my cock rippled with need. Her fingers stroked me up and down, my hold on her wrist not stopping her in the slightest.

This was torture.

Mental and physical torture.

I'd snap soon.

And when I did, I'd terrify her and prove just how much I was holding back last night. Just how much being inside her made all the dark and dangerous parts of me come out to play. I might strive to be better than what I was born to be. I might choose kindness over cruelty, but when it came to her...I forgot who I was supposed to be. I forgot all my promises. I forgot everything good and kind and became everything bad and nasty.

Clinging to my last threads of self-control, I grunted, "You have to stop, *hayatım.*"

"And you have to trust that I'm okay. I'm more than okay. I want you, Aslan. I want the real you. The sensitive you. The violent you."

My eyes flared wide, locking with hers. "You don't know what you're saying."

"I do."

Pressing my nose against hers, I growled, "If I gave you the real me, you'd jump off this boat and never stop swimming."

"Watching you beat Ethan last night was one of the hottest things I've ever seen. Not the violence. Not the blood. But *you*. You protecting me. You honouring me—"

"I wouldn't be protecting you today, Nerida. You put yourself in harm's way. Harm that I couldn't save you from. You're the one I'm angry with, no one else."

"Then show me how mad you are, husband. And perhaps, I'll apologise."

"You're literally going to be the death of me." My bones cracked as she sent another white-hot wave of lust through me. I tried, one last time. My last-ditch effort to keep her safe…from me. "I'm not touching you, wife. Not while I'm seconds away from spanking you instead of loving you."

She tipped her head back and moaned. Loudly. "Do it. I made you worry for me today. I made you watch me do something dangerous. Punish me."

My vision went black. "Another one of your fetishes, *canım benim*?"

"A fantasy."

"A nightmare." I shook my head, planting my hands on her shoulders to push her away.

Only…

My fingers dug into her.

I held her tight and trapped.

"A nightmare that I can't seem to wake up from," I breathed, unable to look away from her mouth. Her pretty fucking mouth that'd sucked me off on this very boat. Her mouth that I'd kissed a thousand times and would always want a thousand more.

Another bolt of energy burned through us.

My hands turned to shackles on her shoulders.

Marching her back to the table, I wedged her against the edge and yanked at the bows of her bikini on her hips. "If I get too strong, you stop me. If I take too much, you scream. If I fuck you too hard, you—"

"Seahorse," she whispered. "I'll say the word seahorse and—"

I didn't let her finish.

I grabbed her chin, held her prone, and kissed her brutally hard.

She moaned and linked her fingers in my hair, her tongue waging war against mine. She didn't submit. She didn't *apologise*. She fought me.

And I snapped.

Knocking her feet out from under her with a swipe of my leg, I caught her and lowered her to the deck. Tourists were close, but they wouldn't see. Not if we stayed down. She gasped as I splayed her, wet and dripping, on the very same deck where I'd given her CPR. In a similar position with her on her back and our lips fused together in life and death.

That memory tried to blend with this.

The terror I'd felt at her blue lips. The horror I'd felt at her limpness.

I'd been so full of panic, so full of illicit love, of fear and loss and *need*.

She'd never apologised for that incident either.

In fact, she'd never said sorry for all the shit she'd made me feel. For all the ways she'd made me fall. All the inevitable, unfightable ways she'd made me hers.

She owed me her life.

On multiple fucking occasions.

My kiss turned harder, bruising both of us.

I sucked on her tongue and fisted her breast with bruising fingers.

She'd been born to torment me.

That much was blaringly true.

Her one purpose was to make me love her more than I could bear, waiting to see just how much despair I could survive at the thought of losing her. I'd spent the past five years pledging my every waking moment to keeping her safe.

But now that we were together—married by stars and auroras—the fear of her being ripped from me, by death or other disasters made my fury *blaze*.

I could spend my entire lifetime fighting to keep her safe.

From everything.

But in the end, the one thing I could never keep her safe from…

Is me.

Feral ferocity roared through me. I fell into a red haze. A haze of passion, punishment, and pain. Biting, kissing, branding my way down her neck, my hand slinked under her back and tore at her bikini bow. She cried out as I ripped the triangles away and threw them behind me.

She shivered as I froze at her bareness. At how hard her nipples were. At how golden her skin gleamed from the sun. With sunshine glowing all around us, she looked exactly like what she'd been on the seafloor. A siren. A nymph. A creature skilled at dooming men and enslaving their mortal souls for all eternity.

Another burst of lusty anger billowed like wildfire in my veins. Ocean droplets fell from my hair as I bent over her and latched my mouth around her left nipple.

I sucked.

Hard.

My teeth teased with barely held restraint.

Her back soared off the deck with a moan.

I wanted more.

I wanted her pleading, begging. I wanted her so undone she remembered nothing but me.

Only me.

My nostrils flared as I wedged a hand on the deck beside her and sucked her other nipple. I claimed it all. I made her writhe. I didn't care if I granted pleasure mixed with pain.

She deserved it.

Deserved to exist in that mind-shattering, body-scratching, bone-aching state that I was so accustomed to.

She made me feel twisted up and flayed alive every fucking day.

She owed me.

Owed me for all the moments and all the longing.

"This is what you do to me every time you put yourself in danger," I growled. With my free hand, I tore at my boxer-briefs, shoving them down my legs. Kicking them away, I snatched her hip and slid her beneath me, crashing my entire weight on top of her. "This is how insane you make me." I pressed my hard cock against her thigh. "This is how desperate you make me." I ground against her. "This is the pain you cause."

She cried out as I spread her legs and shot my hand between them.

Her eyes snapped closed as I sank a single finger inside her.

She was wet.

So fucking wet.

"Shit, Neri." My one finger became two.

"More," she groaned. "God, more. *Please—*"

I drove my fingers as deep as they would go, my knuckles inside her, my thumb pressing hard on her clit, shoving her high, high, high up the mountain of pleasure.

Her moans deepened into a throaty plea. "God—"

"This is what you make me become at the thought of losing you." My grunt mingled with hers, my hand driving relentlessly between her thighs. "You make me wild, wife. You make me dangerous."

"Aslan—" Her head arched as I did things to her. Naughty things, sinful things, but somehow far too innocent for what I truly wanted.

"This is what you make me become when you defy me." Tearing my fingers from her core, I grabbed her cheek and smeared her arousal over her. "Does that turn you on? Knowing that I can't exist without you?"

"Yes. God, yes." Her eyes fluttered as I dragged my thumb possessively over her lips.

"Don't look away," I commanded, my hips slotting between her open legs. "Never look away while I show you who you belong to."

She sucked in a breath as I wedged my elbows on either side of her and looped my fingers in her hair, holding her prone. My hips arched, seeking, beseeching. Driven by instinct, controlled by lust and force.

I found her heat.

I spread her wide.

I trembled on the precipice and her eyes flared with hunger.

"This is how much I crave you. All. The. Fucking. Time."

I thrust inside her.

Brutally hard.

Dangerously deep.

Ice-blue fire burned in her stare as I filled her up, stretched her wide.

Her legs snapped around my ass, holding me, forcing me to give her everything.

I twitched.

I gasped.

My curse of oversensitivity made everything unimaginably intense.

My blood sang.

My cock throbbed.

I could come like this.

Speared deep.

Locked home.

Joined as one with this beautiful, infuriating girl who'd somehow been born with the matching, missing piece of my soul.

Emotion knotted with instinct.

Feelings braided with savagery.

The fatal mixture left me stripped bare, potently aware, and breaking beneath wave after wave of intensity.

"This is how much power you have over me." I rolled my hips, making her feel every inch. "This is how you have me on my knees, Neri." My fingers tightened in her hair, tugging hard, keeping her totally trapped. "But right now...I have you on your back."

She bit her bottom lip, her breathing fast and fluttering.

"I have you spread, wet, and at my fucking mercy...and you know what I'm going to do?"

She gasped and tried to shake her head, unable to move with my fist-hold.

"I'm going to show you what happens when you steal the heart of a guy like me."

I thrust up.

I drove painfully deep.

She cried out as all my humanness vanished as the beast she'd made me become exploded from my darkness.

I rode her.

I bucked into her as my heart cracked, and my pulse roared in my ears. My knees scraped against the deck as our body's smashed against each other. She slipped and skated through puddles of seawater.

We were messy and out of control as I stabbed into her again and again. Fighting, colliding, our grunts loud and animalistic.

My mouth fell wide as a savage roar escaped me.

I dropped my head and kissed her.

She moaned into my mouth, giving me her air, replacing all the oxygen I'd given her when she was fourteen. I'd been a love-struck eighteen-year-old, giving her CPR. Desperate to make her live. Frantic with fear of losing her. Already so fucking aware that if I lost her, that was it.

She was it for me.

I didn't want to live a single day if I couldn't have her.

My hips drove exquisitely hard.

Punishing her.

Imprinting my cock deep, deep inside her.

Never again would her body know anyone else.

I would make damn sure of that.

I would mark her, brand her, own her in all the ways she owned me, so she always belonged, always came home, always remembered me, wanted me, needed me.

A whisper in my head tried to steal the moment.

The godawful terror of what would happen if I was ever caught.

If I was gone, I didn't want her to be alone.

I would want someone else to protect her, love her—

Who the fuck am I kidding?

The thought of her with anyone else? Even if I was alive or dead?

It made me rage.

It made me roar.

It made me pound and pound and *pound* into her, fisting her hair, rutting into her like a savage, ensuring she burned like I burned and craved like I craved.

"This is what you get," I panted into her ear as tingles and painful sparks of an impending release ricocheted down my spine. "This is what you leashed, Neri, the day you found me."

Her fingernails shredded my back as I lost any resemblance of being a man.

She turned as wild as me. As out of control and manic.

She grunted as I fucked her.

Over and over, her cries turning louder, the harder and faster I took her.

Her cries turned to mewls as she stiffened beneath me. Her toes curled. Her head arched. And when she screamed, I silenced her with the deepest kiss, the most controlling tongue.

I gagged her all while a barbaric snarl escaped me as her body rippled around mine with an electrifying release.

She fisted me.
Milked me.
And I didn't stand a fucking chance.
I went with her.
I chased her.
I mounted and rutted and spilled every piece of my body and soul inside her.

My sensitive skin quaked. My heightened awareness shattered.
She was my first and my fucking only.

The sharpest release of my life tore down my spine, spurted up my cock, and made me jerk and shudder within her.

I suffocated my groans with another kiss, forcing her to lick up my desire.
Impulses to keep driving into her ensured I fed her every drop.
Instinct to keep marking her as mine made our ending almost as violent as our beginning.

I didn't want to stop.
I couldn't stop.

I'd let myself go, and it took a monumental effort to gather the parts of me that needed to be caged and swallow them back down where they belonged.

It took a while.

An eternity before my hips finally settled, sated and content in the knowledge that she was well and truly mastered.

She was mine in every way that mattered.

That knowledge was enough to control my raging heartbeat and soften my violent nature.

We clung to each other.
We breathed in each other.

And as the dregs of my humanity returned, horror rippled down my spine for what I'd done. "Shit…Nerida." Pushing up to my elbows, I untangled my fingers from her sun-drying hair. I went to withdraw. "I'm sorry—"

"Don't you dare apologise." She smiled with swollen lips, and grabbed my ass, preventing me from disengaging. With a groan, she stretched beneath me like a well petted cat, our bodies slicking and sticking to each other. My cock pulsed deep inside her, reacting to the way she preened, already thirsty for another taste.

I stiffened as her spine popped and her face flared with discomfort, but nothing could hide the gleam of satisfaction or the smug satedness in her eyes. "So…that's what happens when I steal the heart of a guy like you, huh?"

Part of me was ashamed.

I never wanted to be so hard with her, so desperate or cruel.

But the way she choked on a smile and her gaze glowed with love helped ease the shame rapidly crawling up my throat. "You did want to get to know me better…" I smirked, my cock twitching inside her. "Now, you do."

She licked her lips. "Unfortunately for you, it's made me want to know *everything*. Every part you've hidden from me. Every piece of you that you pretend doesn't exist. I know you loved your father. The one who gave you a love for numbers and sweetness, but…you're not just that son. You're another's too. An heir to someone powerful and cutthroat and frankly, a man who sounds like a monster—"

"That's why I will never embrace that side of myself."

"But don't you see? You're not just him. You're better than him. You're *more* than him. You will never be him because you're already your own person. I'm not afraid of you, Aslan. I will never be afraid of you because that side of you protects me, even while ravaging me—"

"Ravaging you?" I snorted, letting words I didn't want to acknowledge linger between us. "Is that what I did?"

"Pretty sure you went all lion on me."

I laughed under my breath. "I'm well aware of the books you read on your e-reader, Neri. You're not so innocent in all of this."

Her eyebrows vanished into her hairline as she blinked like a sweet little virgin instead of the dirty temptress she was. "You have no idea what I read."

"Oh, I don't, do I?" I nuzzled my nose with hers. "How about the one with the dragon shifter and the joining knot? His mate can't get away as he—"

"Oh my God. How do you *know* about that?"

"I'm on the same account as you. Anna gave me her old e-reader when she upgraded, remember? I get to share your library and read all about French men stringing up Australian girls, using toys and whips and—"

"Oh God, *stop*." She laughed.

"See where I'm going with this?"

Her cheeks blazed bright red. "You think I'm—"

"Hot for domination?"

She groaned and buried her face into my neck. "You said it, not me."

"Your body's been telling me ever since I first kissed you." I stiffened inside her, my blood thickening, my desire swelling. "Why do you think I can barely control myself around you? You smile at me all sweetly. You let me finger you against my door and kiss me with your innocent tongue, but then you go to bed and read some deliciously filthy stuff."

"We could…enact some of that filth if you want."

"Fuck, don't tempt me." I hardened, stretching her all over again, highly aware we hadn't disengaged, just like we hadn't last night—almost as if the thought of being apart was too painful to contemplate.

We were human. We had no magic or primitive mating rituals like in Neri's books. Yet…our hearts had provided a joining tie. A knot that couldn't be undone because it would be far too painful to survive without it.

Words faded, and she snuggled deeper into my arms.

Primordial urges sang down my spine to thrust again, but the aching tenderness of the moment made me roll onto my side and drag her with me.

Her leg hooked over my hip, keeping us as one.

Inside one another.

Our eyes locked.

Our lips sought the softest kiss.

And I couldn't help fearing I'd done something wrong. That I shouldn't have touched her the way I did. Shouldn't have fucked her so roughly. Especially after…

"*İyi misin, karıcığım?*"

She shivered and kissed me again. "I will never tire of hearing you call me your wife. And yes, I'm fine." Her eyes burned like glaciers into mine. "Truly."

"What I did…the force I used, it didn't…trigger anything?"

A shadow swirled over her face, but she held my stare. "I promise you, Aslan. While I'm in your arms, nothing else exists. Your need for me keeps me entirely present. When you're like this…deep inside me, I'm nowhere else. I'm wholeheartedly yours."

My heart swelled. "And you'll let me help if that ever stops being true."

"Always." Slinging her arms over my shoulders, she hugged me tight. "As long as you keep 'helping' me in that way, I have no doubt I'll be cured. Just…don't hold yourself back from me. You've always restrained yourself. I feel it every time you kiss me. Just give me everything, and I swear to you…I'll be okay."

I really should've listened harder.

I should've heard what she didn't say.

Neri had survived one of the worst things a girl could endure.

She wore her bravery to shield her.

She used my love to heal her.

Yet no matter how much I loved her or how fiercely I gave her what she needed…she'd become like me.

Trapped by a past she didn't want to confront.

Preferring to ignore it, hide from it, pretending life could be normal, all while it festered and bled in the dark.

Chapter Forty-Nine

NERIDA

(*Sea in Croatian:* More)

"DID HE SURVIVE?"

I blinked, confused all over again as the past swirled with marine colours, popping painfully into memories. "Pardon?" I rubbed my temples, cursing the faint headache that'd appeared. A headache I was familiar with. I'd been afflicted with them ever since I was twenty. Brought about by the worst moment of my life. A moment far, far worse than the rape. So, *so* much worse.

I would've happily spread my legs for Ethan every night if I didn't have to endure what came next. What came next for Aslan…

My heart wrenched in my chest, my emotions too sharp and vicious. I didn't want to tell the reporters what happened at Christmas. I didn't want to tell them what happened after or about the day when my parents feared I would die from a broken, haemorrhaging heart.

I didn't want to relive it because I'd barely survived it the first time.

"Nerida?" Dylan asked gently, leaning over and touching my knee. "Are you well? Do you want to stop? We can come back tomorrow if you wish."

I patted the back of his hand and forced a smile. "No, no. I'm fine. I know it's getting late, but…I'd rather tell you everything today if that's okay."

"It's no bother to come back tomorrow." Margot smiled, the sun starting its lazy descent toward the horizon. I'd been talking for hours. Lingering on the good, hiding from the shadows that hunted me.

Tomorrow…

No.

It has to be today.

Now.

Because now was the only moment any of us had. If I'd learned anything in my long life, it was that. It was the unarguable knowledge that living didn't happen in the future or the past. It happened right now, and it was up to us to focus and *live* it because if we didn't...it was gone.

Sitting taller, I cleared my throat and asked, "What was the question, Dylan? I want to continue. I'm okay to push on."

He studied me carefully before finally repeating, "Did he survive? Ethan...? Did he survive what Aslan did to him and the midnight swim?"

My lips stretched into a smile. A smile that I hoped wasn't too smug as Ethan was a person, after all. He'd been someone's son. Someone's brother. He'd done something awful and paid an awful price. But I held no animosity or fear toward him anymore. Not like all those years ago. Then I'd drowned beneath feelings I couldn't deal with, ensuring Karma visited us in an equally awful way.

"To this day, I don't know." I stared at my age-stained hands. "He was never found. Just like Aslan's family was never found. All of them vanished without a trace."

"Do you think Ethan was...eaten?" Margot winced. "Could that happen? Could the very shark that you helped with the hook have eaten him as a thank you?"

I smiled. "Perhaps. The ecosystem of the sea doesn't discriminate between flesh from man or whale. What is no longer needed by one is needed by another. The cycle of life is merciless and predictable."

"So...Aslan was never charged with his murder?" Dylan asked carefully.

I winced.

His question was a little too close to what was coming next.

The second incident in the long line of dominos, all lining up ready to crash.

"No. He wasn't. No one knew. Well...no one knew until we told them."

"Wait. Who did you tell?" Margot asked. "I mean...I'm frankly surprised you're telling us, if I'm honest. I know the incident took place decades ago, but...Aslan could still be found guilty. He could spend the rest of his life in jail if they suddenly went looking for Ethan's remains based on this article."

Dylan stiffened. "Margot has a point. Personally, I'm glad Ethan got what he deserved. If Aslan was here, I'd shake his hand for doing what all men would love to do if their wife was hurt in that way, but...it might be risky being so upfront about it, Nerida. Perhaps we should redact a few parts—"

"No. Keep the story in its entirety."

"But aren't you worried—"

"No." I didn't wait for them to ask why I wasn't worried. They wouldn't get an answer to that question.

Margot and Dylan shared a look, deliberating if they wanted to continue with my tale or stay stubbornly on Ethan's possible murder. Not having a conclusion to his survival or demise had always felt like a loose end in the saga of my life.

Had he swum to shore, limped to the nearest hospital, and begged for treatment? Had he lied about why he had a hole in his leg and two missing fingers? Perhaps he was living his own tale, with a wife who had no idea what he'd done, with children of his own. Or…maybe his bones were now coral. Calcified and practically stone, mutated with crustaceans, picked clean by eager fish.

I would never know.

And, depending on my mood each day—on the days I actually spared him a thought, which was never now—I would either hope he'd survived or hope he'd died. I could control the narrative on his ending, giving me comfort, even though, for so long, not knowing if he was still alive gave me nightmares.

Trying to distract them, I said, "Remember those little nudges I told you I was good at following? Those little knowings that seemed to come and go? Well, they started nudging me rather loudly that something was coming. Something painful and hard. An incident that would change the course of our lives forever."

"Something worse than rape?" Margot's mouth fell open.

"Something *because* of the rape." I shrugged sadly. "Something that could've been avoided if only I'd done what Aslan had asked of me."

Margot sat upright, suddenly understanding. "You didn't talk to him…did you?" she asked quietly. "You didn't let him help you through the aftermath.…you shut down."

I gave her a smile, sharing feminine understanding. Women were hardwired to be strong, invincible. It was that conditioning that ended up breaking most of us.

"My cousin was drugged and date-raped." Margot placed her hand over the microphone, muting what she said next from being recorded. "She slept through the entire thing and only found out, thanks to my sister taking her to the hospital. They found at least three men had abused her, according to DNA. She told all of us that she was fine. She said she wouldn't let three faceless men scar her for life. She told us she got counselling. She hid how badly she was hurting. It wasn't until she couldn't hide anymore that we finally knew how much she couldn't cope. It was a long recovery once she reached out for help and actually began to heal instead of hide."

I reached over and squeezed her hand. "I believe all women war with the same choice. The choice of a brave face and burying what happened—all because we believe our strength comes from saying it didn't affect us—or the choice to *let* it affect us. To say we are not okay. To cry. To rage. To break things and ourselves. These days, society is more welcoming of pain. But back then, we were taught our tears only give the bastard more power. By thinking about it, talking about it, or letting the trauma flow through us, we were weak. We weren't moving on. We were letting that moment define us when it was that moment we had to accept rather than suppress."

Sitting back, I held her eyes and put all my honesty on the table. "Aslan would've killed for me. He probably *did* kill for me. Every time he caught my eyes during dinner, with my parents none the wiser, I felt him rummaging around in my soul to make sure I was okay. Each time he touched me, I felt him tearing out the truth that I wasn't as okay as I said.

"It made me feel endlessly guilty. I had him. I was loved by *him*. I had nothing to fear. Nothing to run from. He'd dealt with Ethan. And I'd promised him the night of our wedding that I'd moved on. Aslan had replaced Ethan with himself. The bruises between my legs were thanks to Aslan's possession. His protection. His devotion. Not some bastard's abuse. In the weeks that followed, nothing changed outwardly. Life spilled forward, exams were completed, school ended, and through it all, day by day, I was forced to realise I wasn't as strong as I thought.

"I didn't want to think about it, so I didn't. I didn't want to relive what'd happened on my ex-boyfriend's bed, so I pretended it never did. But…night by night, my mind didn't give me a choice. The nightmares began slowly, sporadically. But once the cracks began in my repression, those nightmares spilled into day terrors. I jumped whenever someone touched me unaware. I stopped going out with friends. I stopped enjoying physical contact with my mother and father. I even flinched a few times when Aslan caught me by surprise to kiss me.

"Oh no…" Margot breathed, knowing exactly where this was going. "That would've killed him."

"It did more than just kill him." I looked at Dylan who listened quietly, making a few notes here and there.

"What happened?" Margot asked, her eyes tight and worried.

"I tried to work through it on my own…with disastrous results. While doing my best to prove how strong I was, I cut Aslan's power off at the knees. He believed his entire purpose in life was to protect me, so when I refused to let him protect me from myself, I made him helpless. His every instinct howled to go to war on my behalf, and when I refused to give him anything to fight, he floundered. He grew more and more frustrated. More and more paralyzed by what I *didn't* say than what I did."

"I can commiserate. There's nothing worse than feeling helpless when all you want to do is help." Dylan chewed on the end of his pen. "You would've been driving him insane. Let me guess…he exploded?"

"Rather spectacularly." I sighed. "And in the worst possible way."

"I don't know if I'm ready for this so soon after hearing about what Ethan did to you," Margot whispered.

"But this isn't the worst thing, is it?" Dylan held my stare. "There's more coming. Worse coming?"

I nodded sadly. "Oh yes. This was just the beginning of our fall. A fall that left us in literal pieces. And I do mean…literally."

Chapter Fifty

ASLAN

(*Moon in Georgian:* Mtvare)

THE FIRST WEEK AFTER WHAT'D HAPPENED ON Low Isles and at Zara's house, Neri almost had me convinced she was okay. We returned to our routine of sneaking around, but instead of dry-humping against my door, I'd shove aside her knickers and sink as deep as I could possibly get.

I'd clamp a hand over her mouth.

I'd ride her hard.

We wasted no time chasing our release, knowing what a dangerous game we played.

I wanted to tell Jack and Anna.

I racked my brains on how best to tell them every night.

This wasn't just about sex. It was for life. We were forever and ever, in all ways, not just this. Even if we couldn't keep our hands off each other.

Sleeping together on that beach had turned us into animals.

Thank God we were both equally as sensitive because our fucking was fast, furious, and almost always ended with us gagging each other with our tongues. Choking on our groans, grunting through endless jerks and clenches, coming together after just a few minutes, snatching precious moments when we wouldn't be missed.

As December crept closer, Jack and Anna got busier, just like they always did. Last-minute requests came in for data for the end of the year. Grants were given for next year's projects. They put in all the hours to clear the decks for their two-week holiday they took over Christmas, waking at dawn and not returning till dusk.

Most days, I went with them.

But on the rare days they didn't need me onboard, I well and truly defiled their daughter. Most of the time, I'd be inside Neri while she still wore her school uniform. It got to the point where she'd return home from school and be bouncing on my cock two minutes later.

On the days her parents were around, we'd wait until Anna was preparing dinner and Jack was in the shower.

Neri would give me a look.

The look.

The one that said '*fuck me, immediately.*'

I'd follow her to her room or she'd come to mine—depending on where her parents were in the house—and it would only take us a few hot kisses, a quick wrenching of clothing, and I'd pin her against whatever hard surface we were close to and shove my cock inside her.

She didn't give me a chance to talk to her properly. She drove me wild with her clawing and pawing, making me drop to my fucking knees to service her in any way she wanted.

I well and truly left virginhood behind through frantic riding, grinding, and pumping. And if Jack knew a tenth of what I did to his sweet Little Fish, he'd rip off my cock and hang it from the one and only palm tree in their front garden.

Not that that stopped me.

We fucked like rabbits.

Nowhere was safe.

Doors, walls, floors, Jack's Jeep, even in the pool with the lights turned off when I was supposed to be helping her with her breathwork.

For a week after our star-witnessed marriage, Neri and I lost ourselves to dirty, frenetic sex.

Twice a day.

Sometimes three times if she crawled into my bed before she went to school—pretending to go running like she sometimes did along the beach, coming to me in tight spandex shorts and a sports bra, acting innocently surprised when I snatched her from the floor, tore off those tempting shorts, and drilled her brutally hard into my pillow.

I couldn't stop burying myself hilt-deep inside her. Couldn't stop the spell she'd cast over me, whispering that each time I took her, I was helping her, keeping her safe from memories, giving her an outlet to heal from what Ethan had done.

I trusted her.

I believed that each time she came to me, I was *helping* my wife, not just fucking her. I was giving her space to be free and move on. She convinced me that my touch burned away Ethan's and my cock eradicated his.

For an entire week, I was naïve.

For two weeks, I was hopeful.

For three weeks, I was wary.

And by the time she sat her last exam and only had a week left of school before she graduated, I couldn't swallow her lies anymore.

She'd been *lying* to me.

Telling me point blank she was okay, when she wasn't.

She was having nightmares.

I could see it in her drawn cheeks and shadowed eyes. Could sense it in the flagging energy and sparkle of her spirit. I tried to get her to talk to me. Truly talk. I cupped her cheeks and kissed her softly when she came to me for primal fucking, trying to use words instead of thrusts.

But she never let me.

She'd flirt and scoff, saying my fears were unfounded, making me doubt what I sensed until I reluctantly gave in.

It always ended with her tugging down my shorts and riding me, all while I murmured that she was safe, he was gone, and I was there for her in every way she needed.

She'd kiss me afterward, accept my offer to talk without talking, and then return to the main house where she'd fall asleep and return to the night where I couldn't save her. The night where Ethan touched what wasn't his to touch and hurt the one girl I would burn the world to fucking ash for.

I tried to pretend her refusal to talk to me didn't hurt.

I didn't put my own shit on top of hers.

I didn't remind her that I knew what she was doing because *I* did it.

Every damn day since the shipwreck, I'd hidden from my ghosts and shoved them deep, deep inside me. I never let myself remember what my father had told me about Cem Kara and my true heritage. I pretended I was the biological son of a math's professor because to contemplate anything else fucking crucified me. I couldn't even admit I wasn't a true Avci because that meant Melike wasn't my sister and that was….that just wasn't possible.

Over the years, I'd become so skilled at hiding, most of the time I forgot why part of me was always sad and twisted. I couldn't recall why I would sometimes wake with pain in my heart or my head full of storms and screams.

I'd become a master at repression, and it fucking killed me to watch Neri learn the same skill.

For most of December, I let her work through her trauma her way. I didn't believe I had any magic to fix her and did the only thing I could by being there for her when she wanted me.

I let her use me.

I let her confuse me.

I let her frustrate me.

But when her nightmares started tainting her days…that was when I started getting angry.

The first time she flinched, her mother had wrapped her arms around her from behind on the deck after we'd eaten.

I'd frozen solid.

That was huge.

That was *terrifying*.

That was a direct admission that Nerida Taylor—Nerida Avci—was hiding something right beneath her parents' noses.

Well, two things, actually...but I could wait.

I planned on telling them right.

I'd even bought a ring.

A ring that cost more than I'd ever spent before.

A ring that I'd snuck into town and trawled every jewellery shop searching for.

I'd almost given up, but just like the necklace with a girl swimming with a sea lion had proven to be designed especially for Neri, a ring had jumped out that was made exactly for my perfect siren.

I couldn't wait to give it to her.

I had it tightly trapped in a velvet box, buried in my sock drawer.

I wanted to get on bended knee in front of Anna and Jack, and propose to her all over again, showing with actions, not words, just how much I adored their daughter. And when Jack and Anna accepted my vow, then and only then, would I tell them we were already married in the only way we could.

I could never make Neri my wife here. She would never wear my last name in this country, but I hoped they'd see that no other man would love her the way I did. No other man would happily kill for her, kneel for her, go out of his fucking mind for her.

But the idea of proposing popped into a nasty bubble as Anna stiffened the moment her daughter flinched. She'd looked at Neri carefully, her loving gaze full of questions. I waited for Neri to break and tell her mother everything. But she made up a lie about seeing a spider and expected us all to believe she was suddenly afraid of Australia's creatures when she'd spent her entire lifetime protecting them.

The second time she spooked, it caught Jack unaware. Their close relationship from when she was little still spilled over into her almost adulthood. Just because she was closer to eighteen instead of eight, it didn't stop him from snatching her around the middle and dumping her in the pool whenever he felt like it.

Before Ethan, she'd squeal and fight back. Happily entering into a splashing war and clambering all over her father's slippery shoulders.

After Ethan, she forced a laugh and swam away. Her splashes were half-hearted and she blamed the stress of exams on her lack of willingness to play.

Jack had caught my eyes as he clambered sadly out of the pool. The pain etching his familiar face had almost had me blurting out what'd happened. If I couldn't help Neri, perhaps he could. I wanted to tell him that his little girl had been abused, and I'd done all I could to make it right. I'd fucking shot the bastard. I'd hit him until he'd cried. I'd cut off his fingers and thrown him overboard.

But I couldn't tell.

It wasn't my secret to spill.

So I kept watching as Neri slowly became afraid of loud noises and innocent touches. I kept silent as she learned to school her reaction so she didn't twitch as badly, smothering her pain ever deeper. Any deeper and it would slice through the very same heart I was trying to protect. It would make her bleed far worse than she already did. And I wasn't sure how much longer I could wait. How much more I could take before I dragged her to a fucking therapist and forced her to talk to someone.

Before it was too late.

I bit my tongue for as long as I could. I used that tongue to kiss her, terrified that she kept demanding me to be rougher, crueller, wilder, all because she was seeking an outlet, an escapism. The days I let her goad me into being ruthlessly hard, I'd choke on shame for leaving bruises on her gorgeous skin, always where her parents wouldn't see.

She'd drive me to breaking point, not leaving me alone until I sucked her nipples so deeply her breasts bloomed red beneath my mouth. Teeth marks would mar her delicate flesh, and I'd die a little inside for causing them.

The nights I marked her were the nights she actually looked relaxed and free from the memories haunting her.

And I fucking hated it.

I hated it because I knew what she was doing.

I'd done the same thing for years.

Her inner pain was manifesting outwardly.

My pain had been losing my family. I'd eased that pain by throwing myself at the servitude of the Taylors, forcing myself to fall for another family, all while abandoning my own.

But Neri hadn't lost loved ones, she'd lost herself.

She'd lost the girl she'd been *before*.

And she used pain to find her.

Pain to make herself come alive again. Pain to fortify the suppressed memories from ever breaking free and swarming her.

I didn't want her to let Ethan win by refusing to let herself heal.

But what could I do?

She started getting angry with me when I pushed. She shut down when I got tetchy. Tension sprang between us that wasn't there before, and I backed down. I bid my time. I obeyed my girl, and did my best to bite my tongue.

But that all stopped the day she flinched from *me*.

A week before Christmas, she flinched.

Fucking *flinched*.

She tried to pretend it hadn't happened. She reached to kiss me in the kitchen, safe to touch me without fear of being caught because her parents were down the street visiting the neighbours.

I'd caught her doing the dishes.

I'd planted my hands on her hips to act out her fantasy of being fucked against the sink. I'd already unzipped. Ready to slip inside her while her hands clutched at bubbles and glasses.

But she jumped a mile when I touched her.

She spun in my arms with wide, worried eyes.

And that was all I could take.

I stormed away.

I slammed my door.

And I knew things were about to get ugly.

Chapter Fifty-One
ASLAN

(*Moon in Nepali:* Candramā)

"YOU'LL NEVER GUESS WHO JUST MESSAGED ME," Neri said with a smile, stepping into my room as if she owned the place.

"Leave the door open," I muttered, saving my progress on my latest language app and closing the second screen where I'd been working my way through a math paper I'd found online that was said to be impossible.

It wasn't impossible.

Frankly, it was easy, and the thrill of completing the page-long calculations had made my brain dance with colours. I'd slipped once—on *The Fluke* when Neri was doing her math homework a few years ago—and told her that numbers felt smooth to me. Liquid and silky, a pleasure to think about and untangle, but when she'd looked at me like I was lying or worse...making shit up, I'd swallowed down the rest of that truth.

The truth being, I didn't just *feel* numbers, I saw them in colour. Technicolour with glowing edges and sparkling curves. Twos were orange, sevens were turquoise. Together, they conjured such a pretty shade that I got goosebumps whenever they appeared in an equation together. I think that was why I was so good at math. It was like a dance to me. A dance where I somehow inherently knew all the steps.

I hadn't told Neri that part of myself for two reasons.

One, I didn't want her to think of me as strange, and two...while it remained my little secret, I could pretend the gift came from my father: the father who'd raised me and filled my crib with number toys and games. I didn't want to think that it might've come from my biological father. That this uniqueness might be hereditary and yet another thing I couldn't escape.

"Why do you want me to leave the door open?" Neri asked quietly, frowning a little at my lack of enthusiasm.

Tossing my phone onto my pillow, I swung my legs to the floor and stretched, popping muscles that'd had enough of manual labour. This week had been insane. I'd spent hours scrubbing *The Fluke* so it was ready for its rest over Christmas. I'd run countless errands for Jack and spent days ordering new stock and supplies for the new year.

Lucky for all of us, tonight marked the start of our official holiday. Neri had finished school yesterday, and Jack and Anna were already celebrating with a bottle of champagne that they splurged on every year. A bottle with a drunk humpback on the label and the words 'Whale Plonk'.

Plonk typically meant cheap and barely palatable wine, but this particular winery loved to use the word cheap when they really meant exorbitantly expensive.

"Aslan…are you okay?" Neri asked quietly, leaving the door open and stepping closer to me with a wary glance.

I didn't want to be mean, but…I couldn't keep choking on it. "You flinched last time we were together, or have you forgotten? I'd hate to make you feel uncomfortable by being alone with me."

She gasped. "You know I didn't mean to. You took me by surprise."

"You would never have flinched before that bastard."

"I was washing dishes. I didn't hear you—"

"Exactly, Neri! You were washing dishes. And I was going to fulfil your very unique little fetish, but in one jolt you showed me that you're *lying* to me."

"I'm not lying—"

"You're not talking to me, that's for damn sure."

"I am. I do. I just—"

"Look. Forget it. It's not my place to get mad." Scrubbing my face, I did my best to stop our fight before it escalated. "Who messaged you?"

"What?"

"You just said I'd never guess who messaged you."

"Oh, right." It took a moment for her to accept the change of topic, staring at her phone in her hands. Finally, she sucked in a breath, accepted my olive branch, and swiped it on. "Here." She passed it to me. "Read that."

I skimmed the text.

Honey: *Heyyyy! So…first thing you should know about me is I suck at messaging. Second thing you should know about me is…I meant what I said when we met in that bar. (Remember? The night you dumped what's his face?) I immediately liked you. I've claimed you as my Port Douglas bestie. I'm so sorry for not messaging sooner, bestie, but…guess what? I told my brother about your idea of him building something on the bottom of the sea (if he wants to find that elusive utopia he's searching for), and he thinks it's a crazy idea. Crazy not possible. Crazy stupid. Crazy let's try! I gave him your number. He'll probably get in touch. He'll probably say he's fallen in love with you within a day 'cause that's what he's like. But don't worry, you can't sleep with this one because he doesn't like tacos. *Snicker.*

My gaze shot to Neri's. "I have no idea what any of that means. Or why you're showing it to me." My heart smoked with leftover jealousy, remembering her with Joel and all the nights I'd had to endure with him over here, sharing dinners and movies and kissing her right in fucking front of me.

"Shit, sorry...scroll down." She tried to grab it. "Wrong message."

"Hang on." I kept her phone out of her reach. "Do I have any reason to be concerned about this brother of hers? Why can't you sleep with him just because he doesn't like Mexican food?"

Her lips curled and the first genuine laugh I'd heard in a while tumbled from her mouth. "Taco is slang for pussy." Her cheeks pinked. "She means her brother is gay. I'm surprised she didn't send a sausage emoji." Her eyelashes came down. "Besides, I'm with you, Aslan. I married *you*. I'm never going to be with anyone else for as long as I live."

Her words tried to ease the pinch in my chest, but I didn't let them. Neri kept pretending things were okay, but they weren't. They were so far from okay that I was starting to lose control.

Leaning closer, she tapped the screen and scrolled to the message below that one. I read it, even though my pulse fluttered with warning from her standing so close.

Honey: *Also...don't freak out, but I had the strangest feeling that I should message you today. I know you were super sad at messing stuff up with your other bestie, and if she didn't forgive you (her loss, by the way. Huge loss. HUGE!), then I'm offering myself up as tribute. Don't know why I had the urge to message you so strongly. Here I am, waiting in line at the store (buying another box of huge-ass condoms for my huge-ass boyfriend who is against all big pharma and doesn't want me on the pill, even though condoms suck), and I had the strangest feeling that you might need a friend. So, friend...let's talk. I'm here. I'm a vault. And if I'm totally scaring you right now, no biggie. I scare a lot of people. So just flow with it and message me anyway!*

With a slightly shaking hand, I passed the phone back to Neri. "She sounds...chaotic. Chaotic but nice."

Neri cradled her phone as if it'd suddenly become immensely precious. "I met her the night you kissed me for the first time. I felt an instant connection with her. I gave her my number but forgot to get hers. I've looked for her on Facebook but didn't have any luck." She sighed, revealing the young girl I'd known since she was flat chested with her head in dolphin-shaped clouds. "I've missed having a girlfriend. I...I can't tell you how glad I am that she messaged. I can't wait to tell her all about us and—"

"You can't tell her about us, Nerida. No one can know."

"Of course, they can know. You're not invisible. It's not like you don't exist."

"For me to exist I have to *be* invisible, remember?"

"Oh, I remember all too well. Each time I think about suggesting we do something, I remember. Each time I think we should go see a movie or perhaps go do something we'd never normally do like horse riding or kayaking or literally *anything*, I remember that you can't. You can't get into most places without ID and we can't do any activities where you might get hurt because you can't get medical treatment. Oh, and if that wasn't enough, if you get caught, you die. So yeah, I remember, Aslan. Believe me."

My temper blackened. "I'm so sorry to be such an inconvenience to you."

She reared back, hurt flaring in her pretty blue eyes. "Why are you being like this?"

I opened my mouth. I tried to explain the anxiety I was feeling. The awful pressure that we were out of balance, and if we didn't fix it soon, something bad was going to happen. "It's nothing," I snapped, unable to be mad at her after everything she'd endured. "Don't worry about it."

"I worry, Aslan. I worry all the time."

"Like I would know."

"*What?* What's that supposed to mean?"

"It means you broke your promise."

"What promise?"

"What promise?" I laughed blackly. "You know what promise."

"All I know is…I came in here wanting to share the awesomeness of having a new friend. Honey seems special. She even feels the same nudges as I do."

"Certainly seems like it." I raked a hand through my hair, struggling to cool my anger, but failing. Dropping my arm, my chin tipped up and I clipped, "I wonder why she sensed you needed a friend, huh? Could it be because you're hiding stuff? Could it be that you're bottling up how you're truly feeling and it's starting to spill out into whatever emotional plane we all exist on? Because I have the same nudges, Neri. Nudges that tell me you aren't being honest with me. You're not talking to me. You're letting what happened overshadow everything you do, and you promised me, fucking *promised* me, that you would talk to me. That you would let me try to help you, but instead, you think you can lie to my face all while I see how you aren't sleeping, barely eating, and constantly looking over your shoulder. You're worse now than the day it fucking happened, and I can't take much more. I can't last much longer if you don't let me help—"

"You *do* help me." Her eyes glistened with sudden tears. "You help me so much."

"By fucking you."

"By keeping me grounded! Whenever I'm in your arms, I can't think about anything else."

"So you're using me to hide." I stood in a rush and slapped my palm against the door. It swung shut with a slam. I winced, hoping Jack and Anna didn't hear.

I'd wanted to keep it open so Jack and Anna wouldn't start getting suspicious on the number of visits Neri paid me. Not that they showed any signs of suspecting.

Then again, it wasn't unusual for Neri and I to be close. We'd spent almost six years in each other's pockets. It wasn't our togetherness or platonic touches that would alert them to our secrets…it would be this.

Us shouting at each other.

A fight that was so unusual it would raise questions.

"If you don't want to talk to me, then you need to find someone else to talk to, Nerida. That is non-negotiable." I marched into her and grabbed her cheeks. My fingertips burned from touching her. My heart kicked. My blood heated.

She licked her lips, unable to look away from me. "I just need to reclaim my body, that's all. And you're helping me do that. Every time you fill me, you're reminding me that it's *my* choice. *My* decision. I feel so safe when I'm with you. Is it so wrong to admit that I need you to keep fucking me…so I don't become afraid of it?"

"Afraid of sex? Or afraid of me? Is that what you think will happen?" I strangled. "That if we stop tearing each other's clothes off that you'll suddenly not want it anymore?"

Tears welled on her bottom lashes. "What if…what if I lose that sense of safety in your arms? What if…what if all I can remember about sex is what *he* did and not what we have?" She didn't give me a chance to reply, whispering, "I-I don't know why I can't stop thinking about it, Aslan. I fully believed I'd be able to snap my fingers and say it's in the past. It was just sex. He didn't even hurt me…not really."

"Didn't *hurt* you?" My fingers dug into her cheekbones. "Fuck, Neri, is that what you're telling yourself? You think he didn't hurt you?" Dropping my right hand, I cupped her breast, immediately finding her thundering heart beneath. "He hurt you right here, *aşkım*. He hurt you where no one can see. It's a wound that has to be tended, just like the burns on your ankles and the bruises on your wrists. But unlike those bruises, you can't hide these with make-up and concealer until they're gone."

She nodded weakly. "I know. I know you're right. I've read online that it's normal for the trauma to get worse the longer I don't confront it. But…I don't *want* to confront it. I don't want him to take anymore from me than he already did."

"But don't you see, Neri? He's taking bits of you every day that you pretend it didn't happen."

She started trembling in my hold. "Do you…is that why you're angry with me? You've been short-tempered with me for weeks. Is it…is it because…he's been inside me?" She choked on things she'd buried. "Am I…is that why you don't want to sleep with me? Why you told me to keep your door open? Why you didn't come to my room last night when Dad and

Mum popped to the supermarket? Do you…" She sucked in a tattered breath. "Do you think I'm…dirty…. That I'm…undesirable after he—"

"Fuck." My ears rang.

My heart stopped.

My fucking knees gave out.

I dropped to the floor, dragging her with me.

She cried out as we collapsed together, knees to knees. Tears burned my eyes at the thought of her fears, her doubts, her awful beliefs that she would *never* have contemplated before. She would never have even entertained such an idea. She knew who she was. She knew the absolute power she had over me.

To think she doubted herself, me…*us.*

It fucking destroyed me.

Rage poured thick and hot through my veins. Aggression raised its ugly head, and I grabbed her cheeks far too roughly. "*Beni dinle, Nerida Avci, iyi dinle—*" Cursing under my breath, I switched my mind from the tongue it automatically went to when my emotions exploded, repeating in curt English, "You listen to me, Nerida Avci, and you listen good. I'm not going to tell you what you cannot say or think because it won't make a damn bit of difference. Your mind is yours to use as you please. I can't stop you from thinking such things. I can't stop you from convincing yourself that what Ethan did to you has made you undesirable, dirty, or wrong."

She winced, but I held her firm and kept going.

"What he did is not your fault. What I did to him is not your fault. You didn't encourage him to rape you, and you didn't force me to hurt him. He preyed on you because he's a cunt, and I hope to fucking God I killed him. He made his choice. I made mine. And now *you* have to make a choice to accept that both of those things happened. They *happened,* Neri. It wasn't a nightmare. It isn't something you can ignore. He. Hurt. You. It wasn't sex. What he did to you was *not sex*, so stop fearing that you'll become afraid of something that is natural and so fucking good between us. What he did is the exact opposite of what we have. And I'm *begging* you to see that. I'm begging you to *allow* yourself to see that. Stop putting on a brave face. Stop pretending he didn't deserve to die and stop letting his voice tear you apart."

"Aslan, stop." She clung to my wrists, trying to get away. "Enough—"

"No, it's not enough. I've been too soft on you. I love you, Neri. I love you so fucking much. I'd do anything to take this away from you and shoulder all your pain, but I can't. All I can do is show you how wrong you are. Show you that I could never think of you as dirty or undesirable. To even suggest that is fucking lunacy."

Dropping my hands from her cheeks, I unbuttoned my jeans and unzipped. Diving my hands into my shorts, I pulled out my cock. Hard and angry, a mirror image of the rest of me. "See what you do to me? See what you've always done? You are the most fascinating, stunning, and by far the most wonderful creature I've ever seen. You put me to shame with your strength and bravery. You're intelligent, kind, and so in-tune with animals that you sometimes make me think you're not human. You blow me away with your aspirations and dreams. You make me lie awake at night with how bright your future is and not a day goes by that I don't wake up with my own fears. A true logical fear that you'll realise I don't deserve you. Because no one fucking does. No one can come close to you, Neri. No one can…because it's *you*."

My voice turned thick and dark. "But you know what? Just because I don't deserve you and just because you're doubting how wonderful you are, I'm going to give you a lesson. I'm going to show you that despite my fury at you for doubting yourself, I can't say no to you. I've never been able to say no. You've tormented me since you were barely old enough to know what you were doing. Your every look makes me throb. Your every touch makes me twitch. And if you don't trust a single thing about your life or who you are right now, then trust in this."

Raising up to my knees, I grabbed her shoulders and flipped her around.

"Aslan—what?" She fell forward, landing on her hands and knees. The floating navy skirt she had on twirled around her thighs. "What are you doing?"

"Giving you what you came here for." Grabbing the hem, I flipped the material over her back, exposing her ass. She wore her typical bikini. This one bronze with white strings.

"Did you come here so I'd fuck you, yes or no?" Undoing the knots on her hips, I tossed the scrap of Lycra away and reared up behind her.

She moaned as I swiped a finger through her wetness, testing her, making sure I wouldn't be the monster hurting her if I did this.

"Answer me, *aşkım benim*." My voice was gravel and stone.

"Yes. I-I used Honey's message as an excuse to come and—"

"Fuck me."

"Yes."

"Remember the word you said on *The Fluke*…the one you'd utter if I got too much?"

Her head tipped forward, her hair cascading on the ground. "Seahorse."

"Use that if you want me to stop." I palmed her ass, fisted my cock, and mounted her with as much finesse as a raging beast.

Fuck

Me.

The pressure of her.

The tightness.

I drove my cock right into the heart of her, the heart that I wished I could heal but couldn't.

She went to scream; I clamped my hand over her mouth from behind. "*Quiet.*"

Her back arched as I folded over her, pressing my chest to her spine.

I didn't just sink inside her.

I speared inside her, stabbed inside her.

Ferally deep. Savagely quick.

I couldn't make her whole again, but I could offer every part of me to repair the parts of her that were missing.

I would do it for the rest of my life and beyond. A pledge of a husband who no longer fought the violent side of himself because it was the violent side that'd protected her. The violent side she needed to keep away her ghosts. The violent side that made her feel safe.

"I'm right here. Deep inside you. Just you and me." I thrust once, shuddering at the slippery, slick connection.

She quivered and moaned beneath me, spreading her legs as if preparing herself to be fucked.

Removing my hand, I whispered in her ear, "*Iyi misin?*"

She nodded, gasping hard. "Yes. God, yes. I'm more than okay."

I rolled my hips, grunting at her tightness, her heat. "You come to me for a cure, yet each time I give it to you, it only makes me sicker."

She choked on a cry, keeping herself as quiet as she could.

We'd never been this stupid, this reckless. Usually, I fucked her against my door, so it would be blocked from her parents walking in on us. But right now, with my cock deep inside her from behind and her panting on all fours, Jack could swing the door wide and catch us.

Catch me riding his daughter like a damn dog, and with the way my fury raged, I'd probably fucking finish before I let him tear me off her.

"I'm sorry, Aslan. Sorry for using you."

I groaned and withdrew right to the tip. "Say that again."

"I'm sorry—"

I thrust indecently deep, shutting her up.

Her first apology.

And I punished her for it.

Planting one hand on the floor, I curled my other around her hip.

I spread my legs for balance, cursed my shorts clinging to my thighs, and let go.

"Fuck," she breathed, accepting my fury, my fear, my endless wish to fix her.

Her hair dusted the wooden floorboards as I pounded hard and painfully fast. Her fingernails scratched as she tried to stay still and my knees found every splinter as I drilled over and over inside her.

My heartrate exploded with every thrust.

The image of her bent over and at my mercy blew my fucking mind.

I couldn't tear my eyes from where we were joined, hypnotised with every withdraw and penetration, my flesh disappearing into her flesh, wet and hungry, hard and thirsty.

We didn't speak.

Too far gone for words.

We couldn't use each other's tongues to shut us up, so we clamped our lips closed and breathed through flared nostrils.

On and on, I hammered into her. Not slowing, not pretending this was anything more than what it was.

A quick, dirty fuck to hold memories at bay.

And something cold and sickening slithered around my heart.

I ignored it as I reached between her legs and found her clit. I shut up the whispers crowding in the back of my mind as I thumbed her swollen sensitivity and groaned at the flutters of her core.

"Come for me. Come on me. Fucking come, Neri or—"

"God—" She groaned and obeyed me.

Her entire body shattering and clenching, drawing me deeper, granting me access to her very soul. I never stopped rocking, driving deep, drawing out every inch of her release.

Only once she went limp and I had to curl my arm under her waist to hold her upright did I let the curse in my blood out to play.

I stopped dampening the sharpness of touch.

I stopped dulling every hot, wet sensation.

I threw myself headfirst into feeling *everything*.

Every ridge of her, every searing, branding heat.

The pressure.

Fuck, her pressure.

Her fisting, feminine pressure was my literal kryptonite.

My body flushed with sweat.

My cock thickened with unbearable size.

And I couldn't fight my overwhelming, devastatingly painful senses.

Rearing up behind her, I didn't care that she face-planted onto the floor. Her hips angled and took me deeper. Her absolute submission while impaled on my cock stole all my humanity.

I came with a silent roar.

My spine shattered.

My cock exploded.

Wave after wave of blistering, brutalising fire spurted out of me and into her, drenching her, coating her, giving her exactly what she needed. Granting her the medicine her body craved by proving that she had me by the actual balls.

She had me strung up and bled dry as I jerked and shuddered, riding out the epic waves of my release.

My heartbeat thundered in my ears as I finally blinked back the dark spots in my gaze and looked down. "Ah, shit."

Neri lay with her cheek pressed against the rough sala floorboards, her hair spread all around her, her eyes closed. For a second, I feared I'd gone too far again, but then I noticed the sated curl of her lips and the rhythmic relaxation of her breathing.

She looked happier than she had since the last time I'd been inside her. And I hated that.

I hated that the bright, brave girl I'd fallen in love with—the girl who taught me how to be happy—now relied on me to give her back that happiness.

Bending over her, I pressed a galaxy of kisses all along her back, hoping they seared into her skin through her white t-shirt, branding her the way she'd branded me.

"*Seni seviyorum,* Aslan," she whispered, squeezing her inner muscles and making me suck in a groan.

"I love you too, wife."

She smiled. "You've made me feel like the most powerful girl alive, simply by throwing me to my hands and knees."

"If only you'd remember how powerful you are when my cock *isn't* dripping inside you."

She chuckled, sounding carefree and exactly like my Neri.

My heart tumbled painfully. *"Benim aşkım sonsuza kadar sürecek, seni her zaman seveceğim. Ay ve deniz şahidim olarak yemin ederim."*

She wriggled a little. "Hmmm, something about the moon and the sea and—"

"I said, my love will last forever. I'll always love you. With the moon and the sea as my witness, I vow it."

"I don't know what I'd do without you, Aslan."

"You'd be fine without me. Just like you were fine before me."

"Before I fell in love with you, I had no idea what I was missing. Now I'm only half a person unless I'm with you."

I kissed her shoulder blades. "But don't you see? You aren't just half. You are double. You have my heart, Neri. You have my soul. Even apart, that means you're not alone. Ever."

"God, when you say things like that to me..." She clenched around me again, doing sinful things to my body.

My hypersensitive cock perked up for more.

I wanted another round.

Glancing at the door, I decided to err on the side of caution. I could stay inside her like we sometimes did. I could wait for my cock to harden and spread her all over again, ready for round two. But we'd already been too long. Jack expected me to help with the barbecue to celebrate our first night of holidays and Anna...she was probably wondering where her wayward daughter was so they could celebrate her finishing school.

That cold slithering around my heart returned, along with the crowd of whispers.

Wincing, I withdrew from my star-given wife and sat back on my heels.

Neri moaned as she pushed up to her hands and threw me a grateful look as I tossed her the tissue box that lived on my bedside table.

I didn't speak as I shoved my half-hard cock back into my shorts and zipped up. Neri cleaned between her legs, found her bikini bottoms, and stood to secure them. Only once her skirt was back in place and I'd gathered her into my arms, did I murmur, "That was the last time, *canım*."

She flinched, leaning back in my embrace to study my eyes. "What do you mean?"

"Christmas is in three days. I'm going to tell Jack about us. I-I have something to give you, and...I don't want to keep hiding anymore. It's a fucking miracle we haven't been caught and I'm not willing to keep playing with fire."

"But...what about—"

"You have my word I'll never tell them what happened to you at Zara's, but you can't keep using sex between us as your cure. It's not working, Neri. I hate that it's not working and I'm not saying I won't keep helping you in any way I can, but...that was the last time you come to me to hide."

"But I wasn't hiding. I was living." Her nose wrinkled with determination. "You don't understand, Aslan. When I'm with you, when I hear you groan with lust and feel how desperately you need me, you give me back every scrap of self-worth he took from me. I don't feel helpless or powerless. I'm not angry or sad or second-guessing every part of that night. I can stop beating myself up for accepting that mug of Coke. I can stop going over and over why—when I've prided myself so many times on my instincts—that they failed me so spectacularly that night." Her voice wobbled a little. "When I'm with you, Aslan, I can just be *me* again. It goes...quiet inside, and I really need that quiet. I'm sick of my mind racing and—"

"The only way it will stop racing is if you face everything you just admitted. Accept that your instincts failed you, but that doesn't mean you can't keep trusting them. Accept that you let societal niceties coerce you into accepting a drink from a total stranger. Accept that he took more from you than you're willing to admit and then...when you've accepted all of that...get angry, get mad, cry, scream, go butcher a tree, because I swear to you, if you don't find a way to let it out, you'll end up like me. Afraid of walking down the street in case I'm caught. Afraid of sleep in case I hear my sister's screams. Afraid of living or daring to dream and fucking terrified of the future because as much as I want to plan a life with you, Neri, I have no idea where to start. What will it look like, or how is it even possible? I want what everyone else has. I want a home with you, a family with you, a long, safe, incredible romance with you, but right now, I have no idea if that can even happen."

Tucking her hair behind her ears, I kissed her cute wrinkled nose. "Perhaps we both have to be a little braver."

She nodded beneath my lips, sucking in a fortifying breath. "Okay. No more hiding."

"No more hiding."

"We face the future. Together."

"Together."

"We tell my parents in three days."

"When we hand out the presents on Christmas night, I'm dropping to one knee."

She shivered. "And we tell the whole world that we belong to one another."

I kissed her. "Agreed."

We smiled and opened my door, and went to her parents with our secret buried tight.

We spent a lovely evening with family, eating, drinking, linked by hearts and promises.

And I went to bed that night with hope.

Hope that Neri would be okay.

Hope that Jack would accept me.

Hope that one day…we could be free.

What a shame none of that happened.

What an utter waste the world said…fuck no.

Chapter Fifty-Two

ASLAN

(*Moon in Lithuanian:* Mėnulis)

10:00 A.M.

CHRISTMAS.

The day that all carols and department stores tried to convince mankind was the greatest day on earth.

It started off well enough.

I helped Jack prepare the lobster that his friend down the street had caught and given as a Christmas present. Neri helped her mother bake a thousand different desserts and the tree that Anna had put up two weeks ago, glittered with garish rainbow lights and silver tinsel that shed all over the tiles.

A small pile of presents waited underneath on a red velvet cloth.

The ring I planned on giving Neri sat on top of the box of craft beer I'd bought Jack and the latest book on underwater photography for Anna.

The morning we spent outside, eating the prawn cocktail that Anna said was traditional on Christmas morning. Jack cracked open a beer at ten o'clock, and pushed one into my hand, despite me trying to refuse.

The Christmas cheer had well and truly infected both the Taylors, and I grinned into my prawn cocktail as the sun shone and the temperature made all of us sweat in our shorts and tropical-coloured shirts. Jack had bought all four of us the ugliest, brightest shirts from some reject store, claiming this was now our Christmas uniform.

Back home in Turkey, I'd be bundled in jackets and scarfs, gathered around the fire with my family to ward off the chill, waiting for New Years to celebrate with friends. Christmas wasn't really done back home, and it'd taken time to get used to the huge production it was here.

What would Melike make of it?

Stop. Don't go there.

Wrenching my thoughts from my constantly haunting ghosts, I returned to hotter climes and forced myself to enjoy the day. I did my best to stay present and not fear what would happen once we all sat down for our big meal and opened our gifts.

The Taylors liked to wait until the evening for present giving.

I had no idea why, and the waiting made me insane.

Seven or so more hours before Jack and Anna found out.

Seven or so more hours that ought to be easy to endure, but somehow became the most excruciating.

Once we'd finished food course number one, Neri cleared the dishes, and Jack dragged me into his office to offer my opinion on the latest echolocation equipment that he was thinking of upgrading to on *The Fluke*. The entire time he pointed out the pros and cons, my ears stayed perked for sounds of Neri and her mother in the kitchen, longing to hear Neri's laughter.

Three days since I'd had her on her knees in my room.

Three days since I'd given her what she needed.

Three days since I'd seen the relaxed and confident version of the girl I'd kill for.

Even though it took everything I had not to go into her room and sink inside her, I'd meant what I said. I was done enabling her.

She needed to face it. Accept it. Deal with it. And move on.

I was aware I was a fucking hypocrite for forcing her to do the very thing I was incapable of doing, but...I'd lived the path she was travelling down, and I would do whatever it took to stop her before it was too late.

"So what do you think?" Jack asked. "Worth the investment?"

Forcing myself to pay attention, I finished my beer and shrugged. "The sonar you have right now seems to work okay. Are the frequencies that much better to justify the upgrade?"

He nodded, pursing his lips. "Good point. I'll pull up the manual of our unit and compare the ranges. Just because this one is newer doesn't mean it's got better mapping capabilities."

"Good idea." I jammed my hands into my beige cargo short pockets, glancing into the corridor just in time to see Neri walk past.

Our eyes caught.

My heart punched me in the chest.

I tripped all over again, drinking in her gorgeous sun-streaked hair, garish flower-print shirt, and white miniskirt.

I smiled.

She tensed before forcing half a smile and darting toward her bedroom.

Her door closed quietly, and Jack moved to my side, staring after his daughter. "Wonder what's her problem? Unlike her to be so quiet on Christmas. She's usually high as a freaking kite and sneaking presents when we're not watching."

He sighed, finished the last mouthful of his beer, then patted me on the shoulder. "Might go ask Anna if she knows anything. My little fish has been off for a few weeks, and I'm not liking it."

I froze. "You...you've noticed she's not herself?"

He frowned. "Noticed? 'Course, I've noticed. She's my baby. If she's not driving me loopy or laughing her head off, then something's up. Ever since she went to see Zara, she's not been herself." He turned to face me. "I know she said that her and Zara weren't able to swallow their differences and the friendship is over, and I know she said she slept on *The Fluke* to have some privacy—without asking permission, I might add—but did she say anything to you when you guys went to Low Isles the next day?"

I forced myself not to flinch.

Neri and I had both agreed to stay as close to the truth as possible about that night. She hadn't come home and after our day swimming on Low Isles in full view of tourists and local fishermen, there was a high probability that someone would recognise the boat and say something to Jack at some point. So...our story had been: Neri had crashed on *The Fluke*, called me early in the morning, and finally gotten me into the sea. Needless to say, Anna had flung herself at me when Neri proudly announced I'd dived for the first time. And she conveniently used the story of the shark and its rusty hook to volley any questions about what'd happened at Zara's.

She was sneaky, my little siren. Sneaky and secretive and a little too clever at spinning a tale.

Swallowing hard, I answered Jack, "Nope, she didn't say anything to me. Obviously, she's sad about the break-up with Zara but..." I cursed myself as lies fell out of my mouth. "I think it might just be everything happening at once, you know? School's ended. University starts next year. She has to move away from you guys..."

Jack nodded with a relieved grin. "Yeah, you're right. She's no longer a kid anymore. Guess I'll never get used to that and, if I'm perfectly honest, I'll forever see her as my little girl who literally rules my heart and soul."

A rock lodged in the back of my throat, witnessing the unconditional love on his face for his one and only daughter.

A flashback of sitting in the back of his Jeep, a few days after I'd been plucked from the sea, all while Neri ran inside to pick up Italian takeaway, tore through my mind.

"You are welcome in my home, on my boat, and in my family but if you **ever** *touch Nerida in a way that is anything more than platonic, you will be on your own so fucking fast you'll wonder how it happened."* *His gaze narrowed.* *"And I don't do second chances."*

My stomach twisted.

Sweat broke out down my spine.

What would he and Anna say later tonight when I admitted that I'd touched Neri in ways that were definitely not platonic. That I'd done things for her that were definitely not legal. And that I wanted to keep doing those things for as long as we both shall live?

"Go and check on her for me, will ya?" Jack patted my shoulder again as he strode into the corridor. "I'm gonna go help Anna with the second course."

He left me on the threshold.

I looked at Neri's closed door, knowing I couldn't do what he asked because if I did, I'd end up inside her.

She'd touch me, kiss me, and use my oversensitivity against me until I submitted and succumbed.

I couldn't fuck her today.

Not while my mind swarmed with the past and our future hung so precariously.

It took everything I had to walk in the opposite direction.

The cold slithering around my heart returned, along with the feral whispers in my head.

If I told Jack and Anna and they refused me, where would I go?

If I told them I'd been with their teenage daughter—even though she was of legal consenting age—would they throw me out or worse…?

Could I survive never seeing them again?

Never being welcome in their house and hearts?

You don't have a choice not to tell them.

Not anymore.

The ring box glowered at me as I walked past the tree.

The ice-cold beer in the esky on the deck promised to dull my rapidly building fear of tonight.

Grabbing a bottle, I sucked the alcohol down, begging it to take the edge off as Jack and Anna laughed in the kitchen and my heart didn't beat right without Neri.

I missed her.

I loved her.

I felt like I'd already lost her.

1 P.M.

"Having fun?" I asked, sitting at the outdoor table where copious amounts of homemade pizzas had been eaten and I'd had the privilege of watching Neri grow, year by year.

She'd had five birthdays around this table and was inching ever closer to her eighteenth in April. Even I'd been forced to smile as the Taylors lavished me with the same treatment a few weeks ago when I'd turned twenty-two.

She looked up, her eyes hidden behind dark sunglasses, a big floppy straw hat on her head to protect her from the searing sun. "Yeah, surprisingly, want to try? It's just like cross-stitch but with diamantes instead of thread." She passed me the plastic pen with a smirk.

I clung to my fifth beer of the day, shaking my head at her offer. "I think I'll just watch."

She laughed, but it wasn't her usual sparkling, effervescent laugh. This was dull and flat, like soda left out too long. Dropping my eyes from her shaded ones, I eyed up the diamond painting spread out over the table. Plastic trays held glimmering rhinestones in every colour, waiting for her to stick them onto the large canvas of a stunning seascape with turtles, whales, orcas, and coral. Moonlight speared through the water with stars twinkling in the sky, turning the entire mood silver and mysterious with mystical pink and green splashes on the horizon.

It meant nothing more than a gift given by a father who knew his daughter's favourite things, yet…the moon on the sea and the stunning aurora australis reminded me all too well of our marriage vows in the shallows of Low Isles. Of the way I'd slid inside her for the first time. Of our promises to always be one.

My heart pinched.

My hand strayed toward Neri's, desperately needing to touch her.

I froze as she looked up.

We shared so many unspoken things, but then she bit her bottom lip, shook her head, and returned to her painting.

Scowling, I did my best to shove aside the fog of blackness. Blackness that'd returned with a vengeance. I hadn't felt its oppressive presence in a while, but all day, it'd gathered at the base of my head, swallowing up my happy thoughts, turning my mind darker and heavier, swirling with ghosts and terrors.

Neri didn't notice my inner struggles or see what I saw when she pressed another jewel against the artwork. She didn't seem to fear what would happen tonight. We hadn't talked about it, or about anything else really. She hadn't told me if she'd had any nightmares recently or if she'd looked online for a therapist.

I wanted so much to talk to her, but sitting at the table beside the open doors where her parents squabbled and flirted in the kitchen was not the place.

So I sat quietly and watched her following the symbols on the graph, slowly making a starfish come alive.

"Nice of Jack to give you a present early." I lifted my bottle to my lips, annoyed to find it almost empty.

The alcoholic dullness that I'd been searching for hadn't arrived. But I'd kept drinking…I'd drunk more in one go than I ever had before, mainly thanks to Jack plying me with three in the pool when he'd come to join me. We'd sat on a rock and dangled our feet in the cool water, discussing his plans for next year's research projects and how he wanted to go back to Southeast Asia.

"Yeah, I think he was surprised that I didn't pilfer something like I usually do. Probably wanted to reward my good behaviour."

"I think he was gutted that you didn't steal a gift, actually. It's practically a tradition that you'll swipe at least one before dinner."

Neri shrugged half-heartedly. "I'm almost eighteen. Little too old for gifts."

"That's bullshit and you know it."

She scowled. "Keep your voice down."

"He asked me earlier if you were okay," I murmured quietly.

"He did?" She paused with her pen hovering over a moon-gleaming dolphin. "What did he say?"

"He said he's sensed you've been off ever since you went to Zara's. He asked me if I knew anything."

She turned into a glacier, her eyes ice chips. "What did you say?"

"Nothing of course. I vowed to you that I wouldn't tell. It's not my place."

"Do you think he suspects?"

"I think he's just sad that you're not your usual self." I finished my beer and leaned forward, whispering in her ear, "*I'm* sad you're not your usual self. I wish…I wish—" Grief grabbed me around the throat.

Fuck, I couldn't lose her.

What if I lost her tonight?

What if, by trying to claim her, I lost her for-fucking-ever?

A moan escaped me, and I dropped my forehead to her flower-printed shoulder. "Neri, I—"

"Who's ready for dessert before dinner?" Anna laughed, leaping through the sliders with a platter full of handmade éclairs.

Neri stiffened.

I ripped my head up, shifting my chair a little farther away from her. I couldn't tame my skittering pulse. I'd been so close to kissing her arm. So, so close to forgetting I couldn't touch her when every part of me begged to erase the awful, sickening distance between us.

Jack exploded out of the house, landing next to Anna, his hands up and a huge grin on his face. "Me. Me. They're all for me. Mine." Snatching the tray from his wife, he dropped his head to the closest éclair, taking a massive bite like a starving animal. He groaned. Loudly. "Hmmm! Soooo good."

Seemed I wasn't the only one who'd had a few beers. Only difference was, Jack got silly, and I got depressed.

Anna snickered and wiped away the chocolate and cream smeared on his nose. "What on earth am I going to do with you?"

"Same thing you do every day, my darling." Jack laughed. "Put up with me and love me even more for my nonsense."

Anna rolled her eyes.

Neri forced a smile.

And Jack looked at me and froze.

What?

What had I done?

What had he seen?

Slowly, Jack came around the table and sat beside me, placing the platter away from Neri's diamond painting.

I tracked him the entire way.

I glowered as he reached over and patted my balled hand on the table. "You're hurting, Aslan."

It was my turn to freeze.

What the fuck?

How did he know?

How much did he already know about me and Neri—

Licking my lips, I swallowed hard. "I don't know what you're—"

"You're missing your family, mate. I see it as plain as day in your eyes." He winced and leaned back as Anna sat down and handed out plates for the creamy, flaky desserts. "I always forget that this time of year would be the hardest for you."

"I'm fine, Jack."

"It's okay *not* to be fine, you know." He studied me. "I lost my parents when I was fairly young too. Car crash when they were driving down to Sydney. But you already know that. I've told you. In fact, you know a lot about us, yet..." He sighed. "We *still* don't know a hell of a lot about you."

I fought my rising temper. "You know everything there is to know about me."

"From sixteen to twenty-two, yes, I'd say we know you better than anyone. But before that...you're not exactly an open book." He smiled sadly. "Do you want to talk about them? Talk about what you and your sister would do on Christmas—"

"We didn't celebrate."

"Oh...well, what *did* you celebrate?"

The rocks were back in my throat, spilling into my heart, creating a landslide that crushed every piece of me. "Let's just focus on today, okay?"

"You should talk about them, Aslan," Anna said kindly. "Make them come alive from your memories."

"My memories already haunt me. I don't need to give them any more ammunition."

"But if you just talked about them—"

"I'd have to relive what happened."

"You could start to heal," Jack said.

"I *am* healed. I'm fine."

Neri huffed but wisely stayed quiet.

Jack and Anna shared a look before Anna murmured, "Melike…that means queen in Turkish, right? That's so pretty—"

"I-I can't do this." I shot to my feet and raked both hands through my hair. "I'm not…eh. I'm not feeling so good." Stalking from the table, my ears rang as Neri said, "Leave it alone, Mum. You know how he feels about talking about them."

I didn't wait to hear Anna's reply.

I stormed into the house and grabbed another beer, all while the clouds of blackness roiled through me, grumbling with thunder, churning with grief.

I felt the ghost of my father urging me to apologise.

I felt my mother telling me it was okay to hurt.

And I felt my sister—the little girl I didn't share a single drop of blood with—urging me to go out there and tell them everything.

Tell them who I truly was.

Who I truly loved.

Who I wanted to become.

But I couldn't.

So I didn't.

And the tension wound ever tighter inside me.

3 P.M.

I sat next to Neri on the couch.

Jack and Anna had gone for a quick walk along the beach before starting the final preparations for the extravagant dinner. Roast chicken permeated the house with rosemary and garlic potatoes. Crisp salads waited in the fridge, and freshly baked baguettes begged for lashings of butter. The lobster Jack and I had prepared earlier was chilling, and when I'd gone to claim yet another beer—*because why fucking not, I need all the help I can get to stay sane today*—the amount of containers and fresh fruit wedged on the fridge shelves hinted that none of us would be escaping tonight without a serious case of overindulgent indigestion.

Looking at Neri beside me, I cursed the approved space between us. She hadn't snuggled closer the minute Jack and Anna had left or tried to pull my shorts down for a quickie.

She merely sat quietly beside me, texting Honey with furious flurries of her fingers while some nonsense played on TV.

Leaning closer, I read her latest thread over her shoulder.

Honey: *Oh, I know. Family dramas are the worst! Christmas always seems to bring out the madness, hey? Cool diamond painting, though! I love doing them. Keeps my idle hands busy.*

Neri: *Think I just want to crawl into bed and wake up when today is over.*

Honey: *Go jump your boy's bones. Go to bed but make it rock!*

Neri: *Hard to jump someone who doesn't want to be jumped.*

Fury unfurled like wildfire. "What the hell, Nerida?"

She flinched a mile as if she'd forgotten I even sat next to her.

"First, what the hell are you doing talking about us, and second, why would you say I don't want you?"

Her forehead pinched with frustration. "You told me you wouldn't have sex with me anymore. Not until I 'cured' myself."

My heart twisted. "That wasn't what I said. I never said you had to *cure* yourself."

"Yes, you did." Pure anger filled her gorgeous face. "Your exact words were, 'this is the last time, *canım*.'"

"I meant last time using me to hide. Not last time we're allowed to fuck."

"Well, I've decided you were right. I need to find another way to get over it. So don't worry, you're off the hook."

"What the hell is that supposed to mean?"

"It means, I don't need your help. I can do it on my own." Standing upright, she fisted her phone and muttered, "I-I need to be by myself for a little while." With a twirl of white miniskirt, she stalked down the corridor and into the main bathroom.

I sat blinking at the empty lounge.

What the fuck just happened?

My heart bellowed to go after her.

My insides bled at the thought of hurting her.

Standing, I swayed a little as the beer finally caught up with me, making everything a little hazy. Balling my hands, and forcing the world to stay upright, I marched after her and banged on the bathroom door. "Neri. Let me in."

"Go away."

"Talk to me."

"I'm done with talking, Aslan. Just like you, remember? You can't even talk about your family, and they've been dead almost six years!"

A chill poured through me. "That's different—"

"No, it's not. You're a damn hypocrite."

I winced, hating that she called me out on it. "Fine, I admit it. I'm a hypocrite. But I'm only trying to keep you from doing what I do. You can't keep burying this, *aşkım*."

"I'm not planning on burying it." A strange noise came from the other side of the door. "I'm dealing with it in another way."

The chill inside me solidified into frost. "What are you doing in there? Open the damn door." Jiggling the handle, I yanked and jerked. "Unlock it and let me in. If you're struggling, then let me help. I'll give you what you want. Quickly. We can be together before your parents get home."

"Go away."

Another noise.

A quiet moan.

"Nerida! Open the fucking door."

She didn't answer.

She hissed as something crashed inside the bathroom.

"What the *hell* are you doing?"

"Fixing myself," she shouted. "You should probably learn how to do the same thing."

I saw red.

I pummelled my fist against the door. "If you don't open in three seconds, I'm gonna break it down. I'm going to bend you over my knee and—"

"Aslan?" Jack appeared at the top of the corridor. "Everything okay?"

Fuck.

FUCK.

Trembling hard, I dragged my hand over my mouth and did my best to swallow down the panic Neri had given me. "Yeah…yeah, everything's fine."

"Why were you yelling?"

"I, eh…too much to drink."

"Fair enough. No more until you've eaten a big meal to soak it up, alright?"

"Yep. No worries."

His eyes flickered past me to the locked bathroom door. "Neri okay?"

"I'm fine, Dad!" Neri yelled. "Just taking a bath."

"A bath?" Jack's eyebrows shot up. "It's freaking two hundred degrees outside."

"A cold one!"

"Get in the pool then, you moron! Stop wasting water." Jack shook his head and rolled his eyes. "Teenagers." Giving me a wave, he stomped into the kitchen; his voice trailed back as he chatted with Anna.

Taking a risk, playing with fire, I pressed my mouth against the door and whispered, "Neri…open up. Let me in. I know something's not right. Let me help."

She didn't reply.

The sound of running water splashed in the bath.

I stood there for as long as I could before Jack came to get me, shoved another beer in my hand—despite his scolding to sober up—and dragged me to the couch to watch some Aussie football.

5 P.M.

Neri finally came out of the bathroom.

She'd stayed in there for over an hour and only appeared in a flash of skin and towel before darting into her bedroom.

I'd stopped drinking.

But it didn't stop the black, dangerous fog in my head.

I'd driven myself mad with fear over what she'd been doing in there.

My stomach hadn't stopped churning, and as much as I wanted to storm into her bedroom and demand she speak to me, I couldn't.

Jack kept me occupied by forcing me to root for his favourite football team and Anna put me to work in the kitchen, carving the chicken and making sure the table was perfectly set.

For two fucking hours, I did what I could to thank the Taylors for yet another year of harbouring me, another year of keeping me safe, all while my heart and soul were with Neri down the corridor.

And by the time she appeared, she took my fucking breath away.

Her hair was sleek and loosely curled in ways she only did when she went out to parties with her friends. The ugly floral shirt was gone, replaced with a skimpy black dress with rose gold stitching across the bodice. Her breasts spilled out the top, her legs went on for miles, and her eyes absolutely hypnotised me.

Black eyeshadow made her seem both sultry and witchy, thick lashes, cheeks dusted with colour, and lips painted an enticing peach. She walked past the back of the couch; I couldn't help twisting to stare after her. She left me in a cloud of frangipani perfume. The scent she knew made me hard as a fucking rock.

Padding barefoot into the kitchen, Neri said softly, "What do you think?"

"Wow, sweetie!" Anna exclaimed as Neri went to her mother. "You look absolutely amazing! You've put the rest of us to shame. I had no idea we were going to eat in our party dresses."

"It's okay. I just felt like dressing up." Neri rubbed her forearms, glancing at her wrists. "Wanted to feel…pretty, you know."

Anna wrapped her arms around Neri. "Sweetie, you are the prettiest girl I've ever seen. You don't need make-up and a little black dress to prove it."

I stood and headed toward the threshold of the living room and the kitchen, drawn to her despite myself. "You're stunning," I choked. "I-I can't take my eyes off you."

I stiffened for Jack's suspicion or Anna's confusion, but Anna just beamed and nodded. "Isn't she just? My little girl, all grown up."

"Bloody hell, Nerida." Jack bowled past me and scooped Neri into his arms. "That's it. Who is this vixen, and what did you do with my little fish?"

Neri laughed, but it was hollow. The sadness in her eyes, even while her lips faked happiness, carved out my heart with a rusty dagger. "I'm still her, Dad. Put me down."

"Nope. I'm never putting you down again. In fact, you're forbidden from going to Townsville next year. I won't survive you not living under my roof. Especially looking like that." He squeezed her until she grunted in his arms. "You're far too precious. No one is allowed to touch you."

"Ha ha." She patted him on his head, ruffling his hair like she used to.

It made Jack tip his head back and stare at her like a love-sick puppy. "You promise you'll visit all the time, right? What am I supposed to do without you driving me up the wall?"

"Dunno. Get a cat?"

He planted a fat kiss on her cheek before plopping her back onto her bare feet. "Nope. Much better idea. I'll clone you. I'll make myself another little fish so this big one before me can swim in the huge open ocean, and I can keep another version of you safe, here, tucked up in my arms forever."

Tears suddenly glittered in Neri's eyes. "You are the biggest sap in the world."

"Only for you, my love. Only for you." Planting his hands on her shoulders, seriousness filled his tone. "You know I'd do anything for you, right, Nerida? Whatever you're dealing with at the moment, you can tell your silly ole' Dad, and I'll do anything to make you happy again."

Neri sniffed, and Anna clutched her hands to her chest, sending soapy bubbles from doing the dishes down her garish shirt. "Ah, Jack. You still know how to make my heart skip."

Jack threw her a wink. "Fancy making another one of these, my darling? I know we said we only wanted one, but this one's flying the coop, and I don't think I'll cope with an empty nest."

Anna chuckled. "I'm over the hill, and you've had a vasectomy. No more. Besides." Anna stepped toward me, wiping her hands on the tea towel hooked in her shorts pocket. "We already have another one. Right here." Wrapping her arms around my waist, she slotted into my side, tiny to my height, slim to my size. "We have a daughter *and* a son. One born for the ocean and another delivered by it."

Neri sucked in a breath, locking eyes with me.

Jack gave a fierce nod. "You're right. You're absolutely right. I hope you realise you're one of us, Aslan. I'm sorry for pushing you before. I know better than to dredge up the past. But I hope you know that we've grown to care for you like you're our own."

Everything inside me howled and clawed.

All the pain, all the grief, all the secrets and the ghosts and the hiding—it all crashed over me like a drowning tsunami.

I buckled.

I couldn't catch a proper breath.

Extracting myself from Anna's embrace, I bowed my head. My legs threatened to crash me to the floor, and I was so close, so fucking close to blurting out everything.

I'm in love with your daughter.
I want to marry your daughter.
I want to be your son…just not in the way you think.

I looked over my shoulder at the ring box just waiting for me to spill out my entire heart, and I couldn't do it anymore.

Rocking on the balls of my feet, I went to turn. To grab the ring. To drop to bended knee. But Neri rubbed her wrists again, swiftly, inconspicuously, and the smallest smear of concealer came away.

And what I saw beneath made my heart wrench to a godawful stop.

Just *stop*.

Dead.

Mortified.

Horrified.

Broken.

I grunted as if she'd sucker-punched the entire life out of me.

Because she had.

She'd fucking slaughtered me.

Her eyes met mine, and the ice-blue clarity darkened with fear.

She knew.

She knew I'd seen.

She knew I was so close to breaking.

"Neri…" I cleared my throat, trying to speak around the shattered glass inside it. "Can I…can I talk to you alone for a minute. Please."

Jack raised an eyebrow, but his faith in me, his blind fucking trust, had him grinning as if my inability to accept his yearly invitation to be his wasn't unusual.

"Planning covert Christmas shenanigans, huh? Fine." Swooping toward Anna, he grabbed his wife and carried her giggling down the corridor. "Tell you what! Let's all dress up! Make an occasion of our last family dinner under the same roof. Go raid your closet, Aslan. Anna and I will be a while."

Anna squealed as Jack buried his face in her neck, marched her into their bedroom, and kicked the door closed. Her throaty laugh hinted exactly what they planned on doing.

I didn't care if they were planning on making out or dressing up, the only thing I cared about was Neri.

My moon-married wife.

The girl who'd just torn out my heart and left it bleeding all over the damn kitchen.

"Neri…" I breathed, drifting toward her, cursing the remnants of alcohol and the fog of day-drinking. I reached for her damaged wrist. "What did you—"

"Not here." She reared back, not letting me touch her. With a thin breath, she braced her shoulders and strode with a ramrod spine all the way to her bedroom.

I followed with my shredded heart dragging all the way behind me.

Chapter Fifty-Three

ASLAN

(*Moon in Ganda:* Omwezi)

I DIDN'T SAY A WORD AS SHE waited for me to step into her girlish decorated bedroom.

I stared at the mermaid bedside light and mosquito net draped over her bed while she quietly closed the door. Her teal blankets and lacy pillows clashed with the pink-lacquered dresser and chipped lemon tallboy.

A lifetime she'd spent in this room.

Evolving.

Becoming.

I'd been inside her on her bed. I'd rutted into her against her door. I'd believed we were fated, all while we'd laughed and kissed and made promises to each other in snatched moments when her parents weren't home.

All that preciousness. All that belonging tore itself into pieces and crushed beneath our feet as I turned to face her.

She stayed by the closed door, clinging to the handle.

No lock.

No way to stop her parents from coming in.

Nothing to prevent me from doing what I was about to do.

As calm as a storm about to tear a city apart, I stepped into her and grabbed her right wrist.

She didn't fight me.

She sucked on her bottom lip as I used the hem of my hideous shirt to wipe away the thick concealer. Redness appeared. Faint streaks of purple. The first bloom of blue.

I wanted to be sick.

Despair splashed like acid on my tongue.

I'd failed her.

I'd fucking failed her that night and all the other nights she'd struggled.

Once every inch of make-up was removed, I let her go.

Silence throbbed around us.

I trembled so hard my teeth clacked as I reached for her left wrist.

She hung in my hold, meek and submissive.

Silent tears coursed down her cheeks as I wiped her gently. As gently as I possibly could, removing her attempts at hiding. Choosing right here, right now, to do what I'd begun to suspect she needed.

I didn't want to do it.

It would butcher me into irreparable pieces.

It would probably cost me my life.

But I would do absolutely anything if it made her whole again.

My ears rang as another blush of red, streaks of blue, and the faintest smudge of black marked her no-longer healed wrists.

The bruises Ethan had given her had faded. She'd used the same make-up to hide what he'd done over the past few weeks.

But these…these were so fresh they glowed.

Every part of me howled.

I honestly didn't know how I stood so still and didn't crumple at her feet.

My voice resembled a slab of granite as I strangled, "You hurt yourself."

Sniffing back her tears, she encircled her wrist and nodded. "I thought…about what you said. About the bruises on my heart not healing like the ones on my skin. I hoped…" She sighed and shook her head. "I thought if I could see those bruises, then I could figure out a way to heal them. I can rub arnica into these. I can hide these. I can press against them and make them hurt, and it stops my mind from going back to that bed with him tying me down and—" Her breath caught; she cried quietly. "It was a stupid idea, but…I just needed an outlet. I wanted to feel pretty, even though I'm damaged. I wanted to feel beautiful, even though being beautiful is what got me hurt. He went after me because he found me *beautiful,* and…I wanted to reclaim that part. I wanted to dress up and not be afraid that if I wore a short skirt or dared to put on eyeshadow that I wouldn't invite another monster to rape—"

Her sobs stole the rest of her words.

My arms snarled to wrap around her.

My entire nervous system stung and snapped to gather her close and give her somewhere safe to shatter.

But I fought those urges.

Those urges were wrong.

I'd tried to help Neri her way…yet it'd only made things worse.

There was another way.

A way that I doubted any psychologist would approve of or ever agree might be necessary for those far too brave to break.

But I had first-hand experience.

So many times, I dreamed of drowning.

So many nights, I begged to die.

If I had been braver, I would've walked into the sea and let it take me, if only to escape the soul-crushing guilt that I'd done nothing to save my family.

The family that'd died *because* of me.

But I hadn't been brave.

I hadn't returned to the source of my agony, so that agony kept on fucking oozing.

But Neri…

I could take her back to that source.

I could throw her back into those nightmares and give her a different ending.

Nausea rushed up my throat as I breathed, "You should've come to me, *hayatım*." The alcohol in my system grew more potent. I felt loose and petrified but also fierce and resolved.

"I tried." Her wet eyes met mine. "You said—"

"If you told me you needed pain, I would've given you pain."

She frowned through her tears. "No, you wouldn't. You would never hurt me."

I shifted a single step into her, pressing her against the door with sheer force of presence, even though no part of me touched her. "Are you so sure about that?"

I shouldn't do this here.

I should take her back to my room where at least we had a few walls and the garden between us and her parents.

But…the alcohol whispered this was wise.

The depression hissed this was necessary.

And the stark fear clawing at my heart made recklessness supersede any and all self-preservation.

I didn't care about myself.

I only cared about her.

And I'd failed her.

Over and over again.

I won't fail her now.

Her eyes narrowed, dancing and searching mine. "What are you saying?"

"I'm saying I know how it feels to be trapped by who you are, trapped by what happened, trapped with no way of getting free."

"Aslan, I—"

"Tell me what you need, Neri."

"I just need you. I need you inside me and—"

"No. Dive deeper. Tell me what you *need*."

"I need…" She wrung her hands, nervousness pouring off her. "I need to feel the pain again. I want it to hurt but on *my* terms. I want it to hurt so I can heal my heart as well as my flesh this time."

"Not enough. Try again."

Anger puckered her eyebrows. "I don't know what you want me to say."

"The truth. Give me the truth."

"You want to hear that I'm sick of feeling this way?" she suddenly hissed, keeping her voice down so her parents didn't hear. "That I'm sick of *being* this way? This isn't me. This anger isn't me. This fear, this hate, this rage…it isn't me!"

"So let it out."

"I can't."

"Yes, you can."

"How?"

"On me."

"What?" Her forehead furrowed. "I'm not going to take it out on you. You deserve nothing but my thanks after what you did."

"I didn't kill him."

She winced. "You shoved him overboard."

"Against your command."

"Why are you saying this?"

"Because I think you're furious at me as well as him. I think you're so tied up in knots you're going to explode if you don't let it out."

She pushed away from the door, trying to move past me. "Just stop it, Aslan—"

"Did I say you could leave?" I shoved her against the door.

Her eyes widened as her back thumped quietly against the wood. "Are you crazy? They'll hear."

"I don't care."

"Since when?"

"Since I saw your new bruises. Bruises *you* did. Bruises *you* caused. I can't think about anything else. I don't *care* about anything else. I don't care this could backfire spectacularly in my face. All I care about, Neri, is *you*."

"We'll discuss this tomorrow—"

"No. Now. Talk to me. Hurt me if you need to. They're going to find out about us in an hour anyway. And if I can give you a break from the pain you're feeling before then…" I shrugged sadly. "I'll do whatever it takes."

"I'm not discussing this with you right before Christmas dinner." Her chin tipped up. "It's been a long day. We're both drained. Let's just—"

"I failed you, Neri. I failed you by not being there. I failed you for not stopping him. I fucking failed—"

"Don't make this about you."

"Use me. Take out your hurt. *On me.* Hurt me, Neri. Hurt me because I wasn't there. Hurt me because I wasn't there to stop him."

"What? No. I don't blame you—"

"I blame myself. I blame all of this on me."

"Aslan, stop it—"

"I'm offering myself up to you to use in whatever way you need."

"What I need is for you to stop being an idiot. You never come into my room when Mum and Dad are in the house. What's gotten into you?"

"What's gotten into me?" I growled. "I just fucking told you, *aşkım*! *You* got into me. *You.* You've torn apart any hope I had that you'll be okay. You're hurting yourself, Neri. You hid in that bathroom and *hurt* yourself. What part of 'I can't fucking breathe seeing you in pain' do you not understand?" I pinched the bridge of my nose, trying to rein in my temper.

I exhaled hard, grunting under my breath, "How did you do it?"

"Doesn't matter."

I looked up beneath my lashes, dropping my hand. "Of course, it matters. It matters a great deal."

"It's done. And…it didn't work anyway, so you don't have to fear me doing it again. I still feel…messed up."

"I know how you can let that mess out."

"Not this again." She bared her teeth. "Those beers you've had are making you reckless. Let's just get through the rest of tonight and—"

"I'm not fucking proposing to you in front of your parents while your wrists are welted, Neri. You need to let go. Let it out. Get angry."

"I can't be angry. Mum and Dad will hear."

"Don't use that as an excuse. You're hiding still. Hiding beneath everything you can. That stops. Right fucking now." I balled my hands. "I can't stand seeing you so sad. I can't stand feeling so helpless. And I think…I think that's your problem too."

She scowled. "My *problem*?"

"You feel helpless."

"No, I don't—"

"For the first time in your life, someone overpowered you, threatened you, and took something that wasn't theirs to take. It slapped you in the face. It forced you to see that you aren't invincible, and now you feel utterly helpless."

"Stop putting words in my mouth."

I stepped into her, wedging my leg between hers, pressing my knee against the door. I never took my eyes off hers as I pushed up, rocking my thigh against the part of her that I'd tasted, kissed, worshipped, and adored. "If he was here right now. If it was his leg between yours, what would you do?"

Her entire body flinched. "Stop it. I don't want to think about that."

"You think about it all the time."

"No, I don't."

"Your nightmares say otherwise." I drove my thigh higher, making her breath catch. "Tell me what he does to you in your nightmares. Does he pin you down? Does he tie you tight? Does he fuck you—"

"Stop!" She shoved me hard.

I absorbed the strike but didn't move.

Instead, I crushed her harder against the door.

My hands landed on either side of her head, planting on the wood, imprisoning her. The tinkling pieces of my well and truly brutalised heart fell into my toes as I whispered in her ear, "You don't want to relive it, but it's the only thing you see. It won't stop until you accept it or…"

She breathed fast as I pulled away a little, looking into her eyes, needing her to see what I was willing to do.

"Or what?" she whispered.

"Or it happens again."

"*What?*"

"You're forced again. Taken again. Raped by a bastard who—"

"Get the hell off me, Aslan. You're drunk. You have to be. I have no idea why you're saying these things. Sober up or get out—"

"Make me." My entire soul screamed fucking murder as I locked my fingers around her fragile throat. "Strike me, hit me, hurt me like you wished you'd hurt him."

She stilled.

Didn't even blink.

My thumb caressed the column of her neck, pressing against her galloping pulse. "I hate that he touched you, Neri. I *hate* that he hurt you. I wished you'd let me rip out his fucking heart for you when I had the chance, but you didn't. You let your goodness get in the way, but this time, I'm not going to let you. Become like him. Hurt me like he hurt you."

"Aslan…let me go."

Nuzzling my nose against hers, I whispered, "Don't ask me. *Make* me."

"I can't. You're far stronger than me."

"But vulnerable in many places." Keeping one hand on her throat, I dragged the other down her body until my fingers joined with hers. She never looked away from me as I guided her palm to the front of my shorts.

To the aching length popping out the top waistband. To the desperately sick and blackly twisted part of me that was turned on, all while fucking horrified.

"Knee me here, and you can get free."

"I'm not going to knee you. Are you insane?"

"I'm the son of a murderer, trafficker, and rapist. I'm not insane, Neri. I'm just embracing my true heritage."

"You're nothing like him, and you know it."

"Are you so sure?" I forced her hand against my throbbing erection. "Would I be hard if I wasn't? Would I be so fucking drunk on taking you like this if some part of me wasn't already evil?"

She squirmed against me, rubbing herself against my thigh as she tried to escape. "I know what you're doing, and it won't work."

"You sure?" I ran my nose down her throat, inhaling her perfume and the telltale sharpness of panic beneath. "You smell of fear. Fear that's overriding the trust you have in me."

"That's instinct."

"Exactly."

"But I know you. I know you'd never hurt me."

"Seeing you hurt yourself has made me a little...unhinged, *aşkım*. Drinking hasn't helped. I'm right on the edge, and I don't think I can stop myself. You need pain, so I'll give you pain. You need to relive it, so I'll make you relive it. I'll take you into the nightmare, Neri, and I'll happily be the monster you need to kill to survive."

"I just need you to love me. That's all—"

"And I do. With all my fucking heart. But that's not enough."

"It is enough. It *will* be enough—"

"Fight me off, wife."

"Aslan, don't—"

"Tell me no."

"Aslan—"

"I won't make it easy for you, but you're strong. You can stop me. You can win."

"I don't want—"

My tongue shut her up.

I threw myself onto her and wedged her against the door.

She moaned into the violent kiss.

She shook her head as I opened wide and claimed her. I licked her deep. I licked her hard. I kissed the girl I'd kissed a thousand times before, but this time, I let all my guilt, all my rage, all my fear tangle tightly with hers.

It was frightening and sickening and a part of me that was my father's son, roared at the freedom. At the overwhelming reaction in my blood and bones to no longer have layers and walls, locks and vaults. To let everything that I'd been hiding from crash free and swarm me.

My hands landed in Neri's hair, yanking her head back, kissing her harder.

For a moment, she melted.

She recognised me.

Remembered us.

I cursed her for licking me back.

But then...her back arched, and a ripple of war worked down her spine. With vicious teeth, she bit me.

I gasped as blood bloomed, staining my teeth and splashing metallic.

"Again," I snarled, crushing my mouth to hers, forcing her to taste me, drink me. "I won't stop until you make me. I won't be gentle. I won't be kind. I'll be exactly what you need me to be—"

She snapped.

A guttural groan echoed in her chest as she threw herself against me.

It didn't even rock me back on my feet.

I kissed her harder, sucking her bottom lip, screaming inside for making her feel so weak, so easily taken.

With a cry of terrified frustration, she did exactly what I told her to do.

She used my thigh between her legs to hold her weight and drove her knee directly into my balls.

I coughed and tumbled to the side.

Stars exploded.

The room spun.

The beer I'd consumed threatened to splash up my gullet, and I dropped to one knee as I cupped myself.

Fuck. Me.

The pain kept getting worse.

Echoing and spreading, burning down my legs and into my belly.

Neri took full advantage of my pain.

Leaping over me, she flew onto her bed and landed on the other side, putting the mattress between us. "Aslan, stop it," she whisper-hissed. "*Enough.*"

All I wanted to do was kneel before her and beg for her forgiveness.

I wanted to gather her close and press endless vows into her hair.

Instead, I shot to my feet and lurched like a drunken bear toward her.

She squealed as I grabbed her damaged wrist.

She fought and scratched as I threw her onto her bed.

She went to scream, but I slammed my hand over her mouth, squeezing her cheeks with awful fingers. Looming over her, I used my free hand to shove up her little black dress. "Fight me off. Prove to yourself that you're strong enough."

Burying my mouth against her neck, I bit her. Hard.

She yelled under my hand and turned into a little hellcat.

Fighting and kicking, wrestling and brawling.

I struggled to keep hold of her.

Genuine surprise widened my eyes as she managed to knee me in the stomach and shove my mouth off her neck. Punching me in the temple—just a graze but enough to make me dizzy—she scrambled up her bed and grabbed hold of her mosquito net, ready to launch to the floor.

"Not so fast." Lashing my arm around her waist, I threw her back down again.

Only problem was, she didn't let go of the net.

The webbing cracked.

The bamboo ring tethered to the ceiling came crashing down on top of us.

We froze for just a breath.

Two fish caught in a net, covered from head to toe.

But then she fought again.

She was slippery and quick, and each time I managed to get a proper hold, she slipped out from under me.

The webbing tangled in my legs. Radiating pain in my cock made me sloppy. The strike to my head made me slow. She was winning. So resilient and quick-thinking.

Pride swelled in my chest.

She was so fucking strong.

If the bastard hadn't drugged her first, he wouldn't have stood a chance.

I needed her to see that.

She needed to believe in that because then she'd know that none of this was her fault. It wasn't because she was beautiful or accepted a drink or went to a house party to get her friend back. She was a victim of cruel circumstance, bad luck, and a rotten fucking criminal.

My heart hammered as she kicked me in the chest, shoved the bamboo ring over my head so the thickest part of the net blinded me, then wriggled to the floor.

I fought with the net, wasting valuable time, struggling to catch a proper breath.

Tearing it away, snarling with fury, I slid off the bed after her. Pillows followed. A blanket caught around my ankle, falling with me.

Grabbing her around the hips, I flipped her onto her back and wedged my entire length over her.

Her eyes burned into mine.

Her cheeks shot red and the bruises on her wrists sent my temper raging. "I hate that you hurt yourself. Fucking *hate* it."

"My body. Not yours." She struck me in the chest, again and again.

I ducked my head to protect myself, unwittingly giving her space to squirm free again. Somehow, she got to her feet and stomped on my chest, shoving me onto my back.

The booze in my system made me sloppy and sick.

I groaned as I looked up at her.

I felt fucking undone, not human.

I wanted her to finish the job, to put me out of my six years of misery, but then the frenzied ferocity faded from her eyes.

And she blinked.

She returned from whatever hellhole she'd been fighting from and tripped back a step. Shaking her head, she wrapped her hands over her mouth as she studied me bruised and battered on the floor. "Oh my God."

I winced as I sat up on my elbows, keeping my legs spread, kicking aside a shell-shaped cushion. "Now do you see, *hayatım*? Now do you trust?" I probed my bleeding bottom lip with my tongue, hissing under my breath. "I didn't hold back. You beat me, fair and square. You are strong enough. So fucking strong—"

With a sharp cry, Neri threw herself on top of me.

Her hands clamped on my sweaty cheeks, and she sat heavily on my straining, bruised erection, her black dress fanning around my hips.

I grunted at the fresh onslaught of pain.

I couldn't catch a breath as she dropped her head and crushed her mouth to mine.

I groaned as her tongue dove deep, claiming me, leashing me...

I didn't stand a fucking chance.

All the tension.

All the need.

It erupted into ice-hot flames, poured fuel on our twisted fire, and shoved us headfirst into lunacy.

I kissed her back.

She cried out, driving me further into chaos, her tongue wild, her hips undulating on mine.

We kissed stupidly hard.

Violent and messy, deep and dirty.

We forgot about everything.

Where we were.

Who we were.

We were frantic and filthy, driven by primal instincts to join, to bond, to fuse so tightly together, we could never be unfused, never be apart, never feel the same horrid helplessness infecting both of us.

The blackness within my soul billowed in size. The depression within my mind blew through me on waves of alcohol. They tried to drown me, but they were nothing, *nothing,* compared to the disease Neri caused.

The bone-deep, soul-sure demonic realisation that I would do absolutely anything for this woman.

I'd turn homicidal.

Suicidal.

My survival hinged entirely on hers, and if that meant slaughtering thousands, so be it.

She moaned and fought me, turning our kiss into something only a devil would like.

She ground herself on my cock, her hands dropping from my cheeks and fumbling against my zipper.

Grabbing her around the hips, I rolled and pinned her beneath me.

I dry-humped against her, hissing at the lingering pain from her knee.

Her diligent little hands kept working, and the sound of my shorts coming undone echoed far too loudly around us.

Common sense screamed into my ears.

Jack and Anna.

If they found us like this...

"Neri. Fuck, Neri. Wait. We can't—"

Her tongue silenced me.

I kissed her savagely back. Our noses nudging, our teeth clacking. "Your parents are—" Kiss and nip and lick. "—down the hall."

"They're doing exactly what we're doing. They don't have a clue." She moaned into my mouth and shoved her hand into my boxer-briefs. "You're the one who started this." She sucked my bleeding bottom lip into her mouth. "So finish it."

I almost came as she fisted me.

My hips drove into her palm against my control, and the blistering ripple of a release quickly centred in my very bruised balls. "Neri—"

"Be fast." Her hand stopped driving me insane, slipping between us to shove her knickers to the side. "Be quiet." Her legs curled over my hips and lashed tightly at the ankles, directly above my ass.

She trapped me against the hottest, wettest part of her, but my shorts were still in the way. "Neri. I can't. I'm—"

"Do it, Aslan. *Please.* I'm begging—"

"I'll give you what you want if you stop squeezing the life out of me with your damn thighs, *canım*. I need to shove my pants dow—"

"Okay, kids. Dinner's ready—" The door swung wide.

Jack stepped, Jack tripped, Jack broke.

Every emotion that a human could feel played over his face in the fastest second as his gaze fell on me between his daughter's legs, the pillows all over the floor, the broken mosquito net, Neri's tears, our rumpled clothing, and worst of all...the bruises and condemning wounds on Neri's wrists.

"*No...*" Jack stumbled, his fancy suit a mockery of the mayhem he'd walked in on. His exclamation was just a breath. A prayer really, begging his eyes that this wasn't real. He clung to the wall as he saw a re-enactment of what Neri had gone through with another man on another night.

"Dad..." Neri choked beneath me.

I shoved off her and leaped woozily to my feet, hastily rezipping my shorts. "Jack...it's not. I didn't. I meant to tell you—" The beer, the fight, the lust—it all swarmed my senses, and I didn't see Jack's punch until it landed squarely against my jaw.

I spun with his force.

I bounced off Neri's bed.

I landed on my knees and blinked back fresh stars.

"Dad, don't—!" Neri cried, tripping to her feet. "It's not what you—"

"You fucking bastard!" Jack kicked me with all his might, his dress shoe crunching against my ribs. I heaved and buckled over, wrapping my arms around where he'd struck. "You fucking *bastard*!" He kicked me again and again, raining pain as I curled up on the floor, protecting my head and face.

"Dad, *stop*!" Neri's scream ricocheted in my ears.

Jack only hit me harder.

Not listening.

Beyond listening.

"What the hell is going on in here?!" Anna bowled into the room. I only saw a blur of a pretty pink dress before Jack's fists pummelled me in the head.

I couldn't speak.

Couldn't explain.

I would never defend myself against the guy who'd kept me hidden and given me a life. Given me a purpose.

So I took it.

I took every strike, kick, and hit, all while Neri screamed and Anna yelled and Jack lost his ever-loving mind on me.

"Call the fucking police, Anna!" he roared, kicking me in the lower back, making me groan.

Footsteps raced out of Neri's room.

"I told you!" Jack snarled. "I *told you* never to touch her. And what the fuck did you do? You drink too much and think you can take what isn't yours to fucking take?!" He kicked and stomped me. "You hurt my daughter!"

"He didn't, Dad. I love him—"

"Shut up, Nerida. Go and find your mother."

"Aslan didn't do this."

"Look at your room! It's destroyed. Look at your wrists! He was on top of you! There are fucking teeth marks on your neck, for fuck's sake!"

"It's not what you think—"

"It's *exactly* what I think." His fists came again, finding fresh spots to hurt. "He was trying to rape you."

"No, he wasn't!"

"I can see with my own eyes, Nerida!" He kicked me again, his force turning sloppy with fatigue. "Don't try to defend him. *Never* try to defend someone like him."

"I called the station," Anna shouted. "They're on their way." A glimpse of her legs came into view as Anna inched closer to Jack and said breathlessly, "That's enough, Jack. He's down. He's not going anywhere. Let the police deal with him."

Jack sucked in a snarl-sob, kicking me once more in the belly for good measure. "How could you, Aslan? How could you fucking do this to Neri? To us? After everything we've done for you?"

I tried to speak.

Blood trickled from my lips.

I tried to breathe.

Pain strangled my lungs.

Agony stole everything.

"Dad, listen to me!" Neri yelled.

Jack spun to face her, grabbing her by the elbows as my vision skipped in and out of focus. Shaking her, he glared at the fresh ligature marks on her wrists. "Did he tie you up? What did he do to you? *Tell me*. Tell me, and he'll never touch another girl for as long as he lives."

"It wasn't him, Dad!"

"You expect me to believe you did this to yourself? Come on, Nerida! Your skin is welted. He did this—"

"It wasn't him. He was trying to help me!"

"*Help?*" Jack laughed with dripping scorn. "*Help?* Fuck, I've been so blind." Horror filled his tone. "How long has he been 'helping' you, little fish?" Tears scratched his throat. "Is that why you've been so off these past few weeks? Did something happen when you went on *The Fluke* together?" He shook her hard. "Tell me! Stop fucking protecting him and *tell me*—"

"It wasn't him who raped me!" Neri yelled. "I-It wasn't him!"

Silence tumbled like snow all around us.

"What…what do you mean…it wasn't him…" Anna choked. "Did someone else…? Neri?"

Neri's quiet sobbed filled the room. "It wasn't Aslan. Okay."

The overwhelming pain faded just enough for me to uncurl from my spot on the floor and look up. Blood poured from a cut on my temple, blinding me in one eye. I caught Neri's water-streaming stare.

I saw her horror.

I witnessed her heart crack.

I knew why she'd tried to keep this secret.

To tell anyone else what Ethan had done only made it more real. To tell her parents that she'd been touched, defiled, abused…

She'd never be able to look at her parents again without them seeing her that way. She'd never be their strong daughter again. Never see their eternal pride and unconditional love without streaks of pity and sorrow.

I couldn't let her lose that bond, that sense of happiness and home.

I couldn't allow her to hurt herself for me.

"It was me," I coughed, wincing and clutching at my probably-broken ribs. "I-I attacked her—"

"*WHAT?*" Neri exploded. She tried to run to me, but Jack lashed his arm around her middle. "That's not true. You saved me. You've *always* saved me. Every damn day of my life since I was twelve, you've—"

"Groomed you and molested you. Right beneath our fucking noses," Jack hissed. "I should never have let him into our house." His stare burned like acid. "I should've reported you the moment we found you at sea."

Sirens sounded in the distance, coming closer, closer.

"At least, I get to rectify that. At least you'll get what you deserve." Jack held Neri as she fought to get free.

"Dad. Don't. Just listen to me!"

Fear drummed through my veins.

Fear that by manhandling his daughter, she'd regress. She'd won against me tonight. Our ridiculous role-play had returned her power that Ethan had stolen.

But if her father kept trapping her, I didn't know what that would do.

"Jack…" I grunted around my wounds. "Let her go."

"Don't you dare tell me what to do with my own flesh and blood, Aslan. Don't you fucking *dare*!"

"Stop restraining her," I coughed and spat blood into my palm, wiping it on my shorts so I didn't stain Neri's cream rug on the floor. "Just let her go."

Sirens echoed so loud, screaming down the neighbourhood.

Fuck.

I needed to run, to hide.

If they catch me—

Grunting with agony, I pushed up to my knees. "Jack…I-I love your daughter. I always have—"

His fist shot into my cheekbone so fast, my head smashed backward against Neri's bed. The room spun. My ears rang.

"Don't you *dare* talk about love, you son of a bitch. You don't know the meaning of it!"

Sirens cut off outside the house.

Terror hammered through my blood.

When I'd forced Neri to accept her strength, I'd been prepared to die for her.

That wish was about to come true.

"Dad, please. Tell the police you're mistaken. Don't let them take him. You can't let them take him!" Neri begged, choking on tears. "He'll die if they deport him!"

"That's bullshit. It's just another lie. Good fucking riddance." Jack dragged Neri toward the door. "Let's go. You'll need to make a statement."

"I'm not going anywhere!" she screeched. "Let *go* of me!"

A loud knock on the front door.

Anna wrung her hands. "They're here."

"Go answer the door," Jack snapped. "I'll wait here with him."

Anna held out her hand. "Neri, sweetie, come with me. You don't have to watch this."

"Don't let them in, Mum. They can't take him away. They'll kill him!"

"No one is going to kill anyone," Jack grunted. "Unless it's me." He shoved Neri toward Anna. "Go with your mother. Now."

"Dad. *Please* don't do this."

Anna tried to grab Neri. "Come on—"

The door hammered again. "Police. *Open up!*"

"Go!" Jack yelled. "Once he's in custody, then we'll talk."

"He didn't do this!" Neri screamed.

"Go, Nerida. I won't ask again!" Jack bellowed.

I struggled to stand.

My left kneecap crunched; my ribs screamed.

Pain made me lightheaded, and I couldn't see straight.

I fell back down.

If I cared more about my own life, I'd fight through the blaze and knock Jack aside. I'd bolt through the house and go.

But…Neri.

I couldn't leave her with this mess.

I couldn't abandon her to parents who would never look at her the same way again.

I would rather die and take the blame, knowing I'd take a piece of her soul with me, than run like a fucking coward.

"It's okay, *aşkım*," I murmured, swallowing another mouthful of blood from the cut on my tongue. "I'll be okay—"

"No, you won't. This is all such a giant mistake." Rushing at her father, she pummelled his chest. "This is all my fault. I've been wanting to tell you for months—"

"*Months?*" Jack grabbed her damaged wrists, making her cry out. "Months?! He's been forcing himself on you for months?" "

"You're not listening to me! He never forced me. Not once! I love him, Dad—"

"Fucking hell, I'm gonna kill him. He's got you so brainwashed, you don't even know what you're saying!" Tossing Neri toward Anna, he roared, "Take her, Anna. Tell the police to get in here quick before I rip his motherfucking balls off!"

"Police!" The knocking turned violent. "Open immediately!"

"Go!" Jack roared at his wife.

Anna left Neri on the threshold and tore up the corridor in a whirl of pink.

Everything inside me stilled, went quiet, prepared to die.

So this was how it ended.

This was how I lost her.

"*Seni seviyorum, karıcığım.*" I forced a smile, hoping I didn't look too beaten, too bloody.

I didn't want Neri to remember me like this or see me being dragged out the door in handcuffs. "Go, Neri. It's okay."

"Fuck that. *None* of this is okay."

"Nerida, go find your mother," Jack roared, rolling up the cuffs of his suit, his knuckles raw and bloody from hitting me. "I'm going to say another goodbye to Aslan."

Neri froze.

Her lips twisted.

Her eyes dried up.

And I saw the decision before she even acknowledged it herself.

"Neri, don't—" I coughed.

Too late.

Leaping for her bedside table, she grabbed her mermaid lamp with its heavy scaled base, yanked the cord out of the wall, and struck her father with all her might around the back of his head.

He groaned and dropped like an anchor to the floor.

His eyes closed.

His limbs went loose.

He passed out.

"Shit." My heart smoked with panic. "Neri, what did you do?"

"Doing what you've always done for me." Landing on her knees beside me, she grabbed my arm and threw it over her shoulders. "Stand up. Right now. *Get up*, Aslan."

Male voices sounded by the front door as heavy boots entered the house.

Groaning, I shut down all my pain and locked away all my weaknesses.

Using Neri as much as I dared, I tripped to my feet and rode out the heavy waves of nausea.

"Stand still. Don't fall." Letting me go, Neri raced to her dresser and grabbed the chair beneath. Wedging it under the door handle of her room, she bolted to her window. "Come on."

Lurching forward, my bones didn't work correctly, but I ignored them. I would walk on shattered legs if it meant I survived and somehow figured out a way to fix all of this.

"I'm not leaving you," I panted as I landed hard against her windowsill.

"You don't have a choice."

"Come with me."

"I'm going to tell them it wasn't you."

"I don't want you doing something you don't want to do."

Tears rolled down her cheeks. "It's my mess, Aslan. I did this. Give me the chance to fix it."

"But—"

"Go." She shoved me. "Go now. Please, just *run*."

The door handle wriggled, crunching against the top of the chair. "Open up," a police officer yelled.

My heart raced. Another wave of nausea.

I glanced back at poor Jack sprawled on the floor.

He didn't deserve this.

None of them did.

I'd done this.

I'd done this because I was my father's fucking son.

Neri pushed me harder. "Go. Get out. Run!"

Something heavy smashed against the door, trying to dislodge the chair.

"*Run*," she hissed. "If you don't fucking run, Aslan, I swear on my life, I'll follow you to Turkey and find you if you get deported."

Rage burned hotly. "You know why you can't—"

"RUN!"

Fighting every instinct not to leave her, I drank in her fire, her ferocity, and fell so damn hard for the girl who fought so vehemently for me.

She'd chosen me.

Over her father.

Over her family.

Snatching her around the nape, I pressed a feral kiss to her mouth, fed her all my feelings, then threw myself out the ground-floor window.

I landed in the narrow vegetable garden ringing the pool.

"Go!" Neri whisper-screamed. "Run!"

I spun and looked at her one last time.

Her door shot open as two male cops spilled into her bedroom.

Our eyes caught.

My heart broke.

I ran.

Neri and Aslan's tale will conclude in Cor Amare, the second and final book in The Luna Duet.

RELEASING: 25th July 2023

Preorder links can be found at www.pepperwinters.com

While you wait for Cor Amare, if you liked this tale, try The Ribbon Duet. The same angst, need, and love can be found in Ren and Della's story.

Other Upcoming Titles…

Ruby Tears
(Dark Romance)
Find out more at:
https://pepperwinters.com/upcoming-releases/

"Ten thousand dollars.
That pitiful sum changed my entire life.
It bought my entire life.
A measly ten thousand dollars, given to my boyfriend by a monster to fuck me.
He took it.
The monster took me.
And I never saw freedom again."

I'm the bastard son of a monster.
My other half-blooded siblings have their own demons…but me?
I truly have the devil inside.
I try to be good.
To do my best to ignore the deep, dark, despicable urges.
But every day it gets harder.
I thought family could help.
I reached out to my infamous half-brother, Q, begging for his secrets to stay tamed.
Instead, he gave me an ultimatum to prove I'm not like our father.
Infiltrate The Jewelry Box: a trafficking ring of poor unfortunate souls, kill the Master Jeweler, free the Jewels, and don't lose my rotten soul while trying.
Only problem is…my initiation into this exclusive club is earning a Jewel all of my own.
She sparkles like diamonds, bleeds like rubies, and bruises as deep as emeralds.
She's mine to break.
I can't refuse.
If I want to prove to my half-brother that I'm not like our sire, I have to sink into urges I've always fought, plunge into madness, and lose myself so deeply into sin that the only one who will be breaking is me.

WOULD YOU LIKE REGULAR FREE BOOKS?

Sign up to my Newsletter and receive exclusive content, deleted scenes, and freebies.
SIGN UP HERE

UPCOMING BOOKS 2023

Sign up to my Newsletter to receive an instant 'It's Live' Alert!

Please visit www.pepperwinters.com for latest updates.

OTHER WORK BY PEPPER WINTERS

Pepper currently has close to forty books released in nine languages. She's hit best-seller lists (USA Today, New York Times, and Wall Street Journal) almost forty times. She dabbles in multiple genres, ranging from Dark Romance, Coming of Age, Fantasy, and Romantic Suspense.

For books, FAQs, and buylinks please visit:

https://pepperwinters.com

DARK ROMANCE

Goddess Isles Series
Once a Myth
Twice a Wish
Third a Kiss
Fourth a Lie
Fifth a Fury

Monsters in the Dark Trilogy
Tears of Tess
Quintessentially Q
Twisted Together
Je Suis a Toi

Indebted Series
Debt Inheritance
First Debt
Second Debt
Third Debt
Fourth Debt
Final Debt
Indebted Epilogue

Dollar Series
Pennies
Dollars

Hundreds
Thousands
Millions

Fable of Happiness Trilogy

SEXY ROMANCE

The Master of Trickery Duet
The Body Painter
The Living Canvas

Truth & Lies Duet
Crown of Lies
Throne of Truth

COMING OF AGE ROMANCE

The Ribbon Duet
The Boy & His Ribbon
The Girl & Her Ren

Standalone Spinoff
The Son & His Hope

STANDALONES

Destroyed – Grey Romance
Unseen Messages – Survival Romance

MOTORCYCLE CLUB ROMANCE

Pure Corruption Duet
Ruin & Rule
Sin & Suffer

ROMANTIC COMEDY written as TESS HUNTER

Can't Touch This

CHILDREN'S / INSPIRATIONAL BOOK

Pippin and Mo

FANTASY ROMANCE

When a Moth Loved a Bee

UPCOMING RELEASES

For 2023/2024 titles please visit www.pepperwinters.com

RELEASE DAY ALERTS, SNEAK PEEKS, & NEWSLETTER
To be the first to know about upcoming releases, please join Pepper's Newsletter (she promises never to spam or annoy you.)
Pepper's Newsletter

SOCIAL MEDIA & WEBSITE
Facebook: Peppers Books
Instagram: @pepperwinters
Facebook Group: Peppers Playgound
Website: www.pepperwinters.com
Tiktok: @pepperwintersbooks

ACKNOWLEDGEMENTS

About five years ago, I reached mental burnout from overworking and letting my mind convince me that life was meant to be suffered and endured. I drenched my body in so much stress, it began to break down. The saying that stress is a killer is 100% true. Thanks to being trapped in my mind and working twenty plus hours every day, I caused a heart condition called PAF. It got so bad, I could barely walk and the 'attacks' would last for up to two hours with my heart palpitating at 210bpm.

When I 'woke' up and realised life is meant to be enjoyed and celebrated—and I put my health and happiness first—my heart no longer needed to remind me to take better care of myself.

Until recently.

For some reason, the start of 2023 didn't go as I planned and my PAF returned. Unlike last time where I tried to battle through it, I stopped, I listened, and I changed again.

I listened to my instincts (I'm very much like Nerida in that way and love to follow those nudges which are almost always right) and turned to yet more techniques of breaking the noise of life. I've been a devout yogi for over five years now. I practice almost every day. I've dabbled with meditation but didn't really take it seriously, until this year. This year, I started cold water therapy with Wim Hof. Began breathing techniques, running, and meditation (on top of yoga and the sauna work I was already doing). And I can safely say, it has put me in the best mental and physical state of my life.

So great in fact that I was averaging 6,000 a day writing this book and it felt like a single minute passed by. Each word was an absolute joy and I seriously felt like I was on some kind of high.

Aslan and Neri popped into my head in a fabulous explosion that never fails to make me tremble with how magical storylines can arrive. In two seconds, I knew their story from beginning to end, felt as if I'd known them all my life, and put aside everything to follow those nudges to write.

In six weeks, I had LUNAMARE. And it was the best book and the best time I've had writing for years! I'm so thankful to you for reading and thankful for whatever nudges told me to write this book.

I'm also so thankful that I was able to share a bit of my own experience in Port Douglas (I've dived on the Great Barrier Reef and explored Daintree rainforest). I was blown away by the gorgeous town and would love to spend more time there.

I am completely Neri in this book and wanted to be a marine biologist when I was younger. I swear I must've been a fish at some point because writing about the ocean and all the magic that exists under the waves feels like going home in a way. If I could, I'd write sea themed books forever.

This was also the first book in years that I've written without beta readers. I wrote it from start to finish and hoarded Neri and Aslan to myself. But…when it was time to share, I'm ever so grateful to Rowan, Cyn, Melissa, Rochelle, Danielle, and Whitney for reading.

I also have a MASSIVE thank you to Betül from Silence is Read for her incredible Turkish translations and her huge help at making Aslan as authentic as possible. She not only helped me perfect his culture, his history, and the incredible background of Turkey, but she made him so much more real. It was an absolute honour to write a character from such a wonderful place and I truly hope it inspires a lot of people to travel to this incredible country!

Betül was also amazing enough to give me a list of phrases and words to include in the back of this book so you can see for yourself the beauty of this language. She went above and beyond and I'm ever so grateful to her!

I owe another massive thanks to Tor Thom and Fiona Clare for the impeccable narration.

Valentine PR, Nina, Kim, and all the fabulous girls for epic promotion.

Jenny for her wonderful edits and eagle eyes.

Cleo for the absolutely gorgeous covers.

Christina for the awesome final proofread.

All the incredible bloggers, tiktokkers, instagrammers, and facebookers who helped review and share.

And…you!

Thank you so much for reading and allowing me to share a small piece of my imagination with you once again!

Pepper

x

TURKISH WORDS & GLOSSARY

Aşkım: My love
Güzelim: My beautiful/handsome one
Sevgilim: My darling/lover
Hayatım: My life (used to express affection for someone significant in one's life)
Meleğim: My angel (used to express love or admiration)
Güneşim: My sunshine (used to express affection or admiration)
Çiçeğim: My flower (used to express admiration or endearment)
Or Kuzum: My lamb (used to express tenderness, gentleness, and affection)
Tosunum: My bull calf (used for young boys or chubby babies by doting loved ones)
Aslanım: Brave (used to signify brave, strong, heroic people)
Kahretsin: Dammit (curse word)
Kafami sikeyim: Fuck my head (curse word that is commonly used. Loose translation: 'fuck me')
Birtanem: My love (used to express a loved one, my only one)
Seni çok seviyorum: I love you so much
Seni seviyorum: I love you
Özür dilerim: I am so sorry
Teşekkür ederim: Thank you (formal with polite meaning)
Teşekkürler: Thank you (informal)
Defol: Get lost, go away (loose translation)

The most common terms of endearment are *Aşkım, Güzelim, Sevgilim, Hayatım, Canım.* These are made extra affectionate by adding *benim* (ben means me and benim means mine).

Aşkım benim.
Hayatım benim.
This intensifies the phrase between close loved ones.

Thank you to Betül for this amazing list and for all her help making Aslan as authentic and as culturally respectful as possible.

I am now head over heels for everything Turkish and can't wait to jump back into Aslan and Neri's world in Cor Amare.

Any errors are mine.

Printed in Poland
by Amazon Fulfillment
Poland Sp. z o.o., Wrocław
13 July 2023

8c9b1394-474f-4b3a-8fab-7020f5c479ddR01